A MOMENT AFTER DARK

JANET RAYE STEVENS

Carolyn —
Enjoy the "Moment"!

Janet Raye Stevens

Great Brook Publishing

A MOMENT AFTER DARK © 2021 Janet Raye Stevens

Printed in the United States of America.

First printing, 2021

ISBN: 978-1-7373103-4-1

www.janetrayestevens.com

Cover Design by Elizabeth Turner Stokes

Acknowledgments

In grateful acknowledgment of the many people who have helped nurture and encourage my passion for history, and in particular my interest in the World War II era, including my parents, my stepfather Everett Harrington, John and Kathy McFarland, Mike and Susannah Bush, and the late, great Nathaniel Mencow, educator, friend, peerless navigator of the B-17 *Betty Boop-The Pistol Packin' Mama*, and one of the greatest of his generation.

Thanks also to the writers and readers whose time, talent, and support have helped me bring *A Moment After Dark* to life: Jenny Applegate, who was there at the beginning, Ruth McCarty, Christine Gunderson, Lauren Sheridan, Tracy Brody, Angele McQuade & the McQ+You crew, and especially Suzanne Tierney and Kari Lemor. More thanks to Elizabeth Turner Stokes for another amazing cover, Amalie Berlin, Shannon Gilmore, my editor Reina from Rickrack Books, and the inimitable Melissa – The Literary Assistant.

For my friend, teacher, and mentor, Glenda Baker, who taught me persistence is key.

Chapter One

Addie Brandt dragged the tall stool close to the coffin and studied the man lying peacefully inside.

"Now, what can I do for you, Mr. Gallagher?" she murmured.

Not much, she feared. Old Gallagher was no John Barrymore. Not even Lionel Barrymore, with his basset hound looks. Addie retrieved the makeup basket Mother had given her the Christmas before she died. Try as she might with her paints and powders, she probably wouldn't be able to make Johnny Gallagher any less unattractive in death than he had been in life.

That irked her. She'd been fond of the man. Not just because he was Uncle Pat's friend. Because he wasn't like the others. He didn't stare or run away when he saw her. He didn't dare touch her—no one in her hometown of Goveport, Massachusetts would touch her—but he'd always given her a kind smile when they met. She'd feasted on those smiles. For that, she owed him a face as handsome as Errol Flynn for his funeral.

1

Addie perched on the stool and got to work.

Gallagher's brown suit smelled of mothballs. The scent mixed with the salty, chill wind blowing off the Atlantic, whistling through the window Addie had cracked open. Father would grumble about the cost of letting the heat escape, but she needed the fresh air. She'd been painting the dear departed, as Father called them, for their family business since she was eighteen, when Mother got too sick to do the job. Addie should be used to Brandt Funeral Home's unique smells after four years. Should, but wasn't. She doubted she'd ever get used to it.

Finished, she removed the towel she'd tucked under Old Gallagher's chin to keep face powder from speckling his white shirt. He wasn't really old, no more than fifty, Uncle Pat's age. Like Mother, too young to meet his maker. Cancer had taken Mother at only forty-three. For Gallagher, it was a bum ticker.

Addie combed the man's few wisps of grayish hair then reached for a small box on the counter that ran along the cement block wall under the windows. Some kind of jewelry, something her uncle's sausage fingers couldn't manage. Uncle Pat had been dressing the stiffs, as he called them, and attending to the more unpleasant aspects of preparing a body for burial for nearly twenty years. The delicate work, pinning on jewelry and buttoning small buttons, had been Mother's job. And now Addie's.

The box opened with a soft click and Addie gazed at the silver rectangle within. A tiepin, probably clipped on Gallagher's brown tie with this suit for weddings, funerals, Easter Mass. She lifted the pin—and gasped as icy cold latched onto her fingers, shivered up her arm, and spread through her veins like a living thing.

Addie's breath caught. *No. Dear lord, please, no.* Her silent plea went unheeded as the strange power that lived deep within her took hold of her waking mind. A thousand needles stabbed her brain. Her vision narrowed, as if she were thundering backward in a train tunnel. Then the world went black, and she plummeted into the gaping abyss of the Sight.

A moment later, the darkness peeled away, like sections of an orange breaking off until she looked up at a sky so blue it stung her eyes. She could taste its sharpness. She smelled warm sea air, mixed with hot metal, oil, gunpowder. Sleepy voices surrounded her, men just waking up. Heat baked her skin and bounced off metal walls of hard steel, joined together with silver rivets.

Looking down, Addie saw she had a man's legs, wearing white trousers. A uniform?

An angry buzz droned overhead. She squinted into the sun as a swarm of metal locusts came into view.

"What in holy hell—?" A man's rough voice came out of her mouth.

Airplanes. They flew in formation, ten, twelve, maybe more. Sunlight glinted off their wings. The first wave broke off and swooped in. The buzz became a roar. An explosion rattled Addie's bones. She staggered. Smoke billowed, choking her. Men screamed and shouted in confusion and panic. Pain.

A man in a once-white Navy uniform, now covered with soot, pounded up. A boy, really, his face twisted in terror.

"Jimmy! It's the Japanese," he cried and scurried away.

Jimmy. Addie had slipped into the skin of a man named Jimmy, on a ship somewhere. Choking on smoke so thick

3

and slick with oil she could almost touch it. Strangling on her own fear. One thought pushed through the chaos: *I've got to man my gun*. She plowed through the smoke, her shoes beating the deck.

Another explosion, like the fury of hell blasting open. The ship heaved. No, it *lifted*, as if a giant hand scooped it up then dropped it into the water again. She fell with a thud onto the deck. Heat seared her palms, scorched through her trousers and singed the skin off her knees. Nearby, a man wearing a suit of flames leapt overboard.

She managed to stand. She shaded her eyes from the glare and looked up. A plane dove through the smoke, the red circle of Japan like an angry eye on its side. *Mother Mary*, she prayed. Staccato flashes of machine-gun fire cut through the noise. Hot beads of metallic hail pinged the deck. A thousand knives of fire pierced her chest.

And then, nothing.

～

"Addie, wake up."

She blinked her eyes open. It took several seconds to realize she was at the funeral home, lying on the cold concrete floor in the basement preparation room. Her uncle, Pat Feeney, had gone out for the afternoon newspaper. He loomed over her, paper in his hand, his ruddy face pinched with worry.

"What happened? Did I fall?" Her hand flew to her throat. Her voice croaked like a sea lion's bark and her throat burned, as if she'd swallowed a lit cigarette. She could still smell the smoke, taste blood in her mouth. Gunfire and screams still echoed in her ears.

"You tell me what happened." Uncle Pat tossed a skeptical look toward the coffin, then back at her. His eyes were blue sapphires, like Mother's, like Addie's own, minus their usual twinkle.

"I don't know." Her voice sounded more normal. She sat up. The burning pain in her knees faded. The stab of bullet holes in her chest slowly subsided. "I think I fainted. I'll never get used to the smell in here."

Uncle Pat settled on the stool and watched her struggle to her feet. He wouldn't offer to help, nor would she let him. She would never let him touch her, never chance triggering the Sight and seeing what the future might be for him. Or for anyone in her family. Not since Mother.

"You're bleeding," he said.

"What?" The screams of the dying grew fainter in her head. The sounds always lingered longest.

He pointed to her hand. Blood bubbled from her fingertip. A perfect red circle. *Jimmy, it's the Japanese*. The bubble burst and blood trickled down her finger.

"You stuck yourself." Uncle Pat scooped the tiepin off the corpse's chest. "With this, I think."

A shudder engulfed her.

"What's got into you, girl? Fainting at the sight of blood. After all these years keeping company with the stiffs?" He held out the pin for her to fasten but she tucked her hands behind her back. He frowned. "Maybe it wasn't the blood? Did you have one of your…spells?"

She shook her head, and he gave her a look that reminded her of Mother. She had always known when Addie lied, too. Uncle Pat knew Addie was afflicted with the Sight. His own son, Michael, the eldest of his four boys, also suffered from it. But no one in the Brandt or Feeney families ever spoke of it. It was as if not talking about it, never admitting Addie and Michael could see the future with a mere touch, would make it go away.

She dug a lace-edged handkerchief out of her skirt pocket. She twisted it around her cut finger as she watched her uncle bend over the body and fumble the tiepin into place.

"This is a school pin, G for Goveport High," he said. "Couldn't belong to Johnny. He never went to school. Went to work in the quarry soon as he got off the boat from Ireland, same as me. Must've been sixteen. This must be his son Jimmy's pin."

Addie went cold. "Jimmy?"

"You don't remember Jimmy Gallagher? S'pose not, he was ahead of you in school. His old man was mighty proud when Jimmy got a diploma. Not that it did him any good, with no jobs in the Depression. Jimmy up and joined the Navy."

She couldn't breathe.

"Should've heard Johnny brag about that." The pin finally in place, Uncle Pat took out a handkerchief and polished it. "The boy's stationed at some place with palm trees and girls in grass skirts. Pearl Harbor, Johnny called it." He scowled at the blood dotting Gallagher's white shirt and slid the tie to the left, hiding the blot. "There, don't that look fine? Let's not bother your da with this bit of nothing, eh? He'll make me wash and starch the shirt, and press it, to boot, and me with a poker game tonight."

Addie wasn't listening. "Pearl Harbor," she murmured.

"Know where that is? Never heard of it, 'cept it's too

far away for poor Jimmy to come home for his old man's funeral."

He kicked loose the wheel locks on the collapsible metal bier holding the coffin and Addie watched him push it to the elevator at the back, near the embalming room doors. Her stomach churned. A dead man's tiepin couldn't trigger the Sight, since Old Gallagher had no story left to tell. His son Jimmy did, however. A most dramatic story. If what Addie had seen of the future came true, Jimmy would soon have his own funeral.

And so would a lot of other men.

～

A ddie escaped as soon as she could. Uncle Pat offered to make her a cup of tea—his treatment for all ailments whiskey couldn't cure—but she declined. She snatched up her brimmed felt hat and red wool coat, tugged on her leather gloves, and fled through the side door to the alley. She didn't tell her father she was leaving.

Still shaking, she hurried up Holmes Street, along a wet sidewalk banked with soot and dirt-coated snow. She crossed Main Street at Duffy the Cobbler's. Downtown Goveport bustled with its usual chaos. Cars, trucks and even a few horse-drawn carts rumbled by brick-front shops and granite office buildings of all heights and widths. Pedestrians rushed past, some carrying brown-paper-wrapped packages tied with string. The air smelled of fresh-caught haddock and cod at the markets. Gulls cawed overhead, circling, looking for scraps.

The sharp sea air bit her cheeks but the tears that

filled her eyes weren't from the cold. How she missed Mother. Nearly two years since she'd passed, and the sting of grief hadn't faded a bit. Mother had understood what Addie went through, because she'd been burdened with the Sight, too. Just a bit, as light as a summer cold, she would say.

Addie had been cursed with more than a bit.

It started when she was a child. Touching someone brought on vague, come-and-go images, like a sail bobbing on the horizon. The Sight grew stronger as Addie grew up, ghostly flickers she could neither control nor understand.

Terrifying, but not as frightening as what happened after Mother died. The Sight had come on like Man o' War thudding toward the finish line. Now, a touch of another's flesh and Addie could see their future. *Live* their future. Feel, smell, and taste what would happen to them. Even holding an object that belonged to another had begun to bring on the Sight. It was as if Mother's death had released the full force of this hellish affliction.

Addie swiped away her tears and picked up her pace. Her toes were frozen by the time she turned onto Pine Street, a road lined with elegant red-brick townhouses, squeezed together like sardines in a can. A gay holiday wreath hung on her family's mahogany front door, with a bright red ribbon that fluttered in the wind.

She climbed the brick steps and entered a spacious foyer with a hardwood floor polished so bright, she could almost see her reflection. On the right was the door to Father's library, to the left, the front parlor, with the stairs and hallway to the dining room and kitchen straight ahead. The rich scent of pumpernickel bread baking drifted through the house. Home had once been as warm and comforting as that smell.

Now, with Mother gone, the house always felt empty. Cold.

Addie hung up her coat and hat in the closet and set her boots on the mat by the telephone table to dry. The front parlor's pocket doors were open and female voices drifted out. In no mood to face Aunt Trudy, Addie tried to tiptoe across the foyer to the stairs. She only wanted to hide in her bedroom where she could be alone. At least until her cousin Marta got home from her after-school job.

"Who is there? Is that you, Adelaide?" Aunt Trudy called out in German.

Steeling herself, Addie stepped into the parlor, a bright corner room with four windows and a thick, coral-colored Oriental carpet. Her heart stung to see Aunt Trudy seated in Mother's wingback chair by the window. The lace curtains behind her diffused the afternoon light. Addie stifled a groan when she noticed her aunt's guests, the elderly Vogel sisters. They perched on the plump sofa, holding glasses of sherry. The room reeked of their rose-scented toilet water.

"You're home early," Aunt Trudy said, still speaking German. She pierced Addie with her stare. Her gray hair was parted in a strict, straight line and pulled into a tight bun. The rest of her was strict and straight, too.

"I felt ill, so I left," Addie said. The ladies tittered. Father insisted they speak only English at home, so her German was halting, not even close to being grammatically correct. "It's nothing serious, Aunt."

She wasn't really Addie's aunt. Father and Eb Brandt were cousins, but when he, his wife, and their two children had arrived from Germany in '34 to live with them, Father had asked Addie to address them as Aunt and Uncle as a gesture of affection and respect.

She felt neither.

"Nothing serious," Aunt Trudy repeated. "But serious enough to leave work." She sniffed then turned to her guests. "You remember my friends, the Vogel sisters. They've come all this way to visit."

The sisters lived in the Germantown section of the city, where Aunt Trudy went to shop and gossip. Addie nodded at them in greeting.

"It is a pleasure to see you again, Adelaide," Fraulein Hannah said. At least, Addie thought it was Hannah. She and her sister Bronya looked so much alike in their simple brown cloth dresses and severe braids wrapped tightly around their heads.

"The ladies were telling me the butcher's daughter is to be married in the new year," Aunt Trudy said. "You remember Margo Abt? You were at school with her."

Oh, she remembered Margo, and no doubt Margo remembered Addie, the way she'd taken such pleasure in teasing her all through high school.

"Please give Margo my hearty congratulations," Addie said, a lie that sounded even more unconvincing in her stilted German.

"It is time she settled down. She's twenty-two, as are you, Adelaide," Bronya, or perhaps Hannah, said. Her voice turned arch. "I suppose you will be next to walk down the aisle?"

Addie held back a bitter laugh. The Vogel sisters, Aunt Trudy, and all of their gossiping friends knew she had no suitors and never would. Her heart ached with loneliness at the certainty of that thought. No man would be brave enough to risk touching Addled Addie, the nickname she'd earned long ago that had stuck like a briar.

Muttering something placating, Addie excused herself and backed out of the parlor, eager to escape. Indignant comments she didn't bother to translate followed her as she dashed up the stairs to her bedroom.

She peeled off her clothes and went to the bathroom to scrub away the smell of the funeral home as best she could. She wished she could erase what the Sight had shown her today just as easily. The images of bodies cut in two, the smell of burning oil, the *crack-crack* of the guns, and the cries of the dying.

Addie had no idea when the awful attack would happen, but her belly would bubble in fear and anguish until it did. And probably for the rest of her life.

She stared at her hollow-eyed reflection in the mirror over the porcelain sink. Sudden anger coursed through her, as hot as the water pouring from the faucet. Anger at Mother, for leaving her so lost and alone. At Father, who willfully ignored her troubles. At her cousin Michael, who'd never speak of the affliction they both shared. Even anger at Jimmy Gallagher, who was going to die, along with a lot of other men, and she couldn't do anything to stop it.

No, that wasn't true. Addie *wouldn't* do anything. She'd learned her lesson long ago. She'd spoken up once before, and she was still paying for it. She wouldn't put herself through that again.

Addled Addie was going to keep her mouth shut.

Chapter Two

"There you are, Jack Dunstan." The petite blonde seated at the rolltop desk swiveled to scowl at him as he came into the apartment. "You've been gone so long I thought you'd flown the coop."

The floorboards creaked as he crossed the parlor to the liquor cart near the window. He poured himself two fingers of scotch and downed it in one gulp while glaring out at the city. In the distance, the rays of the setting sun touched the top of the Washington monument. Sometimes, Dunstan wished he *could* fly the coop. Take off and leave DC and his troubles behind. Especially after today, when he'd gone from one gloomy meeting to another.

"Oh dear, was it that bad?" Virginia said. She straightened the papers and folders strewn across the desk and eyed him with concern. "Get me a drink too, sugar, and come tell me all about it."

He filled his glass again then poured whiskey for Virginia and handed it to her. Nothing but the finest Kentucky bourbon for her. Since she'd joined the team, anyway. When they'd found her, poor and desperate, she would've been grateful for a bottle of rotgut and bail money.

She sipped her drink then patted the seat of the stout wooden chair next to the desk. "Now, sit. Tell me what those mean old G-Men said to make you look so glum."

The chair creaked as he sank into it. Her perfume, something flowery and expensive, drifted over. He studied her. She wore a snug green dress that matched her eyes, all Jean Harlow bombshell, not a hint of subtlety. Appealing, but not his type. He liked his women less glamour-girl, more girl-next-door. Like Madelyn had been. Or had pretended to be.

He shook off the dark memories that threatened to cloud his mind and dug his cigarette lighter out of his suit jacket's pocket.

"You know those meetings are classified," he said, lighting a Lucky Strike. "I can't tell you a thing. Suffice to say, I didn't hear good news. We creep closer to war every day. Doesn't help that every meeting I'm in someone makes it clear J. Edgar and the other brass still haven't forgiven me for what happened."

Virginia frowned into her whiskey. "Small-minded bureaucrats. It wasn't your fault."

He shrugged. "I suppose I should be used to the blame and icy stares after all this time. Should be used to those smirking dollar-a-year men who think I'm a conman, leading a flock of loons."

"Well, at least Radcliffe's in our corner. He might act like we're his redheaded stepchildren, but he keeps our expense account flush."

Not for much longer, if what he'd heard today came to

pass. Their boss, Percy Radcliffe, had announced he was moving over to Bill Donovan's new intelligence operation, the Coordinator of Information Office. That would leave Dunstan and his team without a champion at the FBI. Their operation teetered on the brink of obliteration.

Dunstan took a long pull on his cigarette. He suspected Radcliffe had chosen to move on before he got booted out. Back in '38, an FBI paper-pusher named Woden had talked Hoover into letting him pull together a team of people with special powers to fight crime. Hoover put the team under Radcliffe's wing. A year ago, Woden's true nature had been revealed. He was a Nazi agent, his mission to recruit as many gifted people to his cause as he could.

That treachery had been costly, with Woden escaped, their team in hiding, and Madelyn... Dunstan took another drag. He preferred not to dwell on that.

J. Edgar had been as angry as hornets. A Nazi spy embedded in the agency charged with seeking out and destroying enemy infiltrators left Hoover with egg on his face and searching for a scapegoat. Fingers pointed at Radcliffe.

And, ultimately, at *him*. The man who'd failed to stop Woden's final betrayal.

"Never mind that," Dunstan said, exhaling smoke in a heavy sigh. "Let's talk about your day. Have you found me anyone?"

Virginia looked down at the stacks of manila folders on the desk. "How could I *not* find you someone, when my only assignment lately has been to sit and read all day? Hunting for your precious gifted folks."

Her gripe was good-natured, though Dunstan knew the

job irked her. Madelyn had been the team's researcher. She'd read newspaper clippings and pored over field reports like a detective, searching for stories of unusual events and even more unusual people. With Madelyn gone, the tedious task had fallen to Virginia.

"I know the job's a bore," he said. "But we can't rebuild our team without finding new blood." Not that their team had ever been massive. At their strongest, they'd been an even dozen gifted folks, including him and Virginia. Woden's treachery had cut that number down to four.

Virginia gave a reluctant nod and settled her glass on a well-used 1939 New York World's Fair drink coaster. She opened a folder and riffled through the papers within. "Here's a story from Illinois. A young mother in Peoria lifted a car off her toddler."

Dunstan straightened, intrigued. "Her own kid? A mother's been known to do astounding feats when her child's threatened. Mark that a potential, in any case. What else?"

She put the folder aside and reached for another. "How about this? A Missouri farmer claims to be able to read minds."

He dismissed that with a wave of his cigarette. Even he doubted anyone had that ability. "On to the next one."

Virginia picked up a yellowing newspaper clipping. "Here's a heartbreaking one, an AP story from '32. A place called Goveport, Massachusetts. North of Boston, I think. Girl has visions, sees a missing boy."

He took a sip of scotch. "Nine years ago? Kind of dated."

"That's what I told Rollie in the Records office when he gave it to me. Said he found it in one of the files, a

15

closed case he thought was up my alley." She eyed Dunstan and lifted a thin eyebrow. "Rollie's an odd duck. Considers stories of old murders and terrible crimes bedtime reading."

Like Madelyn. The gloomier the story the better. A wistful smile tagged at Dunstan's lips, remembering that. Stronger emotions crowded in, and he struggled to push them back. Ironic that a man with the gift to erase emotions had so much trouble erasing his own.

"Sounds like the Bureau's the perfect place for ol' Rollie," he said then nodded to the clipping. "Go on, read it."

"Police are denying a city girl's 'vision' led to the recovery of the body of Hugo Nunes, found in a sinkhole near Haines Quarry yesterday." Virginia read with the drama of Ethel Barrymore mixed with Tallulah Bankhead's Alabama drawl. "Police say a thirteen-year-old girl had come forward after young Nunes, also thirteen, went miss-ing. The girl claimed to have 'seen' a vision of her school-mate trapped in a hole. Searchers were not directed to the quarry until yesterday, nearly two weeks after the boy disappeared. Captain Steven Walker defended the delay of the quarry search. The tip came from a child. We all know children are given to flights of fancy. That she named the location is simply a fluke, Walker said."

Finished, Virginia handed him the clipping. "Well? Think she might be the real McCoy?"

"Could be." Dunstan scanned the page. "No name listed. She was thirteen? That'd make her how old now?"

"Really, Dunstan? Good thing you're handsome and so deliciously tall, because math is *not* your strong suit. She's twenty-two, a woman now."

He gave a distracted nod and looked at the clipping again, at the police captain's dismissive words about the girl's claim. Madelyn had said children whose gifts had already come on were rare. Even then, they could barely control their ability, much less understand what was happening to them. If this story was true and not a hoax, the girl had some inkling of her gift at a young age. She must've been terrified. And cut to the bone when the police ignored her warning.

"Poor kid," he said. "I wonder if she ever reported another vision."

"I could call the newspaper and see what they know."

"I've got a better idea." A selfish idea, to be honest with himself. "Let's go up there and find out."

Getting out of town would get him away from the accusing stares and take that target off his back. For a few days at least. And, if luck was with him, he might find the girl. If his luck held, she could turn out to be legit.

He took another drag, warming to the idea. He could use some good luck now. He hoped to convince Radcliffe to take the team with him to the Coordinator of Information Office. Hoped Bill Donovan would see the benefit of taking them on. After the disaster with Woden, Dunstan needed something concrete, something big to prove the operation's worth to both men. A woman with the ability to see future events, especially in a time of war, might clinch the deal.

"Pack a bag, Virginia." He knocked back the rest of his drink. "We're heading to Goveport."

"We? Kindly leave me out of it. I'll have no part in what you plan to do to that poor woman."

"What? I want to help her, like I helped you." And hopefully help himself out of a jam.

She scoffed. "Help her? You mean you want to *use* her. One of these days, Dunstan, you'll realize us gifted folks are real people, not puppets on a string for you to manipulate."

"Speak for yourself. I've seen you manipulate more than one puppet."

Her laughter gurgled like water in a country stream. "Because *you* told me to, you monster. Besides, you know I'm in full control of my gift now. Plus, I'm older—"

"Yeah, twenty-five's positively ancient."

"Same age as you. And there's a difference between twenty-five and twenty-two. Besides, this woman may not want to be found. She may not want your so-called help."

"Virginia..." His cigarette ash had grown as long as a kite's tail. He flicked it into the glass ashtray on the desk. "War's coming. Not a matter of *if*, it's a matter of when. If this woman has the gift of sight, we'll need her. And I need you and your special talent too, so let's go." She looked mulish. "You've been complaining about sitting here with nothing to do, here's your chance."

She brightened. "Can I get a new wardrobe?"

He snorted. "On our government budget?"

"A new hat then?"

"Are you *trying* to get our allowance cut off? No unnecessary expenses." He tipped his head toward her bedroom, on the far side of the team's suite of rooms in one of Washington's oldest apartment buildings. "Now, go pack."

She snatched the clipping from his hand and placed it on the pile of folders. "I hope this girl's a knockout and you fall head-over-heels for her. Will serve you right to have someone pulling *your* strings for a change. Sometimes I think you don't have a heart at all." She gasped in sudden distress. "Oh, Dunstan, I didn't mean it. You know how emotional my gift makes me. I know you're still—"

He held up a hand, cutting her off. "Forget it. I've gotten over that."

She nodded, seeming to buy his lie. And it *was* a lie. He'd never get over Madelyn, or what Woden had done to her. Never get over the way his heart seemed to have been torn out of his chest, chopped to bits, and burned to ashes for good measure. Leaving behind a gaping hole filled with grief, guilt, and a solid determination to never again open himself up to that kind of pain.

Even if this woman in Goveport turned out to be as gorgeous as Greta Garbo and wealthy to boot, he would steer clear. He was only interested in her gift, if she had one, and how she could use her ability to help her country. If that should help him, so be it.

"Go on now, Virginia. Pack a bag." He crushed out his cigarette and stood. "We'll catch a train to Boston first thing in the morning."

Then on to Goveport, in search of the mystery woman. If her gift turned out to be real, she could be the key to saving the team.

And saving Dunstan's neck.

Chapter Three

Addie changed from her sober work clothes into a flowered day dress and a pair of cotton gloves, then sank onto her bed in the room she shared with her cousin Marta. Addie had always felt comfortable in this small, tidy space. Patchwork quilts Aunt Trudy had stitched covered the narrow beds, matching oak bureaus stood on either side of the closet, a spindly chair sat in one corner, and Marta's cedar hope chest rested under the sole window.

Addie plucked *Rebecca* from the vanity table between the beds, leaned back against her pillows, and opened the book to the page she'd dog-eared to mark her spot. She tried like heck to focus, but even Daphne du Maurier's lush prose couldn't distract her from the gruesome Sight that had battered her brain day and night since Monday. She gladly put the book aside when Marta rushed in ten minutes later, home from her after-school job.

Her cousin tossed her school bag onto her bureau and

flopped onto her bed, shooting Addie a grin. They were both blue-eyed blondes, but the resemblance ended there. Marta was petite, slim and delicate-looking, like Aunt Trudy, where Addie was tall and broad-hipped like Mother.

"Schulman's was a *madhouse* today." Marta kicked off her brown-and-white saddle shoes without unlacing them then crisscrossed her legs, her pleated skirt stretched over her knees. "Every old crab out Christmas shopping swarmed the perfume counter, wanting me to spritz them with a sample."

Addie gazed at her cousin fondly. Marta had come to America seven years ago at the age of ten, so she didn't have much of an accent. Except for when she said words like *spritz*.

Marta leaned toward the vanity table and opened the drawer, pulling out a pack of Marlboros and a pocket lighter.

"Careful, Marta." Addie glanced toward the closed door. "You don't want your mother to catch you smoking in the house."

"I'm not afraid of my mother," she said, but she sprang off the bed and darted to the window, opening it a crack. An icy breeze pushed in, stirring white curtains edged in hand-tatted lace. Marta sank onto the hope chest and clicked the lighter, touching the blue flame to her cigarette. She took a deep pull. Tobacco crackled and the tip glowed red.

A red circle.

Addie shuddered violently as the Sight's images flared in her mind again, pushing away all other thought.

"Something wrong?" Marta exhaled, peering at Addie

through a cloud of smoke. "You look like you saw a ghost." She stiffened. "You had a vision, didn't you?"

Addie could only nod. They'd been friends since Marta had come to live with them, when she was a scrawny thing with a big curiosity and eager to learn everything about her new country—and about Addie. Her cousin had wormed the truth out of her long ago.

Marta threw her cigarette out the window and rushed over. Addie's bed barely dipped as she perched her slight weight on it. "I've wondered why you've been so pale and jumpy lately. Tell me, what did you see?"

Addie gazed into her cousin's concerned blue eyes but could see only the cerulean blue sky over Hawaii. The whine of airplanes on the attack buzzed in her ears and the hot lead of bullets seemed to spear her chest.

Another image came to mind, from when she'd accidentally touched Marta's hairbrush a few months ago. Addie as Marta standing inside a tent, with rain beating against the canvas. She wore an olive-colored jacket and trousers. Sweat pooled under her arms. The smell of rubbing alcohol stung her nose. All around her, men moaned. Blood slicked her hands and waves of anguish flooded her heart.

The vision hadn't made any sense at the time. But after what the Sight had shown Addie two days ago... A new knot formed in her stomach.

"My heavens." Marta grabbed Addie's gloved hands and squeezed. "It's terrible, isn't it? I see it in your face. Won't you tell me what you saw?"

"You're hurting me." Addie's fingers had gone numb.

Marta released her hold, but not her gaze. "You *must* tell me. I won't budge until you do."

Addie sighed, almost in relief. "Have you heard of a place called Pearl Harbor? Do you know where it is?"

Marta frowned. Clearly, she hadn't expected a geography quiz. "No. Is it important?"

"Very important." The story poured out. Tears spilled down Addie's cheeks as she spoke about the ship, the planes, the terror, and the bullets that would end Jimmy Gallagher's life. "Jimmy and so many more men. Bleeding, screaming. Dying." She swallowed more tears. "It was horrible."

"Oh, Addie. You *have* to tell someone."

Addie gave a grim smile. "I just did."

"I mean, tell someone in authority. You can stop it. You can save lives."

"You know no one will believe me."

"They will. Last time, they didn't believe you because you were so little. And you *were* right. That's why people shun you, because of their own guilt. They'll listen to you now."

She wished that was true. "I don't know when it's going to happen. Maybe not for years."

"Or sooner. You've read the newspapers. You know everyone talks about war, and what the Japanese are doing in the Orient. Besides, it doesn't matter when, you know it's *going* to happen and that's enough."

"It's not enough. I'm—"

"Scared. You have this incredible ability inside you, yet you hide from it. You think people will mock you. You fear what your father will say. He's desperate to keep what you can do a secret, to keep you locked away in that funeral parlor. He doesn't encourage you to go to college, find a husband or anything. It's almost like he's—" Marta cut off and a pretty flush burned her cheeks.

Like he's ashamed of me, Addie thought. No, that wasn't quite it. As if he was *afraid* of her. That's why Father had always been so distant, and even more so since Mother's death. Why he'd been so furious when he'd discovered she and Mother had gone to the police about Hugo. And why, after the circus that had followed, he'd forbid Addie and her mother from even speaking of her strange affliction. Because what Addie could see, feel, and sometimes even taste scared him to death.

But not as much as it scared her.

Marta took her hands, gently this time. "Addie, this is not the time to shrink with fear. Think of those poor men. Think of what they'll suffer, what their families will suffer. You *must* do something."

Addie trembled under Marta's pleading gaze. Her cousin had a tender heart and a passion to make things right. She recalled the baby bird Marta found outside their house years ago, shivering, clinging to life. She'd made it her mission to nurse that bird back to health, and she had. She'd fixed the little thing through sheer force of will.

Addie shook her head, wishing she had one iota of Marta's courage. "I'm sorry, I can't."

"You can't? You *won't*." She released Addie's hands and scowled. "Sometimes I just don't understand you. If *I* had the power to stop such a terrible thing, I would."

Marta bounced off the bed and huffed out of the room to go wash up for dinner. Addie watched her go, knowing truer words were never spoken. If Marta had the Sight, she would change the world. Whether the world was ready for it or not.

Cousin Hans served himself a heaping portion of Aunt Trudy's *mohnnudeln* then passed the bowl to Addie. She scooped a smaller amount of the buttery noodles made from poppy-seeds and potatoes, trying her best to ignore Marta's disapproving glares.

At the head of the dining room table, Father sipped his wine and gazed fondly at Hans, who seemed to inhale the noodles without tasting. "I see work is good for your appetite, Hans," he said, his accent nearly gone after twenty-three years living in America. "Has it been busy at the construction site?"

Hans looked up from his plate and grinned Marta's grin, the only thing he shared with his sister. At twenty-four, he was a copy of his father, minus thirty pounds—tall, blocky build, brushy blonde hair and solemn blue eyes.

"Busy, and how," Hans said, his accent more pronounced than Marta's. "The fire tower's a big project, but we're moving lightning fast." He stuffed a forkful of roast beef into his mouth. "When it's done, it'll be twice the size of the tower near Haines Quarry, with a view for miles. Spotters can watch for fires in several towns."

Uncle Eb sat up, his keen gaze on his son. "Interesting. The spotters will also have a view of the seacoast, to watch for foreign ships."

He spoke with barely an accent. Father had told Addie he'd attended a British school before the war, which explained his impeccable English. Still, that didn't keep Uncle Eb from railing against Father's rule that no German be spoken at home, especially at the dining table.

"And you, Marta?" Father said, quickly changing the subject. "How is school?"

Marta chased a slippery noodle around her plate with her fork. "*De*-lightful. The cafeteria had liver and onions for lunch today. Did you know the home economics classes prepare our meals? I swear those girls go out of their way to find the worst recipes to experiment with. I said no thanks and grabbed a hot dog from the vendor outside Schulman's instead."

Father chuckled then turned his attention to Addie. He sipped his Riesling wine, eyeing her still-full plate with a frown. "Aren't you hungry, Adelaide? Your aunt will be offended if you only pick at the delicious meal she's prepared."

She glanced at Aunt Trudy, seated across the table next to Marta. Light from the chandelier highlighted the silver threads in her hair and the lines around her eyes. Why would her aunt be offended? She picked at her food all the time. Addie couldn't recall seeing her eat more than a few morsels at any meal. No wonder she was so thin.

"Or are you unwell?" Father continued. "You left work early Monday. You've been as listless as a sloth since. Is something wrong?"

If only he was truly interested in what ailed her. "I'm fine, Father, it's just—"

"I heard encouraging news on the wireless in the parlor earlier," Uncle Eb cut in, interrupting Addie as he always did. At least it put an end to Father's inquisition. "Our army is now close to Moscow. The Wehrmacht will crush the inferior Communist forces in no time."

Addie frowned. Uncle Eb could barely contain his glee.

He'd been licking his lips with delight since the German army had invaded Poland and the European war had begun.

"You underestimate the tenacity of the Soviet forces, Eb," Father said. "And the deadly power of a Russian winter."

"Bah," he spat, brushing that off with a wave.

Father's chair creaked as he shifted and shot him a challenging look. "Well, suppose you are right. Suppose the Russians capitulate, and England falls too. What then? The Reich has become an insatiable beast. Will Hitler set his sights on us next?"

"Us?" Uncle Eb's upper lip curled. "Can you not feel even a small amount of pride in what our people have accomplished? The German people, I mean."

Addie smoothed the linen napkin across her lap. Marta rolled her eyes. Aunt Trudy plucked at a piece of pumpernickel bread like a nervous sparrow. Hans's gaze jumped between the two men, seated at opposite ends of the table.

"They are not my people, Eb." Father sliced into his roast beef as if performing surgery, a slight scowl the only sign of his annoyance. "*These* are my people now. My daughter..." He gestured to Addie with his knife. "Your children, our neighbors. Americans all. You forget that, much to our peril. You know German Americans have fallen out of favor with the onset of war. To crow over the Reich's victories invites ruin on us. We can't afford to push away any more business."

Uncle Eb's expression tightened. "You fear these neighbors whose business you covet. You fear losing profits to the point you forget who you are. You are a *German*."

"And you're a fool," Hans snapped. "You were destitute and without work in that Germany you love so much. If Uncle Otto hadn't paid our way here and given you a job, we would've starved. And what do you do to thank him? You insult our new home and shirk your work duties every chance you get."

"Hans, that'll do," Father said, but Addie could hear admiration in his voice.

"I won't be silent, Uncle. *He's* the reason you've lost customers." Hans stabbed a finger at his father. "He broadcasts his love of Hitler and everything that monster stands for to anyone who'll listen. Can you blame people for shunning us? For going elsewhere to bury their dead? It's *his* fault."

Uncle Eb eyed Hans stonily. "I should've answered the call from the Fatherland and sent you home when you completed school. You'd have done your duty, joined the army and distinguished yourself as your friends back in Germany have."

Addie cringed at his malicious tone. She would've been completely cowed if her father had spoken to her like that. But not Hans. He laughed.

"You're going to get half your wish, Father." He looked around the table, connecting gazes with each of them until he had everyone's attention. "I made up my mind. When the fire tower's finished in January, I'm going to join the army." He stared straight at his father. "I'm joining the *American* army, Father, and you can't stop me."

Marta gasped. Aunt Trudy finished obliterating the piece of pumpernickel bread. Uncle Eb slumped, deflating like a punctured tire. Father eyed Hans with a mixture of dread and approval.

Hans went back to his meal. His fork tinged against the plate, like an anvil's clang in the stunned silence. Addie had never seen his future and now she didn't need to, if he followed through and enlisted. What the Sight had shown her of Marta's future crystallized. She would become the nurse she'd always wanted to be, but Marta wouldn't be working at an ordinary hospital, she'd be tending the wounded near the battlefield.

Anxiety roiled in Addie's belly. War was coming to America and both her cousins would be in the thick of it. In harm's way. If what she'd seen came to pass, Hitler wouldn't be turning his sights on America, his Japanese allies would. A horrendous, crippling assault that would demand retaliation. It would mean war.

Addie had the power to stop it.

She gazed at Father. Though only forty-seven, he looked much older. His shoulders drooped and worry lines marred his once-smooth face. The war abroad had dealt a blow to his business. Mother's loss had struck an even greater blow to his heart. With all his troubles, he'd probably be furious if she revealed her ungodly affliction to the world.

But what did that matter with so much at stake? Father had seen war, fighting for Germany. She heard him cry out sometimes at night, as he relived the horror of battle in his sleep. Surely he'd understand. If she could warn about the attack, somehow stop it, she could save lives, maybe prevent a larger and nastier war from starting. Keep her cousins safe here at home.

Wouldn't that be worth Father's embarrassment, or the loss of a few more customers?

Marta caught her eye and nodded, as if reading her

thoughts. This was bigger than Addie's petty fears. Already a pariah, what more harm could she inflict on herself? She couldn't waffle or fret any longer. She had to raise the alarm.

She had to tell someone.

Chapter Four

Addie slipped out of work at lunch and ankled up Holmes Street and five blocks down on Main to police headquarters. She flapped her coat all the way to get the smell out. Her story would smell fishy enough without the added stink of embalming fluids. Marta had offered to skip school and go with her, which would've been thoughtful if Addie hadn't known her cousin would welcome any excuse to miss algebra class. She'd declined the offer. No use in both of them getting laughed at.

Butterflies raged in Addie's belly as she gazed up at the four-story brick building. Bars covered the windows on the lowest level. At the top of a steep flight of stone steps, a transom window over the door bore the words *Goveport Police* in sea salt-eaten gold letters.

Cold bit through her leather glove as she held the iron rail and started up the steps. Fearful memories surged. Addie, a nervous girl of thirteen, climbing these steps, clinging to Mother's hand. The dismissive way the policemen had treated them that day. The frightened stares, the whispers, and the schoolyard teasing she'd faced after Hugo's body was found. And in the weeks and months after that, the desperate folks who had knocked on their front door, begging Addie to help them find buried treasure and straying husbands.

Father had forcefully sent them away and the furor had subsided over time, but the way people still sidled away from her on the street, she had little hope the legend of Addled Addie had faded from the memory of the Goveport police department.

At the landing at the top of the stairs, she reached for the doorknob and almost leapt over the rail when the door flew open. Two flatfoots in knee-length wool coats and hats with earflaps burst out of the building.

Addie willed herself calm as the men passed, then she stepped into a large, square, wood-paneled room with a flight of stairs on the left and benches against the wall on the right. Police officers sat at cluttered wooden desks lined up in rows, or they milled about in the area beyond a long reception counter. Telephones rang, typewriters clattered, men talked. Cigarette smoke hung like clouds overhead, trapping the smell of sweat, coffee, and a hint of whiskey.

A hush fell as every man in the room turned and stared. Addie had been prepared for laughter or curious looks, but this ogling, men assessing her as a woman, was something unexpected. She wasn't sure how she felt about it. Flattered or offended? Perhaps a little of both.

"May I help you, miss?" the pale young man at the counter said, standing as she approached. His stool was tall, he was not, and Addie found herself looking down.

Here goes nothing.

"I want to report a crime. Uh, not a crime. An attack I think will happen. Soon. Maybe not soon, but it'll happen." The cop's expression went from polite interest to dismay. She imagined Marta by her side, telling her to spit it out, for pity's sake. "I think there's going to be an enemy attack on a Navy base, and I want to tell someone so they can stop it."

That got his attention. It got everyone's attention. Typing ceased, conversation stilled. The short cop's eyes narrowed. *He thinks I'm pulling his leg.*

"What's this, Officer Pellerin?" A pudgy man of about forty strode up. He had sergeant stripes on his uniform and carried a cup brimful of steaming black coffee.

"Sergeant Gillis, this *lady* thinks we have time to waste on false reports of a ridiculous nature," Pellerin said.

Gillis eyed her with clear blue eyes. "Please, come with me," he said after a moment.

He swung open a hinged wooden gate connected to the counter, granting her access to the male domain beyond. She followed him to the back, acutely aware of being watched. Gillis stopped at a paper-strewn wooden desk and nodded at the chair next to it. Addie sat, smoothing her coat over her knees, grateful she had her back to the staring men.

The sergeant settled into a creaking chair and took a sip of his coffee. His lips puckered in distaste. "Cripes that's bitter." He shot Addie a rueful look. "The wife's got me on a reducing diet. No sugar, no cream." He set the coffee mug on his desk and got down to business. "Now, would you care to repeat what you told Officer Pellerin, Miss...?"

"Brandt. Addie Brandt," she said, her voice shaking. The sergeant stiffened. "Do you know who I am? Do you also know what...what some say I can do?"

"I've only been here a couple years," he said. "But I've heard your name bandied about. Something about a lost boy years ago, about you somehow knowing his location. I don't put much stock in rumors. I want to hear what you have to say."

"What if I said the rumors are true? That I have a strange talent." She nearly choked on the word. Movie stars and artists had talent. She did not. If the Sight was anything, it was a curse. "I see flashes of the future, with a simple touch." She held up her hands, safe inside her gloves.

"All right. Let's say your claim is true and you've somehow glimpsed the future. You're here today to... What?"

What, indeed. "To warn you, I suppose. So you can warn others and maybe stop the terrible thing I saw."

He picked up a chewed-up pencil and held it over a notepad. "Okay, shoot."

She glanced around. A curly haired blonde of about twenty-six hunched over his desk across from the sergeant's. His pencil scratched busily, but Addie suspected he listened to them. And so did the officer riffling through a filing cabinet drawer, the Negro janitor mopping up spilled coffee, and everyone else.

Asking themselves one question—is Addie Brandt insane?

She turned back to Sgt. Gillis. Might as well finish the job and remove all doubt.

"There's an American naval base in Hawaii, in the Pacific Ocean. I've seen..." She swallowed. "I've seen an attack, a horrible attack from the air."

He looked up from his pad. "You don't say? And when's this attack's going to happen?"

Her heart sank all the way to her toes at the skepticism in his voice. *He's humoring me.*

"I don't know, Sergeant," she said. "All I know is it'll be morning. The Japanese will send dozens of planes, maybe even hundreds, and they'll bomb and they'll shoot and they'll kill—" Her throat closed. She couldn't choke out another word.

"The Japanese are going to bomb a Navy base? An *American* base?"

Addie gazed wearily at the source of the outburst, the curly haired policeman across the aisle. He had a round, cherub-like face with rosy cheeks and long eyelashes, but his expression was anything but pleasant.

"I've heard some strange stories in my life," he said. "But that's slug-nutty. Wouldn't be surprised if the Krauts attacked, with Hitler in the driver's seat. But the Japanese? Poppycock."

"It's what I saw," Addie said in a small voice that sounded desperate to her own ears.

"Did you see pink elephants too?" he said with a snort. "Why don't you go home and sleep it off."

"Knock it off, Pete," Sgt. Gillis said, but Addie suspected he agreed with the young man. She was drunk. Or hysterical, or just plain loony. Probably everyone thought that.

"You must believe me." She fought to contain her

distress, and her growing anger. She'd rather be sent to blazes than show how much this Pete had upset her. "I wouldn't have come here if I wasn't serious. If I didn't believe the threat was real."

"I'd like to believe you," Gillis said. "But I told you, I'm new in town, moved here to be closer to the wife's family. Now, in New Hampshire where I'm from, we had a lady come in once a week and predict all manner of mayhem. She knew names, dates, places right down to longitude and latitude, but the one thing she didn't have was proof." His gaze dipped to her hands, folded on her lap. "Do *you* have any proof?"

"Proof? You mean you want me to demonstrate my...talent?"

Pete snorted with laughter. "Like a penny-a-fortune seer at a carnival."

"Pete, I told you to knock it off," Gillis said, sterner this time and Pete's smug grin vanished. The sergeant turned back to Addie. "Yes, Miss Brandt, I'm afraid that's exactly what I want. Proof."

"It-it doesn't work in that way. There's no guarantee I'll see the same images, have the same vision, or have a vision at all." Well, she'd never tried to summon the Sight. Why would she, when it always muscled its way in, like a rude neighbor crashing a party.

"Well then." The sergeant's blue eyes narrowed. "What do you expect me to do?"

Addie's anger threatened to boil over. "Can't you call the Navy or the FBI or someone?"

"And tell them what? A fanciful girl thinks there might be a strike against one of our naval bases at some point in the future? I'm sorry, dear, that's not what police work is. I can't call anyone without something solid to go on." He held out his hand. "Or some kind of proof."

She stared at his palm as if it held a bomb. Touch him? What good would that do? If the Sight showed her a vision, it would most likely be terrible. And whatever she saw might not happen until next week or next year. She shook her head and the sergeant frowned.

"Bah! I thought as much. Why don't you run on home, Miss Brandt, and forget this foolishness?"

Addie lost the battle to hold her temper. Marta liked to say never get a German angry. Or an Irishwoman. The blood of both pumped furiously through her veins.

By golly, she'd do it.

Cool air tickled her skin as she stripped off a glove and reached for the sergeant's hand. Silence fell in the precinct again. Everyone watched her. Pete licked his lips. Addie's hand hovered over Gillis's. She felt his skin's warmth and she cringed. She hadn't held anyone's hand since Mother's, years ago. The day the Sight showed her Mother was going to die.

But she had to. With the fate of so many men hanging in the balance, with the future of her cousins at stake, she *had* to touch him. She'd give him his proof, and let the Sight do its worst.

She pressed her fingers against his. Instantly, darkness as black as pitch blanketed her mind. Her body seized. Images flashed. Terrifying sensations beat against her brain. It took every ounce of strength she had to tear out of the Sight's grip.

She opened her eyes to see Sgt. Gillis smirking at her. "Well? Where's my proof?

Addie scrabbled her glove back onto her hand and shot

out of her seat. The chair legs squawked against the floor-boards. "I-I can't," she said hastily. "I'm sorry."

"Crazy as a loon," she heard Pete say as she snatched up her pocketbook and dashed away. "Shame. She's a real looker."

Gillis's reply carried across the room after her. "All the nutty ones are."

Burning with fury and humiliation, Addie flung open the front door and slammed into a wall. No, not a wall, a man. A powerfully built man, with shoulders as broad as an anchor filling his overcoat and a chest apparently made of iron. She felt its firmness under her palms. She looked up to see a face like Dick Tracy in the funny papers—all angles. Razor sharp jaw, full lips, crooked nose, black hair under a fedora perched at a rakish angle. And eyes the color of brown sugar. Curious eyes that kept her gaze a moment too long.

"Whoa, sister. Where's the fire?" he said, his voice as deep as the ocean. He smelled like the ocean, too. Fresh, salty-sharp, like he'd been born on Pott's Beach.

She laughed bitterly. Couldn't help it, after what the Sight had inflicted on her in the heartbeat she'd held the sergeant's hand. Addie as Gillis, bent over a body, at the foot of a massive structure engulfed in flames. An ear-splitting pop rent the air and she looked up. The structure shuddered then chunks of burning wood splintered and plummeted down.

She'd ripped herself out of the vision before the fatal moment the scorching embers crashed onto her. Or Gillis, rather. But she knew with certainty the sergeant would die a brutal, fiery death.

Somehow, she made it around the big man she'd

slammed into, mighty glad her hands were covered and she couldn't make contact with him. She'd had enough of the Sight for one day.

Besides, she did *not* want to know what could fell a giant Redwood tree of a man like him.

Chapter Five

If Dunstan had to slam into a woman fleeing police headquarters like her hair had caught fire, then this was the dame he wanted to run into. A tall, leggy beauty, with honey-gold hair that tumbled over her shoulders, plump lips meant for kissing, a lush, curvy body meant for a whole lot more, and eyes as blue as a September sky. Troubled eyes. Deeply troubled.

He quirked an eyebrow, intrigued. She'd gotten bad news in there. Maybe a relative had gone missing, or a husband pinched for poaching.

He and the beauty did a confused two-step before she righted herself and bolted down the steps. When Dunstan entered the police station, he saw why the girl had run like she'd just busted out of an asylum. The joint was in an uproar. Laughter, hooting, excited chatter, as if the whole place had just won the Irish Sweepstakes.

"Can I help you, mister?" the kid at the front desk asked, chortling.

"Can I help *you* is the question," Dunstan said. "What's going on? You fellas get hold of some giggle juice?"

The cop let out a blat of laughter. "I think the girl who just left must've. Comes in, claiming she can see the future. Said she saw some kind of attack."

Dunstan glared toward the door. Was that beauty he'd knocked into outside the woman he'd come here to find? *Damn*. He'd been too busy admiring her to get a read on her. He swiveled and eyed the desk clerk, a thundercloud coming over him. He itched to pick up this pipsqueak and throttle his mocking hide until he turned as blue as his uniform. Then take on the rest of these dopes.

He tamed his inner beast—a struggle—and demanded, "Who'd she talk to?"

The kid wiped his streaming eyes with his sleeve. "What's it to you, bub?"

Dunstan leaned forward, just enough to crowd the fella. It had the desired effect. Pipsqueak sobered, and quick.

"It's *everything* to me. Now, who did she talk to?"

❧

"Look, I know he's busy, but for Christ's sake, this is important."

Dunstan tucked the base of the old-fashioned candlestick telephone under his arm, tipped the earpiece against his ear and winced at the squawks on the other end of the line.

"Yes ma'am," he said. "I'm sorry, ma'am. I know there's no need to blaspheme, but there *is* a need to hurry." He sighed as the secretary asked for his name once again.

"Jack Dunstan." A long pause. *Nuts*. She had no idea who he was. "Tell him it's about Operation Mind Reader."

He could almost see the secretary's mocking sneer. Their team's code name made him want to sneer too. Radcliffe had saddled the group with that ridiculous moniker long before Dunstan had been recruited. Nobody could read minds. At least, he'd never met a gifted person who could. His team member Pearl could bend animals to her will. Garrity had the strength of an ox. Virginia could make any warm-blooded creature fall for her. Madelyn and that bastard Woden had their particular talents, but none of them could read minds.

Addie Brandt came the closest. *If* her gift was real.

Dunstan bit back a curse. If he'd gotten to the police station sooner, he could've spoken to her. Instead, he'd spent the morning haunting every eatery and smoke shop in Goveport, trying to learn as much as he could about the girl. He went to the cops only when he had a name, Adelaide Brandt, known around town as Addled Addie. That cruel nickname made him burn.

"One moment," the old biddy on the other end of the line said finally. Dunstan heard the clunk of the handset being dropped on her desk and the tick of heels retreating across tiled floor.

He paced as far from the telephone table as the phone's cord would let him, then back again. The steam radiator pinged a jazzy tune, trying to heat the suite's parlor. Damned ineffective. The cold seeped through the window cracks. He'd taken this shabby suite of rooms, with two postage-stamp-sized bedrooms, a tiny kitchen, and a parlor with a sagging sofa and an even droopier armchair, because it rented by the week for a low rate.

The Savoy Hotel was also out of the way, easier not to be noticed. Not that he'd been laying low today as he browbeat that wheezing Sgt. Gillis for information, right there in front of Goveport's finest.

The door opened and Virginia breezed in, carrying several packages and a hat box. She removed her perfectly serviceable winter hat, edged with some poor bird's missing feathers.

Dunstan pressed the telephone's mouthpiece to his chest. "How much did you spend?"

"You want me to look my best, don't you?" She hung up her coat in the small closet, tossed her hat on the shelf next to his gun holster, and closed the door. "You know I can't do my job properly unless I look like a million bucks."

He couldn't help a grin. Even if Virginia's gift didn't work on him, she was persuasive.

"Who're you talking to?" She opened the hatbox and removed a green confection dotted with silk flowers.

"Radcliffe's office. I found our girl."

"My goodness that was fast." She put on the hat and gazed at her reflection in the mirror hanging by the door.

"I take no credit. She practically mowed me down outside the police station. She had a vision and went to the cops. They didn't believe her."

Virginia met his eyes in the mirror and frowned. "Fools. Wait, a vision?" She spun around. "Is that why you called the boss?"

"Not calling him to chat." He nodded to the pack of Luckys and his lighter on the stub-legged coffee table in front of the sofa. "Light one up for me, will you?"

He watched her shake a cigarette free and flip the

lighter's lid, her polished red fingernails against the silver surface. The lighter had been a gift to him from Madelyn for his birthday after they'd met in Sarasota. When he was happy. Before he knew the truth.

Virginia lit up with a choking cough—she didn't smoke —then popped the cigarette into his mouth. He took a deep drag, trying to calm the riot in his gut. If Addie Brandt was right, and he didn't warn Radcliffe and the boys in Washington in time, then...

Disaster was too light a word for what could happen.

"Have you confirmed the girl's got a gift?" Virginia asked.

"Not exactly. From what I found out, she never went to the police again after the incident with the boy." He exhaled heavily. "So that could've been a fluke."

Virginia set her new hat on the coffee table then headed for the liquor cart. One good thing about this place, a well-stocked bar. She held up a glass, but he declined. Not now. He needed a clear head when he spoke to Radcliffe.

"Perhaps what the girl saw *was* a fluke." The bottle clinked against the glass as she poured herself a whiskey. "Or maybe the poor dear was frightened. Dunstan, I was terrified when my gift made itself known, and I was nineteen. She was thirteen, and they probably laughed at her."

Still laughing at her. The memory of those flatfooted fools ridiculing her and the mocking way some of the townsfolk had spoken of her heated his blood to boiling.

Damn it all. He'd always been driven to play the hero, the protective knight in shining armor. Woden had known that. So had Madelyn, and they had both used that need to snare him. He wouldn't let himself be

44

caught again. But the way Addie's wide blue eyes had looked at him when they'd collided, distraught and filled with pain, had stirred something in him he thought long dead.

A voice crackled over the phone line. Radcliffe's secretary, bringing him back to the matter at hand. She didn't have good news for him.

"Gone for the day?" Dunstan repeated, irked. "But I've *got* to talk to him. It's a matter of national importance. Yes, ma'am. I understand. Would you tell him I called? I'm at the Savoy Hotel in Goveport, Massachusetts. Tell him to telephone me right away."

He hung up and dropped into a chair. *Now* he needed a drink. Virginia seemed to think so too. She stuck a glass full to nearly overflowing with cheap scotch into his hand.

"What do we do now?" she asked and settled on the sofa, resting her whiskey glass on her knee.

The question most on his mind. What should their next step be?

Drink in one hand, cigarette in the other, he got up and went to the window. He stared out at the city, built on a hill so steep a small earthquake could send the whole place sliding into the sea. Brick apartment houses and granite office buildings crowded next to the Savoy here at the top of the hill. Farther down, a number of piers and wharves jut out into the bay. A maze of tenements hunched by the water's edge.

Where the fishermen lived. Dunstan knew those tenements. Clapboard tinderboxes, beaten down by New England weather. The peeling paint, kerosene lamps, water that ran cold in the summer and frigid in the winter. He knew because he'd grown up in such a place.

"First thing," he said. "We assess if the girl truly has a gift."

"If she does, what then?"

"I recruit her."

"That'll be easy as pie." Virginia let out a dour laugh. "And if she isn't gifted?"

He shrugged. He'd begun this search as a selfish journey to salvage his team's reputation. To hopefully find someone with a gift powerful enough to keep Operation Mind Reader alive. But the situation had suddenly turned ugly.

He drained his drink in a fast gulp.

He hoped the Brandt girl would turn out to be as batty as the cops claimed. Because if she had a gift, if she'd truly seen the future, then all hell was about to break loose.

Chapter Six

Michael Feeney cursed.

He could tell all kinds of things about the future with a single touch, but he'd be damned if he could predict whether his ancient Model T Ford would make it up Atlantic Avenue's steep incline. He pressed the gas pedal and the engine coughed and wheezed like Jack Benny's old Maxwell, threatening to give up the ghost.

"Get a horse!" one of the two dozen men who'd hopped off the city bus hollered.

The fella's companions guffawed and jabbed each other in the ribs as Michael's jalopy sputtered by. They all headed to the same place as Michael, the fire tower construction site on Goveport's north end.

By some miracle, his car reached the worksite's access road. He crept along the deeply rutted dirt track through the trees and pulled up moments later at a broad, open space near the top of the cliffs. This area used to be stuffed with pines until the monster hurricane that had eaten up the East Coast in '38 had knocked them down. FDR's Civilian Conservation Corps had hauled away the upended trees, clearing the area. Maybe why the government chose to build the fire spotting station here, so close to the ocean.

Michael killed the engine but didn't get out. He took his silver flask from his jacket pocket and knocked back his first belt of the morning. Second drink, to be honest. He couldn't leave the house without a shot of Old Crow. Couldn't get through the rest of the day without whiskey to dull his senses, either. Not since that day the Sight had crashed over him like a vengeful wave.

Six years ago, that was. The day he'd touched his brother and had seen a future that terrified him so much, he hadn't dared touch a living soul since. Six years since he'd shaken Da's hand or hugged his ma. The last time he'd kissed a girl.

The last time he'd been sober.

He took a healthy swallow and another for good measure, then put the flask away and climbed out of the car, heading for the fire tower. The day had dawned clear and cold. The tower's wooden skeleton, girdled by a multi-level scaffolding, shot up into the cloudless sky. With the frame complete, the workers had begun laying on planks for siding, leaving space for windows.

The men streamed in from the road. They were dressed like Michael—boots, dark green work shirt and trousers, heavy jacket with a thick collar, and a union suit underneath to keep their fannies warm. They set their lunch pails on the picnic table near the supervisor's office and got to work. Soon, their mixed babble of German, Italian, French, Portuguese, and English filled the air, nearly drowned out by the pound of hammers on wood.

Michael took attendance, dealt with any problems that cropped up, kept things on track. Charlie Chester, the project supervisor, rolled in around ten in his spanking new car. Pushing fifty, with the gray hair to prove it, he wore a fancy suit stretched over his big belly and acted like the day could begin now that he'd arrived.

"Feeney, I wanna talk to you!" he bellowed.

Michael hustled over and followed him inside the supervisor's office, a one-room shack with a metal desk, a couple of file cabinets, and a wood-burning stove that was never lit. Though the building sat a good hundred yards from the construction site, Fat Charlie wouldn't take the risk of a fire getting out of control.

"What's on your mind, sir?" Michael asked. His breath puffed a cloud into the icy room.

"Time, that's what." Fat Charlie stood on the other side of the desk. Sunlight beamed through the windows, making him look like a ghostly W. C. Fields, with his pale, fleshy face and balloon nose. "We're moving along, but we need to speed the work up. The men are slower than turtles stuck in molasses. You know as well as I do the job's got to be done the first of January, no later."

"That deadline's always troubled me, sir," Michael said. "What's the rush? Why New Year's Day? Fire danger's low in winter. The spotting tower won't be useful until the warmer months. Why do we have to hurry? Aren't you worried a rush job will lead to shoddy work?"

Fat Charlie propped his fists on the desk and leaned toward Michael. "I'm more worried Uncle Sam will start breathing down my neck, Feeney. The Forestry Service wants the station in operation next month, and I'm going to make damn sure to deliver." He shifted and pasted on one of his fake smiles. "I know I'm riding you and the rest of the fellas. And I know it's winter and getting on to Christmas. Everyone's got their minds on fruitcake and pretty girls in red instead of work. But this is an important job. We've *got* to meet the deadline. Tell the men to pitch in and get it done."

Michael frowned. Not like the men weren't already working hard. "This is an important job how, sir?"

He'd asked that question before. He may be just a dumb Mick, but even he knew a fire spotting tower didn't need to be so tall. Or built so close to the ocean's edge. Or in need of two radio rooms and so many lookout points. Something was up. Why else would his boss demand the cops send a squad car to check on the site every night when they'd all gone home?

But Fat Charlie was in no mood to answer. Not today, or any other day.

"Never you mind," he said, one eye narrowed, warning Michael to lay off. "Just do as I ask, son. *If* you want to be foreman on my next job."

Michael muttered, "Yes, sir," and backed out the door into the cold. He hated when Charlie got in a crabby mood. Hated scuffles and arguments of all kinds. Strange that he'd ended up foreman, buttering up his boss and telling everyone else what to do when he just wanted to be left alone.

He took another snort and went to tell the men to get moving, on the double.

When lunch break came, Michael shaded his eyes from the sun and watched the crew put their tools aside and climb down the scaffold. The temperature hovered around freezing, but most of the fellas had worked up a sweat and shed their wool jackets and gloves. Sawdust clung to their trousers and boots.

His gaze lit on Hans Brandt on the top level, just finishing up. The kid swung his hammer like a cudgel. He wasn't cut out for this kind of work, but because they were cousins of a sort—Addie's mother had been Da's baby sister, the first Feeney born in America—Michael wouldn't tell Hans so, to keep peace in the family.

Most of the men gathered around the picnic table to eat, except for the colored fellas on the crew, who hunkered down by a tree stump with their meal. Michael wouldn't eat with any of them. Though he wore gloves and was halfway to pickled, he still wouldn't risk triggering the Sight by getting close to anyone.

Besides, the fellas were sore at him today for pushing them to hurry up and they needed time to cool off.

He grabbed his lunch pail from his car and headed toward the cliffs that overlooked the Atlantic, where it met the Perkins River. The river flowed from the west, cutting between the rocky outcropping where Michael stood and even steeper cliffs across the way. Far below, the tide rushed in, gushing into the river's mouth with muscular force.

He sat on the cold ground and uncapped his flask, taking generous sips as he chewed on his ham sandwich. Seagulls swooped by, squawking, begging him to toss them a crumb. A bitter wind whipped up from the ocean, stinging Michael's face. The sun sparkled off the water, lighting the dense growth of pines at the clifftop across the river like a painting. Funny how that bastard of a hurricane had spared most of the trees over there and knocked them all down here.

A flash of light in the trees caught his eye. Michael squinted, seeing another flash, sun glinting off metal or something. Maybe an intrepid hiker's walking poles. Could be sunlight bounced off a deer hunter's rifle, though the deer usually grazed further inland, near the quarry.

Or someone could be spying.

On them.

Unease prickled down his spine. He looked back at the construction site. Finished with lunch, the men drifted back to the fire tower. There was something odd about that structure. Something Fat Charlie wanted to keep secret.

A secret someone else might want to know.

Charlie had left the site a while ago, headed to town for a long lunch as he liked to do. Should Michael tell him about the flashes when he got back? What would he tell him? He'd seen a twinkle of light, nothing more. Michael squeezed the flask in his hand. Maybe he hadn't seen anything at all. Whiskey did a dandy job keeping the Sight at bay, but it also made his brain as fuzzy as hell.

He closed the lid on his lunch pail and screwed the cap on his flask. Best to keep his mouth shut. Speaking up wouldn't change anything, wouldn't stop a bad thing from happening. If he thought it would, he'd shout from the treetops what the Sight had shown him of his brother Danny's fate. He couldn't change the future any more than Addie could have when she warned about that missing boy. It had gotten her nothing but grief. And a kid still died.

Michael tucked the flask back into his pocket, tucking away his suspicions, too, and any thought of speaking up.

Then he went back to work.

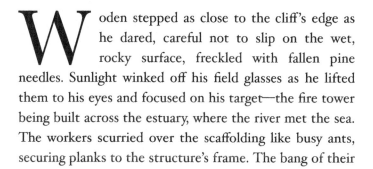

Woden stepped as close to the cliff's edge as he dared, careful not to slip on the wet, rocky surface, freckled with fallen pine needles. Sunlight winked off his field glasses as he lifted them to his eyes and focused on his target—the fire tower being built across the estuary, where the river met the sea. The workers scurried over the scaffolding like busy ants, securing planks to the structure's frame. The bang of their hammers striking nails were like pistol shots echoing off the cliffs.

"Impressive," Woden said. "The project is moving along apace, even in this cold weather." He handed the binoculars to Falcon, who'd come up beside him.

"A pity they'll never complete their task," Falcon said, looking through the lenses. "If our mission is successful."

Woden frowned at the uncertainty in Falcon's voice. "There is no doubt our mission will succeed."

"I still wonder about choosing Hans for this task. Are you sure he can be turned?"

Annoyance flared in Woden's core, igniting his gift. He loathed being questioned by anyone, especially an underling. "The boy will do as I command," he bit off. And so would Adelaide, when the time came.

The sudden sound of a person crashing toward them through the woods cut off further discussion.

"That would be Smith," Woden said, his irritation growing. Their local contact, making more noise than a bull elephant as he made his way up the path from the road.

Ordering Falcon to stay out of sight, Woden moved through the trees toward a clearing where the Wentworth property stood, an abandoned Colonial-style home that served as their meeting place.

"That hill could challenge a mountain goat," Smith said, wheezing and puffing as he rounded the corner of the decaying house.

Woden ground his teeth. The trek up from the street was no challenge to a man as fit as himself, but Smith seemed to have little familiarity with exercise. At least his contact spoke German, as instructed. The man's English was flawless, and they were alone except for Falcon hidden nearby, but Woden was taking no chances.

"How inconvenient for you to have to exert yourself, Smith," he said. "Come, tell me what has happened to require this urgent meeting."

"I'm sorry, but it's about Addie. You told me to let you know if—"

Woden held up his hand. "*Adelaide*, if you will." Addie was a childish name. Adelaide was the name of a warrior, a woman of untold power.

"Yes, of course, Adelaide." Smith mopped perspiration from his brow with the back of his hand. "You wanted to know if she did anything unusual from her daily routine. She visited the police station yesterday. To report some kind of vision."

"Continue," Woden prodded, intrigued.

"She claimed she saw an attack by the Japanese on a naval base in the Pacific."

Woden stiffened. He didn't doubt Adelaide's gift of

sight. He had confirmed her ability himself. But would the Reich's erstwhile allies dare attempt an act of aggression so bold?

"No one believed her, of course," Smith said. "Just another tale from Addled Addie."

Woden's irritation blossomed into anger. His fearsome gift awakened. Curse these small-minded people who feared and belittled what they didn't understand.

"Do you think Addie, er, Adelaide could be trouble? Or a risk to the operation?" Smith licked his lips. "I could get rid of her."

Woden leveled a cold gaze at him. "Don't be a fool. She's part of my plan. She's the reason I chose to stage this mission in Goveport. Continue to keep watch on her, but do *not* harm her. Is that clear?"

Smith grunted a *yes*, as if disappointed he wouldn't be allowed to murder the girl.

Woden bit back a snarl. Smith wasn't his first choice for this mission. Though passionately devoted to their shared cause, the man's pride and tendency to argue with his betters were infuriating. However, he'd gone to the trouble of placing Smith here and putting him in a position where he could keep watch on Adelaide. He had to rely on him. He didn't have to like it.

"Is there anything else we need to discuss?" Woden demanded, eager to end this meeting.

Smith narrowed his eyes. "Yes. A G-man visited the police station yesterday, shortly after Adelaide left. He asked questions about her. Man called Dunstan."

"Dunstan? He's found his way to Goveport, has he?" Woden spoke with cool disinterest, though the anger simmering in his blood flared at the mention of that name.

After Woden had convinced the FBI to establish a special division of gifted agents and to place him in charge of building the team, his real operation had begun—turning those assets to the Nazi cause. His results lagged behind his counterparts in London and Moscow, but Woden had felt confident he could prove his worth.

Then the disaster last year. Dunstan had exposed him, and he'd had to flee.

Woden curled his hands into fists. He'd fallen out of favor with his superiors in Berlin because of Jack. Now, with his last chance to prove his worth hinging on this mission, Dunstan had come on the scene to muck it up.

"Is this Dunstan one of you?" Smith asked. "I mean, is the man like you? Is he a...?"

Freak. The word Smith had left unspoken. *Is he a freak like you?* Woden's fury grew, fed by his fears about Jack and Smith's scorn. His vibrations rumbled and his gift demanded to be cut free of its leash and attack.

Struggling to hold the urges at bay, he pinned Smith in a hard gaze. "What difference would it make if Dunstan was *like me*, as you say?"

Smith's blue eyes returned a defiant stare. "It might make a difference, if the man's dangerous. I need to know if he poses a risk to our plans."

Dark energy surged into Woden's hands. His fingers twitched with the burning need to turn the force of his fury onto this fool. "Do *not* question my authority," he said between clenched teeth. "Leave Dunstan to me. *You* focus on the mission."

"The *mission*," Smith mocked. "What's so important about that fire tower, anyway?"

Woden glared. "Is *that* what you think it is?"

"That's what everyone in this stinking city thinks it is. What everyone says it is. You've been bloody stingy with details of this job, so what in hell am I supposed to think?"

Woden's control broke and he could no longer restrain himself. His anger spiked, his power snapped loose of its chain, and his rage exploded.

"Be *silent*," he ordered, and thrust out his arms. Energy shot from his fingers and drilled into Smith's mind. He corralled the man's thoughts and wound a phantom noose around his neck. He squeezed his hands into fists and cinched the noose so tight Smith's eyes bulged. Gasping for air, Smith dropped to his knees. He gouged at his throat, desperate to loosen the invisible rope that crushed his windpipe.

Woden let his gift flow. Hatred and rage rushed through his blood like a riptide. His skin burned and his nerve endings popped. His anger coiled around his vibrations and shot from his fingertips in fierce waves he could almost taste. Exhilarated and engorged with fury, filled to the core with gritty pleasure, he watched Smith writhe on the ground.

"You will think what *I* tell you to think," Woden bit off. "And *nothing* else. Do you understand?"

Smith gave a terrified nod.

"Breathe." Woden threw open his fists, releasing his victim. He drew back. Physically. It took more effort to retreat mentally. His vibrations hummed with excitement as they cooled. His energy and his anger slowly receded. The satisfaction that had filled him dissipated into nothingness, leaving him empty and craving more.

Smith rolled over, choking and coughing, then staggered to his feet. "You're a real bastard," he croaked, rubbing his throat.

Woden let out a grim laugh. "I have to be, to keep the mission on course. Now, if you're finished insulting me, I have your next assignment. Find me a boat and a skilled man to pilot it. A man who can be counted on to keep his mouth shut. Can you complete this task for me?"

Smith glowered. "Bah! I'm trained to hunt and kill, not play errand boy."

"I am aware of that," Woden said, his temper heating again. "I know you're impatient. I am as well. But you must follow my instructions. There can be *no* missteps for this mission to succeed. In time, your skills will be in great demand. You will spill blood before this is through, I guarantee."

That seemed to placate Smith, and Woden dismissed the man before he gave in to his urges and throttled him again.

"Dunstan's no doubt trying to rebuild the team," Falcon said, joining him after Smith stalked down the path leading to the road. "He's here to recruit the girl."

"He's not going to get her. Adelaide is *mine*." Woden needed her. Not for the mission to succeed, but for his own future. "You leave Jack to me. Now, go," he ordered, wishing to be alone. His attack on Smith had drained him, and he did not want to show Falcon his weakness. "I'll contact you when I have details on the boat."

Falcon handed over the binoculars and left without another word. Eager to escape Woden and his anger, no doubt.

Woden tucked the field glasses into his overcoat pocket and waited until Falcon disappeared from sight.

Only then would he allow himself to feel the pain. Gasping for breath, he slumped against the wall of the house, dislodging chips of peeling paint. He eased off his gloves and examined his aching hands with a furious frown.

They were getting worse. Swollen fingertips stained blue-black. His palms and the backs of his hands criss-crossed with protruding, inky veins that burned as if a thousand hornets had pierced his flesh. The bitter result of giving in to his rage and unleashing the tempest inside him, in exchange for a few moments of pleasure.

Had he learned nothing from his father's fate?

Woden and his father had been blessed with a mighty gift, the ability to control minds. Such power had demanded a price. A vengeful demon lived inside him, compelling him to unleash the fullness of his energy. A hungry demon he found more and more difficult to fight. Father had nourished that beast with abandon. It had eaten away at him until there had been nothing left but a charred, soulless husk of a man, filled with rage.

Woden flexed his hands. The pain slowly ebbed, but the blue-black stain on his fingertips remained. It had spread, too, oozing along his skin past the first knuckle. Smith's fault. The man had pushed him beyond control. He'd had no choice but to punish him. Woden wouldn't let that happen again. Wouldn't give in to the demon next time. Wouldn't indulge in his vulgar cravings. There was too much at stake.

He put on his gloves as he strode back up to the cliff's edge. Holding the binoculars gingerly, he focused once more on the construction site, and Hans, high on the scaffold. The first move on this mission's complicated chessboard. Despite Falcon's doubts, Hans would be the perfect pawn. The boy's plan to take up arms in defense of America and not his German homeland had earned him Woden's contempt and had sealed his fate. He deserved what was going to happen.

Woden shifted his gaze to a tall, slender man with dark hair standing at the base of the structure, speaking with one of the workers. Michael Feeney, Adelaide's cousin, who shared the girl's gift of sight. Feeney would be a useful asset, but any effort to recruit him would have to wait until after Woden had secured Adelaide.

She was his top priority. She possessed something her cousin did not, something of vital importance.

She was German.

The success of this mission would help restore his superiors' faith in him, but bringing them a girl of German blood, born with such a valuable gift, could vault Woden into a position of power within the Reich's intelligence apparatus. Perhaps earn him an audience with the Fuhrer.

If he could turn attention away from his increasingly visible malady. Or find some way to cure it. He squeezed the field glasses with aching fingers, well aware the Fuhrer did not tolerate failure. Or imperfection.

Perhaps Dunstan could be of service in that respect. There must be a way to harness Jack's energy to cure his ailment. His ability to drain emotion had successfully quelled Woden's rage. Surely the man's peculiar gift could be used to rid him completely of the compulsion eating him up inside. If so, there would be no limit to his power.

Woden headed back to the clearing, his spirits lifting. First, he must attend to Hans and the mission, then Adelaide. He felt confident he could convince her to join his cause and travel to Germany with him. She seemed a woman of biddable temperament, from what he'd observed.

Bringing Jack into the fold would be the challenge. Dunstan could not be as easily manipulated as a woman. He must proceed with caution and spring a trap Jack couldn't escape. This time, Woden would win.

Then it would be checkmate, the end of the game.

Chapter Seven

"That's the fifth time you've swept the floor today," Uncle Pat said, coming down the stairs from the viewing rooms above.

"Really?" Addie would never know it from the amount of flower petals, leaves, dirt and even beach sand she swept into the dustpan with her broom.

"Yes, *really*." Uncle Pat carried an arrangement of dried sea grass and carnations across the room to the counter under the windows. He plunked the vase next to the sink and turned to her. "You been cleaning like a dervish all day. Something bothering you?"

She shook the dustpan into the bin. "I'm fine," she said.

Not a lie. Something didn't bother her, *everything* did—her humiliation at the police station, what she saw of Sgt. Gillis's fiery future, her certainty about an assault on Hawaii, and the cold fact that no one believed her. Well, Marta believed her. So would cousin Michael if Addie told him about her vision. He'd believe her, and also call her a fool for sticking her neck out like that. He'd be right, of course. She'd accomplished exactly nothing by going to the police.

Uncle Pat clucked like a disapproving chicken. "You are *not* fine. You're pale and fidgety and worrying yourself to skin and bones. Take a break, go get something to eat."

Addie frowned. She didn't want to go out into public after yesterday.

"Don't give me that look." He jerked his chin toward the door. "Go on. I'm sick of seeing you mope around here. I know you miss your ma. Lord knows, I do too. But it's time to put the past away. You got to get out there and live. Be daring."

A sandwich at Sal's, the only restaurant she felt comfortable enough to go to, didn't exactly qualify as daring. But her uncle was more stubborn than all her Feeney relatives combined, and Addie knew he wouldn't let it go.

"All right," she said with a sigh. The cupboard door's hinges squawked like hungry seagulls as she opened it and put the broom away. "If you think Father won't mind."

"He's gone out. Where, I dunno. Maybe haunting the morgue looking for customers." He winked. "He'll never know you're gone."

She peeled off the white cotton gloves she now wore at work at all times to protect against a repeat of the tiepin incident. She replaced them with her leather winter gloves. She put on her hat and coat then left through the side door into the wide alley where they parked the hearse. She climbed the hill, breathing in Goveport's unique smells, a mix of sea air, car exhaust, and fish. Always fish.

Wet snow began to spit as she reached Main Street. An

icy wind whipped under her skirt and rippled over her stockings. She wished she had the guts to wear the wool trousers Marta had gotten for her on sale at Schulman's, but Aunt Trudy would faint dead away to see her leave the house in men's clothing. That never stopped Marta, who traipsed around town in trousers and Hans's old Brooks Brothers shirts. Addie knew Marta didn't even like wearing pants. She did it simply to be difficult.

The bell over the door jingled merrily as Addie stepped inside the warmth of Sal's Luncheonette, a cozy place on the ground floor of a tall granite office building. At noontime the place would be hopping, but now, after two, the crowd had thinned to a few businessmen at tables and three women in winter hats in one of the booths along the side wall, shopping bags and packages at their feet. They looked up as she entered then put their heads together, whispering.

About her, she feared.

Addie dusted snowflakes from her shoulders and crossed to the Formica counter, where a smattering of customers huddled over their meals—a plump older woman in wool trousers, a Negro man in overalls, and a teen in a beanie cap, slurping Coca-Cola.

Addie steered toward her usual seat, the swivel stool at the end of the counter, away from the others. Her mouth watered and her stomach growled at the scent of fresh-baked Italian bread and Sal's minestrone wafting from the kitchen. Uncle Pat was right about one thing, she had been worrying herself thin. Her skirt's waistband slid easily. She vowed to eat until she popped.

She smoothed her wool skirt under her bottom as she sat and shrugged off her coat. Her gloves stayed on. Rosa

Conti, the waitress, bustled over with a coffee pot and a cup. Tall and buxom, with crooked teeth and black hair as shiny as polished onyx, Rosa wore a pale green dress and white apron.

"Now look what the cat dragged in." Rosa set the cup in front of Addie and filled it with steaming coffee. "Haven't seen you in a dog's age."

"I know it's been a while," Addie said, pulling a paper napkin from the dispenser and wiping down her cup's rim. "Work's been really busy."

"Sure. I bet folks are just *dying* to get into your place."

"Oh, Rosa, that joke's terrible." Addie swallowed a mouthful of the bitter coffee. "And so is this."

Rosa laughed, a cross between a snort and a whinny. Addie laughed too, her mood lightening. She shied away from most other public places, but she always felt comfortable at Sal's. Because of Rosa. They'd met the first day of high school and, despite being opposites in many ways, had become fast friends. Rosa, a fisherman's daughter from Fisk Village, Addie, from a privileged family up by Colby Park, had one thing in common, something that had forged a strong bond—both were picked on and bullied by their classmates.

"So, what'll it be?" Rosa said. "Oh, why do I even ask? You'll have the usual, tuna salad."

Addie splashed milk into her coffee and took another sip, skimming the menu board on the wall over the swinging kitchen doors. Dozens of sandwiches and dinners were listed there, the blocky letters coated with grease and soot and probably sand accumulated over the years. Sal's menu never changed, but maybe *she* should.

"I think I'll try something different today," she said.

Rosa's dark eyes popped. "Well, bust my buttons. That's a surprise. Next you'll tell me you're taking up wing-walking."

"Guess I'm turning over a new leaf. What do you recommend?"

"How about a hamburger? Or the liverwurst?"

Addie wrinkled her nose, her usual reaction to liverwurst, or anything with *wurst* in the name. Sometimes she thought she wasn't German at all. "I'll have the mine-strone. Didn't you say Sal's is the best in town?"

"*Everything* Sal cooks is the best in town. But don't tell the old sourpuss I said that."

Rosa's heels clacked on the black-and-white tiles as she moved to the kitchen's service window to put in Addie's order. Then she rustled through her pocketbook on the counter and came back, carrying the coffee pot and a small box.

"Glad you stopped in," she said. "Saves me a trip down the hill to drop this off. You know how your funeral parlor gives me the creeps." She placed the box wrapped in blue paper dotted with snowmen into Addie's hand. "Merry Christmas."

Addie grinned in delight. "You're quite the early bird. I haven't even shopped for your present."

Rosa waved that off. "There's still three weeks 'til the big day, you've got time. But don't forget. I could use some new stockings, hint, hint."

She could use some new work shoes, too. Addie had noticed how rundown her Oxfords had gotten, with worn heels and frayed laces.

"What are you waiting for?" Rosa said. "Open it."

Addie peeled the paper off the box and removed the

lid. A brooch in the shape of a swan nestled inside, backed with silver and studded with glass beads.

"Oh, my. It's beautiful," she murmured, touched. They'd exchanged gifts at Christmas for years, usually something inexpensive, like lipstick or a handkerchief purchased at Woolworth's. This gift must have cost much more. Money Addie knew Rosa didn't have. She'd dropped out of school at sixteen when her father died, to go to work to support her mother. She'd been slinging hash at Sal's ever since, living on her tips.

Rosa beamed. "I ran into Marta at Schulman's." She refilled Addie's coffee. "She said you like swans, so I thought you might like that."

Addie fastened the pin on her sweater, fumbling since she wore gloves. Marta had gotten that detail a bit wrong. Swans reminded her of Mother, who had adored the creatures and had a dozen figurines she'd displayed atop her bedroom bureau. But Mother had never owned a swan brooch.

"I do like it, thank you," Addie said, vowing to buy Rosa the best brand of stockings Schulman's had to offer for her gift. Ten pairs of stockings, even. "It's lovely, and so thoughtful—"

"Oh, murder!" Rosa whacked Addie's arm. Hard. "It's *him*."

She followed Rosa's gaze to see a man as tall as a Redwood and with shoulders as broad as an anchor step into the restaurant. Addie gasped. The man she'd banged into at the police station yesterday.

Rosa twittered with excitement. "He's new in town. He come in yesterday and was *quite* attentive. Asked all kinds of questions. I think he's got a crush on me."

The man made a beeline for the counter. Despite half a dozen empty seats, he sank onto the stool next to Addie. She shrunk away. Didn't mean to. It was instinct at this point. His overcoat smelled of wet and a tinge of mothballs. He tossed his snowflake-speckled fedora onto the counter and removed his gloves. Puckered scars ran up the backs of his hands and wrists.

Rosa greeted him with a broad smile. "Hello, big fella. Back again already?"

"I couldn't stay away, Rosa," he said, words that clunked with insincerity. At least to Addie.

"Oh, Dunstan, you're fresh." Rosa plucked a coffee cup from under the counter and put it in front of him, filling it to the brim. "See anything you like? On the *menu*, I mean."

He flashed a grin and asked for the meatloaf special. With a saucy wink, Rosa wriggled away. He tugged a newspaper out of his coat pocket and slapped it on the counter. He shook a cavity-inducing quantity of sugar from the dispenser into his coffee, picked up his spoon, and stirred lazily as he scanned the headlines.

Addie sipped her own coffee, watching him as subtly as she could. Now that she had a good look at him, she could understand Rosa's wriggling and flirting. He would grab any girl's interest. Not handsome—it would take all Addie's skills to paint that granite face handsome—but striking. In his mid-twenties, he had a solid jaw, cheekbones sharp enough to cut through steel, tan skin, well-defined lips, intriguing brownish-gold eyes, and muscled thighs that were apparent through his snug trousers.

One side of the man's mouth quirked, an oddly boyish grin for someone seemingly carved out of stone. Addie flushed. Did he know she was admiring him?

He stopped stirring and slurped coffee out of his spoon, then placed it on the counter. He turned to her. "I seem to keep running into you, Miss...?"

Addie couldn't decide what insulted her more, that he'd assumed she'd happily chat with a stranger in a diner, or that she was still a Miss. She straightened, putting a bit more distance between them. She was about to give him a sneer worthy of Aunt Trudy when Rosa hurried over, carrying Addie's order.

"Dunstan, this is Addie Brandt." She practically threw the minestrone onto the counter. Soup spilled over the bowl's edge into the saucer underneath. "Addie, meet Jack Dunstan."

Rosa's eyes flashed a warning. Addie frowned. She would never dare do anything as disloyal as flirt with a man her friend had set her sights on. Not that she even knew how to flirt.

"Pleasure to meet you," she said coolly. "What brings you to Goveport, Mr. Dunstan?"

"No mister, Addie, just Dunstan," he said. "I'm an insurance man. I help folks prepare for the future."

She raised an eyebrow. This "Just Dunstan" didn't look like any insurance man she'd ever met. They were usually squirrelly little men trying to figure out how not to pay out on policies.

"Will you be staying in town long?" She tugged another napkin from the dispenser and cleaned off her soup spoon before stirring her minestrone.

"I'm staying for a bit, I suspect," he said. "Depends on the folks I meet, and how receptive they are to what I have to sell."

His gaze shifted from Addie to the hovering Rosa. He

flashed her an oily smile. Now *that* was like a salesman.

Rosa let loose another whinnying laugh. "Oh, Dunstan. If you're selling, I'm buying."

Two plates filled with food appeared in the kitchen's service window, followed by Sal's bald head. "Hey Rosa, get back to work. You got other customers you know." He banged the little bell.

"Hold your horses," Rosa snapped, but Sal had already vanished back into the kitchen, like a turtle into its shell.

She hurried away and Dunstan swiveled toward Addie. "Your last name is Brandt? That's German, isn't it?"

Addie choked on a mouthful of minestrone. She remembered what Father had said about the growing animosity toward German Americans. Could this man be attempting to bait her? Or was he simply rude?

"It might be," she said. "Though I fail to see why my name or anything else should interest you."

"It interests me because of that." He stabbed a finger at his newspaper, at headlines reading *Japanese Threat Greeted With Bluster* and *Russians Beat Back Nazi Offensive*. "We'll soon be in this war. People will have to choose a side. Are you one of those German nationalists who think Herr Hitler is the bee's knees? Or are you red, white, and blue through and through?"

Maybe just red, as in seeing red. This man's impertinent questions had gotten her dander up. "You certainly are curious, Mr. Dunstan."

"It's just Dunstan. And I'm a curious fella, or so they say." He flashed another boyish grin. "So, what is it, Addie? Which side will you stand up for? Your ancestral people? Or will you work to help Uncle Sam win the fight that's coming?"

She put down her spoon, fully annoyed now. "Why don't you take me downtown, officer, where you can grill me properly?"

He laughed, a deep rumble, like a wave crashing into a cave. "Fair enough." He lifted his cup and eyed her over the rim. "Guess I'm pushing too hard."

She should ignore him. He was rude and strange. Yet, something about this back and forth with him seemed to... irritate her, yes, but also *excite* her. Engage her. She'd never had a conversation like this with a man before. The few times she'd spoken with a man close to her age, the subject was a corpse. Certainly no man had ever asked for her opinion, about anything.

"If I tell you where I stand, *Mister* Dunstan, do you promise to leave me alone?"

"Doubtful."

Her lips twitched. "At least you're honest. Well, then, speaking for every part of me, my German side and my Irish side, and the American I'm proud to be, I don't want us to fight at all. War means death and I hate death."

"That seems ironic, coming from a woman who works where you do. You're surrounded by death every day."

She blinked. "How do you know where I work?"

"You have a chatty friend." He tipped his head toward the kitchen window. Rosa bent down, bottom thrust out, yelling through the opening at Sal. "I've learned a lot about everyone in Goveport the short time I've been here. You're the one who sees things."

Addie cringed. She'd told Rosa about the picture show that played in her head, but Rosa had never laughed or teased her about it. It stung to discover she'd been spreading gossip about her.

"I'm sure you're mistaken," Addie said.

"I'm sure I'm not. Rosa says you've seen her future. That you tried to save a boy's life long ago. You tried to warn the police about something yesterday. Something bad."

Addie pushed the minestrone away, no longer hungry. And no longer amused. He knew why she'd been at the station house. Of course he knew. The police had laughed her out of the building just as he'd entered. Every man in there had probably been busting to share her strange story. And if he knew, how long before everyone in Goveport knew?

Everyone, including Father.

"Don't get sore," Dunstan said. "I'm not one of *those* people. The ones who mock you. I get why you went out on a limb like that. I'd have done the same thing. I hate war too. Folks think it's all about glory. It's really about death, and a lot of pain. I was too young to remember the Great War, but I remember what came after. Not a family on my block went untouched. Husbands and brothers injured, sons who never came home. Mothers and wives brokenhearted. Children left to grow up without a father."

The clench of his jaw, the tightness in his voice moved her—he spoke about himself.

"*That's* war, Addie, and I'd give my last breath to stop it happening again. To make sure it wouldn't even begin. I think you feel the same way. That's why you tried to warn them. Fools wouldn't believe you, but I do. And I'll listen to anything you have to say." The briefest pause and then, "What did you tell them?"

"Mr. Dunstan, just what line of insurance are you in?" she asked, nearly breathless.

He held out his hand. "Why don't you find out?"

She looked down at his palm, free of the scars that marred the back of his hand. Smooth, tanned skin, criss-crossed with so many lines a palm reader could be employed for months studying them. What did he want her to see? Was it worth the risk? The terrible images of the attack had haunted her for days. Why would she touch him and invite yet another horrific Sight?

"Addie, look at me," he coaxed. She did, surprising herself. He held her in his gaze. "I *know* you can do this. Trust me."

His deep voice rolled over her in a gentle wave. Trust, a heavy word. She'd never allowed herself to trust anyone. Least of all a man she barely knew. And yet... A soft, pleasant hum, like a cicada on a summer's evening, thrummed in the back of her mind. She couldn't deny she felt drawn to him. Felt at ease looking into his golden-brown eyes. Should she risk touching him?

"Am I interrupting something?"

Addie jumped. Dunstan scowled and his hand disappeared. The glare he aimed at Rosa would've warned her if she'd been looking at him. But she wasn't. She frowned at Addie, eyes sparking with hurt and jealousy. Addie flushed with guilt, as if Rosa had caught her and Dunstan cavorting completely naked.

Rosa turned to Dunstan and pasted on a smile. "Here you go, hon." She placed a plate in front of him, piled with a slab of meatloaf and mashed potatoes dripping brown gravy. She laid out his silverware. "You finish that, and I'll bring you a huge piece of apple pie for dessert. I baked it myself."

"Why, I love apple pie," Dunstan said. "Did you really make it yourself?"

His abrupt change shocked Addie, from his piercing gaze and impassioned way he'd spoken to her, to this almost mocking flirt.

"Oh, yes," Rosa cooed, leaning forward a little. "I bake the pies every morning. There I am at the crack of dawn, kneading the dough, rolling it out. Slaving over a hot oven, just for you."

Dunstan laughed and Addie would've laughed, too, if she wasn't so rattled. She happened to know Sal got his pies from Stein's Bakery three blocks down. Rosa didn't have to lift a finger, save to open the box.

Dunstan's coffee spoon on the counter caught Addie's eye and she got an idea. A nutty idea, but after all that heated talk and a half-eaten bowl of minestrone, she wanted her questions answered. What did Dunstan hope she'd see if she'd touched his hand? His spoon might give her the answer. She'd probably get away with swiping it. The way Dunstan and Rosa flirted and carried on, they probably wouldn't notice if she stole all the silverware in the restaurant.

Addie dropped some coins on the counter, picked up her coat and slid off the stool. She whizzed through a silent Hail Mary and in a flash, she dropped the spoon into her coat pocket and slipped away.

Addie walked rapidly along the sidewalk. An odd sensation tickled the back of her neck, as if someone strode close behind her. Wondering if Jack Dunstan had abandoned Rosa to follow her, she glanced back. She saw a dozen or so pedestrians bundled against the cold, hurrying about their business, but no Dunstan.

Annoyed at herself for such a fanciful thought, she turned at the corner. The snow had picked up and a wintery haze obscured the view of the Atlantic and the fisherman's memorial at the bottom of the hill.

She soon reached the Federalist-style building that housed Brandt Funeral Home, standing there like an old friend. Comforting, with its cinnamon-red bricks that had weathered a hundred winters, stone steps up to the front door, and a green awning over the entrance. Black shutters bordered the windows on the floors above the basement level—the viewing rooms on the first, Father's office and the casket display room on the second, the empty apartment where her family had once lived on the third, and the stuffy attic, filled mostly with cobwebs.

Addie ducked into the alley between Brandt's and the Denman building, headed for the basement entrance. The overcast sky cast a gloomy gray pall over the long, cobblestoned passageway. Thankfully Uncle Pat had flipped on the light over the side door. The hearse faced outward, parked in its usual spot by the embalming room doors, its headlights like two round, surprised eyes staring at her.

Addie stepped into the preparation room and headed straight to the bathroom under the stairs. She locked the door and closed the toilet lid. Why did men *always* leave the seat up? She sank down and took the spoon out of her pocket, still wet with coffee and no doubt tasting of sugar from the entire stalk of cane Dunstan had stirred into his drink.

She laid the spoon on her lap and slipped off her gloves.

You truly are addled, Addie Brandt. How had she gone from quivering over Sgt. Gillis's demand that she show him proof of the Sight, to stealing silverware like a petty thief, hoping to peer into Jack Dunstan's future? Probably not what Uncle Pat had in mind when he'd encouraged her to be daring.

She stared at the spoon, glinting in the overhead light. What would she see? Something awful? She didn't like the man, but she didn't wish him ill.

Was his future tied to Rosa's? Years ago, Rosa had badgered Addie into predicting her fate. Usually, the Sight showed dark, unpleasant visions, but when Addie had held Rosa's hand and slipped into her skin, she'd seen her old and plump and happy. Seated on a sofa beside a gray-haired man, watching a motion picture on a rectangular box hung on their parlor wall.

Could Dunstan be that man?

Perhaps she would find out. She reached for the spoon handle then stopped. No—the spoon's bowl. The piece he'd touched to his mouth might work better. Trembling, she braced for an onslaught to her senses and stroked her thumb across the smooth, rounded end. She opened her mind to the Sight and...

Nothing.

She shifted and tried again. Still nothing. She held the spoon tight and concentrated. Her heart hammered.

Sometimes the Sight showed her clear, explosive pictures. Sometimes confusing images, fuzzy and abstract, like an out-of-focus film. But most times she saw something, heard something, felt something.

This man? Nothing. Just a hazy gray field. A calm, hollow stillness.

Like a corpse.

Chapter Eight

Dunstan stayed to finish his meal. He'd paid for it, no use letting it go to waste. Besides, the food tasted damned good. Like mother used to make. Somebody's mother, anyway. His own always had more important things to do than cook for her kids. Like search for the escape that could only be found in a bottle.

He pushed his empty plate away and lit a cigarette. He'd followed Addie to Sal's with one goal in mind—to determine once and for all if she had a gift. He'd barely sat down next to her when he had his answer. His brain started buzzing like a beehive, the usual response when two gifted people got close. He didn't even have to concentrate to feel her vibrations.

He'd felt something else, when Addie had looked at him, her eyes sparkling with annoyance and a bit of mischief. When she'd made him laugh. Desire, yes, but it went deeper than that. A pang of...longing. And a burst of hope. He hadn't been hopeful for a long time.

Then he'd bungled the whole thing by pushing her too

hard, too soon. How many times had Madelyn warned him his impatience was rash at best, dangerous at worst? And how many times had he ignored her?

He took a hard drag. Now what?

He'd finally gotten Radcliffe on the phone this morning. His boss had given him an earful for zipping off to Massachusetts without a word, a tirade that quickly turned to interest when Dunstan told him about Addie's vision. But before Radcliffe would go to his superiors with Addie's warning, he demanded the one thing Dunstan couldn't give him.

"I want *proof*," Radcliffe had hollered into the phone. "You know how many crackpots contact the FBI every day spouting vague shit about someone blowing up the Statue of Liberty? I can't talk to Hoover or anyone else without proof. I need details, dates, the size of this so-called attack force before I can sound the alarm to anyone."

Dunstan crushed out his cigarette. Details he might be able to get from Addie, but proof? How could he do that? He didn't even know how Addie's gift worked, never mind how he could prove her vision to be true.

The only sure way to confirm her claim would be to wait until the attack occurred. Then it would be too late to warn anyone.

Rosa shimmied up to him. "You ready for that pie now, hon?"

She pouted when he turned her down, pouted some more when he turned down her offer of something even tastier when her shift ended. He hated giving the girl the brush-off, but she'd served her purpose, giving him plenty of information on Addie, her family, and just about everyone else in town.

Dunstan drained his coffee and went in search of Virginia. He found her where he'd dropped her off, in Schulman's department store. She beamed at him from the escalator as it carried her down from the second floor, its wooden steps clacking. She tottered toward him through the throng of shoppers, carrying so many packages she could barely see over the top of the pile. That girl had a problem. She truly did.

"Don't look to me for help carrying that load," he grumbled when the store's revolving door spit them out onto the sidewalk.

"I wouldn't dream of it, sugar."

He steered her toward their car, a block away. Snow fell, but it hadn't started to stick. Virginia's heels tapped out a rapid patter on the wet pavement.

"Well? What happened?" she asked.

"Addie's the real deal," he said.

"That's good, right?" Virginia gasped, out of breath from hurrying to keep up with his long strides.

Dunstan slowed his pace. "It's good I've confirmed her gift, but bad if what she saw is even slightly true. I tried to get her to talk, to get the information Radcliffe wants, but she's damned skittish. I thought if I could get her to try and read me, she might relax enough to open up." Maybe would've succeeded if Rosa hadn't barged in. "But she didn't bite."

Virginia stopped so fast her pile of packages nearly toppled. "Dunstan! You didn't ask that girl to touch you? In a public place? A man she'd just met?" She let out a mystified laugh. "How you don't get beaten to a pulp every day, I don't know. Well, I do know. If you weren't so monstrously tall and burly, maybe someone would knock some sense into you." She shook her head. "I suppose she ran away like a frightened rabbit?"

"She ran, but I don't think she was frightened." More like intrigued. She'd palmed his coffee spoon like a seasoned sneak thief. That took gumption. He grinned, imagining her tucked away somewhere with the spoon, trying to see his future. What he wouldn't give to see her face. "Maybe there's hope yet."

"You think we can fix it?"

He relieved Virginia of her packages and they started walking again. "We *have* to fix it. Radcliffe insists we find out what she knows."

"What do you have in mind? And if you say bust into her house like a bull in heat, I'll poke you in the eye with the heel of my shoe. You can't force her to trust you. You have to be more subtle. Woo her, soften her up."

"You mean pretend, play games. You know I hate that. I prefer to be direct."

"Then you're in the wrong line of work. Aren't spies supposed to be sneaky and the like?"

He would have to give in. And he hated to give in. "What do you suggest I do?"

"Get her to go somewhere she won't suspect you're trying to weasel something from her."

"How? Rosa says she never goes anywhere besides work and that restaurant."

"Then let's *make* her go somewhere. I'll help. You brought me here. I might as well earn my keep. There must be someone I can put a love whammy on."

They passed a row of sandwich board signs touting all sorts of entertainment for the weekend. One screaming headline caught his eye, *Swing with the Jim Penney Quartet!*

Friday & Saturday Night at The Oceanside! An idea popped into his mind, spurred by three words in smaller type that appealed to his expense account, *No Cover Charge*.

"Virginia, did you know Addie has a cousin? Good looking fella, if you like the blonde, Teutonic type."

She smiled up at him. Snowflakes had settled on her hat and hair. "I like them well enough to keep listening."

They'd reached their car, a black Ford coupe they'd picked up in Boston. Balancing the packages on one hand, Dunstan opened the door and Virginia climbed in. He handed over her shopping loot, which she arranged around her feet like a mother bird feathering her nest.

He slid into the driver's seat, started the car, and told Virginia his idea on the way back to the hotel. Together they worked out a plan. A ridiculous and convoluted scheme, involving Addie's cousin Hans and Rosa.

Dunstan didn't like manipulating either of them. Or Addie. But he had to. He hadn't been able to prevent what happened to Madelyn and it weighed on him every day. If what Addie knew could stop a tragedy, if she could help save lives and stall the inevitable march toward war for even a day, he would use everyone and everything in his power to do it.

Chapter Nine

Michael Feeney's Ford rattled as it bounced through an icy puddle on the dirt track. Someday, he felt sure the doors and all four wheels would fall off as he hit one of these deep ruts. At nineteen cents a gallon, he could barely afford to fill the gas tank, never mind more costly repairs. He prayed his junker would stay in one piece until he landed his bonus when the fire tower job wrapped up.

His car jounced past the men leaving the worksite, headed toward the main road. They tossed him angry stares and Michael didn't blame them. He'd pushed them hard today. The crew were weary and worn out, despite Saturday being a half-day shift.

He came out of the woods and turned left onto Atlantic Avenue, where the street reached a dead end. Even with the massive cleanup of fallen trees and rebuilding that followed the 1938 hurricane, the land and the few houses up here still looked as if they'd taken a beating from Joe Louis.

Michael's car puttered down the avenue toward home, where he lived with his parents and three younger brothers. His brothers had jobs and steady dates and would be getting hitched and moving out soon, but Michael figured he'd live with his folks until the end. Seemed like he'd frozen in time the day the Sight had come home to roost. Unable to move on with his life, unable to think about anything but his fear and a future he couldn't change.

He'd been out fishing with his younger brothers in Da's skiff with the pinhole leaks. His brother Danny, the youngest at twelve, had reeled in a fat cod. The fish twisted on the line, mad as hell. Michael had leaned over to help. He'd closed his hand over Danny's and...

He'd blanked out. Dark as pitch. When he came to, Michael was Danny. He didn't know how, but he knew beyond a shadow of a doubt he'd crawled inside his brother's skin, felt what he felt, saw what he saw.

Michael had been through a lot of scary stuff that year —the grease fire in their kitchen that sent them running into the night, the kid next door who'd died of polio, and his good pal Jerry Daly, mowed down by a bus. But what he'd seen of Danny's future that day on Da's boat had frightened him so much, he shut himself off, vowing never to let the Sight come again.

The sun came out from behind a cloud as he neared the bus stop, shining a halo of light on the most beautiful doll Michael had ever seen.

"Hell's bells," he said, adding an appreciative whistle.

He slowed his car for a good look. A tiny thing in a dark green coat with big buttons and wide lapels, she had tight gams, a heart-shaped face, upturned nose over pouty lips, and angelic blonde curls under a hat that looked like a chimney pipe.

Waiting for the one o'clock bus to town, no doubt, but Jesus, what was a looker like her doing all the way out here? Should he stop? Not that he'd try to make time with her. He wouldn't risk the Sight elbowing its way in if they should accidentally touch. But he could offer her a ride. The girl looked frozen to the bone.

He pulled the car to the left side of the road and lowered the window. "Need a lift?" His warm breath sent a cloud into the cold air. "Could be a while before the bus gets here."

She stared at him with big, surprised green eyes, and thin eyebrows raised sky high. "Beat it, fella, I've got a date."

He barked a laugh. "You're a saucy one. What's a Southern belle like you doing up in this wintry place?"

She seemed about to spit at him again then stopped and tilted her head. Her perfume drifted through the stink of car exhaust. Soft and delicate, like her. The scent made Michael's brain buzz.

Her eyes darted to the left and she frowned. "Look, you'd better go."

"Are you afraid of someone? Your old man?" That burned him. She didn't seem the type to take a man's fists. "Come on, doll, get in." He started to open his door.

"No." She held up her hands, stopping him. She wore no gloves. Her hands were small, her nails tipped with polish so red it looked like blood. "I'll be fine, but you *must* go."

"If you say so. I hope the fella you're waiting for is worth it."

Michael pressed the gas pedal, almost relieved she'd turned him down. He'd have tortured himself with her beside him the whole way to town, thinking of the sinful things he'd like to do with her but couldn't. Not unless he wanted to haul a host of unwanted visions into his brain.

Besides, he already had a date. A date with a fifth of whiskey and he didn't want to be late.

Dunstan thumbed his cigarette lighter's spark wheel, keeping an eye on Virginia from their car. He sat up in alarm when a beat-up old Ford chugged into sight from the access road and slowed as it passed the bus stop.

"Keep moving," he muttered, then groaned when the car stopped.

The driver rolled down his window to speak to Virginia. Was the fella trying to pick her up? Dunstan trusted her to deal with the man, but he clenched his fists and didn't relax until she sent him on his way. Dunstan ducked as the jalopy wheezed by and down the hill.

Moments later, a couple dozen figures stepped out of the trees and turned onto Atlantic Avenue. The men from the worksite, including Hans Brandt, their target. He dragged along behind the others, his shoulders hunched from the cold. The kid listed to starboard, as if his lunch pail weighed him down.

At the bus stop, the men swarmed around Virginia like wolves in heat. She shook them off and zeroed in on her quarry. She didn't waste a second. She lifted a cigarette to her lips, followed by a sultry rendition of, *Got a light, mister?*

Hans struck a match. Virginia touched his wrist to guide his hand, the cigarette tip flared red hot, and it was done. A helpful stranger had become an ardent lover.

Dunstan still marveled at how her power worked. A simple touch turned the fella to putty in her hands. Smitten and so starry-eyed the man would barely notice Virginia, who didn't smoke, coughing like a consumption patient as she drew on that cigarette. Not for the first time, Dunstan was heartily glad Virginia's special talent didn't work on him.

Soon, the bus lumbered up the hill, spitting exhaust, and squealed to a stop in front of the waiting horde. Hans helped Virginia aboard, hovering as if she were a delicate flower whose petals could be easily crushed. She flashed a grin in Dunstan's direction as she disappeared inside the bus, immensely pleased with herself, the little minx.

He ducked out of sight again as the bus made a U-turn and rolled by him back down the hill. Then he sat back and lit his cigarette. Burning tobacco crackled as he took a long pull. Virginia had done her part in this ludicrous plan, his turn to reel someone in next.

He studied his lighter, ran his thumb over his monogram and the smooth surface, hot from the flame, thinking of Madelyn. She hadn't needed any special abilities to catch him. He'd walked into that trap eyes wide open.

Madelyn Cooper, of the Beacon Hill Coopers. Old money and strict manners, finishing schools and debutante balls. Born and bred in Boston, not far north of New Bedford, where Dunstan grew up, but oceans away from his hardscrabble, hand-to-mouth childhood.

And yet, he'd dared to believe a girl like that had fallen in love with him.

He worked for a traveling carnival when they met, putting his broad back to good use, sometimes exercising his fists on unruly customers. Madelyn and Woden had come to the carnival in Sarasota to look into Garrity the strongman's claims of uncommon strength. They'd left Florida with two gifted people for the price of one.

He'd fallen for Madelyn hard and fast. She was magnificent. Beautiful, smart, ruthless. Woden's star pupil. Dunstan became her heroic knight, determined to save her from the melancholy that plagued her. The bitter cost of her gift. She could incapacitate a person with grief and guilt, but her vibrations bounced back, filling her with sorrow. It weighed her down like an anvil. She'd needed him and the relief he provided.

"Jack," she'd sigh, fingers pressed to her temples. "Make me well."

He'd done as she asked and absorbed her pain. He loved her, how could he not? The only woman to ever show him tenderness, or to seem to care for him. He would do anything for her. Except he could never make her truly well. He could only offer temporary relief, only give her a few moments peace.

He became like the drug to an addict, to her and to Woden. Dunstan hadn't seen any of that. He'd seen only Madelyn, and her need, and how he could help her. How much he loved her.

And trusted her.

He let out a bitter breath, exhaling smoke that filled the car.

They'd put him to work training new recruits, helping them discover their power and teaching them to use it. The logical job for him. As a neutralizer, no one's power could work on him, and he could keep them in line. He liked his job. It helped that he'd never thought twice about what happened to the new agents after he turned them over to Woden to be sent into the field.

As it turned out, he should've wondered. Woden had done his damnedest to turn them to the Nazi cause, to use their gifts to spy on Uncle Sam and even commit sabotage. Dunstan didn't know how Woden had done it, bribery or blackmail, but the man had convinced a half dozen agents to join him. The ones who refused disappeared or turned up dead.

Until Dunstan had found out. Found out everything, including Madelyn's role in the traitorous scheme.

He took another deep drag. Now, here he was. Older, no wiser but much less trusting. Determined to get a naïve young woman to trust him. If he could convince Addie to let him test her gift or talk about her vision, what then? If what she'd seen could somehow prove an attack was imminent, he doubted Radcliffe would simply thank her and send her on her way. He'd use her as surely as Woden had used Madelyn.

Dunstan jammed the lighter into his pocket. He couldn't think about that now. He started the car. Better to hand Addie over to Radcliffe than let the other side get to her. He swung the car around, aiming toward downtown. Better for Addie to become the government's pawn than sharing Madelyn's fate.

Better that than ending up dead.

Chapter Ten

S aturday used to be busy at the funeral parlor, but they'd had only one viewing this morning and Addie got to come home early. After lunch, she curled up in the leather chair by the library window with a cup of tea, determined to finish reading *Rebecca*. But once again she had trouble focusing.

She couldn't keep her mind off Jack Dunstan.

Who was he? Why had she been so drawn to him? Why had she gotten no Sight from that spoon? Could it be because she'd touched an object and not the man himself? Since the incident with Hugo, she'd *always* gotten a Sight when she touched another's flesh, but this new wrinkle in her strange ability had only recently reared its ugly head and she had yet to figure it out.

The first time, Addie had been dusting upstairs in the viewing rooms a few weeks after Mother's death, so list-less and bereft she could barely lift the dust rag. Thinking she couldn't bear to go on. She'd spotted a pair of eyeglasses under a chair, left behind by a mourner at a wake the evening before. When she picked up the glasses, the Sight had latched on. She'd slid inside a young man's mind, saw him years later as an older man, standing over his own mother's casket, his face wet with tears.

The man's grief had coursed through her, and so had his fearful thoughts. How could he live without his mother? His anguish had magnified Addie's own sorrow and threatened to overwhelm her. She'd dropped the eyeglasses as if they were made of fire.

She'd been careful after that, though she couldn't avoid accidentally touching an object and setting off terrifying images and sensations, like when her fingers had brushed Marta's hairbrush. Or when she'd held Jimmy Gallagher's tiepin.

And now, with Jack Dunstan's spoon, her fickle affliction had shown her nothing.

Addie picked up her teacup with a shamrock design and sipped a mellow afternoon tea made the Irish way, with lots of milk. She wished her cousin Michael would talk with her about their shared burden. With Mother gone, only he understood what she went through. But he wouldn't say a word, preferring instead to muffle the Sight's effects with alcohol.

The front door slammed so hard it shook the house, making her jump. Her teacup rattled in its saucer.

"Addie," Hans called. Hollered, actually. "Addie? Where are you?"

"In Father's library," she shouted back. She hopped up from the chair and had almost reached the door when Hans flung it open. He burst into the room wearing a grin as wide as the Atlantic Ocean.

Addie caught his mood and grinned back. "Hans, what's the ruckus? What's happened?"

"Addie, I met a girl. A *marvelous* girl."

He couldn't have surprised her more. Hans was devastatingly handsome, even the cousin whose braids he'd once tugged could admit that, and he'd dated a lot of girls. But he'd never spoken of any girl in such a way. Could he have fallen in love at last?

"That's terrific," she said. "How? When? Oh, I have so many questions."

He laughed. "I have no answers. It happened so fast. We met at the bus stop. Today, just now, on my way home from work. She's the most beautiful girl I've ever seen."

He'd just met the girl? At the bus stop? Could someone be smitten in such a short time? Dunstan's face popped into Addie's mind, and she just as quickly booted him from her thoughts.

"She's terrific, Addie," he continued, beaming. "Solid as they come. A real homebody. Wants marriage and children and everything a girl could want, and can you believe it, she loves to play cribbage."

"Sounds charming. Does this paragon have a name?"

He nearly blinded Addie with his smile. "Virginia," he breathed. "Virginia Beach."

"Virginia Beach? Truly?"

"I know. It's an odd name." He suddenly sobered. Closing the door, he lowered his voice. "There's a rub. You know I don't care what Father thinks, but she's worried he won't like her because she's not German."

"That could be a problem." Addie doubted his father would like her even if she were German. Unless the girl declared a mad passion for the Nazis and all they stood for, Uncle Eb wouldn't like her at all.

"Will you...will you come meet her?" he asked. "You know Father is still angry with me for my decision to enlist. Virginia thinks you can help sway him. If you could put in a good word about us with him, there's no way he'll object to our being together."

As if Uncle Eb would listen to her. "Well, after everything you've said, I'm dying to meet your girl."

"Swell. How about tonight?"

"*Tonight?* Isn't that a bit sudden?"

"I don't care. I want you to meet her now." He ran his fingers through his brushy blonde hair. Addie worried. He seemed on a rollercoaster of emotion. "Virginia wants to meet you too. She suggested the Oceanside Club. She's telephoning before supper to confirm. Shall I tell her it's a date?"

Addie didn't know what horrified her more, the thought of going to a nightclub thronged with people or the impropriety of Hans meeting his date there. "Won't you pick her up at her home?"

He shook his head. "Can't. She's staying with her aunt. Very prim, doesn't approve of her walking out with men." He turned giddy and frantic again. "We have to meet on the sly."

Addie frowned. Bold enough to make a date with a stranger he'd met at a bus stop, sneaking behind her aunt's back seemed downright shocking.

But what did she know? She had no experience with the opposite sex, except one horrible kiss in eighth grade when Karl Dahlgren had grabbed her after school. While he slobbered all over her face, the Sight thrust her inside an older Karl, as he stuck pins into a field mouse then tossed a lit match onto the poor creature. She'd felt his pleasure at his nasty deed. Frightened and repulsed, she'd shoved Karl away and ran as his laughter and spiteful taunts followed her down the hallway.

So, Addie couldn't judge her cousin's behavior. She couldn't refuse him either, considering the way he fidgeted and shifted from foot to foot, impatient for her answer. How could she deny him his happiness?

"All right," she said. "I'll come along and meet your new friend. Tonight."

He grinned, as excited as a child at Christmas.

Addie scooped up her book and carried her teacup to the kitchen. Aunt Trudy snatched both cup and saucer from her to wash them and Addie went up to her bedroom. She opened the closet door and dug through the dresses and skirts hanging in her half of the small space, hoping she could find something suitable to wear. Doubtful, since she rarely went out.

She spotted the grim black crepe she'd worn to her mother's funeral. She took it out of the closet and laid it on her bed as Marta burst into the room and slammed the door.

"Mother's getting on my nerves." She flounced onto her bed. "Told me I *must* go with her to Germantown after school next week. She says she's going to buy me new shoes. I'd *love* a new pair. I've worn out the heels on my best pumps running all over creation at work. But I know that's really an excuse for Mother to play matchmaker. The shoemaker's son is home from college, working in Herr Friedrich's shop until the new year. Mother thinks it would be *de-lightful* if we met."

"Would that be too terrible? You'll need a date for the spring prom. He could be a nice fella. Could be handsome."

"I don't care if he looks like Cary Grant and invites me to ten proms. You *know* I want to go to nursing school, and I can't do that if my mother hitches me to a husband before I'm even eighteen." Marta grabbed her pillow and flung it across the room. It smacked her Shirley Temple doll, sitting on the chair in the corner, minding her own business. "Why won't Mother understand? I don't want to get married. Not now, not *ever*."

Addie nodded. She admired Marta's grit but didn't envy the fight she'd have with her mother in the coming months. Aunt Trudy might be small, but she was as fierce as a dragon and always got her way. Addie suspected even Uncle Eb feared her.

She smoothed the skirt of her mourning dress spread across her bed. How had her cousins' once dull lives suddenly become as dramatic as a radio soap opera? First Hans, falling in love with a stranger in an instant. Now Marta, declaring she would never get married, not even to a college man.

"What are you doing?" Marta straightened, her keen gaze on the black dress. "Did someone die? I mean, someone you know, not at work. Are you going to a funeral?"

"No, nothing like that." Addie quickly spilled the details of Hans meeting Virginia and inviting her to meet his new love at the nightclub tonight.

Marta hopped off her bed and hurried over. "Well, well, I didn't think my brother had a single romantic bone in him." She poked through the outfits on Addie's side of the closet. "I imagine this girl must be *very* pretty for Hans to go so dizzy over her so fast." She pulled out a flowered summer frock and held it up in front of Addie. "No, out of season and too plain. You need something with more gas, something to make a fella's eyes pop."

She tossed the dress on top of the one on the bed, wooden hanger and all, and threw herself back into the hunt.

Dismayed, Addie watched the pile of discarded dresses grow. Why did she need a dress that would make anyone's eyes pop? She'd only agreed to go out tonight as a favor to Hans, to meet Virginia, not to meet men. Like Marta, she knew she would never marry, but for a different reason. She could never allow herself to get close to anyone. Not with the Sight guaranteeing disappointment for her and any unfortunate man she set her heart on.

So why did Jack Dunstan keep filling her thoughts? Sure, he was attractive and interesting and had spoken to her like a real person and not some sideshow exhibit, but she had no interest in him. Not in *that way*, at least. She barely knew him.

And, heavenly days, she couldn't be sure she even *liked* him.

~

Addie's legs quaked as Hans escorted her to the nightclub's entrance. She was about to enter an unfamiliar place, filled with people. A doorman in a red coat with gold buttons opened the door with a flourish. *I'm doing this for Hans*, she reminded herself and prepared to follow her cousin inside.

"Hans! Adelaide!" a voice called.

Hans stopped and looked past her. He broke into a mischievous grin. Addie followed his gaze. A stout young man in an overcoat that reached nearly to his ankles hurried toward them.

"Hans, you didn't tell me you invited Wilhelm," she said. "Is this a setup date?"

He grinned again. "I want you to be as happy as I am, cousin."

Addie wouldn't use the word *happy* to describe Hans. Not the way he'd paced about the house, waiting for Virginia's telephone call. Or the way he had repeatedly pestered Addie to hurry and get ready so they wouldn't be late. Frenzied, on the edge of hysteria. So completely unlike the normally staid and serious Hans.

More than ever, she wanted to meet Virginia Beach. That made her nervous enough without Hans's school chum to entertain. Still, Mother had raised her to be polite. She greeted Wilhelm warmly as he bustled up in a cloud of Vitalis hair tonic and dimples.

"Good evening, Adelaide." He seized her gloved hand and shook it like he primed a pump. "I hope you don't mind that your cousin invited me to make up a foursome."

"Not at all," she lied, letting him take her arm and lead her through the door.

Inside the club, the clashing smells of perfume, cologne, cigarettes, and liquor hit Addie like a solid wall. The roar of voices and laughter and the wail of a swinging band nearly deafened her. Despite her fears, her mood lightened, and her heartbeat kicked up with excitement.

They checked their coats. Addie smoothed her skirt. Her mourning dress and all the others had gone back into the closet. Instead, she wore one of Mother's fanciest frocks, a taffy-colored velvet with a plunging neckline and a flared skirt. Marta had the brilliant idea of looking through a trunk in the attic, stuffed full of Mother's clothes Father couldn't bear to throw out. Though a bit rumpled and somewhat dated, the dress fit Addie's curves perfectly. She had never felt so glamorous and feminine.

Not that Hans or Wilhelm spared her a glance as they followed the head waiter to a table at the back of the cavernous club. A hundred tables ringed a dance floor in front of a small stage for the band. Christmas lights dangled from silk canopies covering the high ceiling. More lights snaked above huge picture windows that must've offered a lovely ocean view during the day, but only darkness on a winter's night. A single light cut through the inky blackness outside, the revolving beam of Mackey Lighthouse.

Addie knocked elbows with dozens of people as she squeezed by chairs on the way to their table, making her glad she wore gloves and a dress with long sleeves. Wilhelm pulled out her chair and they were no sooner settled than a waitress in a short skirt and netted stockings arrived.

"What'll it be, fellas?" she asked, as if Addie were invisible.

"Glass of Rheingold," Hans said.

"Sorry," the waitress said. "That's off the menu. Scott, the owner, has declared all German beers the enemy. Got a local brew, one hundred percent American."

"Bah!" Wilhelm spat, scowling.

Addie bristled, equally offended, but Hans let out a

giddy snort. "That's fine," he said. "I'll have a glass of that and keep them coming."

Wilhelm muttered that he'd have the same. So, reluctantly, did Addie. She preferred wine. Good wine. She suspected German wines were off the menu too.

The band struck up "Stardust." Couples ebbed off the dance floor and others flowed on. Soon, Hans's face lit up and Addie turned to see a moss green feather attached to an equally green skull-cap hat bobbing through the room toward them. The hat sat on thick blonde curls framing a saucy face. Virginia Beach bounced along on wedged heels that added several inches to her petite frame, with shapely legs and a generous bosom cinched into an evergreen voile dress Marta would duel the Devil to get her hands on.

The men stood as Virginia arrived, wrapped in a flowery scent. Hans clasped her small hand in both of his. Her gloves matched her outfit, as green as her sparkling eyes. Addie's heart sank. She'd considered using the Sight to find out about Virginia when she shook her hand, but the gloves put an end to that plan.

Goodness, what was happening to her? Only days ago, the Sight terrified her beyond all reason. Now she schemed to use it on every person she met. She'd be pawing Wilhelm to investigate his future next.

Virginia gave Hans a warm, playful smile. "Hello, handsome," she drawled in a voice from south of the Mason-Dixon Line. How far south, Addie couldn't be sure.

"Hello, darling," Hans said, as moony as a lovestruck calf.

Addie had never seen him act so goofy. She cleared her throat. Hans jumped, as if he'd forgotten she was in the room. Or anyone else, for that matter.

"Virginia, meet my cousin, Addie Brandt. Our friend, Wilhelm Schmidt."

Wilhelm slapped his heels together and snapped a nod. Correct and courteous, but uniquely German and likely to get him pummeled if he wasn't careful.

"Glad to know you, Miss Beach," Addie said as the gentlemen took their seats.

She looked at Addie with nearly as much curiosity as Addie eyed her.

"Please call me Virginia and drop the Beach. Really, my name makes everyone giggle. Virginia Beach. See? You're smiling. My parents were silly people who thought it hilarious to give me such a cockeyed name. Shouldn't bellyache though, my brother's name is Sandy. Sandy Beach, isn't that too much?" She beamed at them and then at the waitress, who'd arrived with their drinks. "Oh goody. I'll have a Manhattan if you please."

Addie liked her. How could she not, with such a sunny, breezy manner? She could almost see why Hans had been smitten so fast.

"Hans tells me you're visiting family in Goveport," Addie said. "Do you plan to stay long?"

Virginia shook her head vigorously, though every curl stayed firmly in place. "Not long, Addie, a week or so." She gave Hans an adoring look. "But I hope to spend as much time with this fine fella as I can while I'm in town."

Hans colored and Addie was certain Virginia had squeezed his knee under the table.

"Hans, you beastly boy, why didn't you tell me your cousin is so beautiful?" Virginia went on. "And such a snazzy dresser. Your dress is delicious, Addie. Every man here is just eating you up. You *must* tell me where you found it."

Addie straightened the silk orchid hairclip at her temple then fiddled with the swan brooch Rosa had given her, pinned to her dress. Her suspicions and doubts melted away. The couple were clearly an example of opposites attract, Virginia's bounciness the perfect antidote for Hans's soberness.

The waitress returned and placed Virginia's drink in front of her.

"No cherry?" Virginia pouted at her cocktail. A Manhattan she'd called it, a reddish liquor in a tall-stemmed glass.

The waitress lifted a shoulder. "This ain't New York, sister."

A whinnying laugh drowned out Virginia's response. Addie looked up to see Rosa sashay up to their table. She wore a snug red dress and a red rose in her sleek black hair, which was piled to an impossible height. She clung to the arm of a tall man with broad shoulders.

Addie's heart launched into a vigorous jitterbug—Jack Dunstan.

He stood out in the crowd. His size, of course, but also what he wore, a casual black suit when the other men were in more formal attire. His suitcoat hugged his shoulders, his trousers molded to his strong legs.

Addie's cheeks heated. She flushed some more at the bold way his gaze swept over her, lingering a beat too long in certain places. Annoyance flared. The man was simply too much, ogling one woman with another woman on his arm.

"Lookee who's out on the town," Rosa squealed, her

gaze on the brooch. "I'd never believe it if I didn't see it, Addie Brandt at the Oceanside. Who's this handsome fella?" She shifted and ran an appraising look over Wilhelm. "Addie, you're the slyest girl that ever walked. I didn't know you had a steady. Ain't that a pip?" She tugged Dunstan's arm. "Well, see you in the funny papers. Come along, Dunst—"

"May we join you?" Dunstan plucked a chair from another table and pushed Rosa into it before the question was out of his mouth. He grabbed one for himself and shoved in next to Addie before anyone could answer. The chair, a delicate thing with spindly legs, groaned under his bulk. His thigh bumped against hers. His scent, Lifebuoy soap and a hint of the beach, washed over her, making her dizzy.

"Addie, you remember Dunstan?" Rosa's eyes were like black pebbles, boring into her.

Addie nodded, her throat dryer than the desert. Introductions were made. Wilhelm gave Dunstan a hearty hello, Hans, a vague wave.

"Pleasure to know you, Mr. Dinstan," Virginia said, dabbing at the corners of her mouth with her gloved fingertip.

An uncomfortable silence followed, broken by another laugh from Rosa.

"Look at the mob of us," she said. "Squished together here tighter than a girdle. What a mismatched bunch of loonies. I think we need a drink." She swiveled. "Where's the waitress? She's awful slow. Sal would fire her fanny in a heartbeat. There she is. Hey, girl! Over here!"

Rosa waved madly. The waitress snaked toward them through the tables, her tray held aloft.

"Goodness, Addie, you're looking peachy tonight," Rosa said after she and Dunstan had ordered drinks.

Addie could barely manage a nod in response. Dunstan stared at her and didn't look away, not even when Rosa took a cigarette from a slim case and held it to her lips. Rosa had to clear her throat twice to get his attention.

He lit her up with a lighter he took from his pocket. Silver, with grooved lines and a monogram. Fancy. Too fancy for a man like him. A gift no doubt, from someone who didn't know him. Or someone trying to impress him.

"Look at all the swells." Rosa exhaled smoke and ran her bright-eyed gaze over the crowded room. "I always wanted someone to bring me to this ritzy joint. And now I'm here."

"A fire trap," Dunstan grumped. "This place would go up in ten seconds if someone torched it."

Virginia glared at him. Rosa scowled. "Dunstan dear, don't be a wet blanket," she said, picking tobacco off her tongue.

"Let's dance," Addie heard Hans whisper to Virginia. A moment later they moved toward the dance floor.

Another awkward silence. Dunstan shifted his brooding gaze to Wilhelm. Addie wondered if he'd start grilling Wilhelm about his loyalties as he had her. He'd get an entirely different answer. Though Wilhelm spoke excellent English, he and his family had only been in America since '37 and still spoke of their home country with pride.

"Wilhelm," Dunstan said instead. "Do you mind if I dance with your date?"

Addie stiffened, surprised.

Wilhelm tore his attention away from watching Hans and Virginia dance. He tipped his head toward Dunstan.

"What? Oh. No, go ahead. I mean...if Adelaide doesn't mind."

"*I* mind," Rosa snapped.

Dunstan ignored her. He ignored Addie too. He took her arm and before she had a chance to say *boo* he plowed through the crowd toward the dance floor, tugging her behind him.

"You could've asked *me* if I wanted to dance," she said, raising her voice to be heard over the music and noise.

He glanced back. "Didn't want you to say no."

Addie's face went hot again, unsure she would have, given the chance. "Shouldn't you dance with Rosa instead of leaving her all alone?"

"She's got Wilhelm. Unless he drowns himself in his beer to escape her chatter."

Of all the rude men in the world, he was the rudest. "Must you always be so blunt?"

"I'm honest, not a poet, Addie." He pulled her into the center of the dancing couples and faced her, his lips twitching. "Look at us, sparring like an old married couple when I'm supposed to be charming you. As you've noticed, I have no charm."

The sparkle in his eyes warmed her thoroughly, contradicting his entire argument. And when he took her in his arms, one hand closed over hers, the other pressed firmly against her lower back, she barely resisted the urge to fan herself. She'd helped Marta practice at home for school dances, so she knew the steps, but no man had ever held her like this. Her belly fluttered and a strange, soft hum rippled through her brain.

The band struck up an old favorite, "Cheek to Cheek,"

easy to foxtrot to, but Dunstan steered her into a rumba of sorts. He repeatedly stomped on her feet.

"You dance divinely," Addie said sweetly.

"My apologies," he said, equally insincere.

"You should apologize to Irving Berlin. You're not doing his terrific rhythm any justice."

He grinned. "I like a girl who speaks her mind, even if it is to insult me." His expression turned serious. "I like to speak my mind too, Addie. I hoped I'd run into you tonight. I need to talk to you. I'm not an insurance salesman. I work for the government. I lead a special group of people in Washington. People like you. I want you to come work for me."

Addie frowned, confused. "What're you talking about?"

"I'm talking about your future. You tried to warn the police about your vision. That took a spine of steel. You have what it takes to be on my team. What do you say? The hours are long and the pay stinks. But the people are great, and your country needs you. *I* need you. With your ability to see the future, you might help us stop a war."

"Is this a joke?" Addie glanced over her shoulder to see if Hans watched them. His idea of humor ran toward dropping frogs down a girl's blouse, though he'd been acting so strangely today, she wouldn't be surprised if he'd put Dunstan up to such an odd prank. But Hans held Virginia close and swayed to the music, happily occupied elsewhere.

"No joke," Dunstan said. "I know people who can do something about the attack you saw." His Adam's apple slid up and down nervously as he swallowed. "But there's a catch."

Ah. There was always a catch. Dunstan reminded her

of those cut-rate casket salesmen who tried to fast-talk Father into buying their product before he could notice the pieces didn't quite fit together.

"Do tell, Mr. Dunstan," she said with awful politeness.

He glanced around suspiciously at the other dancers. "I need you to tell me how your visions work," he said, lowering his voice. "I need details, as many as you can recall." He jerked his head toward the rear door. "Let's go somewhere we can be alone. You can tell me everything. I can test you, too, get an idea of your skills, and maybe some kind of—"

"Proof," she said, cutting him off. "That's what the police demanded. Before they laughed at me."

"*I* won't laugh. You can tell me everything you saw, in your own words."

The brutal images flared into her mind before she could stop them. The sting of bullets cutting through Jimmy's body. The sounds, the explosions, men screaming. The smells. Dunstan watched her, his eyes darkening. That strange hum in her brain pulsed louder.

"Addie, you can trust me."

She searched his face. That word again. A word more powerful than love and hate combined. "Why should I trust you?"

"Because I'm like you." He stared into her eyes. "I know what you're going through. You're not alone. There are a lot of us out there."

Us? Addie had always thought Mother, her cousin Michael, and she were the only poor fools saddled with the Sight.

"You have the Sight?" Her heart thudded. Could that

be why he seemed to be following her, why she felt so connected to him when she got close to him?

"No." He huffed in frustration. "My gift is different. It pales in comparison to yours. *Your* gift is special."

Addie's feet froze mid-step and she wrenched out of his hold. Any flame of trust he may have ignited snuffed out in an instant, with that one word. "*Gift?* You're lying through those pretty white teeth. If you were truly like me, you'd *never* call it a gift. It's an affliction. A horrible disease."

"Addie, don't be a dunderhead." The couples around them flashed concerned glances their way and he lowered his voice further. "Let me help you. I'll show you how to use your power. You'll never be afraid of your gift again. But you *must* trust me. Let's go someplace we can talk—"

"Ain't you the sweetest couple," Rosa said, her voice dripping vinegar. She'd pushed through the crowd of dancers and stood with her arms crossed and her foot tapping, but not in time to the music. She glared at Addie, her expression brittle and hurt. "Are you making time with my man, Addie Brandt?"

The other couples had given up all pretense of dancing. They stared and snickered. Addie was not amused. Neither was Dunstan. He pinned Rosa with a look that had turned to steel.

"Not on your life, Rosa." Addie's voice trembled with anger and humiliation. "As far as I'm concerned, you can have him. Goodnight, Mr. Dunstan."

She hurried away. Virginia called to her as she flew past her and Hans, but Addie didn't stop. Didn't want to talk to her, or anyone.

Oh, Addie, you fool.

Mother had warned her to avoid people like Dunstan. They were worse than the people who mocked her or begged her to help them after Hugo's body had been found. Men like Dunstan wanted to *use* her, wanted her to perform for them as if she were a trained seal.

She'd been so caught up by Dunstan's attention, by the excitement and curiosity about the Sight his words had awakened in her, she'd forgotten Mother's wise advice.

But Addie had come to her senses.

Chapter Eleven

Dunstan's car bumped along a narrow street close to the waterfront, into the heart of Fisk Village. Or Fish Village, as Rosa said the natives called it. "Chattanooga Choo-Choo" played on the radio and Rosa sat beside him. Close beside him. Her tongue slid over her waxy red lipstick, and she cast him hungry looks.

"Up here, on the right," she murmured, gesturing toward a hulking tenement building squeezed between two other hulking tenements. Dull lights dotted some of the greasy-looking windows, but most of the other occupants had gone to bed.

He pulled up to the curb and bolted out of the car before Rosa could move in. She was a looker and it had been a while since he'd had female companionship, but he wasn't interested. He had another woman on his mind. They'd left the Oceanside Club immediately after the disaster with Addie, and he had to get back to her.

"That was fun," Rosa said as she took his arm and he walked her to her door. "We should do it again sometime."

He muttered something evasive. He was a goddamn heel for leading the girl on, for using her in this ridiculous scheme. He should put an end to their fictional romance here and now, but he could think of nothing else but getting the hell out of there. A biting wind whipped off the ocean, the stink of rotting fish hung in the night air, and boats creaked against their docks, bringing it all back. Bitter memories of bitter times. A past he didn't care to remember. Not now, not ever.

They reached Rosa's front steps. She turned to him and fiddled with the buttons of her coat, a threadbare brown thing with frayed cuffs. "You wanna come up? I got my own room and Ma's asleep."

He gazed at her upturned face. Poor kid. Trapped in this dead-end life, grasping at anything that might dull the ugliness. He knew how that felt, and he'd left home at fifteen to escape it. He hoped Rosa would find her escape too, maybe with that fella Addie had seen in her future. She deserved to be happy.

"Sorry, not tonight," he managed. He kissed her forehead, a kiss an uncle would give his favorite niece, and said a brusque goodbye.

Then he hightailed it out of there.

Minutes later, he parked as close as he dared to the Oceanside. He killed the engine and the headlights and waited in the darkness until Addie and the rest of her party exited the club. She stood awkwardly next to Wilhelm, clearly antsy for her cousin to say goodnight to Virginia so they could go home. Dunstan suspected it'd be a long wait. Hans had attached himself to Virginia like a leech on a wound.

The pale light from the streetlamp illuminated Addie's

soft blonde hair brushing her shoulders. She'd buttoned her coat, hiding her luscious curves, outlined by that dress to an almost obscene degree. God, she was beautiful. He hadn't noticed a woman in that way for a while, had sworn off dames altogether after Madelyn. But when he'd held Addie close as they danced, when he'd gazed into those warm eyes and seen a blush touch her cheeks...

He'd wanted to kiss her. There, on the dance floor. Wanted to whisk her away so they could be alone. And not to talk. At that moment, he hadn't given a damn about her vision, or Radcliffe haranguing him for details, or Rosa, or anything.

He'd only wanted *her*.

He lit a cigarette. Jesus, he was slipping. Letting the lid off his own feelings, loosening his hold on the emotions he'd absorbed from others over the years. Letting his desires overpower the needs of his assignment.

Wilhelm said something to Addie then gestured as if trying to get her to go with him somewhere, maybe around the corner to neck. She shook her head and Wilhelm scowled. That kid should throw in the towel. He had as much chance with Addie as he had walking on the moon. Dunstan had felt her fear. It drove her to keep people at bay, to crawl inside herself and close the door behind. He'd gotten that door to open a crack tonight, only to have it slammed in his face.

Thanks to his own stupidity.

Virginia finally freed herself from Hans and started down the street. She toddled past Dunstan in their car without a glance. She would double back when Hans and Addie and the third wheel had left. She knew what she was doing, and she did it well.

Dunstan's cigarette had burned down to the dog end by the time Virginia climbed into the car.

"Quick," she said. "Before Hans gets the idea to come back and find me. I told him I'd catch the bus at the corner."

He started the engine and maneuvered the car into late-night traffic. "Was it that bad?"

"Not really, as tonsillectomies go. I didn't get so much as a whiff of a gift in him, but his mind is completely open. He'll be easy to manipulate if we need him for something."

Dunstan wished Hans's cousin was half as easy to control. "Virginia, you're heartless."

"We both know that's not true." She removed her gloves and held her hands in front of the dashboard heater. "Hans barely knows anything of Addie's ability, but I got a few interesting tidbits out of him. Life in the Brandt home is far from peachy. His daddy's a Bund member, in total sympathy with the Nazis, but I suppose you know that. Hans says his folks treat Addie like a poor relation. And get this, he says he's never seen Addie's father hug or kiss her or give her any kind of affection. Not even when her mother passed away. Isn't that the saddest thing you ever heard?"

Sad, and infuriating. Dunstan rolled down the window and flicked his cigarette into the wind. All his miserable youth he'd longed for the kind of family he saw at the movies. Fresh-scrubbed, bright, happy in their tidy homes. An illusion. He knew that now. The more he traveled looking for the gifted and the more he got to glimpse beyond that front door, the more unhappiness he found.

Virginia settled back against the seat. "Mind telling me

what happened on the dance floor? Did you get fresh with Addie? She stormed off in quite a huff."

"You know me better than that." He turned at the intersection, taking the corner smoothly. "I talked to her. She heard me, opened up some to what I had to say, but she got the wrong impression. Thought I'm trying to use her."

"Well, aren't you?"

He scowled. "I'm trying to stop a war."

She sighed. "Poor Addie. Her vibrations are in *complete* chaos."

"I know." He'd felt her turmoil the whole time they were close, especially when he'd asked her about the attack. Fear had shrouded her like a storm cloud. "She doesn't trust anyone. Least of all herself."

Virginia sliced him a glance. "You like her."

He snorted and she let out a laugh that would've been endearing if it didn't annoy him so much.

"You can't fool me, Dunstan. I saw you looking at her. Your face simply crackled with excitement. When you two were dancing, I thought the sparks would ignite the whole place. And here you are now, downright devastated you hurt her feelings."

"I don't care about Addie's feelings. I care about her gift and how she can help us."

Virginia laughed again. "You're a terrible liar. You like her. There's no shame in that. It's about time Cupid poked you again."

"Lay off of that romance mumbo jumbo, will you? My business with Addie Brandt is strictly that, business. She's an asset to be used, nothing more."

Her face fell and Dunstan cursed his stupid mouth.

Virginia fed off the first blush of love and the excitement of new romance. She didn't want to hear his cynical booshwa.

"Sorry," he muttered.

She sniffed. "Now you listen to me and listen good. Not every girl's a scheming wench like Madelyn. Certainly not Addie. She's sweet."

Yes, sweet. Also unworldly, vulnerable. And unaware of the seductive power she possessed. Madelyn's opposite.

Madelyn had known what she wanted. Her father worked in the diplomatic corps and had secured her a job in the press office her senior year in college. She'd approached Woden at a government function and joined his team before the ink had dried on her diploma from Bryn Mawr. Seasoned and well-trained by the time Dunstan had come on board, she knew the risks, understood the sacrifice of a life of subterfuge.

She'd chosen her path. Dunstan's job was to force that path on Addie.

Their car puttered up behind a Standard gasoline truck stopped at a traffic light. The silence stretched until they moved again.

"Well, what's next?" Virginia asked, her tone still frosty.

He eyed her, tempted to apologize for real this time. He decided to let her be angry with him a little longer. She enjoyed it so much. "We try again tomorrow."

"Tomorrow? But it's Sunday."

"Do you think our enemies care about that?" They'd reached their hotel. He slipped the clutch and mashed the brake. "The Japanese, the Nazis, or whoever's behind whatever Addie saw won't take a day off." He turned to Virginia, fired up. "And neither will we."

Chapter Twelve

The Christmas tree had been delivered yesterday, a sturdy balsam that reached the parlor ceiling. They'd moved the wingback chairs aside and put the tree in the front windows. The fresh smell mixed with the sweet scent of Father's pipe tobacco. Orchestral music played on the radio and a dozen ornament boxes rested on chairs and side tables as the family gathered to decorate the tree.

A cozy family scene. As cozy as Addie could ever hope for these days, with Mother gone.

Father strung the lights. Marta chattered as she hung up glass snowmen and paper reindeer. Hans grinned from ear to ear as he helped his sister. No doubt thoughts of sugarplums and Virginia Beach danced in his head. Aunt Trudy took her time with each ornament, making sure they dangled from their branches *just so*. Uncle Eb didn't join in. He sat on the sofa with a glass of eggnog, looking on with an odd, calculating smirk.

Addie bent over a box to unwrap her favorite ornaments, brought to America from Germany by Father. She wore her cotton gloves, and she had to be careful the delicate painted glass balls, stars, and cones didn't slip from her hands.

She tried to keep her mind on her task, but Jack Dunstan kept crowding in. Last night, he'd demanded they go off somewhere *alone*. To talk, supposedly. About her vision and coming to work with him, about people with so-called gifts, and about the power he claimed to possess. Was any of that true? Did he really work for the government? Or had he been playing with her, a gullible girl who blushed as red as an apple when he looked at her?

Tissue paper crinkled as Addie unwrapped a red, blown-glass swan with a fluted tail. Mother's favorite. Bittersweet memories of Christmases gone by pushed all thoughts of Dunstan from her mind.

When she was little and they lived in the apartment in the funeral home's top floor, she'd help her parents decorate the tree each year. Addie would hold the swan and Father would lift her up while Mother told them where to hang it. Mother would wait until Addie had almost got the ornament in place then pretend to change her mind. She'd do it again and again and Father would fly Addie all around the tree like an airplane, until they all three collapsed on the floor, laughing.

Addie straightened and looked toward Father to find his gaze on her. A host of expressions flashed across his face. Grief, regret, even guilt.

He held out his hand. "Come, Adelaide. We will put it on the tree together."

They hadn't hung the swan since Mother took ill. After she passed, it seemed somehow wrong to put it up without her. But this year... She heard Uncle Pat's voice in her ears, *time to put the past away*. Time to move forward. Mother would prefer her beautiful swan shimmer in the lights on the tree rather than sit in a box. Addie went over to Father and handed him the ornament.

He held it gently, as if fearing it would break. "Where do you think Mother would've liked us to place this?" he asked, his voice deep with sorrow.

Her throat closed. She'd been so wrapped up in her own loss she hadn't thought of how much he must miss her. "I don't know where," she said. "Mother never could make up her mind."

That coaxed a smile out of him, something she hadn't seen in a long time. "How about there, by the wooden soldier?" he said.

Addie swallowed tears as together they hung the swan in a place of prominence on a high branch. Afterward, Father gazed at her a long time. He didn't hug her or even take her hand, yet she felt more at ease with him than she had since Mother died. Maybe even since before she'd gone to the police with her vision about Hugo and became Addled Addie.

She began to unpack the next box of decorations, her mood somewhat brighter.

After all the ornaments had been placed on the tree, Addie and Marta dropped tinsel over the branches. The silvery strands made of lead reflected the light from the hot, red and green colored bulbs. Uncle Eb, still on the sofa, watched them with that same peculiar expression. Hans leaned against the wall, smoking a cigarette. Aunt Trudy stood beside him with an ashtray, to make sure no ashes fell onto her immaculate carpet.

The telephone in the foyer jingled. Father had settled into his chair with his pipe. Before he could move, Aunt Trudy put down the ashtray and marched out of the parlor to the stout-legged telephone table in the front hall.

"Brandt residence. Who is speaking?" she demanded, and Addie and Marta exchanged amused glances. If Aunt Trudy hadn't married Uncle Eb and dedicated herself to cooking food she rarely ate, she could've had a fine career as an executive secretary. Or perhaps an interrogator in a prison.

The mystery of who would dare telephone on a Sunday was soon revealed. Virginia Beach, calling for Hans. He practically broke an ankle rushing to pick up the receiver. Not long after, he hung up and beckoned to Addie to join him in the foyer.

"Virginia wants to go to a picture show later today, and she wants you to join us," he said, giddy and out of breath.

"Truly?" Addie lowered her voice, well aware the whole family listened from the parlor. "I would think she'd want to be alone with you."

His grin didn't falter. "Apparently she's as crazy about you as she is about me. What do you say? Tell me you'll tag along."

Addie said she would, though she doubted she had a choice. Hans's beloved had insisted she join them, and Virginia's wish was his command.

"**M**y goodness, it's cold," Virginia said, her teeth chattering. "I declare, I could never get used to this horrid Yankee weather."

"At least it's not snowing." Addie stamped her feet to warm her cold legs. Someday she'd buck up the courage to wear her new trousers, but she was glad she hadn't today. She'd look like a frump next to Virginia, all dolled up as if they were going to a nightclub again, and not to a late afternoon movie at the Bijou.

"I'm so glad you could join us." Virginia laced her arm through Addie's. "And I'm glad you're feeling better, too. A shame you had to leave the Oceanside so quickly last night."

Not quick enough. Addie had wanted to get as far away from Dunstan as possible, but her departure had been considerably slowed by all the goodbyes Virginia and Hans had to say outside the club. Not to mention the kissing. And Wilhelm, pestering her to come away with him for some mysterious reason that may also have involved kissing.

"It was just a headache," Addie said, only half-lying. Her head had hummed the whole time she danced with Dunstan, and more so when they had argued. Even now, that strange buzzing sensation still tickled her brain.

"Good," Virginia said. "Oh, I don't mean good that your bean was thumping, I mean I feared Mr. Dunstan had said something to upset you." She peered at Addie keenly. "What *did* he say?"

Addie studied her. Perhaps Virginia wasn't as flighty as she had initially thought. Burying the sudden urge to tell her everything, Addie turned to Hans with a smile when he returned with their tickets. He handed Virginia hers as if he presented her with a precious gem.

The doors opened and they joined the crush of people waddling like penguins into the building. The smell of freshly popped popcorn permeated the carpeted lobby, so strong Addie could almost taste the butter. Ushers opened the inner doors and the crowd spilled into the large theater filled with cushioned velvet seats. Masks of comedy and tragedy hung on either side of the screen and intricate gold scrollwork decorated the high ceiling.

Hans took off his hat and they shuffled into a middle row. Addie sat sandwiched between her cousin and a silver-haired man who smelled of garlic. She shed her overcoat as the lights dimmed and the chatter faded. The thick, red velvet curtains whooshed open, and an image flickered onto the screen.

Addie settled back, determined to block all thoughts of the outside world from her mind. The newsreel came on first, making that difficult to do. War news. Shaky film footage of Japanese soldiers advancing into what the announcer called rubber-rich territories of the Far East, followed by grainy images of a Soviet warship at sea and bombed buildings in London.

The Sight's horrific images pushed into her mind. She pushed back.

Next, a Three Stooges short that darkened her mood for another reason. Hans guffawed and the old man next to her snorted with laughter. Virginia leaned forward and caught Addie's gaze with a sad shake of her head. What was funny about three grown men poking each other in the eyes?

Birth of the Blues, the main feature, came on next and

Addie truly began to relax. The story wasn't such great shakes—jazz musician Bing Crosby romancing singer Mary Martin while Jack Benny's butler Rochester cracked wise—but the hot jazz music got her toes tapping.

Near the end of the picture, Addie felt something. More like *sensed* something, over her shoulder. A glance back revealed Jack Dunstan in the row behind her. Light from the film flickered over his angular face. Addie frowned, but her heart did a delighted two-step.

"Are you following me, Mr. Dunstan?" she said in a scolding whisper.

He startled as if surprised to see her and leaned forward. "*Mister* Dunstan? Come now, Addie, I thought we were friends after dancing a lindy together last night." His voice rumbled in the darkness.

"Was that what we were doing? I thought it was a foxtrot."

He chuckled softly, sending shivery waves up her spine. Darn it, she wanted to be angry with him. She *was* angry. But her body disagreed.

"Frankly, my two left feet don't know the difference," he said, and the silver-haired man hissed for quiet. Dunstan shot him a glare then gazed back at Addie. "I really need to talk to you. Give me two minutes—"

Suddenly, the film stopped. The clarinet's wail became a moan as the sound faded. The house lights popped on, spreading a ghoulish white light over the packed house. Addie squinted and sat up straight. A nervous buzz filled the theater. Several people called out from the balcony above, asking why the film had stopped.

The Bijou's manager, a scrawny man in a gray suit and a red bow tie, took the stairs to the stage two at a time. The man's Adam's apple bobbed wildly as he cleared his throat and called for attention. The hubbub died down.

"Please, everyone." He paused, seeming to struggle for words. "There's been a..." He cleared his throat again. "Could I ask that all military personnel in the theater report to their posts?"

Concerned whispers rippled over the audience, becoming a roar. Gasps, exclamations, questions. Addie's insides twisted.

"What's the problem?" a man near the front shouted.

The manager held up his hands, imploring the crowd to quiet. Addie closed her eyes and prayed for strength. She knew what he would say next.

"There's been an attack." The manager's voice cracked on the word. "An attack on an American Naval base."

A stunned silence followed. Addie glanced back at Dunstan. He went as still as death, as solid as stone.

"The situation is dire," the manager said. "Please, will all military men report for duty? Now."

A man in an Army uniform seated on the right stood. He shuffled from his row and up the aisle, his face grim. The silent crowd watched him go. Then a panicked commotion seized the theater.

"I knew those krauts would turn on us someday," the man next to Addie blurted.

"Tell us what's happened," a woman in a straw hat cried, her voice shaking.

"Yes, tell us," several others called out.

"I don't know." The manager passed a shaking hand over his face. "I truly don't. There's been some kind of attack from the air, somewhere in Hawaii. The Navy is there, on site. I'm sure all will be well."

He sounded as if he didn't believe his own words. Addie certainly didn't. Nothing would be well again.

The manager made no mention of turning the movie back on and no one asked. The theater emptied. People scurried up the aisles to the exits amid a confused babble, sobs, nervous tittering.

Hans stood and wrapped his arm around Virginia's shaking shoulders. She stared at Addie as if in pain. Tears dug a trail down her powdered cheeks.

"Come on, Addie. We've got to get home," Hans said, gathering up his overcoat with his free hand. He sounded scared and years younger.

Still seated, Addie gazed up at him. There was no reason to hurry home, or to hurry anywhere. But she stood and followed him and the weeping Virginia up the aisle.

"Addie, wait." That came from Dunstan, caught behind several chattering women, trying to get to the aisle. She saw him vault over the seats to the next row as the crowd swept her into the lobby then out into the cold.

Outside, people darted to-and-fro and hung on one another for support. Some desperately tried to hail a cab or find a newspaper. Cars sped up and down the street. Horns honked. Voices shouted. All around Addie, shocked, tear-streaked faces.

It was her fault. Addie Brandt, the seer of death. She could have stopped it if she'd had more courage. If she'd pushed harder for someone to listen to her. Or if she hadn't been so quick to cut Dunstan off.

Hans released Virginia and stabbed his arms into his overcoat sleeves. The collar folded under itself, but he didn't seem to notice. Virginia melted into the crowd after Hans said a hasty goodbye. He raced toward Uncle Eb's

Packard, parked at the end of the block. Addie hurried after him, fearing he'd leave without her, and she'd have to walk home.

"Addie."

Dunstan again. Everyone raced about, feet pounding the pavement in panic. Frightened out of their wits. And he calmly cut through the crowd toward her as steady and commanding as a warship.

"It's not your fault," he said, as gentle as a mother's kiss. He reached for her, and a soothing hum blanketed her brain. The waves of anguish inside her began to ebb. "We need to talk. Come with me."

Uncle Eb's Packard screeched up next to her in the street. Hans leaned on the horn and motioned frantically for her to get in.

"What's the point, Dunstan?" She backed away from him, away from the comfort he offered. "Jimmy Gallagher's dead." Hot tears stung her eyes. "They're *all* dead. It's too late."

She got into the car. Hans slammed the gas pedal and the car shot into traffic before Addie could close the door.

They barreled toward home.

Chapter Thirteen

I t happened.

Dunstan focused on that one hard, cold fact as he watched the black Packard with Addie inside tear around the corner. The attack happened, just as she had predicted it would. His mind reeled, stunned, devastated, a shipwreck on the shoals, battered by the surf. No hope of rescue.

"Dunstan, let's go," Virginia said, suddenly by his side. She plucked at his coat sleeve.

It took several seconds for him to digest what she'd said. He blinked as if he'd just woken up and offered her his arm. She walked beside him, holding on tight. People ran and shouted and sobbed all around them. The air smelled of car exhaust and burning rubber.

"Do you want to get something to eat?" he asked, not really hungry. "There's a chop suey joint up the street that looks open."

Virginia shook her head. "I couldn't swallow a bite. Let's go back to the Savoy."

"I guess Radcliffe has his damned proof now," he muttered as they strode toward the car. Addie's gift was the real McCoy, proved in spectacular fashion.

Dunstan balled his fists, furious. He directed some of his anger at Radcliffe for dragging his feet but aimed the bulk at himself. For not pushing Radcliffe harder to raise the alarm, for playing games with Addie instead of being direct, for letting her slip away.

They passed a newsboy in a wool cap, hawking a one-sheet extra. Dunstan tossed the boy a nickel and scanned the page the kid handed him. Virginia looked on. The news was bad, worse than even his cynical brain could imagine. An unknown number of men dead, hundreds injured, ships and planes destroyed, fires burning out of control. Chaos.

Virginia unsnapped her handbag's clasp, took out a silk handkerchief, and dabbed at her eyes. "Oh, lord. It's simply too, too horrible."

"Imagine what Addie must feel. Even if her vision had shown her only a fraction of that."

Addie blamed herself. He'd felt it, seen it on her face. Stricken, riddled with guilt and a heavy dose of horror. Moments ago, he'd done something he vowed never to do without permission. He'd pushed her. Couldn't help himself. He hated for her to be in such pain. He'd pushed into her mind and shrouded her fear, offering her some comfort when he wished he could've taken her in his arms and held her until the unspeakable images and terror had faded.

"Poor little thing." Virginia's hold on his arm tightened as they crossed the street at the corner. "If only someone would've listened to her. If only the police had taken her seriously. If only we'd done more, or Radcliffe had warned someone." Her Alabama drawl became more pronounced as her agitation deepened.

"Please, don't, Virginia." She sounded like him after Madelyn's death. Spewing enough *what ifs* and *should haves* to fill an ocean liner. He whipped himself that way now. "It's done. We need to look forward, figure out our next step."

She sighed. "I assume Radcliffe will call us back to Washington."

"Not without Addie he won't," Dunstan said. They reached the other side of the street and turned toward their car. "She's proved her worth. A woman who can predict what the enemy might do in a week's time, or a month's time will be valuable. He'll want her. And so will everyone else once word gets out about her. Every enemy agent in the country will slither out of their holes and descend on this town looking for her. Maybe even Woden himself."

"Woden!" Virginia cried. "I thought he'd run back to Germany with his tail between his legs."

"Maybe. Maybe not. You know what he can do. You think the Nazis would keep him out of the field with a gift like his? When he knows so much about our intelligence operations? Especially now."

"Oh no. Addie! Woden will turn her as sure as he turned Madelyn."

"*Don't* get ahead of yourself." He spoke as much to himself as to Virginia. "I'm just saying Addie could be in danger. She needs our protection. No way in hell am I letting any foreign thug get his hands on her. Woden or anyone else."

Virginia looked up at him, her brow still furrowed with worry, but said nothing. Seconds later they got to their car, one of the few vehicles left by the curb. Everyone had fled the downtown. Gone home to be with family or to an open restaurant, to listen to the news, to find comfort in one another.

Addie had most likely done the same. She probably thought her role in this gruesome turn of events had ended now that her vision had come to pass. She had said it herself, *It's too late*. The deed was done.

But Dunstan knew with cold certainty, for Addie, it was only the beginning.

Chapter Fourteen

The radiator spit steam as it sent waves of heat into the parlor. Addie lay on the rug, chin propped on her palms, staring up at the radio as she had when she'd listened to *Little Orphan Annie* as a child.

The whole family had gathered round, Father in his chair by the Christmas tree, Marta sitting cross-legged next to Addie on the floor, Hans in Mother's chair, and his parents as far apart as possible on the sofa. A gloomy silence hung over them, as thick as the cream frosting on one of Aunt Trudy's chocolate cakes.

The radio crackled with H. V. Kaltenborn's nasal voice, reeling off increasingly grim news. The president had called an emergency cabinet meeting, with leaders of both parties asked to join them. Secretary of War Stimson had ordered all men on active duty to appear in uniform. Reports from Honolulu confirmed at least five men killed. Many more were feared dead and injured at Pearl Harbor and the surrounding area on a Hawaiian island Addie had never heard of. *Oha-oo*, the reporter called it.

Addie knew more than five men had been killed. Cut down by gunfire or blown to bits by bombs that had fallen from hornet-like airplanes. More men burned in the fires that followed or choked by the thick smoke that billowed in black clouds across the water.

She shuddered. The most horrifying image she'd seen in a lifetime of disturbing visions had come to pass.

It's not your fault, Dunstan had said. Now that the shock had worn off, she could see that. She'd tried to warn them. At the very least, she'd tried. Still, it weighed on her shoulders like Atlas balancing the world. She wanted her mother. Wanted her so much her insides ached. Mother would hold Addie in her arms, murmur in her ear softly and ease her through this nightmare.

"Are you all right, Adelaide?" Father asked, gazing at her with his brows drawn down.

She most certainly was *not* all right. And Father most certainly would be furious to know why. "I'm fine, considering." She managed a weak smile.

Father touched a match to his pipe and took a long pull. The tangy-sweet aroma of burning tobacco swirled around Addie, making her long for Mother even more. Long for the days when they were together, and the world was bright. Now, the world had tipped upside down.

The radio hissed and whined. Addie strained to hear a reporter at the Capitol, announcing the Japanese had issued a declaration of war against the United States.

"It is no joke," the reporter's tinny, almost frantic voice blurted from the radio speaker. "It's real war."

Father pulled his pipe from his mouth and released smoke with an angry sigh. "This should finish off our business. It won't be war with just Japan. Germany will be in it soon enough."

He glared at Uncle Eb as if he had personally launched the attack. Addie glared too. Her uncle's gleeful yearning for war had come to hellish fruition. Uncle Eb sat erect and proud, showing no sign of dismay or guilt.

Not so Aunt Trudy. She'd been paler than pale since Addie and Hans had rushed home from the picture show. She stared at her son with anguished eyes. She didn't even make a peep when ash from Hans's cigarette fell onto the carpet.

"Germany and Japan are allies," Father said. "They will have to declare war. Whether or not Hitler wanted a fight with America, he's got it now. He's got no choice but to follow the emperor's lead."

"Bah," Uncle Eb said. "The Fuhrer follows no man. He leads. And he would never lead *our* people in aid of the Japanese."

Father glowered. "Hitler doesn't think of the people. He thinks only of power. He lusts for war and spilling the blood of young men."

"Hush." Aunt Trudy clapped her hands over her ears. "Be silent, please."

She spoke German, but Father replied in English. "I can't be silent, Gertrude. We can't avoid the truth. Not anymore."

He gazed at Hans with a distressed expression. Hans took a hard drag on his cigarette, staring at nothing. Addie marveled at her cousin's composure, after his near panic at the theater.

"But why should a war be bad for business?" Marta

131

asked, filling the strained silence that followed. "People will still pass on. They'll need a proper burial."

"I expect Bannister's will get the bulk of business now, my dear," Father said. "No one will want a German burying their dead. Nor will anyone allow the enemy into their home to prepare a loved one for their final journey."

The radio signal faded. Marta reached up to tweak the knob and an announcer on another station reported that sections of Los Angeles were under attack. He ticked off a list of other places the Japanese had also bombed, the Philippines, Malaya, Hong Kong. Addie thought she would upchuck right there on the rug.

"Where's Malaya?" Marta asked, smoothing her wool skirt over her knees with shaking hands.

"It's in the Pacific, like Pearl Harbor," Hans said, his voice flat, emotionless. He put out his cigarette in the ashtray on the cherry wood side table and sat up straight, his gaze skimming them all. "I'm going downtown tomorrow to enlist." A chill ran down Addie's back. Aunt Trudy moaned. "I'm sorry, Mother. I know I said I'd wait until construction on the fire tower was complete, but after what happened, I can't. I'm going to enlist now—"

A sharp rap on the door cut him off. Addie jumped. Everyone did. Another knock tore through the taut silence.

"Who is it?" Aunt Trudy clutched her breast like Lillian Gish in a silent film melodrama.

"Really, Mother, how could any of us know?" Marta said, her acid tone undercut by the frightened wobble in her voice.

"I'll get it," Father said unnecessarily as he stood. No one else had moved.

A moment later, muffled voices drifted into the parlor from the front door. Who could it be? Father said they were the enemy now. Addie was tempted to clutch her bosom dramatically, too. Footsteps sounded on the hardwood as Father returned to the parlor.

"Adelaide, there's a man to see you," he said, as if announcing the end of the world.

It took a moment for that to sink in. A man. To see her. The faces of Addie's relatives mirrored her surprise. Her belly flipped and her heart pounded to think that Dunstan had followed her home, bold and brash, and he now stood at the door, waiting for her.

"Adelaide, did you hear me?" Father said. "There's a man to see you. A policeman."

～

"A policeman?" Uncle Eb's watery blue eyes widened, and his face went as white as fresh fallen snow. He swung toward Addie. "What does he want?"

"I'm sure it's nothing," Marta said, locking eyes with her.

Addie stood, her legs shaking like Jell-O. A policeman at the door. It had to be connected to her vision. He'd come to arrest her. She had much to answer for. She'd known about the attack, hadn't she?

She followed her father into the foyer and gasped in surprise to see not the police chief or even Sgt. Gillis at the door as she'd feared, but the younger man, the officer who'd mocked her. Pete, the sergeant had called him.

Peevish Pete, Addie would call him. He'd been terribly unkind.

He wore galoshes, a topcoat over his uniform, and a supremely uncomfortable expression. Probably due to the suspicious glower Father directed at him. And Addie's own frown. What on earth was he doing here?

His blonde curls ruffled as he swept off his brushed-brim hat. "Miss Brandt. I don't know if you remember me. I saw you a few days ago at the police station."

"How could I *not* remember you?"

A blush as red as a new rose bloomed on his cherub cheeks. He cleared his throat. "I should say so, after the way I treated you. I've come to apologize."

"Oh." How foolish to think he'd come to arrest her. After all, what had she done to be arrested for? "Why, yes, that's nice of you, um, Officer...?"

"Bowdoin." He brightened. "Officer Peter Bowdoin. Call me Pete. I'm truly, truly sorry for the way I treated you and for what I said."

Father's gaze moved between her and Pete, his eyes hot with questions. The rest of the family in the parlor were no doubt straining to catch every word too.

Pete glanced at her father then back to her, clearing his throat nervously. "I'd like to talk to you more in depth, Miss Brandt. Would you care to come with me on a short walk? Please?"

Addie had become quite popular, with all these men begging her to come talk with them. Pete, Dunstan, and even Wilhelm at the nightclub. At least Pete was polite about it, unlike Dunstan, but she still wondered at this man's motives. She looked at Father. His frown told her he suspected Pete's motives too.

"I'm sorry," she said. "Some other time, Pete."

He dipped his head. "I understand."

From his frustrated puff of cheeks, she thought he didn't understand at all.

"Well, I should get back on my beat," he said. "The chief called us in. The mayor's ordered us all on extra patrols, to keep an eye on the coast and all. I only wanted to stop here and, well, apologize." He eyed Father and twisted his gloved hands. "I suppose I should go."

"Yes, you should," Father said, and Addie barely got in a goodbye before he shut the door in Pete's face.

She turned on him. "Why did you do that?"

"I'll ask the questions, if you don't mind. Would you care to tell me why a...a *policeman* came to my house in the middle of the night, demanding to see my daughter?"

My house, my daughter. Like she was his possession. "It's not the middle of the night, Father. It's not even nine o'clock, for pity's sake."

He scowled at her then frowned toward the parlor. Everyone stared at them, listening eagerly. Uncle Eb eyed her as if she'd committed a crime. Marta, the only one in the family who knew the answer to Father's question, cowered on the rug.

Father turned back to Addie, his eyes boring into hers. The warmth she'd felt between them as they hung the swan on the tree earlier today had faded, replaced with chilled anger.

"Adelaide, tell me. Now," he said, his voice soft but commanding. "What did you do?"

She was tempted to shiver in fear like her cousin under Father's stern gaze. Cringe like a child who'd done something wrong. Instead, she got mad. Angry at him. Angry at the police and all the others in this fish-stinking city who wouldn't believe her, who treated her like a freak.

Angry with herself, for letting them.

A sob rolled up her throat. She looked at Mother's photograph, hanging between several others on the stair-well wall. It had been taken a few months before she fell ill. She wore pearls and her hair swept up. Mother had faced the greatest challenge of her life with grace and courage.

Surely Addie could be half as strong.

She choked back the tears and clenched her fists, digging her nails into her palms until they stung. Then, she straightened her back and told her father what she'd done.

Chapter Fifteen

"Feeney, get over here!"

Fat Charlie's bellow startled the seagulls searching for crumbs around the worksite. They took flight, their wings beating furiously as they soared over the fire tower and disappeared into the clouds.

Michael hustled to the office, exhausted and annoyed. He'd been up all night listening to the news, drinking, dogged by memories of what the Sight had shown him of Danny's future. After yesterday's attack, he knew with certainty the vision would soon come true.

He plastered on a questioning smile and faced his boss, who stood in the office doorway.

"I want you to keep a close eye on the men from here on out," Charlie said. "Especially the krauts."

Michael frowned in confusion. "Keep an eye on the men? Why?"

"We're going to war, son, that's why." He plucked a cigar from his wool coat's breast pocket. A half dozen were lined up in there like a picket fence. "We got a bunch of

137

foreigners on the crew. Germans and Eye-talians with accents as thick as my wife's ankles. A man who claimed to be an American yesterday might feel he owes something to his fatherland today. Might think a little sabotage is in order. We're on a tight schedule and I don't want any heinie hothead to toss a wrench into finishing the job."

Michael scanned the men ranged along the many levels of the scaffold. They were anything but hotheaded this morning. The mixed jabber of languages was muted, the thud of hammers on wood almost listless. The crewmembers were as stunned as Michael, wondering—and fearing—what would happen next.

He turned back to Charlie. More than ever, Michael wanted to ask what could be so important about the tower someone would gum things up with sabotage. But he didn't say a word. At this point, probably for the best not to know.

Instead, he simply nodded, adding, "Yes, sir, I'll keep a lookout."

"Good." Fat Charlie touched a match to the cigar. His cheeks bulged as he puffed. "Now, tell me, how many men are we down this morning?"

"Seven. I doubt they're sick. I suspect they went downtown to enlist." Along with half the men in Goveport, including Michael's three brothers. Watching them hug Ma and walk out the door before the sun came up had stabbed him the heart. Especially seeing Danny go, knowing what Michael knew.

Charlie snorted. "Damn right they went to enlist. I'd be first in line if they'd take me." He slapped his big belly. "But I got work to do, and so do they. Go get 'em."

"Sir?"

"Look, Feeney, I need every able-bodied man on this job. Uncle Sam needs this tower finished by New Year's or even sooner. You go find those men. Tell them they can join up as soon as the job's done. Tell them I'll give 'em a bonus if they get their asses back here by noon. But keep that under your hat." He jerked his chin toward the men at work. "I don't want the rest of these fellas to hear about it and stick their hands out for more money."

Michael set out for downtown right away. He puttered down Atlantic Avenue and inched his car across the Perkins River bridge, which connected the northern tip of Goveport with the rest of the city. His turtle pace didn't make the driver behind him happy, but with the pavement slick and icy, Michael wouldn't go too fast and risk skidding off the bridge into the water below.

He steered his jalopy into a parking space on Main Street fifteen minutes later, much to the relief of the lead foot still on his tail. The Packard zoomed by. Michael hoofed it the rest of the way to City Hall, a huge brown-brick building with fan-shaped granite steps leading up to brass-faced oak doors.

He arrived to quite a scene. People packed every inch of City Hall's steps and along the sidewalk in front all the way to Dwight's Corner. A few women, but mostly men. White men and colored men and everything in between. Some in sharp suits and overcoats, some in raggedy sweaters and dungarees. Some carried hunting rifles.

All anxious to go get shot at.

Michael's throat went dry. How many of these men would share his brother Danny's fate?

Every vivid moment of that Sight, the images, sounds, and smells flooded his mind. Michael as Danny, trudging along a rutted road, churned-up with snow and mud. His nose twitched at the smells of wet wool, oil, and sulfur. Bitter cold licked at his limbs, though he wore a heavy wool Army uniform and coat. He peeled off a tattered glove with a shivering hand and blew warm air on white-tipped, frozen fingers. A crack of gunfire broke the morning still. Something bit his jaw. His knees buckled and he fell. Blood pooled by his head in the snow.

Then, blackness.

No amount of cheap whiskey had ever been able to blot out the cold fact that Danny was going to die.

Michael searched for him and for his other brothers, Tommy and Pat Junior, but couldn't spot them. He saw some of his workers off to one side, Hans and Joe Cavacco among them. He shouldered through the sea of men toward them.

Suddenly, Hans pitched forward, as if pushed. He bashed into another man.

"Watch it, you dumb kraut," the man snarled.

A heavy stillness fell over them, the way the air pressed down before a storm. Then Hans pounced on the man like a hawk on a mouse. He knocked him flat and locked his hands around the man's throat. Hans choked him, and to add to the punishment, he bashed the poor fella's head against the pavement.

The crowd swung toward the brawlers, howling in rage. Catcalling and shouting slurs. Michael hung back, determined to stay out of the scrap. A man bumped against him and grabbed his arm. Michael's head hummed, then hurt like hell, as if someone had taken a buzz saw to his brain. His blood heated to boiling. Common sense fizzled and he suddenly lusted to dive in, to join the mob calling for Brandt's hide.

He sucked in air between his clenched teeth. Christ, had he gone bats? Had everyone? Michael shoved away his fierce anger, ignored his aching head, and elbowed toward the fighting men. He grabbed Hans by the collar and yanked him upright. Hans swung his fists at the air, growling and cursing.

Then, as if someone flicked a switch, the fight ended. Men stilled. Silence, save for the rumble of traffic rolling by and the poor strangled fella on the ground, coughing.

Hans shot out of the mob. Michael stepped in his path. "What happened?" he demanded.

"Get out of my way." Hans's eyes were wild, spitting fire. "Leave me alone."

He shoved Michael aside and bolted. Michael watched him run, scratching his head. Hans was a quiet kid, not one to start a brawl. Now, the boy's father picking a fight, he could see. Everyone knew Eb Brandt was Hitler's biggest fan and unpleasant to boot. But Hans? It didn't make sense. Michael's own sudden anger didn't make sense either.

No time for thinking. He put all the questions away until later when he could have a snort and mull them over properly. Then he went to round up the other fellas.

Woden moved down the street from City Hall and turned to watch the brawl. He breathed in the rage, feasted on the fury. It hadn't taken much to aggravate Hans and the men around him.

They were already angry. A touch here, a brush there, a whispered word in a hairy ear, and they erupted, out for blood.

All except Michael Feeney. Woden had to push him twice before anger took hold. Even then, Feeney had quickly shaken off his rage. Impressive—and infuriating. Falcon had reported the man not only shunned his gift, he smothered his vibrations with drink as well. Surely the alcohol had blocked Woden's attempt to rile him. Woden refused to believe a man so feeble in character as Feeney could have the strength of mind to resist his power.

He'd ponder that later. Now he needed to end the fight and concentrate on his real quarry. He held out his gloved hands palms up and curled his fingers, pulling back as if he tugged a heavy weight toward him. He pulled back with his mind, too, and the rage he'd pushed into the crowd seeped away.

His pleasure leached away as well, replaced with searing pain. Pushing such a large group of people had taken a toll. Daggers of fire stabbed his fingers and the veins in his hands throbbed. Woden had no time for such weakness. Hans flew by him, and he hurried to catch up. He'd only just begun to stoke the boy's fury and he had to complete the job, no matter the strain on his body. He needed Hans seething and out of control for his role in the mission to succeed.

"Son, wait," he called in German, hoping the boy still remembered his native tongue.

Hans ceased his headlong rush and turned. His eyes widened in recognition, but Woden held up his hand before he could speak.

"You're furious, Hans." Woden reached out with his

power. His vibrations trembled as angry energy poured from him into Hans's mind. "I heard what those men called you. Such vile names. Smears on our people. They're small men. They *deserve* your contempt." He worked rage into Hans like fingers kneading dough, with care and thoroughness. "They deserve your hatred."

Hans nodded stiffly, obediently. His expression twisted with raw emotion.

"You could kill every one of those men and you would be justified," Woden said, his voice low, cajoling. "You can't trust them. You can't trust your lover, either. She lies to you. She loves another man."

Hans balled his fists and let out a whine. Woden's vibrations burned but met resistance and his energy didn't fully latch on. He felt Virginia's power sizzling deep inside the boy's mind, holding tight. Dunstan was clever to use his blonde Cupid in his attempt to get to Adelaide. He must compliment him on such an amusing ploy when he caught up to him.

"Your lover's been pretending since you met," Woden said. "She's playing the virgin, while all this time, she shares another man's bed. They laugh at you. As those men you work with laugh at you."

He crawled deeper into the boy's mind, pushed in anger until it broke through the remnants of Virginia's gift. Joy and happiness shattered like shards of glass and Woden swooped in, filling him with blood rage.

Hans barely breathed now. His expression had turned feral, his eyes glassy. Woden ignored his own pain and fed greedily on the fury pulsing off the boy. He had him now, fully. If he gave the command to kill a passerby, Hans would rip the man's throat out.

"You must hold on to your resentment and groom your rage, Hans. Let it build against our enemies. Bide your time until you can have your revenge."

Hans nodded, his eyes glimmering.

Woden bent to whisper in his ear. "You'll have your chance to make a statement no one will forget. You'll make me proud, make your family proud. Your homeland will be grateful. You want that, don't you?"

"*Ja.*" Hans licked his lips. "More than anything in this world."

Woden smiled. The boy's German wasn't so rusty after all. "Good. Let us go and talk."

Chapter Sixteen

A wintry wind gusted into the preparation room as Father entered through the alleyway door. He stomped snow and sand off his feet and adjusted the stack of newspapers he carried from one arm to another. He'd been running out all day for the hourly extra editions cranked out by the city's three papers.

Addie glanced up from her stool by the windows, but he didn't look at her. Didn't speak to her either. Hadn't spoken to her since last night when she'd told him about her vision and her trip to the police station. He'd gaped in fear and disbelief as she spoke. When she completed the tale, he'd thoroughly scolded her for bringing attention to herself at a time when attention wasn't welcome, then left her standing alone in the front hall.

He'd insisted she ride with him to work this morning instead of walking or taking the bus, probably out of shame for her to be seen in public. A brittle silence hung between them during the drive and even now, as he dropped one of the newspapers onto the counter in front of her. He walked across the room and disappeared up the stairs. She watched him with an aching heart.

Just when she needed her father's understanding most, he'd abandoned her.

Addie swallowed her hurt and bitterness and spread the newspaper in front of her. Her small problems paled in light of the headlines splashed across the page and the bleak news that poured from the radio on the table near the embalming room doors.

The country was now at war.

President Roosevelt had named yesterday, December seventh, as a date that would live in infamy. He called on Congress to act. Within an hour, they'd declared war on Japan. Germany and Italy were expected to support their ally and issue their own war declaration against the United States at any moment.

Addie scanned the rest of the newspaper. The damage from the attack was still being tallied. The pages were filled with grainy photographs of wounded men on stretchers, battleships belching black smoke, sailors with grief-stricken faces. The firsthand accounts of the horror at Pearl Harbor described a nightmare. So many men dead, hundreds more missing, misidentified, or badly burned. It could take weeks, maybe months, for all the dead to be accounted for.

She shuddered to think of how long Jimmy Gallagher's mother would have to wonder in anguish about her boy, and the many mothers who would share her pain. She wanted to go to Mrs. Gallagher and tell her about her son. To give the woman some peace, at the very least. And perhaps to ease Addie's own guilt.

But Father wouldn't allow it. He'd told her to speak of the Sight to no one.

One person she *really* wished to speak to had probably left the city. Dunstan had offered her help and she'd told him to get lost in no uncertain terms. Several times. Now that the attack she'd warned about had happened, he'd no doubt given up on her and gone back to Washington.

Addie sighed, heartsore, exhausted, wrung out. She didn't want to think about Dunstan or her guilt and regrets for another second. What's more, she didn't want to be *here* anymore, enduring Father's silence and fearful glowers.

He'd told her to stay put, but why should she? They had no work today, and no one in a mood to do work if they did. Father had been in and out and Uncle Eb hadn't even bothered to show up. She'd seen him leave the house this morning at his usual time, climb into his car and drive away. To where, she had no idea. Uncle Pat was here though, in the embalming room with some of his poker friends. She'd heard arguing and coarse laughter, glasses clinking, and occasional curse words most of the day.

Addie pushed the newspaper aside and slid off her stool. She exchanged her cotton gloves for her leather pair and put on her hat and coat.

"I'm going home," she called to Uncle Pat, receiving a muffled goodbye in reply.

The door thumped shut behind her and she hurried down the alley to the sidewalk. She stopped to button her coat. Fog had rolled in. At the bottom of the hill, a ghostly shroud cloaked the memorial to fishermen lost at sea. The foghorn at Mackey Light moaned a warning. She turned left and hustled up Holmes Street in the gloomy murk.

She reached Main Street and crossed at the intersection. It had been only twenty-four hours since the world had turned upside down, yet everyday life went on. Cars and buses rumbled past. Men in suits or work clothes went about their business, women pushed baby carriages and darted in an out of the shops as if it were a normal day.

With one exception. All eyes were on her, the girl who knew about the attack. Or it felt that way.

Addie shook off her guilt as best as she could and rushed on. The smell of fish and diesel oil lessened and traffic thinned out as she reached the city's residential section, populated by houses dating back to Goveport's glory days as a bustling seaport. Large colonial-style homes with widow's walks stood next to tiny saltboxes of no more than four rooms.

She walked past Colby Park, passing the entrance, with its twin granite gateposts, each topped with a carved clipper ship at sail. Father used to bring Mother here to watch the sunset, carrying her into the park when she got too weak to walk.

Tall, thick lilac bushes acted as a natural fence around the park and shadowed the sidewalk. The back of Addie's neck prickled as the wind whistled eerily through leafless branches that looked like grasping fingers. She walked faster. The fog added to the gloom, making it hard to see, and the distinct *tap-tap* of footsteps hurrying behind heightened her jumpiness.

A man suddenly burst out of the bushes. She slammed into him. Strong hands closed around her upper arms. She swallowed a shriek as a face came into focus.

"*Pete,*" she said in relief and annoyance. He wore his police uniform and coat, and his cheeks were red and chapped from the cold, as if he'd been walking a beat all day.

"Addie!" he cried, steadying her. "Did you see him? There was a man lurking, through there, in the park." He glared into the lilac bushes. "He might've been lying in wait for you..." He shot her a meaningful look.

Addie shivered. Jeepers, was he serious? She'd feared word about her failed warning would spread and people would curse her name, but would someone actually skulk in the bushes, waiting to accost her? She often walked home this way. Anyone could've followed her.

She squeezed her gloved hands together, trying not to panic.

"I think he's gone now," Pete said. "Still, I should walk you home, just to be sure."

"Oh, thank you," she said. "But I don't want to keep you from your job."

"*You* are my job. Your safety, I mean."

He shot her a knockout smile and her heart fluttered. He could be charming when he put his mind to it. He offered her his arm, but she declined. They fell into step side by side.

"Addie," he said after a short silence. He sounded nervous. "Let me apologize once more for my terrible behavior at the police station. You meant to help, and I acted the fool—"

His mouth snapped shut when a wheezing jalopy pulled up across the street and Addie's cousin Michael leaned out the open window.

"Hey, Addie," Michael bellowed, banging his fist on the car door. "Hop in. I gotta talk to you."

~

Dunstan cursed under his breath.

He'd spoken to Radcliffe last night and the man had been more than clear—lasso Addie as soon as humanly possible and get her down to Washington. Dunstan had been following her at a discreet distance since she left the funeral home, trying to figure out how to do that. He wasn't about to grab the girl and stuff her into the trunk of his car. He wasn't a gangster's muscleman. Not anymore.

He watched Addie walk, briskly and with purpose. He liked that. Hell, he liked everything about her, the reason why he wanted to tell his boss to call off the whole cock-eyed plan. When Radcliffe got his paws on her, he'd order her locked in a room to test her ability for days on end. Order *Dunstan* to do it, probably. She'd be forced to touch dozens of nefarious individuals. Inviting all kinds of images to invade her mind, none of them pretty, he suspected. Addie would be chasing butterflies after only a week.

He snorted, disgusted with himself. He'd come to Goveport looking for a star who could save his team. He'd found her, and now he couldn't be sure he wanted her. But the die had been cast. Radcliffe would send someone else if Dunstan couldn't come through, and that man wouldn't care about Addie's feelings. Wouldn't care about her at all.

Ahead, a policeman popped out of the bushes and approached Addie. Anxious, Dunstan snapped to attention and hustled forward. She seemed to know the man, so he slowed somewhat, hoping to the cop hadn't noticed him following her. He'd had enough run-ins with the police to last a lifetime.

A car struggled by him up the hill. Dunstan recognized the jalopy and its driver, the man who'd tried to cuddle up with Virginia at the bus stop Saturday. He stopped and hung halfway out of the car's window, waving and calling to Addie. Christ, did that fella drive around town trying to pick up dames all day?

Dunstan moved forward again, but too late to play the hero—smiling like she knew this fella too, Addie dashed across the street to the car. The cop watched her climb inside, looking as aggravated as Dunstan felt. Could the cop be jealous?

Dunstan frowned. Was he?

The Ford disappeared in a cloud of exhaust, heading toward Addie's home. Dunstan put his anxiety away. Taming the worry that tried to push out of the locked vault in his brain took a little longer. He'd stuffed all the emotions he'd absorbed from other gifted people into that dark hole, but it was damned hard work to keep them bottled up in there.

He turned and headed back down the hill. He'd shadow Addie again tomorrow. Hopefully by then he'd find a way to convince her to come to Washington.

Hell, he had to find a way to get her to talk to him first.

Addie hugged herself for warmth. Michael's car had no heater. It seemed colder in here than outside.

"Who's the flatfoot?" Michael moved the gear shift and his car stuttered forward.

"Just some young man I met."

She swiveled to look back at Pete through the ice-frosted rear window. He gazed at Michael's car with an odd expression before turning to frown at the bushes. Addie's stomach tightened. Who could Pete have seen in there? Had she really been in danger?

"You can't fool me," Michael said, flashing a wicked grin. "You have a sweetheart."

"Michael, you know that's not possible."

She faced forward again and glanced at her cousin. A sweetheart wasn't possible for him, either. Breathlessly handsome, with black hair, a strong jaw, and blue eyes as devilish as Uncle Pat's, no one would suspect the turmoil behind those eyes. That's why he drank, to escape the Sight. It broke her heart to see him live his life from afar, sitting in the back row.

Speak for yourself, a voice inside her chided. She'd hardly lived at all.

"You said you wanted to talk to me?" Addie said, more waspish than she'd intended. "What about?"

"About Hans. He had a fight today."

She stiffened. "A *fight*?"

"More like a brawl. Like a Fish Village bar on payday."

"That's not like him at all."

"No, it's not. I never seen Hans like that. He just

snapped. Then he ran away, still angry. Don't know what set him off. Maybe he's gassed up over Pearl Harbor. Tempers are red hot right now. I heard a mob attacked that Chinese restaurant downtown last night. Windows smashed. Some damage inside too." Michael snorted in disgust. "Hotheads thought they were Japanese and were out for revenge."

"How *awful*. Sounds like something those fascists do, attacking people, burning buildings. I hope no one was injured."

"A Chinaman got his teeth bashed in before the cops came and chased the mob away. Trying to protect his property."

Addie trembled. "The poor man."

"You Germans are next, I suspect."

"Gee thanks, Michael. I'm greatly comforted." Sarcasm aside, she suspected he was right. Hadn't Father said as much yesterday, as they listened to the news of the attack? Perhaps that explained her father's anger with her. He understood—and he feared—the suspicion and hatred soon to be directed at them.

"Hans isn't messed up in any of your uncle's shenanigans, is he?" Michael asked, turning the corner onto Pine Street. "Maybe they got him riled up enough to start a brawl."

Hans involved with Uncle Eb's deplorable friends in the Bund? Not possible. She shook her head. None of what Michael had said seemed possible. "Hans isn't like those men, or the hooligans who attacked the restaurant. He doesn't go around starting fights or smashing windows. He's gentle, even-tempered. Wouldn't hurt a fly."

"That poor devil he throttled would beg to differ.

Addie, Hans got so mad, I swear he coulda killed that fella. I seen it with my own eyes. Don't know *what* would've happened if the fight didn't just...stop."

Addie leaned back against the seat and rubbed her pounding temples. This story grew more horrifying by the moment.

Michael snorted. "Funny thing is, the fight happened at City Hall, where Hans was waiting to join up. Waiting to go fight."

"What were you doing at City Hall? Were you there to join up too?"

"Hell no. You gotta have an exam to enlist. Just thinking about being half naked, doctors pawing me, triggering the Sight—" He shuddered. "Well, hell." He stopped the car in front of her house and turned to her, his gaze piercing, filled with unease. "How do you do it, Addie? The Sight's a merciless son of a bitch drunk. How do you get through a day sober? I was you, I'd be scared all the time."

She gave her cousin a weak smile. "What makes you think I'm not?"

His eyes widened. "Damn." He reached over and popped open the glove box. Light glinted off a small bottle nestled inside. Michael pulled it out and pushed it at her. "Have a snort. It'll put that bastard in your brain to sleep."

She eyed the half-empty bottle and the light brown liquid inside, tempted to take a swig. Maybe she would have, if she didn't hate the taste of whiskey. What possible good could getting drunk do for her, anyway? Dull her senses for a few hours, wake up with a headache tomorrow. And still be afflicted with the Sight. Still afraid. No closer to understanding that thing than she did now.

Addie turned down Michael's offer with a shake of her head, thanked him for the ride and got out of the car. She glanced back as she darted up the steps to her front door. Her heart wrenched to see him uncap the bottle and take a drink before he drove away.

Chapter Seventeen

Marta had asked Addie to meet for a late lunch after school and Addie moved at a brisk pace along Main Street. Not to outrun the cold, but to escape the stares of the people she passed. A matronly woman in a wool coat crossed the street when she saw her coming, a middle-aged man in a fine suit spat on the sidewalk, and a younger man eyed her like a ravenous bird of prey as she passed, giving her the creeps.

Clearly, the news had begun to spread about her fore-knowledge of the attack.

Perhaps she should've obeyed Father and stayed out of sight at work. But with no customers and nothing to do, the place was as dead as, well, a funeral home. When Marta had telephoned from school between classes, desperate for a way to avoid going to Germantown with her matchmaking mother, Addie had jumped at the chance to escape.

Out of breath and jittery by the time she reached Sal's, she stepped inside and steered toward a vacant booth. She dropped into the seat facing the door, so she could watch for Marta. She placed her pocketbook beside her and unbuttoned her coat. The swan brooch on her blouse caught the light. And Rosa's attention.

She came over, carrying a cup and a full coffee pot. Her pale-green dress and white apron spoke of the long day she'd had, coated with food stains every color in the rainbow.

"It's a wonder you can show your face in here, after the other night," she said, filling Addie's cup. "Dancing with my date, leaving me to twiddle my thumbs all alone at the table."

Guilt heated Addie's cheeks. She would have preferred Rosa's anger over the hurt in her eyes and bitter disappointment in her voice.

"Rosa, I'm sorry. I didn't mean to. It was just one dance." A dance she heartily regretted. If she'd had more fortitude and told Dunstan no, Rosa wouldn't be shooting daggers at her now.

"Hmph," Rosa said, only slightly mollified. She slid into the seat on the other side of the booth and placed the coffee pot on the table. "I s'pose you're right, but just so you know, Dunstan's crazy about me. We're stepping out tonight, and he's got me dated up for the rest of the week, too."

"Oh." Addie's heart squeezed. There went her theory that Dunstan had left the city. He didn't need her anymore and had turned his attention to someone more interesting.

"In fact..." Rosa grinned like the Cheshire cat. "I think he might be the fella you saw in my future."

That upset Addie even more, though she couldn't

understand why. She hid her dismay behind a forced smile. "Gee, that's wonderful. I wish you both the best."

"Maybe you can find out for sure if he's the one."

"Oh *no*. I can't do that." Addie glanced around the restaurant, at the smattering of customers bent over their coffee and sandwiches. "Especially not in public like this."

Rosa leaned forward and narrowed her eyes. "Yes, you can. I *know* you can. I heard you did some fortune telling for the cops the other day. What's more public than that? You told them about seeing Pearl Harbor, and went on to read Fatty Gillis's future, too. Though if you saw anything more than a couple of Sal's lasagnas in that flatfoot's future, I'd be surprised."

"I did *not* tell the sergeant's fortune. I only went to warn about—"

"Something that came *true*," Rosa spat. "I wanna know if my future will come true too. Am I gonna marry Dunstan?" She stuck out her hand, her dark eyes offering a challenge. "After the way you were flirting with him the other night, I think you owe me that."

Addie trembled as she gazed at Rosa's outstretched hand. Her fingers were puckered and cracked from dishwater and mopping up spills. Her fingernails were chipped. She worked hard for little pay then went home to her mother who did nothing but nag and complain. And drink. Not the happiest of lives. If Addie could assure her Dunstan would be the man to take her away from all that, wasn't it worth swallowing her fear and willingly inviting the Sight into her mind?

She slowly removed her right glove and pulled in a deep breath to bolster her courage. She held Rosa's hand. Darkness closed in and the Sight rushed at her like a hurricane tide. The images and sounds from the vision she'd seen years ago began to take shape, Addie as an older Rosa cuddled next to a gray-haired man on a sofa. A screen hanging on the wall showed a Technicolor movie of a wagon train rolling across the prairie under a blue sky. The smell of cigarette smoke and peppermints filled the small room.

Addie tried to turn her head, to see if an older version of Dunstan sat next to Rosa, when the peaceful scene abruptly shattered. Rosa, the gray-haired man, and the cozy parlor exploded into tiny pieces that blew away like glittery ash. An instant later, Addie crashed into a cold, murky void. She tried to swim back to the safety of the parlor but had no control. Her senses dulled. She couldn't see anything. Couldn't hear, smell, or taste anything either. Terror enveloped her and swathed her in a sinister cocoon, pulling her down, drowning her in fear.

She ripped out of the Sight, drained, struggling to catch her breath.

"Well?" Rosa asked, pinning her with a keen gaze. "What did you see?"

Addie had no idea. She pressed her hand to her belly to still the churning, as confused and disturbed by the vision as when she'd touched Sgt. Gillis. And twice as frightened.

"I... I don't know." Addie shuddered, struggling for calm. "I couldn't see anything clearly."

Rosa huffed. "Maybe you didn't *want* to see anything clearly."

The door opened and Marta burst into the restaurant. She spotted Addie and rushed over.

"Here I am, the late Marta Brandt," she said, peeling off her gloves. "Late, and *very* sorry. Got to gabbing with

Janie after school and simply lost track of time. Hello, Rosa."

Rosa gave her a clipped nod, picked up the coffee pot, and slid out of the seat. "Thanks for nothing," she directed at Addie and stalked away.

Marta took Rosa's place on the other side of the booth. "What was that about?"

"Nothing." Something, actually. Her gaze followed Rosa as she crossed the room to the counter. Something confusing and unsettling.

"Are you sure, Addie? You seem upset."

She looked back at Marta, wondering if she should tell her what had happened. Would she understand? Would anyone? She doubted even Dunstan could understand the cyclone that swirled around inside her head.

"I'm fine," Addie said after a moment. "Just hungry, that's all."

"Well, I think a hearty meal will help with that. Hopefully I'm not so late you have to go back to work and don't have time to eat."

"No, I have time. There's nothing to do at work. Plus, I prefer not to be in Father's company at the moment. He's still upset with me."

Marta scoffed. "He should be proud of you for doing what was right, rather than treating you like a secret to be hidden away."

"That's exactly his plan for me. To keep me hidden. He seems to think I'm some kind of Lorelei, luring sailors to their death with my powers. He doesn't want me to go out at all. As you can see, I've obeyed his command to the letter."

Marta grinned. "I think I like this new Addie. Can you

lay into Mother next and tell her to quit pestering me about the shoemaker's son?"

That got Addie to smile. Her cousin always had a way of making her feel better. Making everyone feel better. "I'll see what I can do."

Marta skimmed the menu board on the wall. "What do you recommend? Something fast. I have to be at the store by four thirty. If I'm even one second late, the floor manager, Miss Revere, will report me to the office, the old battle-axe."

"Why don't you try the tuna salad? I usually get that."

"Sold!" She unbuttoned her coat and took it off, revealing a snazzy red blouse with a floppy bow at the throat and a dark green skirt. Her shoulder-length hair curled under on the ends, and she'd tucked one side behind her ear with a red bow.

"Look at you," Addie said. "Wearing Christmas colors. So cunning."

"Red and green puts customers in a jolly mood, and happy to spend more money. Or so Miss Revere tells us."

Addie sipped her now-cold coffee, starting to relax, and they chatted until the waitress came to take their order. Not Rosa, who was either busy or still fuming at Addie, but Sally, a skinny woman twice Rosa's age, with bleached blonde hair and a slap-dash beauty mark painted above her upper lip. She yanked a pencil from her hair bun and scowled at her notepad as she scribbled down their orders, as if she disapproved of their choices.

Sally puttered away and Marta tipped the creamer over her cup, lightening the dark liquid inside.

"Schulman's will be busy tonight, with Christmas coming," she said. "Why don't people do what I do and shop in October? Of course, I always get the same thing, a tie for my father and a silk scarf for Mother. Don't know what I'll do next year. I heard silk will be hard to get, maybe even rationed. Silk's used to make parachutes, you know, so you can kiss your usual gift of stockings goodbye now that..." Marta sobered, her voice falling to a hush. "Now that we're at war."

At war. Two words Addie had feared and now would be hearing for who knew how long to come.

Marta sipped her coffee, looking pensive. "It's funny how you don't notice things until they affect you. This war's been going on for two years. Terrible things have happened in the Orient, in Europe. Boys I knew in school back home are carrying rifles and marching off to battle. And yet I've shut it out. Even with my father going on about our glorious homeland and Hitler, I've barely paid attention. Ignored it all."

"I know what you mean. I've told myself we're safe here in America. It won't happen here. And now it has." And Addie had been powerless to stop it.

"We were fooling ourselves." Marta met Addie's gaze full-on. "But I can't ignore the world anymore. It's time to do something." Her tone, and her expression, had gone dead serious.

"And by *something* you don't mean serving coffee at the Red Cross, do you? Like my mother did in the Great War."

Marta's eyebrows drew down. "You know me better than that. Janie Carlson says they'll need nurses, just like the last war. Maybe twice as many. I intend one of them to be *me.* I'm going to do everything I can to become a nurse, no matter what Mother has to say about it."

"And your father?"

She dismissed him with a wave of her slim hand. "He won't care. He cares only for himself. And the Bund. And Hans. Father cares a *whole lot* what my brother does, but he hardly notices me. Whatever Mother wants for me, he'll agree. As long as the man she chooses for me to marry is German and a Lutheran, of course."

She sipped more coffee then tittered nervously, not as calm and collected as Addie had thought.

"I'm going to have it out with my mother," Marta continued. "I'm going to tell her just because she's found being chained to a stove fulfilling, doesn't mean *I* have to follow the same path. I'm not cut out to be a hausfrau."

"No, you're not." Addie's lips quirked. Aunt Trudy kept a tidy home and was proud of it, but her daughter could burn water. "What if your mother's dead set against it? How will you pay for nursing school?" Her aunt wasn't the parsimonious sort, but she might threaten to keep her pocketbook closed out of spite.

"I can always join the Army, like Hans. Or whatever the equivalent is for girls. I've got some savings. If the Army won't take me, I can pay my own way to nursing school. As long as they let me pay on installment." She flashed Addie a grin. "I'll have to wait until May, when I turn eighteen, anyway. Never fear, I'll figure the whole thing out by then."

Addie nodded. It looked as if the vision she'd seen of her cousin's future would come to pass. Marta would become a nurse, and someday find herself in that rain-soaked tent with wounded men all around her. *If* the Sight held true. After what had happened with Rosa, how could Addie be sure?

"I *know* you'll find a way," she said firmly, pushing those worrying thoughts aside. "And you'll be the *best* nurse there ever was."

Marta beamed so bright she could have blinded the sun. "I'm glad at least *one* person in our family believes in me."

Sally returned, with an impossible number of plates lined up along her arms. She crashed some of them onto their table and moved on to her other customers without a word. Rosa sailed by a moment later with the coffee pot.

"Don't mind old Sally." She smiled at Marta as she topped off her coffee. "I'd say it was her bunions acting up, but truth is, she's just plain mean." She looked at Addie and her smile faded. She stomped away, ignoring Addie's empty cup.

"*What* is going on between you two?" Marta asked, her expression keen with interest. "She seems as mad as an alley cat."

"It's nothing. A misunderstanding, that's all." Marta scowled and Addie relented. "She asked me to use the Sight, to see if I could tell her about her future. I couldn't focus. It was a mistake."

Marta's scowl softened. "Oh dear."

"She heard about my vision and what I told the police. Soon everyone will've heard. I expect to be getting more requests like Rosa's. People wanting me to tell their fortunes, nasty phone calls, people calling me a witch and worse. That's what happened after Hugo." Addie suddenly didn't have much of an appetite. She pushed her plate away, her sandwich untouched. "I doubt it will be any different now."

"This *is* different, though. People will take you seriously now. Including the police, those pigheaded fools. You were *right*. Pete Bowdoin isn't the only policeman who owes you an apology." Marta put down her sandwich, her gaze on Addie. "This is your chance. I have to wait until I'm old enough to do what I want. You're lucky, you can act *now*. You can use your power to help *right now*."

Addie shifted uncomfortably. Marta made it sound so simple. "I'd like to help, I honestly would. I *want* to stop another terrible thing from happening, but... I barely understand how the Sight works or what it's telling me." That became clear when she'd tried to discover Rosa's future. "I don't know how to control my power, and frankly, it scares me half to death."

But...did it have to be this way? Addie remembered what Dunstan said to her the other night. *I'll show you how to use your power. You'll never be afraid of your gift again.* Could he help her? Was it possible not to be afraid? She'd been running away from the Sight for so long, she couldn't imagine embracing it.

"I know you're scared," Marta said. "I would be too if I could do what you can. But I think the time has come to put fear away. You've been given this unusual ability. You can't ignore it anymore. We're at war. You can use your power to help in the fight."

Marta's cheeks reddened as the impassioned speech poured out, reminding Addie of something else Dunstan had said. *Your country needs you. I need you.* Was that still true now that the attack in Hawaii had happened?

Only one way to find out.

"Marta, you shouldn't train to be a nurse. You should become a lawyer. You're as persuasive as Clarence Darrow." Addie drew her plate close to her again and applied herself to her sandwich with gusto, feeling hopeful for the first time in forever. She would go on the hunt for Dunstan. She had a *lot* of questions she hoped he could answer.

She looked toward Rosa, at a table in the middle of the room, coffee pot in hand as always. She smiled down at a young man with a hundred freckles speckling his face. The first thing Addie would have to figure out—how to find Dunstan without Rosa finding out she was looking for him.

Addie and Marta finished their lunch then ankled to Schulman's, several blocks away. Slush coated the sidewalk, gray clouds hung in the sky, but Main Street was gay. Dressed for Christmas with wreaths on shop doors, metal snowflakes suspended over the street on wires, and huge red and green ball ornaments that hung from the streetlamps, brightening a somewhat gloomy afternoon.

Addie shifted her pocketbook to her left hand and linked arms with her cousin. They strolled along, kicking at slush piles, window shopping, cooing over shoes and hats they couldn't afford. Soon they turned the corner at O'Brien's Smoke Shop. Schulman's huge granite building loomed ahead, four stories high and spread out nearly to the next corner.

Shoppers thronged the sidewalk. Children crowded in front of the store's display windows, gazing at the wonders within—a tiered display of dolls and toy trucks in one window, in another, a jolly mechanized Santa Claus tucked a present under a Christmas tree shimmering with tinsel. Still more pedestrians swarmed the vendor carts at the curb. The smell of grilled hot dogs and roasted peanuts tempted Addie, despite her full stomach.

She spotted Sgt. Gillis at the hot dog cart. Speaking of policemen who should apologize for not believing her. She banished the peevish thought as soon as it popped up. Addie had glimpsed his future, and it wasn't pleasant. She should warn him. He'd no doubt believe her now, except what she'd seen when she held his hand had been so vague, she didn't know what to tell him.

What if she touched his hand again to try to get a more detailed Sight? Would the images be the same, or have changed like with Rosa? Addie nearly growled in frustration. More questions for Dunstan.

Marta turned to Addie when they reached the store's entrance. "You coming inside? There's a sale on Chanel perfume. *The* perfect gift for your favorite girl cousin."

"Aren't you my only girl cousin?" Addie said.

"That I am. All the more reason for you to splurge on something extravagant for me."

"Your offer's tempting. I haven't even started my Christmas shopping yet, but I've got to go. It's nearly dusk and Father will be cross I've been gone so long." She took both of Marta's hands and squeezed them gently. "Thank you for what you said and for your faith in me. You've given me a lot to think about. How did you get to be so wise?"

"Just lucky, I guess." Marta laughed, but her eyes grew moist. "Now let me go before Miss Revere comes and carries me into the store."

Addie watched the revolving door swallow Marta up, then headed down the sidewalk, lost in thought. How could she locate Dunstan without asking Rosa and igniting her jealousy again? He must be staying somewhere in the city or at one of the seaside tourist cabins, though most of those drafty shacks were shuttered for the winter.

An idea struck. She'd first run into Dunstan at the police station. He'd known about her conversation with Sgt. Gillis. Perhaps he'd told Gillis where he was staying. She spun and doubled back, walking briskly through the throng of pedestrians toward the hot dog cart. Her heart sank. The sergeant had left.

"There's that girl," a woman shouted. "Hey, you!"

It took a moment to realize the woman meant her. Addie stopped. Two women of middle age bustled up. They both wore cloth coats. One wore a knit scarf over her hair, knotted under her chin.

"Is it true?" the woman with the scarf demanded, moving closer.

Addie opened her mouth, but nothing came out.

"Is it true you knew about the Japanese? You knew about them hitting Pearl Harbor. You knew and coulda stopped it." The woman's words poured out in an accusing wail. Dark circles rimmed her eyes, and a violent shade of red tinged her nose, as if she'd been crying for days.

Addie's stomach seized. She backed away several steps and bumped against one of Schulman's display windows. The tinny strains of "Jingle Bells" and the *clack-clack* of a toy train sounded behind the glass.

"They say you saw it in your mind. Saw the whole thing." The woman's chin quivered. New tears sparkled in her eyes. "You coulda saved everyone. Coulda saved my Jimmy."

The blood drained from Addie's face. Lord in heaven, Mrs. Gallagher! Pedestrians stopped and gathered around them, pressing in, trapping her. Addie held up her hands protectively.

"She's a Brandt," a man yelled. "They're a bunch of Nazi crooks."

"Slimy kraut," someone shouted, and the chant rippled across the agitated crowd.

Mrs. Gallagher's grief-stricken voice cut through the noise. "You coulda saved my Jimmy. But you didn't."

"I tried," Addie cried, as Jimmy's mother sobbed. "I-I tried to warn them. They wouldn't listen. They wouldn't believe me."

"You people got what you wanted," Mrs. Gallagher's friend snarled. "War. Death. More bodies to bury."

The crowd swelled. They hissed and catcalled, as if Addie were a villain in a melodrama. They surrounded her and shouted epithets, their faces grotesque masks of fury, like in a horror house. The heat and smell of a hundred bodies choked her.

Fear pulsed through Addie's veins. She shoved to the right, then to the left, trying to escape, but the angry horde penned her in. Arms flailed. Someone scratched her cheek. Another person batted her hat and it flopped to the ground. Hands tugged at her pocketbook. Addie pressed against the window so hard she feared the glass would shatter.

Suddenly, a young tough in a moth-eaten sweater and smelling of liquor muscled through the mob and lunged at her.

Addie gasped in terror as his clenched fist flew at her face.

Chapter Eighteen

Woden gorged himself on the hatred. Feasted on the fury and the fear like a starving man desperate for sustenance. His vibrations ached with pleasure and throbbed with an almost carnal lust for more. More anger, more terror and rage, more and more and more...

And still that hungry demon within him could not be satisfied.

"If you're going to get Adelaide, now's the time," Falcon said, creeping up beside him. "Isn't that your plan?"

Falcon's words pricked the blissful cocoon around Woden like a pin to a balloon. The waves of pleasure skimming along his vibrations dissipated and he took a shaky breath.

Minutes earlier, he'd moved stealthily among the crowd outside the store, pushing them as he had the men at City Hall. As before, a simple task. Anger and fear still simmered in everyone's breast, growing more potent as the drumbeats of war increased. He only had to stoke the rage of a few, and the others joined in, directing their venom at Adelaide.

Woden wanted her vulnerable. Wounded, sliced by the vindictive fangs of the mob. He wanted her so frightened that when he swept in and rescued her, she'd be more than grateful. Open to him and his power. So malleable in her fear, he could easily turn her to his cause, and she would agree to join his team by the end of the day.

That couldn't happen if he continued to wallow in his lust. He needed to put his base pleasures aside and focus on his plan. He pinned his gaze on Adelaide through the undulating crowd. She cowered against the store windows, right where he wanted her. Should he allow the thug he'd hired to menace her to strike her? Or should he rush in and rescue her in the nick of time? Women enjoyed such romantic gestures. It could help in softening the girl's feelings toward him.

Suddenly, Falcon stiffened and bolted from the scene without a word.

Alerted, Woden cast a frantic look over the mob to see what had spooked his underling. His gaze fell on something that fired bullets of fury through his veins. A confident, muscular hum pierced his brain and drowned his vibrations.

"Verdammt!" Woden muttered. He wouldn't get the chance to save Adelaide.

Dunstan got there first.

~

A ddie put up her fists, desperate to defend herself, when the tough in the ratty sweater suddenly disappeared. A pair of hands seized the man by the neck and jerked him away so fast his porkpie hat flew off. A dark figure filled the void, putting his broad back between Addie and the mob like a protective shield.

Dunstan.

"That's enough," he commanded. "Be still. All of you."

He swept an arm in front of him, as if drawing a curtain over the crowd. Addie peeped around him to see their furious expressions fizzle in an instant, like he'd thrown a blanket over a blazing fire. A calm murmur rippled, and the ugly pall melted away.

The horde began to shuffle off. Some hung their heads sheepishly. The tough in the ratty sweater dashed into the street, swallowed up by traffic. Mrs. Gallagher's friend put an arm around the grieving mother's shaking shoulders and led her away.

Addie clutched the strap of her pocketbook and struggled for calm. Her heart raced. Her blood rushed like a flooding river.

"You alright?" Dunstan demanded.

"Yes, I suppose." She eyed him. His legs trembled and he sagged, barely able to hold himself up, like the Scarecrow in *The Wizard of Oz*. His normally tan skin had gone as pale as moonlight. He panted, as if he'd just run up a mountain and couldn't catch his breath. Was he going to faint? She could never catch this big man if he did. "Question is, are *you* alright?"

"I'm fine," he bit off. "Just...concerned. What the hell happened?"

"I'm not sure." She glanced toward the street where the tough had fled. Fear rose again. "They started yelling, then everyone was *there* and angry. Like they wanted to rip me apart."

"Just like that?" His eyes flashed as he scanned the area. He glowered at passersby, at the parked cars and the vehicles rolling by.

"What are you looking for?" Addie asked, frowning in confusion.

"An old friend," he said. "He's partial to theatrics, and what happened here seems right up his alley." He turned back to her, his fierce expression softening. He bent to scoop up her hat and pushed it into her hand. "You should get home. You've had a scare. Let me give you a ride."

"Oh, that's not necessary." She shook slush and wet dirt off her hat, deciding not to put it back on. "I'm headed back to work. I'm going to walk."

He scowled. "The hell you will. *I'll* drive you." He took her arm and urged her forward. He moved with an unsteady gait, but his anger seemed to have had abated, and his breathing had almost returned to normal. "My car's down there."

She let him lead her away.

~

oden watched Adelaide disappear into Dunstan's car. He cursed as his opportunity to capture the girl disappeared as well.

He could blame the mob, or Falcon, or the seductive

power of his own gift for distracting him from his goal. For his failure. Could, but wouldn't. The blame lay squarely on Dunstan's shoulders. That gorilla had swooped in like a hero in one of those Hollywood moving pictures and rescued her before Woden could even blink.

How could he have missed Dunstan lurking nearby? He'd searched for the man before riling the mob, had felt for his peculiar vibrations, but it seemed he'd gotten better at disguising himself. When Dunstan stepped in, Woden had no choice but to retreat, to abandon his plan to grab Adelaide or risk exposing himself.

He stalked toward Smith's Packard, waiting for him at the curb. He climbed into the back seat. "Drive," he growled, rubbing his hands together, trying to ease the pain, struggling to quell the demanding demon inside him.

Smith started the car with a roar and met Woden's gaze in the rearview mirror. "I thought the girl was coming with us. What happened?"

He glared at Smith. Jack Dunstan had happened. What's more, the man suspected Woden had been behind the crowd's anger. He'd seen the way Dunstan had scoured the area, searching for him.

"I *told* you to drive," he ordered.

Smith guided the car into traffic and Woden slumped against the seat, utterly drained from using his power on such a large group. He yanked off his gloves and frowned at his throbbing hands. Jack had succeeded in besting him there too. He'd seen Dunstan weaken after pushing the crowd, but the man had rallied with enviable speed, while knives of pain still shot through Woden's hands, scorching his fingertips like fiery nubs of coal.

He closed his eyes, frustrated. Jack would no doubt

stick by Adelaide's side after this incident and it would be difficult to get close to her. He'd keep Smith and Falcon on her trail, looking for an opportunity to secure her, but he must devise another strategy, perhaps find someone the girl trusted to aid him. Someone she would never suspect.

At the moment, he must turn his focus to the next stage of the mission. With what had happened in Hawaii, the Americans were scrambling to tighten security on both coasts. The timetable would have to be accelerated.

He leaned forward. "Did you find a man like I asked you to, Smith?"

He saw the man's blue eyes squint in confusion, reflected in the windshield mirror. Woden grimaced, his anger flaring once more. Smith was as dense as darkness. If he hadn't been assured the man would kill on command, he'd have throttled him by now.

"A man," Woden snarled. "A man with a boat. Did you find him?"

"Oh, yeah. Fella named Maheu. He was a bootlegger back during Prohibition. Now runs a fishing boat out of Fisk's Landing. In the daytime, at least. Anything else you need he'll smuggle in or out at night. For a price."

"A steep price, no doubt."

"Steep as a mountain," Smith said. "He wants a thousand. Five hundred up front, another five when the job is done."

Woden snorted. The fisherman knew the plan hinged on him and he would gouge them for every last penny. Greedy, unprincipled men like Maheu were the lowest of the low. Woden loathed working with such creatures, despised depending on them even more. But he must bury his dislike and deal with such inferior people if he wanted to see the plan through.

"Tell the fisherman I'll meet his terms," he said through gritted teeth. "Arrange a meeting."

He sat back again and pondered his next steps as the pain in his hands subsided. He would find a way to make Maheu regret demanding such an exorbitant sum. He'd get Adelaide, and Dunstan too. This time he would catch his slippery old friend. And with a plan that would cause Jack maximum pain. A trap he couldn't escape.

Woden blamed Madelyn for Dunstan getting away last time. She'd embraced the cause early on. Recruiting her had been far easier than he'd anticipated, in fact. Jack had been her one weakness. She'd begged to be allowed to handle the effort to turn him, and the result had been disastrous.

This time, Woden would take charge and there would be no failure. No mistakes. No escape. This time, he would break Dunstan, leave his reputation in tatters, and destroy him once and for all.

Chapter Nineteen

Addie stared out the window as Dunstan's car chugged along Ocean Boulevard, a broad road that snaked along the shoreline. Rickety piers and docks flashed by, and boats of all sizes bobbed on the water. The Atlantic was as gray as the sky and quite choppy today.

Addie's emotions churned, as unsettled as the ocean. Her pulse had returned to normal but the events at the store still crowded her mind. Jimmy's heartsick mother, accusing her. The man in the ratty sweater, the shouts, the mob wanting to hurt her.

Dunstan coming to her rescue.

"Thank you again for helping me back there," she said, feeling awkward and shy.

"You were in trouble. I stepped in." He flashed a heated look. "I take care of my people."

Yes, his people. The ones with the gifts. He'd made it perfectly clear the other night the only thing he found interesting about a meek undertaker's daughter was her so-called gift.

"But I'm not one of your people," she said.

"Not at the moment. You're joining my team. You just don't know it yet."

He was the cockiest man she'd ever met. Why did she like that so much? She shifted, trying to still her racing heart. Trying to remind herself that the bold, brassy scent she smelled in the car was Rosa's perfume. That he was Rosa's, not hers.

"Dunstan, I want to ask you something." She wanted to ask a *lot* of somethings, actually, but one question demanded an answer the most. "And I want a straight answer. None of your dancing around."

A dark eyebrow shot up. "You told me yourself I can't dance."

"I mean it. This is important."

He sobered. "What is it?"

She hesitated, looking out the car window again. The waterfront had given way to a long stretch of sidewalk protected from high tides by a sturdy seawall, built after the big hurricane had swamped the old wall and washed it out to sea.

She turned back to him and plucked up her courage, hoping her question wouldn't sound nutty. "Dunstan, are you dead?" To give him credit, he didn't laugh. If he'd laughed, she would've sunk right through the floor of the car.

"Why do you ask that?"

"Because, as you know, and as everyone else in the world now knows, I can see a person's future with a touch. Not just see. I *live* the moment. I slip into that person's skin, and I feel, see, touch, taste, and even smell what they do. I *am* them, if that makes any sense."

His jaw went rigid, and he nodded, encouraging her to go on.

"Used to be I had to touch someone, but recently, when I touch an object that belongs to them, I get a vision. I held a tiepin. That's how I knew about the Pearl Harbor attack. I wanted to know about you, so I stole your spoon from Sal's. But when I touched it..." She paused a moment, weighing her words. "Nothing happened. No visions, no sounds. *Nothing*. That's not normally what happens. Normally I see... Well, frightful, horrible things most of the time. Just *horrible*." Something flickered in his expression. Empathy, maybe. "So why didn't anything happen when I held your spoon?"

She watched him. He didn't speak. He stared ahead at the road, as if gathering his thoughts. They passed the fisherman's statue and reached Holmes Street. Dunstan took the corner with ease and squeezed the car into a parking space a half a block down from the funeral home.

"Remember I told you I had a gift too?" He pressed the clutch and turned off the engine. "*That's* my gift. It's different from yours. Very different. I could try to explain it from now 'til next week. Or you can let me show you."

He turned to face her full-on, gazing into her eyes. That soft hum that always tickled her brain when near him intensified. His knees were inches from hers, separated only by the gear shift. Excitement shot through her. So did fear. She *wanted* to learn about Dunstan, about the others, about herself...

Why did that scare her so much?

"All right. Show me," she said, her teeth threatening to chatter.

A long, maddening pause, then, "Take off your gloves,"

he said, his voice rough, husky, as if he'd asked her to take off her clothes.

She held his gaze and bit the tip of her tongue as she slowly pulled off each glove, then held out her hands, palms up. He reached for her then stopped. His hands trembled. He seemed as nervous as her. That somehow made her feel better.

"Go on," she murmured.

He slid his palms over hers. The scarred patches on the backs of his hands looked as rough as storm-beaten pavement, but his palms were smooth and warm against hers. She sucked in a breath as something hot and hungry sparked deep in her belly. Her pulse throbbed and she knew the Sight had nothing to do with it. It was *him*, touching her. His scent, warm and fresh, filled her senses. His tobacco-sweet breath brushed her face. She felt as light as gossamer.

"Remember to keep breathing, Addie." His voice gently teased. He closed his hands around hers. "Now, open your mind."

Her eyes were open but as she let the Sight in, the familiar blackness veiled her vision. A moment later, the dark peeled away and she stepped into a blue-gray mist, as if she stood on Pott's beach on a foggy day. The hum in her brain grew louder, a steady but soothing and tranquil drone.

"What do you see?" she heard him ask, as if at a great distance.

"Nothing. Not a blessed thing."

"What do you hear? Smell? Taste? Feel?"

She shook her head at each word except for the last. A sensation pulsed through her, one she'd never felt when touching someone, not even Mother. Peace. Freedom. No fear at all. Could Dunstan feel it too?

"Part of my ability *is* that nothing," he said. "I'm a neutralizer. No one's ability can work on me. Your gift takes energy from others, mine absorbs it. I'm blocking your vibrations that are reaching out to me and trying to get inside my mind. Your energy hits a wall that returns nothing, free of emotion. That's *my* gift, Addie."

She smiled. "Oh, Dunstan. I feel as if I could float away."

And she would too, if not for him holding her, strong and steady. Who knew that a man who showed her nothing could make her feel so much something?

Happiness, and a palpable sense of relief filled Addie's mind. Dunstan felt it racing along her vibrations. Even a cynic like him couldn't help but be touched by that, the release of emotions that had probably been out of her reach for so long. Kept at bay by the fear that fueled her energy. That terror now reached into his mind and tried to latch on, to find the fear in his future. His own energy easily blocked hers, telling him she had no idea how to control her gift.

They had a *lot* of work to do.

He released her hands. "Come back to me now."

She blinked, coming out of the Sight, as she called it, looking somewhat dazed.

"You have an amazing ability, Addie," he said, and meant it. He'd never met anyone who could do what she could. Her description of living in another's skin had chilled him to the core. "And I have a lot of questions. Do you get a vision every time you touch someone?"

"I think so. I've avoided touching people, so I can't be sure. When I do get a Sight, it varies. Sometimes I see fuzzy, unclear things I can't figure out. Sometimes an image, or a smell that makes no sense. Sometimes I see things clear as a bell. As for touching objects?" She shrugged. "I don't know if it happens every time. I haven't exactly been eager to find out."

She sounded worried, liked she feared disappointing him. "It's okay, we'll figure it out. When did you have your first vision? Was it the boy, Hugo?"

She nodded. "It may have happened when I was younger, but seeing Hugo was the first time I became aware of it. Aware I wasn't like other people."

"What did you see?"

She hesitated a second. "I held Hugo's hand during a game at school, and then I *was* him. I was at the quarry and fell into a hole. It was dark. I cried and shivered with cold. I still remember how scared I...*he* was. I didn't understand at first, but when he went missing a few weeks later I knew. I told Mother, and then... Well, you probably know the rest."

She looked down at her hands. Dunstan sat still and silent, fearing the least sound from him would stop her from letting out what she'd bottled up for a long time.

"After Hugo, I tried to ignore the Sight, but it grew stronger the older I got. Accidental touches showed me futures filled with scary things. The cashier at the grocer's being beaten by her father. My mother, near death." Her voice caught. "After...after Mother died two years ago, the

Sight grew stronger. That's when touching objects started bringing it on."

She shuddered. Dunstan wished he could absorb each horrific image she'd seen and erase every tear the Sight had caused her to shed. He settled for a terse nod. "Intense emotion, trauma even, seems to be what triggers a gift to manifest or intensify. Your mother's loss..."

He fell silent, thinking of Virginia and what she'd suffered at the hands of her not-so-loving husband. Madelyn and the boating accident in which her brother died, and she'd nearly drowned. He didn't know what had brought on Woden's power, only that it had something to do with the man's father.

Addie sighed, as if mystified. "Dunstan, what is this thing inside of me? How does it work? How did we get this way?"

"Our team doctor says our brains are like a misfiring engine, chugging out vibrations of kinetic energy that feed on the energy of others." She looked confused and he didn't blame her. "Sounds highfalutin, but I think Dr. Philbin doesn't really know either. Not sure anyone does." Except maybe Woden, who'd been seeking out and studying gifted folks for years. "As for where our gifts came from, the Doc thinks it's a family trait, passed down, like blue eyes or big ears."

"That makes sense. Mother had the Sight, and so does my cousin Michael, though he ignores it completely. Honestly, he's more afraid of the Sight than I am."

That got Dunstan's interest. "I'd like to meet this cousin of yours."

"I don't know if he'll want to meet *you*." She laughed softly, a sweet sound that quickly faded. "Dunstan, this doctor you mentioned. Does he think there's a way to cure us?"

"I don't think so." He shifted uncomfortably. "Would you if you could? Take a cure if there was one, I mean."

She chewed that question over, giving him time to do the same. Would he get rid of his gift if he could? Kayo the emotions he'd absorbed that constantly slammed a battering ram against the locked door in his mind? That would eliminate the threat of those feelings busting free, but it would also change him. Take away who he'd become. For the first time in his life, he had a purpose. He was worth something. He wouldn't want to lose that for anything. And he hoped Addie wouldn't either.

After a long time, she met his eyes again. "I don't know. I don't know anything, least of all about the Sight. Do you really think you can help me learn how to control my...gift?"

She'd dropped the word affliction. Progress. "Yes. It'll take some work. You're going to have to concentrate hard to corral your emotions. From what you've told me, seems like your vibrations seek out fear and suffering above all."

"Well, *that's* pleasant." She tipped her head, studying him. "Is that why I feel afraid all the time? Aunt Trudy says I'm just a nervous Nellie."

"That's the dark side of your gift. Whatever emotion fuels our vibrations bounces back and stays with us. If you're not careful, it can drag you down." He took her hands again. "You can learn how to use your energy—your vibrations—to control the Sight. Controlling the fear that bounces back will be more difficult. You follow?"

"Sort of." Her vibrations clouded as doubt pushed in. "But I'm not sure I can be so cool about it. What happens if I can't take control? While inside the Sight and out of it? What if the fear or vibrations or whatever you call it gets the upper hand?"

"I can't control that. That's up to you. But I promise I'll be near, and if you need me, I can give you this."

He brushed his thumbs across her soft fingers, stroking gently as he reached into her mind. She straightened in surprise and her face lit up with a radiant glow. His heart tugged and he couldn't help a grin.

"Oh," she said. "It's like floating on a cloud. For the first time in years, I'm not afraid. I feel at peace. Are you doing that? Is this part of your gift?"

He nodded. "I can absorb whatever emotion's troubling you. I pushed into your mind and took in your fear. That's how I quieted that mob at the store. I drained their anger and left them with nothing until they could come to their senses. A *lot* of work to tame so many people, and the more intense the emotion, the harder it is to do. But in this case, it worked."

Thankfully. He squeezed Addie's hands and released them, glad she hadn't been harmed.

"Is that why you seemed ill?" she asked. "I thought you might faint, and I never would've been able to catch you."

He flushed, reluctant to admit any weakness. "My gift's like pushing and pulling at the same time. Absorbing so many emotions takes a lot out of me."

And the emotions never truly went away. Sometimes he felt like he lived in a volcano, with fragments of Woden's rage, Madelyn's grief, Virginia's love potion, and now Addie's fear boiling inside him. Emotions he could never let out. If he did, they would swallow him whole.

"It's easier to focus on just one person," he said. "And

with the gifted, my power is intensified. Our vibrations are chaotic. I can pull out the chaos and block your energy, leaving you with a still nothingness that gives you peace. Even bliss."

That was what had made him so attractive to Madelyn. To Woden, too, and why the man had wanted so desperately to turn him.

Addie searched his face, her expression puzzled. "You held my hand, but you didn't touch anyone at Schulman's. How could you push them?"

"Most of our people need to connect for our power to work. Like you." Like Virginia, who would have hordes of people panting after her day and night if she didn't need to touch skin to make her love power work. "Some others, a rare few in my experience, don't need to touch at all. Physical contact makes the job easier, though."

"What about the others? The people on your team. What kinds of gifts do they have?"

He shifted and sat back. How much should he tell her? He hated to be evasive, but he also didn't want to scare her. Maybe that mob at the store had gotten riled on its own. Tempers were hot after the attack at Pearl Harbor, and Addie knowing about it made her a convenient scapegoat. Then again, maybe the mob's fury had been tweaked. By someone with a gift.

Dunstan hadn't felt Woden's presence there, but he'd been so focused on Addie he might've missed any signs. The man was skilled at masking his vibrations, too. Could he be here? He gazed into Addie's eyes, burning to think that bastard had set his sights on her.

"Addie, listen, there's something you should know. Something you *need* to know. You have the power to block someone from your mind. Even me. If someone tries to push into your head, you have to push back. If they get in, they can control you."

She frowned. "How will I know?"

"You'll know. It'll feel like someone's stabbing your brain with a pitchfork. And you can tell when someone with a gift is nearby. You feel that?" He tapped his temple. "That buzz? So soft you can barely hear it unless you're listening for it. If you concentrate extra hard, you can *feel* their vibrations—"

He stopped. Confusion wrinkled her brow. That lesson could wait for another time.

"Addie, if you feel that buzz, you know one of us is close. If you think that fella's dangerous, *run*. If you can't, and he pushes into your head, do your damnedest to build a wall around your mind. Keep him out, no matter how hard he pushes. Fight him. Your life may depend on it." Her vibrations went pitch black. Damn it, he'd frightened her. "I know you can fight any threat. You've got the strength."

He saw a flicker of trust in her gaze, and something else that ignited a spark in his heart. Feelings he'd kept buried since Madelyn's death. Feelings he'd been avoiding and should continue to avoid if he planned to work with this woman. He would *not* go through what had happened with Madelyn again.

And yet... He couldn't look away, caught in the depths of her warm blue eyes.

"I'd better go," she murmured. "It's getting dark. Father's probably sent out a search party to look for me."

He gave a faint smile and moved away, trying to ignore the sting of her rejection. She picked up her gloves, hat, and purse. He started to get out of the car to open her door.

"Wait," she said, and he swung back toward her. "There's something I should tell you. I had a Sight, a vision, days ago. When I was at the police station. I have no idea what it means. Maybe you can help me figure it out. I saw Sgt. Gillis trapped in a fire. It could be soon, or something that'll happen years from now. But now, with the war, I've heard people talking about sabotage and—"

"What did you see?" he said, all business now. He sat back and lit a Lucky, listening as she described her vision. Not much to it—a structure, the heat of the flames on her face, a lump that may have been a body at Gillis's feet, and the structure collapsing.

"Could it be sabotage?" she asked when she'd finished. "With Sgt. Gillis caught in the fire. Maybe killed by it."

"Or maybe Gillis will cause it."

"Why would a policeman do something like that?"

"Addie, I've been around long enough to know never to trust anyone. Present company excluded," he added with a grin. He crushed out his cigarette in the dashboard ashtray. "Do you remember anything else? Was it daytime? Night? Cold?"

She closed her eyes. "Night. I was outside, wearing an overcoat. The flames were so *hot*." She put her hands to her cheeks, as if to cool them, then opened her eyes. "If only my vision had been clearer, I might know more. Enough to save the sergeant from such a horrible fate." She paused. "Unless the Sight only shows me what *will* be, not what *can* be. Was the Pearl Harbor attack destined to happen, whether I sounded the alarm or not? Can the future be changed?"

He wanted to answer that but couldn't. "I like to think we can stop bad things from happening. Or at least we can try."

She nodded, looking grim. "What if I try again? If I could touch something that belongs to Gillis or the man himself, I might learn more. Something solid to go on."

"I'd pay good money to see you tackle that guy." He chuckled. "But that's not a bad idea. Leave it to me. I'll get you something of his. Somehow."

"Will you let me help?"

That was unexpected. He peered at her eager face. Did he want to risk that? Risk *her*?

"Don't look at me like that," she said. "I *want* to help. You told me my country needs me and I'm ready to do my bit. The Sight's been playing with my mind for as long as I can remember. I tried to save Hugo, but I failed. I failed at warning about Pearl Harbor. I don't want to fail anymore."

"I'm just going to swipe Gillis's coffee cup or something. Anyone can do that. You have a more important job. Why waste your time on such a piddling thing?"

Her face clouded over. "Is that all you want me for? My gift? You don't think I can help in any other way?"

"No, that's not it. It's just——" What? His own fears? He'd already lost one asset under his protection. He didn't want to lose another. "Addie, this is a tough game. What if Gillis *is* up to something? Bringing you along could be risky. Look what happened at the store."

"Dunstan, I want to *do* something. You wanted me to come work for you. How will I know if I'm up to the task if I don't take any risks? If *you* don't let me take any risks?"

He tried a different tack. "Spy work isn't anything like in the pictures. It's a tedious job. Boring, even."

She sighed. "Well, which is it, Mr. Dunstan? Risky or boring?"

His lips quirked. Maybe he'd underestimated her. And she had a point. She needed a chance to prove herself. He needed to give her that chance. It was past time he put away his fears and bitter memories of what happened to Madelyn. Past time he stopped doubting himself at every turn. Time to move forward.

"All right. You win, Addie, you're on. With one condition." Her happy smile vanished as quickly as it had come on. Dunstan hated to do this, but he wouldn't drag her into even a hint of danger until he knew what he was getting himself into. "You let me test your ability first."

She frowned. "There isn't time. What if that fire happens tomorrow? Or in a few days?"

"All the more reason for me to test you. I don't know much about the Sight or how to interpret what you see and hear. A test will help me understand, and also help *you* understand the depths of your gift."

"And *then* you'll let me help with Sgt. Gillis?"

He gave a terse nod, and her frown became a satisfied smile.

They sketched out a plan—he'd have her touch a series of objects to see if her gift picked up anything—then set a time for him to meet her at work the next day. She argued they could meet somewhere else, but he put his foot down. After the incident at the department store, he was determined to keep an eye on her.

Arrangements complete, Addie put on her gloves, her gaze intent on the movements. "One more thing. You don't think Rosa will mind us spending time together, do you? I mean, it's for a good reason."

Dunstan cursed inwardly. He had no one but himself to blame for Addie believing he and Rosa were a couple. He'd have to tell her the truth about how he'd used Rosa to get to her. But not now. That would instantly crush her newfound trust in him.

"Rosa's a swell gal, she won't mind," he said, nearly choking on the lie.

Addie practically flew up the street toward the funeral home. So much had happened in the space of an hour, her head spun. Learning about her ability hadn't been as scary as she'd thought. In fact, it was liberating. She'd broken through the fear that had kept her cowering her whole life. She understood now. The Sight wasn't an affliction or a curse.

She had a gift.

So did Michael. He didn't have to drown the Sight anymore. His ability could be controlled. She'd have to tell him about their gift and Dunstan and what he had called her *vibrations*. And how he could help them both.

Later. When she came down from the clouds.

Dunstan had done that, made her feel as if she could walk on air. She wanted to hug him and thank him a dozen times over for helping bring her into the light. Maybe even kiss him. Of course, that would *never* do. He didn't want her to kiss him. He had Rosa for that. He probably drove like a madman at this very moment to go to her for their date tonight. He wouldn't give Addie a second thought.

She turned the corner into the alley and scuffed to a stop. Her father stood in front of the hearse, broom in hand, sweeping up glass. She sped down the cobblestones, her heart in her throat. The hearse windshield had been shattered. Glass sprayed across the vehicle's front end like slivers of ice. The headlights had been smashed too. The light over the door glinted on the glass strewn on the ground.

Father swung on her, his face a storm cloud. "*Where* have you been?" he demanded. "You said you were going to lunch with Marta. It's after five. I've been worried about you."

With good reason, Addie thought. A chill shivered down her spine at the memory of the man in the ratty sweater about to attack her. And he would have, if not for Dunstan.

"I'm sorry to worry you, Father," she said, contrite. "What happened?"

"What does it look like happened? Hoodlums chucked bricks through the hearse window and kicked out the headlights." The broken glass clinked as he swept with furious strokes.

Her shoulders sagged. He spoke as if it were her fault. At least it felt that way. "Father, you should call the police."

"I will *not*. No one is to know, Adelaide. If anyone asks, tell them icicles fell and broke the window. We cannot afford to call attention to ourselves."

Call attention to *her*, he meant.

He swept the glass from under the vehicle's tires and pushed the whole pile against the building. "Wait for me inside, child, before you catch your death of cold. I will be done soon."

He didn't look at her and she didn't argue or offer to help. Why bother? He would be furious with her forever for what she'd done. For bringing notoriety to the family, for turning suspicious eyes on them and ruining his business.

She huffed toward the door and threw it open, more determined than ever to go with Dunstan tomorrow and take his tests. If only to prove to Father that the Sight was something more than a shameful secret to be feared. To show him she'd done the right thing by warning about the attack, so perhaps, for once, he wouldn't frown when he looked at her.

To prove herself to Dunstan, too. She'd heard doubt in his voice as he countered her arguments for wanting to help. He feared she wasn't up to the task. Why else would he demand she let him test her skills? His uncertainty threatened to make her doubt herself, the *last* thing she wanted now that she had begun to embrace her gift.

Tomorrow she would pass any test Dunstan threw into her path, and then some. Tomorrow she would prove she could do the job.

She would show him and Father and everyone else that she wasn't Addled Addie anymore, the girl frightened of her own shadow. She was the Addie Brandt who'd come to life in Dunstan's car. A plucky, brave woman who knew she had so much more to offer, who could do something important with her life.

She would prove it to them—and to herself.

Chapter Twenty

Addie left the funeral home well before noon, the time she and Dunstan had planned to meet. Father and Uncle Pat were upstairs going over expenditures, looking to cut costs for the lean times ahead, giving her the opportunity to slip out before Father could stop her. She understood his concern, especially after the hearse had been vandalized yesterday, but she would *not* let his fears keep her from making this big step forward.

She waited by the front steps, watching for Dunstan's car. The day was brighter than yesterday, the blue sky free of clouds, but pretty cold. She rubbed her gloved hands together and stamped her feet to keep warm. Pedestrians passed by at a brisk pace, coats buttoned up to the neck. Some gave her a curious once-over as they hurried past, but thankfully no one stopped to speak to her.

Her luck ran out when a heavyset man wearing a moth-eaten wool coat and a limp fedora strode up. About fifty, his fleshy face red from cold and exertion, he stepped so close Addie could smell the mint-scented gum he chewed. She stiffened and her heartbeat sped up.

"Adelaide Brandt, right?" he asked, staring at her as bold as brass. "I'm Benny Hirtle, with the Goveport Herald. Rumor has it you predicted Pearl Harbor. People say you can see the future." He dug a pencil and a notepad out of his coat pocket. "Care to comment on that?" He flipped the pad open with a flick of his wrist and gazed at her expectantly.

A reporter. An unexpected wrinkle in her new notoriety. She eyed him warily, unsure what to say or do. With Father's anger already simmering, he'd boil over like a teakettle to discover she'd spoken to a newspaperman.

"Cat got your tongue?" Hirtle shifted his wad of gum from one side of his mouth to the other. "You were chatty enough with the police last week. Surely you can spare a word or two for me." He jerked his head in the direction of Main Street at the top of the hill. "Let's go somewhere warm. I'll buy you a cup of coffee. That ought to loosen your lips."

His words were more of a command than an invitation. And he must think her a fool. She'd never go off with a strange man. Especially a man from the Herald. Uncle Pat called that newspaper a fish-wrapper full of lies. Whatever she said, the reporter would no doubt twist her words.

"No thank you, Mr. Hirtle. I have no comment."

"Bah." His dark blue eyes narrowed. "Don't be difficult, sis. Come on, it'll only take a minute."

He pressed in and she edged away, nervous, about to dash down the alley to safety, when Dunstan's Ford screeched up to the curb. He flew out of the car and reached her side in a flash.

"Beat it, bub," he snarled and Hirtle scuttled away.

Addie turned to Dunstan, both relieved and annoyed. Relieved the oily newspaperman had retreated, but annoyed he'd only done so because Dunstan had swooped in and scared him off. Like the crowd yesterday at Schulman's.

How could she prove herself capable if the man she wanted to convince had to keep stepping in to rescue her?

T hey left his car at the curb and hoofed it up the hill, walking fast. Dunstan welcomed the brisk walk. Seeing that vulture looming over Addie had wound him up tight and he needed to burn off his anger.

"Are you *sure* that fella was a reporter?" he asked again, as cool as he could manage.

"Yes. Well, I think. I've never seen him before, but I'm not usually hounded by the press."

Not until word had spread about her warning. And her ability. All the more reason to get her out of town, go where no one knew her. Keep her with him, so he could protect her. Something he'd failed to do for Madelyn.

"Addie, we don't want a repeat of yesterday. You might want to..." He tapped a finger to his hat brim, indicating she should hide her face. She tipped the hat at an angle and brushed her dark blonde hair over one eye like Veronica Lake.

They moved on. Church bells chimed twelve as they reached the top of the hill and turned left, headed toward police headquarters.

"Tell me about your mother," he said, offering her his arm. "And this cousin you said has the Sight, too. Either of them ever use it?"

She slipped her hand into the crook of his elbow. "No. Michael doesn't want anything to do with it. He had a scare years ago. Saw something awful, though he won't tell me what." She lowered her voice, as if spilling a shameful secret. "He drinks, you know. To make the Sight go away."

"Makes sense. Alcohol mutes the senses, and a gifted person's vibrations." Madelyn had known that. She'd soothed her sorrow with gin before she realized his ability to absorb her emotions could lift her spirits without the hangover afterward. "And your mother? Did she think of the Sight as friend or foe?"

"She saw only brief flashes of the future when she touched someone's hand, and I think she saw only pleasant things, nothing like what happens with me. But still, Father forbid her from using her gift." A sad smile touched her lips. "She'd sometimes sneak and read people, anyway. Oh, not for money. She thought God had given her the Sight to help people. She thought I should use my gift to help people, too."

Gift. She had used the word—twice—without hesitation. She was coming around. "That's why you went to the police, to tell them about Hugo Nunes. To help."

She nodded. "It was Mother's idea. They put me in a room and questioned me. I was so scared. My mother got annoyed at the way they treated me. They thought I was lying, or insane. Father was *livid* when he found out what Mother had done. He'd just bought the funeral home from Mr. Callahan and feared he'd lose business when word got out. He was right, as usual. People shunned us, called me names, as if Hugo's death was somehow my fault."

Dunstan frowned. Woden used to say fear made people act like fools. Woden had spouted a lot of pompous bull-shit, but that bit he agreed with.

"Then there were the others," she said. "They came around, begging me to help find things for them. Mostly money. Mother felt sorry for them. It was the Depression, people were desperate. Father wouldn't let them in. He scolded Mother. I heard them arguing. After that, she never read people again, never pressed me about using the Sight again, either. But I know she would've wanted me to warn about Pearl Harbor. I think she'd be glad I'm trying to help now." She gave him a sidelong glance. "What about you? When did you realize you had a gift?"

"I wondered when you'd get around to that. Truth is, I didn't even know I had an ability until..." Until Madelyn had helped him figure it out. "Until I was recruited to the team."

"Does anyone else in your family have a gift?"

"Not that I know of. I haven't seen anyone in my family in years."

"Oh." She gazed up at him, a pained look in her eyes. "Don't you miss them?"

He shrugged, trying to brush off his bitterness. "Not much. I had a brother. He died of the influenza. My father was killed in the war. Never knew much about him. My gift could've come from him or my mother. Maybe both. She married an ass named Donnelly when I was young. He owned a bar in New Bedford. They had their own kids to worry about and Donnelly didn't much like worrying about me. The only family member I liked was my uncle Jerome.

He made sure I went to school, even when I didn't want to." He paused, emotion closing in. "He died when I was fourteen. I left after that. Haven't seen my mother since."

"Golly," Addie said softly.

He hadn't meant to spill his guts, but he blabbed to her like a sinner to a priest. Next, he'd be bawling over every bitter moment of his misbegotten life. His childhood. His mother, so drunk she could barely walk. Uncle Jerome's lingering death from tuberculosis. The beatings Dunstan had taken and the beatings he gave. Madelyn and Woden. How he'd used Rosa, and Virginia's role in the whole charade.

No, none of that. For now, he had to keep his mouth shut. When he'd fully won Addie's trust, he'd tell her everything. One thing at a time.

"Let's get out of the cold," he said, gesturing to a coffee shop on the corner.

They stepped inside and he hustled Addie to a table near a window, where he could keep watch on police headquarters across the street. A cloud of cigarette smoke hung over the crowded room. He added to the smoke screen by lighting a Lucky as soon as they sat.

Some of the customers eyed them. A couple of men in fancy suits lingered on Addie. Could be admiring her—she looked edible in that hat and form-fitting red coat that hugged her bottom—or their interest could've been more sinister. Whatever the reason, Dunstan itched to pummel them both.

He put a leash on his temper and turned his attention to a button-nosed waitress in a blue dress who'd ambled over. She looked to him for their order.

"We'll both have coffee," he said. "She'll have a donut."

The waitress left and Addie huffed, a mixture of annoyance and amusement. "Well, that was high-handed. What if I wanted a sandwich or the pot roast special?"

"No time for a big meal," he said. "We've got work to do. And we need to be ready if Gillis comes out." He gestured to the window and the police station across the street. The midday sun brightened the sooty, red brick exterior of the building. Stairs steep enough to give a mountain goat second thoughts led up to the entrance.

"Why don't we just go inside and ask to see the sergeant?" Addie said. "I could take off my gloves, pretend to faint, and have him catch me. Easy as pie."

His lips tugged at the comical image that conjured up. "Nothing doing. We wait and watch. If and when we see Gillis, we follow him and look for an opportunity to get close. If he doesn't come out, we go home and come back tomorrow."

"Why are you so nervous all of a sudden?"

Good question, with a simple answer. No way on God's green earth would he allow her to set foot in that station-house. Those fools had ridiculed her *and* her warning. They might tear into her just to relieve their guilty minds. Might tear into him too. It was damned certain Gillis and the other cops hadn't forgotten him storming in there, waving his badge, questioning them about Addie.

"I don't like butting heads with cops," he said.

"You don't? I can't believe there's *anyone* you don't like to fight with."

She flashed a teasing grin. He took a deep drag. He wished she wouldn't keep being so...adorable. He already struggled to stay detached, all business, and she didn't make the effort any easier.

"Truth is, Addie, I stay far away from the police." He exhaled heavily, pushing out a cloud of smoke. "Got a cop's nightstick to the head when I was thirteen. I deserved it, I guess. I was a kid with sticky fingers, and theft is theft. But my brain's still rattling from that blow. I don't care to repeat the incident."

"Sounds like you've lived an exciting life."

"Wouldn't call my life exciting. More like hanging on by my teeth." Grifting, a little card sharking, fighting, consorting with shady characters. Looking out only for himself. Then he'd met Madelyn and Woden, and his life suddenly had a purpose.

Their waitress returned with two cups of joe and a plate holding a fat jelly donut dusted with sugar, which she put in front of Addie. He crushed out his cigarette in the ashtray and dropped three sugar cubes into his coffee, stirring vigorously.

"I'm sorry to be so nosy," Addie said, tearing into her donut. Strawberry jelly dribbled onto her chin, and she wiped it off with her napkin. "Sometimes I forget how lucky I've been. Even growing up with the Depression on, I had everything I could ever want."

Not everything. She'd had to live with the fear of her gift, and of who she was. Not to mention a father who disapproved of her. From what he'd learned these past few days, Otto Brandt was a cold prig. It was a miracle Addie's spirit hadn't been crushed long ago. If Dunstan ever met the man, he'd tell him that to his face.

Enough brooding and delay. Time to get down to the meat of their meeting. Time to test her skills.

"Are you ready, Addie?" Her expression turned guarded as he slid his coffee spoon across the table to her. "We'll start simple. Reach out and try to isolate my vibrations on this."

She gave a reluctant nod and took off her gloves. She picked up the spoon and her body went rigid, as if caught in some kind of a seizure. Her breathing slowed and her pupils diffused as she stared at nothing.

"I feel a calm stillness," she murmured. "Is that you? I don't feel anyone else. Wait. I feel some vague ripples of emotion. Our waitress, I think." She met his gaze, her own defiant. "Have I failed the test? Are you disappointed in me?"

"No. Now I have some idea how your gift works. From what you've said, the Sight hunts for something dramatic to latch on to, like fear and death." She stiffened so he hurried on. "The waitress's future will probably be as dull as a cloth coat. Or maybe the Sight's hazy because people's vibrations fade over time."

"Or it means this restaurant does a good job washing utensils between customers."

He snorted a laugh. "Yeah, could be that."

He reached into his overcoat pockets and pulled out the test objects he'd selected earlier. His fingers brushed his lighter, still warm from recent use. *That* stayed in his pocket. Virginia had used it to light his cigarette only days ago. He didn't want to risk Addie picking up on her vibrations. Not before he could explain Virginia's connection to the team.

"Give these a try." He placed several items on the tables in front of her—his leather gloves, a nickel he'd gotten for change from the old goat at the newsstand, and his Uncle Jerome's pocket watch.

He wanted one more thing, an object used recently. He

scanned the tables for something to nab, but the efficient busboy, a lanky young Negro kid, had scooped up every dirty dish and fork within a ten-mile radius. Nearby, a man of about fifty gulped the last of his coffee, tossed his wadded-up napkin on the table, and left. Dunstan lunged for the cup before the busboy could whisk it away.

He set the cup between the nickel and the watch. "There. Ladies' choice. Which is first?"

Addie looked over the selection like a child disappointed in her Christmas presents. She picked up his gloves first. She closed her eyes this time, her long eyelashes brushing her cheeks. Her posture stiffened again, and she let out a soft moan.

Dunstan watched, fascinated. During his carnival days, he'd seen lots of so-called seers and fortunetellers perform all kinds of theatrics and phony-baloney trances, but he'd never seen anything as authentic as Addie slipping into the Sight. Or as mesmerizing.

She ran her hand along the gloves and tipped her head, concentrating. "I'm...a woman behind the counter at Woolworth's," she murmured.

Where he'd bought them. On sale, too. "Go on. Open your mind, let the Sight do its job."

She took a deep breath and squeezed the gloves with both hands. "I smell perfume, hear voices, the ding of an elevator bell. The salesgirl is leaning on the counter, writing a letter. I hear the pen scratching across the paper. I see the date, 1944, but can't see what she's written. She's...sad." Addie sat back and gazed at him with a troubled expression. "I'm sorry, I felt her sadness, but couldn't figure out why."

"Will you quit worrying?" That came out gruffer than

he'd intended so he added a smile that only seemed to alarm her more. He grabbed the gloves and stuffed them back into his pocket. Damn it, couldn't he do anything right with this woman? "We're making progress. Besides, I bought these gloves a while ago. I'm surprised you felt any vibrations at all." His gaze dipped to the other items. "Okay, which one's next?"

Her hand hovered over the nickel then she shifted to the cup and gave him a questioning look.

He nodded. "It was used only a minute ago, might give you some stronger sensations."

She took it by the handle and picked it up, closing her eyes once more. She stiffened then gasped. "You're right, the Sight is strong. I'm a man. An old man." She lifted her free hand as if gazing at it through her closed eyes. "My skin is wrinkled and spotted with age. I'm walking down the street. Moving slow because..." Her breath turned ragged. She touched her chest. "The pain." She stiffened and her head jerked back. She whimpered in sudden agony. "Oh, Dunstan, it *hurts!*"

"It's not *you*, Addie. Step away, feel and see it from the outside. Keep the emotions at bay." He seized her free hand and held tight, as if that would anchor her. She gave a shaky nod and her breathing slowed, becoming steadier. "Who are you?" he demanded. "Where are you?"

Her forehead crinkled and her face scrunched in concentration. "I don't know. I...I'm on a city street. It's not Goveport. Boston, I think." She stiffened again. She squeezed his hand, her face contorted in pain. "Dunstan, I'm scared."

He winced. She didn't have to tell him that, he felt it.

Terror coiled around her vibrations like a noose. He wanted to abandon this ridiculous test and pull her into his arms and comfort her. Or use his gift to leech away her fear and push calm into her brain. But he held back. Easing her trouble would neutralize the vision when they were finally getting somewhere.

He leaned forward, forcing her to continue. "Don't stop. Corral your energy, Addie. Stay in the Sight, but move away from the fear, and the pain. What do you see? Give me details. What's going on around you? Can you tell when this is happening?"

She took several breaths and slowly swiveled her head as if looking around, her eyes still closed.

"It-it's winter. People are wearing boots and overcoats, hurrying along the sidewalk. I'm in Boston. I see the gold dome of the state house at the top of the hill." She let out a groan as another wave of pain shuddered through her. "There's a newsstand. Magazines. Newspapers with the same headline. *Three rock and roll stars killed in plane crash*. The date is clear, February 3, 1959... *Oh!*" She tore her hand from his grip. "I can't... C-can't take another step. I'm... I'm—"

Her hold on the cup loosened and it crashed to the table, shattering. She twitched and shuddered and clawed at her chest. Her tongue lolled like a panting dog's. She choked and gurgled, in the throes of a fatal coronary. Her vibrations banged and pulsated with the most powerful fear known to man.

The fear of death.

"Addie!"

Horrified, Dunstan seized both her hands and muscled

into her mind. He pierced her vibrations, determined to drown them with every ounce of calm he could muster. A fierce battle. Her gift fought him as hard as an ornery bluefish hooked on a line. He switched tactics and pulled instead of pushed. He yanked the pain and fear from her brain and into his own, swallowing the emotions whole. Rivers of terror rolled through his mind. He clamped his teeth, bit his tongue, and fought the urge to cry out.

The flood tide ebbed, slower than he would've liked. He held tight to her hands and didn't let go until the final wisps of her fear settled into a dark spot in his mind. The restaurant had gone still. Dunstan barely registered the customers, the waitress, and the busboy gaping at them. He had eyes only for Addie. She slumped in her chair. Sweat dotted her forehead and her chin quivered, but her gaze on him held strong.

"Did I pass the test?" she asked.

He stared back at her, unsettled, drained. Nothing compared to how she must feel after such a violent emotional assault. The remnants of what she'd just endured would linger in her brain, sometimes for days. Sometimes forever, if Madelyn was any guide. And shit-heel that he was, he'd made Addie go through it just to satisfy his doubts.

"Yeah, you passed," he said, grimmer than grim.

Scowling, she looked out the window then straightened. Dunstan followed her gaze to see the police station door bang open and Sgt. Gillis step into the opening. The sergeant swung his scarf around his neck and lumbered down the steps.

"Shall we get on with the real work?" Addie asked, her voice arch. She didn't wait for an answer. She leapt from her chair and hurried to the door before he could order her to stop.

"Son of a bitch," he muttered, reaching through the bits of broken coffee cup to grab Uncle Jerome's watch. He dropped a dollar bill on the table and raced after her, so stunned he didn't ask the waitress for change.

Chapter Twenty-One

Rosa tapped her foot, wishing the old man behind the counter would stop flapping his gums and hurry with her order. Though Sal had sent her to pick up an apple pie from Stein's Bakery, he'd tan her hide if she took too long getting back. Why he'd gotten it into his head to send her out for a pie during the lunch rush she didn't know. He'd been damned crabby about it, too.

"There'll be rationing, like the last war," Old Stein said, wrapping red-and-white-striped string around Rosa's pie box. He tied the knot with bent, stiff fingers. Arthritis, like Ma.

"Even more rationing, maybe," his son, Young Stein, said. He banged the cash register keys with his fist, ringing up a sale of bread sprinkled with seeds and woven like one of Addie's braids. "This is gonna be a big war, with us fighting the Japanese too." He flicked a dark look at Rosa. "And the Italians."

She grabbed her pie box from the old man and turned toward the door, glad Sal paid on account, and she didn't have to go to the register. She didn't have nothing to do with this stupid war, why did Young Stein have to give her such a nasty look?

She bumped into a man in the doorway and almost dropped the pie box. A broad-chested fella in his mid-thirties, with a square face and small eyes, he seemed familiar. She could say that about a lot of folks, though, since practically everybody in town came to Sal's and she might have waited on him at one time. She had no interest in finding out if she'd met him or why he stood like a statue in Stein's doorway, not with the sudden headache that banged at her brain.

The pain made her even madder. She glared at the big oaf and did something she would never do to a man, especially a man dressed in such an expensive-looking coat.

She snapped at him.

"Watch where you're going, you dope!" She shoved by him, rushing out of the bakery and up the sidewalk at top speed.

The sunlight hurt her eyes. Her anger simmered. Anger at the man for being so clumsy, at Sal for making her miss lunchtime tips by sending her out into the cold after a pie, at Ma for being stinking drunk half the time, for belly-aching about every little thing the other half.

Rosa jerked to a stop so fast she nearly dropped the pie. Should she believe her eyes? There, across the street and down the way, was Addie Brandt. With Jack Dunstan. They tore off up the sidewalk past the police station, going somewhere in a hot hurry. Somewhere *she* wasn't invited. Somewhere alone.

"Makes you furious, doesn't it?" a voice said into her ear. "Seeing her, with him?"

Rosa swung to see the big oaf from the bakery. He stared at her like a hungry wolf thinking she would make a dandy dinner.

"Shove off, mister," she said. "I'm not interested."

"You're not angry with me," he said, as blunt as could be. "You're angry with Adelaide. She's making a play for your man, right under your nose. And he's falling for her seductive tricks."

Rosa's headache got worse. A screechy whine sounded in her ears. The fella was right. Dunstan had been red hot and ready until Addie came into the picture. Then, nothing. No visits to Sal's, no dates, though yesterday she'd told Addie different to keep her from getting ideas.

Rosa glared down the street, in the direction her supposed friend had gone. That little schemer. She'd probably been planning to get her hooks into Dunstan from the moment she'd met him.

"You see the truth," the man said, nodding. "She's betrayed you as easily as she's betrayed her country. Adelaide is a Nazi agent. She has been working here in America to help the Germans."

Doubt and uncertainty poked through the pain in Rosa's head. Addie a spy? Hardly seemed possible. That meek little mouse would never do anything wrong.

"You question me?" The man sounded surprised. "My dear, every word I tell you is true. I'm a government agent. We've been after the Brandt family for a long time. Adelaide especially. She's been using her powers to aid the enemy. She's dangerous and needs to be stopped."

Rosa's head ached and ached. Her belly burned, too, like a hot knife had been stuck into it and twisted hard. Her doubts fell away. She believed what this government man said. Completely. Addie was a spy, a traitor. Rosa had known it all along, deep down.

"Here's my predicament, Miss Conti," the G-Man said. "I want to bring Adelaide in, but she will know she's caught if she sees me, and she'll flee. You, she trusts. You're her friend. She will go along with you willingly. Of course, your country will reward you handsomely for your help." He reached into his coat and took a wad of bills out of his inside breast pocket. "There will be an additional reward when you deliver her to me."

Rosa eyeballed the money in his hand and licked her lips. She'd never seen so much dough. With that kind of scratch, Ma and her could move out of their Fish Village dump, find something with real plumbing. She could buy some new clothes and even new shoes. She'd pitch her shabby old Oxfords in the rubbish where they belonged.

She shifted her gaze to the G-Man's beady little eyes. He watched her with a greedy smile. Her headache faded but her rage didn't. It crashed into her like a breaking wave, drowning all other thought and feelings.

Yeah, she'd take the money. In return, all she had to do was turn Addie over to him. Addie the spy, the traitor. A fair bargain.

Rosa snatched the bills from his hand.

Woden shuddered as Rosa stalked away, taking her fury and his pleasure with her. His vibrations drained quickly, leaving him spent and regretting his encounter with Miss Conti had been so brief. He'd sensed a deep reservoir of anger when his mind had first touched hers and after he'd pushed her, her rage flamed from her every pore.

He could feed off the girl for weeks, satisfying his own needs and his demon's base desires. Perhaps he would, once she brought Adelaide to him. Rosa wouldn't be the first innocent he'd mesmerized and kept by his side to indulge his hunger.

Sharp lightning bolts singed his fingers, warning him away from such foolhardy thoughts. Reminding him not to put his gift at risk more than he had to. Especially now, with so much on the line.

Rosa's steps slowed and she glanced back with a worried look, as if afraid he'd chase her down and demand his money back. He wouldn't think of such a thing. She was about to prove valuable at twice the price. He nodded, gave her a ghost of a smile, just enough to encourage her, tweaking her need to please him.

She moved on and Woden preened, impressed with his own cleverness using Adelaide's trusted friend. He'd orchestrated the scene perfectly. A visit to Sal's restaurant, a slight push to instigate an argument over a pie, and Rosa had been sent from the restaurant to the bakery in minutes. She'd been neatly tangled in Woden's net mere seconds later.

There'd only been one hitch, when Dunstan and Adelaide had fled the restaurant before Rosa could see them huddled together at a table like old friends. Or new lovers. Her anger and jealousy had been kindled none-theless, and he'd pushed into her mind and latched on, bringing her fully under his control.

He waited until Rosa vanished from sight, then strode in the opposite direction to meet with Smith, despite the temptation to follow Dunstan and Adelaide. He had to admit, his old friend's antics had piqued his curiosity. What game did he play, dragging the girl all around town?

Woden supposed it really didn't matter. Let Dunstan enjoy himself while he could. Adelaide would be his soon. Miss Conti would see to that.

Chapter Twenty-Two

Dunstan made sure they followed Sgt. Gillis at a safe distance, far enough that the man wouldn't notice, but close enough not to lose him.

"He should go into politics, the way he gladhands," Addie said after Gillis stopped for the tenth time to chat with a merchant or pedestrian. "He told me he was new in town. How does he know so many people?"

"Cops make it their business to know people," Dunstan said, worried about what they would do when Gillis reached his destination. Addie couldn't just lunge at him and grab him in broad daylight. Especially after what happened in the coffee shop. What if she touched Gillis and got trapped in the Sight again? What if she couldn't distance herself from the fear or break away? Dunstan might not be able to free her this time.

He slapped his thigh in frustration. He could've kicked himself for agreeing to a plan he hadn't thought through. For agreeing to let Addie come along. He wanted to swing around and drag her out of there. She'd never go for it, though. He'd quickly discovered Addie had a mind of her own. Once made up, she could not be stopped.

Dunstan shoved those worries away as Gillis turned at the corner. The policeman picked up his pace, not as friendly with passersby now.

"He's got somewhere to be, an appointment maybe," Addie said.

They sped up, moving along in silence. After a while, she stopped and caught his gaze. Her eyes widened with alarm.

"Dunstan, he's headed for Germantown."

"Keep cool. Could be police business that takes him there," he said, but still his nerves sparked. His body went on alert.

They moved on. Gillis had pulled ahead. "We're losing him," Addie cried and started to run.

Dunstan caught up and grabbed her arm. "Stay with me," he barked, earning him a scowl.

They raced after Gillis, pushing by shoppers and businessmen. Car horns honked. Buses rumbled by, belching exhaust. At the intersection, their quarry disappeared around a corner. They followed.

"Holy crow." Dunstan jerked to a stop, yanking Addie back.

A mob stormed up the intersecting street, straight at them. Fearing they were after Addie, he shoved her behind him. He reached for his gun in its shoulder holster under his coat. Then he heard the men hollering, "Remember Pearl Harbor," and singing *Over There*. The marchers carried painted signs reading *Volunteers for Uncle Sam* and *Enlist Today!*

A parade. A goddamn parade through the heart of Germantown.

Addie tugged his sleeve. "They're German. Most of them, anyway. I recognize some of the boys from school. What're they doing?"

"Trying to make a point?" he said. "Germany's going to declare war any minute. They're trying to show which side they're on."

The rest of Germantown worked hard to make a point too, cheering them on in a near frenzy. People lined the street waving small American flags. Still more flags flapped from every building and doorway. Onlookers hung out second and third story windows, shimmied up lampposts, and stood on the hoods of cars, hooting and bellowing.

Dunstan squinted at the crowd. "Where'd Gillis go?"

"Swallowed up, like Jonah," Addie said. "Wait! There he is."

She pointed. Gillis weaved through the marchers as he tried to cross the street. Impulsive Addie darted after him.

Dunstan grabbed at her coat collar and missed. He shouted for her to stop. She didn't. Couldn't hear him. Or ignored him. Harsh memories of Madelyn's end came on hard. So did the thoughts of the mob attacking Addie yesterday. There were five times as many people here, most of them men. A crowd could turn ugly in an instant.

Desperate, Dunstan waded into the eddying swarm after her. His gut clenched. The terror he'd absorbed from Addie's Sight sizzled in his brain, magnifying his own fear for her safety. Struggling for control, he shoved people out of his path like Moses parting the Red Sea, but it was no use.

She was gone.

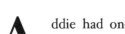

Addie had one goal—to keep Sgt. Gillis in her sight. She plunged into the parade of men after him and saw him step up onto the opposite sidewalk.

"Dunstan, there he goes." She glanced back and twittered in irritation. She'd thought he followed right behind her. She looked about, stood on tiptoe trying to find him, but couldn't see him. A fine time for Dunstan to bend down and tie his shoe.

Now what? Retreat, or chase after Gillis? Which would Dunstan choose? No, which should *she* choose? She plowed forward, buffeted by men of all shapes and sizes, smelling of B.O. and beer and fish. A flagpole whacked her in the head. Men shouted in her face and stepped on her toes, but she made it to the other side.

She searched, scouring the sidewalk in both directions. Up one way, she saw Wilhelm leaning against a wall, talking to a man who had his back to her. The other way, a man who looked like Uncle Eb stepped out of a restaurant. The reporter who'd pestered her earlier popped out of an alley. All around her, dozens of familiar faces, but not the one she was looking for.

Finally, she spotted Gillis. His policeman's hat bobbed through the crowd. She paused for breath before giving chase. What should she do when she caught up to him? Make off with his hat? That would be easier than trying to grab his hand or somehow touch the man himself. Then what? She had no idea.

Her stomach roiled with uncertainty. She suspected she'd failed Dunstan's tests, though he'd insisted otherwise. Touching the gloves had showed her nothing but dim images of a salesgirl watching the clock, anxious for her shift to end. The Sight had been strong and clear with the coffee cup, but she'd gotten so caught up in the horror of the man's future, Dunstan had to pull her out. Proving him right. She didn't know how to control her gift.

She didn't know anything.

Despite her doubts, Addie hurried forward. At the very least, she had to *try*. She'd get a Sight from Gillis all on her own. That would show Dunstan she was more than just her gift.

Her shoes smacked the pavement as she ran. The crowd thickened. She pushed through, seeing more people she knew. Gillis came within reach. The back of his neck above his coat collar was exposed. She'd touch the ruddy skin below his hairline and hope for the best.

Panting, nearly out of breath, she tore off her glove and reached out. She tripped. Or someone stuck out a foot to make her trip. She stumbled and banged to the ground. Her knees scraped the pavement, shredding her stockings.

A broad-shouldered figure silhouetted by the sun suddenly loomed over her. She looked up. The man grabbed her arm and yanked her to her feet.

Wilhelm, much stronger than his doughy frame would've led Addie to believe.

He kept hold of her arm. "Come with me, Adelaide," he said in German, giving her a tug. "I will take you some-where safe."

"I'm fine, Wilhelm," she said in English and shook off his hand, irritated by his stilted, dour manner, as dramatic as Greta Garbo. She peered ahead, searching for Gillis. "I'm actually quite busy, so if you'll excuse me?"

"Addie!"

She spun to see Dunstan rush up to her, his expression thunderous. Had he been worried about her?

"Dunstan, where have you been? I found Gillis, then I lost him. Oh, you remember Wilhelm—" She turned back to Wilhelm, but he'd vanished into the crowd.

Dunstan didn't notice. He seized her in a hug so crushing she could barely breathe. He pushed her out of his embrace just as quickly and gazed down at her.

"Christ, Addie. I thought I'd lost you."

She trembled at his heated voice and his expression. On impulse, she touched his cheek with her bare hand, ran her fingers over his cool skin and the hint of stubble. A strange, new sensation rippled through her. His energy, or vibrations, or whatever Dunstan called the electricity that seemed to shiver between them. She beamed at him, elated by the discovery of a new facet of her gift, moved by the concern for her she felt simmering inside his brain.

Perhaps he *had* been worried about her.

∼

After they left Germantown, Addie asked Dunstan to bring her home instead of back to work. They had no customers, so why return and face empty caskets and Father's gloomy frowns? She'd call and let him know she'd gone home, so he wouldn't worry. Or worry less, anyway.

Dunstan pulled up outside her house, turned off the engine, then opened the door to help her out of the car. Addie took his hand, and though she once again wore her gloves, the heat of his touch seemed to sear her skin.

"You okay?" he asked, walking her the short way to her front steps.

She turned to face him, hoping he hadn't noticed the blush spreading over her cheeks. "I just fell and scraped a knee, Dunstan, nothing serious."

"What about what happened before, in the coffee shop? You hauled in a lot of negative energy. I hope it's not weighing you down."

The fear still shuddered through her, though she didn't want to admit it. "I'm fine. Tip-top, A-One. Ready to try again tomorrow."

"You sure you want to?"

"I want to. I know we'll find a way to catch Gillis tomorrow. If not, we'll go after him the next day and the next until we do." Until she succeeded, not failed.

"I think I've created a monster." He laughed, a wonderful, deep laugh that tickled her down to her toes. "All right, I'll come for you tomorrow at the same time. We'll do more work on blocking your fear. And this time, you'll stay with me, no running off. That's an order."

She nodded, then silence fell. They gazed at one another. She thought of what he'd told her earlier about his family, the hurt in his voice when he'd spoken of his mother and his uncle Jerome's death. She thought of how he'd rescued her in the coffee shop and the way he'd looked at her in Germantown after they'd been separated.

And the way he looked at her now, with an amused glint in his eyes. A giddy sensation tugged at her heart, filling her with tenderness and affection. For him.

"Well, goodbye," she murmured, her cheeks growing warm again. "See you tomorrow."

She darted up the steps, closed the door and leaned

against it, ecstatic and dismayed all at once. How had it happened? How had she gone from wishing the man would simply go away, to an almost overwhelming need to prove herself to him, to this...this what? What were these exciting but unsettling feelings coursing through her?

"*Scheisse!*" exploded from the parlor.

She crashed down to Earth, shocked to the core to hear Aunt Trudy's voice. Cursing. Now Addie *knew* the world had flipped upside down. Aunt Trudy never cursed. Even in German.

"*Scheisse!*" her aunt blurted again.

Intrigued, Addie tossed her coat onto its hook, kicked off her boots and hustled into the parlor to discover what could have caused her proper aunt to let such a sound escape her lips. She found Marta balanced on her tiptoes, her arms stretched up to hold a thick black curtain over one of the front windows. Aunt Trudy stood atop a step-stool, attempting to secure the curtain around the brass rod with a large safety pin.

Ah. The source of the profanity—her aunt had stuck herself. Several times.

"Come on in, Addie, we're getting ready for the battle of Pine Street," Marta said with a grin. She wore a green sweater, plaid skirt, and wool stockings rolled down to her ankles in the new fashion. "And I'm getting a lesson in how to curse like a German sailor."

"What're you talking about?" Addie padded across the carpet and relieved Marta of the drapery. Taller than her cousin, she could reach the curtain rail if she stretched. It made the job easier for her aunt, but, jeepers, she'd never held a piece of fabric so heavy.

"We are under orders to hang blackout curtains," Aunt

Trudy said. "Also, we are not to leave linens to dry on the clothesline after sundown." She snorted like a champion filly told she'd have to bunk with the ice wagon nags. "*That*, you girls know, is something I would never do."

Addie shot Marta a puzzled look.

"On account of the entire German navy being off the coast of Goveport," her cousin said. "Ready to blow us to bits if they see a light in the window or a pair of bloomers flapping on the line."

"Marta, shame on you." Aunt Trudy worked the pin into the thick material with no damage to her fingers this time. "There is war. The entire city is to be under blackout."

"Really, Mother, why would the Nazis want to shell us? There's nothing but broken-down fishing shacks in Goveport. If they want to do real damage, they'll hit Boston. Or do you think our German cousins aren't smart enough to figure that out?"

Aunt Trudy clucked like an irritated hen. She finished securing the fabric around the curtain rail, the pins lined up in a neat row. Addie helped her down. Marta moved the stepstool, and they began again at the next window. She and Marta lifted the length of fabric and tossed one end over the thick rod. The world outside disappeared.

"Your uncle was supposed to come home early to help with this task, Adelaide," Aunt Trudy said. "But I suppose he is too busy with work?"

Addie glanced at Marta. Uncle Eb hadn't bothered to show his face at work all week. She thought Aunt Trudy knew that.

"Probably over in Germantown," Marta said. "Plotting with his pals in the Bund and making trouble."

"Marta," her mother warned, but Addie thought her cousin had hit on the truth. She was sure she'd seen Uncle Eb as she chased after Sgt. Gillis today.

Marta turned a sly smile on her. "So, cousin, are you going to tell me about that excruciatingly tall fella who dropped you off? I saw you with him out the window."

No. Addie didn't want to tell her. She wanted to keep Dunstan as her delicious secret. Even from the cousin she adored. "Oh, he's nobody. Just a friend."

"Nobody my foot. You were positively mooning over him."

Addie shook her head in denial, her cheeks flaring as hot as the sun yet again.

"Who do you speak of?" Aunt Trudy asked. "Does your father know this man, Adelaide?"

Marta rolled her eyes and Addie cringed. If she wouldn't tell Marta about Dunstan, no way would she tell Aunt Nosy.

The front door burst open then shut with a bang, making them jump and saving Addie from further interrogation. She looked into the foyer to see Hans shrug off his coat and toss it in the direction of a hook.

"What's eating you, sourpuss?" Marta demanded.

"Leave me alone," Hans blurted. In German.

He clomped across the foyer without removing the rubbers covering his shoes. Busy securing the last of the pins into the curtain, Aunt Trudy didn't notice. Thankfully. Hans looked as if he'd bite her head off if she complained. He disappeared down the hallway toward the kitchen and the back of the house. The door to the old sewing room that had been converted to his bedroom slammed a moment later.

"He's been *such* a pill all week," Marta said, frowning. "I think they turned him down. You know, when he went to enlist."

Perhaps. Or maybe his brief romance with Virginia had busted up. That would explain his fall into such gloomy depths. And perhaps explain what had spurred the fight Michael had told Addie about. But surely not. Hans had known Virginia for too short a time for his emotions to be on such a treacherous roller coaster.

Addie followed Marta to the side windows and picked up another heavy drapery. *Speak for yourself.* She hadn't known Dunstan for much longer, yet her heart raced and her belly flip-flopped just thinking about him.

She sighed, bemused. Cupid seemed to have an odd sense of humor, the way he'd been shooting his arrows willy-nilly at the Brandt family these days.

Chapter Twenty-Three

Rosa upended the last of the chairs and placed it seat-down on the table, clearing the way for the night man, Luigi, to wash the floor. She massaged her lower back, sore from such a long day, and moved through the kitchen to the back room to get her coat. It smelled like potato peels and garbage back here, though the place had been scrubbed clean, including every pot, pan, and utensil in the joint, set out to dry on the counter beside the sink, ready to return to work tomorrow.

She was running late. Sal's closed at four-thirty, but the last customers of the day seemed to have taken root in their chairs and wouldn't leave. Her headache had eased, but she'd been in a foul mood all afternoon, so it was a short trip to the end of her rope. She'd vamoosed those lollygaggers out the door with some choice sharp words.

Sal had chewed her hide for that, but she'd told him to go pound sand. She had more important things to do than pour coffee refills and get her fanny pinched by creeps who'd leave her a nickel tip, tops.

She had to go catch a spy.

Rosa untied her apron, scowling at the blots of tomato sauce and gravy staining the once-white fabric. She'd have to scrub extra hard tonight to get those spots out. She stuffed the apron into her coat pocket. Her fingers brushed the wad of cash at the bottom. Or she could buy herself a new one now that she had some money. She could buy ten new aprons and twenty pairs of shoes with the rest of the dough she'd get when she did what that beady-eyed G-Man had asked her to do.

Bring Adelaide to me at the Wentworth house when darkness falls, he'd said. *There will be an additional reward.*

That burned her bunions. The very idea she needed a reward to get her to turn Addie in. Addie Brandt was a spy, a Nazi agent, determined to do her country harm. She *had* to be stopped. Rosa would do it for free if she didn't need the money so bad.

She changed into her boots, plucked her ragged winter coat off its hook, then left through the rear door, slamming it shut. She scuffed down the narrow alley to Main Street and hopped a bus to the north side. She got off at Colby Park and ankled it the rest of the way to Pine Street. She peered at the house numbers, looking for Addie's address, forty-six.

She'd never come up here before. Addie had never been to her dump either, but that was because Rosa never invited her. Addie had asked her dozens of times to come over, but Rosa could never bring herself to dirty the doorstep of a nice home in such a nice neighborhood.

She found the right number and, not wanting to smudge the brass knocker polished to within an inch of its life, she rapped on the door. Hard. After Rosa exchanged words with a tiny, hatchet-faced German lady, Addie stood on the threshold, looking as guilty as sin.

As she should, the traitor.

"Rosa. P-please come in," Addie said, sounding awful scared. Maybe she knew Rosa was on to her. The wicked never rest easy, Ma liked to say.

"I'm not interested in coming in," she said firmly. "I came here for one reason, you scheming rat. You should be *ashamed* of yourself, Addie Brandt."

"I know." Addie fiddled nervously with the swan brooch, pinned to her white blouse. Rosa wished she'd never given it to her. Wished she'd save her money. "Rosa, before you chew me out, will you listen to what I have to say?"

"Of all the nerve! What could you say to make what you done any less awful?"

Addie's shoulders drooped and she looked like she might bawl. "It's not like that. We're just working together. As colleagues. I meant it when I said I have no interest in him. I never did. And I never would."

Rosa frowned, confused. Was she talking about Dunstan? At a time like this? "What's that got to do with—"

"Please believe me. Dunstan doesn't want me. He wants you. I-I'm sure of it." Tears sprang to her eyes. "I would never let a man come between you and me. *Never.* You're my friend."

Rosa went still. The beady-eyed man's words echoed in her mind. *Adelaide trusts you. She'll go with you willingly. You're her friend.*

Addie was Rosa's friend, too. Her only friend. The only girl in school who'd been kind to her. She'd never teased

Rosa about her tattered stockings and clothes she got from St. Michael's charity bins. She'd never called her *fast* when she walked out with boys, like everyone else had.

She locked eyes with Addie and her fury ebbed like the tide. She couldn't do it. Couldn't betray her friend, couldn't turn her in no matter what she'd done. Something light and good elbowed into the blackness that had blinded Rosa like a widow's veil since she'd bumped into that G-Man. She tried to latch onto it, but her headache came back, stabbing her as sharp as a fisherman's gaffe. She winced in pain.

Addie's eyes went wide. "Are you alright? You look ill. Won't you come in and sit down? I'll make tea. We can talk."

Rosa shook her head and stepped back from the door. "I'm sorry, Addie."

"Rosa!" Addie's puzzled cry trailed after her as she dashed down the steps and sped away.

Rosa hurried back to the bus stop. Her head throbbed so hard she feared it would burst. She swiped tears from her eyes and her stomach griped like she'd eaten spoiled fish. But she wouldn't go home and cry about it. She'd made up her mind. She would meet that G-Man as planned, without Addie. She'd tell that creep he'd have to find someone else to bring her to him.

Rosa wouldn't do it. Addie was her friend, and friends stick together.

∾

Dusk had turned the sky pink as Rosa made her way up the path from the street. Ahead, she saw the old Wentworth place peeping through the pine tree branches, set back from the cliffs that overlooked the ocean. She used to come up here to neck with some of the more interesting boys after school. No fear of being caught. Not a soul had lived here since the Wentworth's lost their money in the stock market crash and had abandoned their summer home.

She stepped over a fallen branch. A mess of overgrown ferns, shrubs and briars grew wild, clogging the path, threatening to trip her up. The house was in worse shape —every window on both floors busted, the shutters broken, holes in the roof. Funny place for a government agent to hide out, waiting for her.

That got Rosa seeing red. He'd expected her to drag Addie into the woods and all the way up here? Even meek as sheep Addie would've bellyached at that.

A bramble snagged on her stockings. She cursed in annoyance as she bent to set the silk free. Voices drifted from the front of the house. She straightened, puzzled. She'd thought the man would be alone. Ignoring Ma's voice ringing in her head, warning her to take care, Rosa crept along the side of the house. She hid behind a tangled forsythia bush and peeped around the corner.

In the fading light, she spotted two men in the clearing, dressed in overcoats and hats. The G-Man and... Victor Maheu? What was he doing up here? As far as Rosa knew, he barely set foot on dry land outside of Fish Village.

"Saturday night, on the high tide," she heard Beady Eyes say. "Wait for my signal, then deliver the goods."

Rosa scrunched her forehead. What were they talking about?

"What if it's stormy?" Victor asked. "Awful treacherous navigating that cove in rough water. Especially in the dark. Could be dangerous for me and my boat."

"How is that my concern?" Beady Eyes said, as crabby as could be. "You'll be there. On the high tide. Is that clear?"

Well, if that didn't put Victor in his place, the wad of bills that changed hands sure did. Bigger than the bundle the man had handed over to her. Where did a government man get so much dough to throw around?

"Saturday, then," Victor said and grinned, his toothless mouth like an empty cave.

He stuffed the money into his pocket and left. Rosa ducked behind the forsythia as he passed by close to her.

"I know you're there, Rosa," the G-Man said after Victor had gone. "Come out, child."

He spoke like he thought her a simpleton. That got her steamed. Ma talked to her like that. Sal, too. Everyone did. Except Addie. Rosa smoothed her coat, threw back her shoulders, and walked over to the man, jittery and angry at the same time.

"You heard every word?" he asked.

"I sure did. Not like you were keeping quiet. If you're thinking of buying fish from Victor Maheu, you better think again. Sal never buys from him. He tries to pass off last week's haul as fresh catch—" His icy look shut her up. Her heart sank. "You're not buying fish from him, are you?"

"No. I'm not." His voice went as cold as January. "Where is Adelaide?"

Rosa gulped. Pa had talked to her like that, right before he would grab the strap and wallop her good. Well, she never let Pa see how much he scared her, and she wouldn't show this fella either, government agent or not.

She took a deep breath and stiffened her spine. "I changed my mind."

He didn't speak for a long time, then, "You disobeyed me?"

"I guess I did," she said with glee. He sounded surprised, like no one had ever told him to go jump in a lake before. "Something smells fishy about this whole deal and I ain't talking about Victor Maheu. Why'd you ask *me* to drag Addie up here? If she's such a dangerous criminal, why bring her up to this dump and not straight to jail?"

He didn't say anything. Just stared at her like she was a bug in an experiment. That got her fuming even more.

She dug into her pocket and yanked free the cash he'd given her. Though it hurt like the dickens to give up so much money, she stuck out her hand. "Here, mister. I come to give you your money back."

Now he laughed. A cruel laugh that raised the hairs on her arms.

"My dear, you are a delight. You have so much anger in you I could feed off you forever." His smile faded. "Unfortunately, I can't indulge my needs now. You defied my orders to bring Adelaide to me. Worse, you recognized Mr. Maheu, putting my mission at risk. I can't let you go, can't allow you to breathe a word of what you saw here." The look on his face turned mean. "In fact, I can't allow you to breathe at all."

He tugged off one of his fancy leather gloves and reached out his hand. She gasped. His fingers were as charred as hot dogs burned on the grill.

"What's wrong with your—?" Her voice stopped. Her windpipe closed. Collapsed. She couldn't speak, couldn't get in a single whisk of air. She clawed at her neck, trying to loosen the ghost hand that squished her gullet. Anger and alarm washed away, replaced by terror. It filled her chest, pinched every bone, every muscle, every inch of her body.

The man stepped closer and took a deep breath, as if smelling her. "Ah. *There's* your fear." He stroked her neck with blackened fingers as hot as a fireplace poker. Her throat squeezed tighter. He grinned, greedy and full of lust. "Walk," he commanded, pointing toward the cliffs with that hideous hand.

She did. Lord help her, she did. Away from the house and through the trees. She tried so hard to make her legs stop, but she couldn't. Something hot and bitter shot through her blood and she tingled all over. It numbed her brain and her body moved on its own. She clumped along the dirt as stiff-legged as a puppet on strings.

"Very good," the man said, awful pleased with himself. "Now, run."

She obeyed.

Holy Mother, what's happening? Her shoes thudded on the hard ground and slipped on wet stones. Her ankle screamed with pain, but she didn't slow. The money she still held flew from her hand, fluttering away like green butterflies. Her apron fell out of her pocket. Pine branches whipped her face and tore at her hair. Blood oozed. She wet her underpants and kept running. Her lungs burned.

Pins and needles poked her brain from lack of air, and still she ran.

"Stop!" he cried.

She skidded to a halt at the edge of the cliff. Angry, white-capped waves beat against the jagged rocks below.

"It's lovely, isn't it?"

Rosa cringed. The man stood next to her. She tried to pivot, to run away, but she couldn't. Her feet were planted as if stuck in cement. At least she could breathe again.

Confusion punched through her fear. "W-what do you mean?" she asked, drawing in ragged breaths.

"I mean this." He made a sweeping motion with his arm. The view, she guessed. The ocean and the sky, touched by the last purple-pink wisps of daylight. Ma loved this time of day. When the chores were done, and the drinking could begin. Rosa sniffled. She wanted her ma right now, more than anything.

"Nature thrives," he said. "No matter how far man advances or tries to tame the elements, nature will always prevail. Nature is more powerful." He frowned at his blackened fingers. "Nature overcomes man, and eventually destroys us all."

What was he talking about? "Let me go," she demanded, struggling to make her limbs move.

"You know I can't."

"Who...who are you?"

He stuck out his chest, nearly busting his buttons. "I'm Germany's most powerful weapon." He shifted and pointed one of those burned up fingers downward, toward the water churning below. "Now, *walk*."

Rosa fought him with all with all her might, but her foot lifted and reached out over the cliff, hovering in the air. A frigid wind rushed up under her skirt. Seagulls swooped and squawked, watching her.

The G-Man watched her too, his eyes glassy with lust. "Go on," he breathed.

Rosa's foot began to step down. Her head clanged in agony. Fear held her like a fist and tears streamed down her face, but she squashed the whimper that crawled up her throat and bit back pleading words. She would *not* let him see her beg.

She shot him a glare as sharp as a pitchfork. "Go suck an egg, you Nazi freak!"

Then she fell.

Chapter Twenty-Four

A ddie shuffled the paints and powders inside her makeup box. She'd rearranged the case twice this week, but she had to do something to keep herself occupied. To keep her mind on anything else but where it wanted to be.

Dunstan.

When Rosa had appeared on her doorstep yesterday, she'd assured her old friend she didn't have even a smidge of interest in the man. A complete lie.

Addie glanced at the clock again. The hands moved with maddening slowness as the time crawled closer to noon, when she and Dunstan were scheduled to meet. She couldn't believe the way her body tingled in anticipation. She fairly *glimmered* all over, like tinsel on a Christmas tree.

"What's got you so giddy?" Uncle Pat asked, tucking the broom he'd been sweeping with into the cupboard. "I never saw anyone so happy about going out of business."

She sobered. That was unfair. She hadn't been so

wrapped up in her thoughts she'd failed to notice business had evaporated. Father spent the days circling the empty viewing rooms upstairs like a distressed ghost.

"I'm not *happy*, Uncle Pat. I'm just—" She bit back the rest of her words. Father stood at the bottom of the stairs, his suit rumpled, his tie askew, his manner as stern and ill-tempered as it had been all week.

"You're just what, Adelaide?" he asked.

She lowered her gaze. Father didn't want to hear her answer. If she were to tell him a man she'd just met occupied her thoughts day and night, that she seriously considered leaving Goveport with that man, and also schemed with him to pick a policeman's pocket in an attempt to read the cop's future...

Well, he'd probably end up in one of his own caskets.

"It's nothing, Father," she said hurriedly. "Uncle Pat's just making a joke."

He frowned. "I'm pleased you two can find something to laugh about, considering our situation." Addie flushed guiltily as he shifted his gaze to her uncle. "It's clear you haven't heard. There's been an official declaration of war from Berlin."

Uncle Pat slammed shut the cupboard door. Shock and sorrow flooded Addie, though she had expected this news since Sunday.

"We are the enemy now," Father added, sounding exhausted. "The reaction has been swift. The city coroner just telephoned to inform me he will no longer refer the bereaved to Brandt Funeral Home."

Addie gasped. Uncle Pat cursed. "Hell, Otto, that ghoul can't do that."

"He can, and he has."

"Well, we don't need the coroner's help," Uncle Pat said. "We'll have scads of business soon. I hear half of Bannister's men are joining up. The rest'll probably get drafted. How's Bannister gonna plant a stiff without help? Unless he hires girl pallbearers, he'll have to turn customers away. Folks will *have* to come to us."

"You needn't be so glib, Pat. You know what it means for those men enlisting to serve. For your own sons."

The air seemed to still as the two men eyed each other. Addie shuddered, more than grateful the Sight didn't show her the past. The two men had been enemies in the Great War, but each must have suffered a great deal.

Uncle Pat cleared his throat, his bluster gone. "I'm sorry Otto. I'm just so steamed up."

"As am I." Father glanced at her, then turned back to her uncle. "Pat, will you excuse us a moment? I wish to speak with Adelaide."

Addie quaked. What did he want to talk to her about? Something so secret he had to send Uncle Pat away. She hoped her uncle would say no, but knew he always did what Father asked him to. With a brusque nod, he headed for the embalming room. Father watched him go, waiting until the wide, thick door closed with a decisive click before turning back to her.

"I heard about what happened at the department store the other day," he said.

Anger flared. He sounded disappointed in her. She slipped off the stool and moved closer, facing him. "What do you want me to say, Father? That you were right? That my careless blabbing about my gift brought this on? That

I've caused the broken windows and lost us more customers? That *I've* hurt our family?"

His eyes widened and he took a step back. He shook his head. "You misunderstand. I have no care about that or anything else. I am concerned about *you*."

"You have a funny way of showing it." She crossed her arms as she did when she didn't get her way as a child. "You glare at me like you're furious. Like I scare the pants off you. Like you think I'm a monster. Or a f-freak, like my mother!"

"Adelaide, *stop*."

She snapped her mouth shut. Tears stung her eyes. Father reached out with shaking hands but stopped before touching her and sighed in frustration.

"Child, I don't think you're anything of the sort," he said, a gentle note tempering his gruffness. "I never thought that of your mother either. You don't know this, but we almost didn't get married. Her family was against me. She was Catholic, I was not. And a German, so soon after the war where I was an enemy. A poor, immigrant gravedigger. Your grandparents, rest their souls, thought I was beneath her. I *was* beneath her. She was...everything."

He ran his fingers through his thinning gray hair, looking weary.

"When your mother took sick, I felt so helpless. I loved her more than I can say, and I couldn't do anything to protect her or make her well." He gazed at Addie and his eyes misted over. "I love you, too, daughter. I know I have trouble showing you that, but it's the truth."

A sob caught in Addie's throat. She'd never heard those words on her father's lips before.

"I'm concerned for your safety, Adelaide. *Greatly*

concerned." He took a deep breath. "As children, Uncle Eb and I visited the old folks in the country. We heard whispered stories of an aunt called Frieda. She lived in a village near Hanau. She claimed to have the power to heal. It was said she cured people of all manner of ills. Some believed in her gift, most did not. A parlor trick at best, witchcraft at worse. Then she claimed to have snatched a girl who'd breathed her last from the arms of death. The villagers erupted at this blasphemy. Anger grew but Frieda refused to renounce her claim of otherworldly power. She was shunned and attacked, pelted with garbage. Her children were taken from her. One night, a mob dragged her from her bed..." He gazed at Addie intently. "They beat her to death."

Fear nestled in Addie's throat, making it hard to swallow. Poor Frieda. Punished because she refused to hide her true self. "Father, do you believe she had a gift?"

"In my business, death is final, so I'm inclined toward skepticism. But having known your mother, and you, well..." He sighed. "But it doesn't matter what I believe. It only matters what the mob believes. That's why I forbid your mother and you from exploring your power. To protect you from *them*. The very thing you face now. Derision, anger. And, yes, violence. That is why I've tried to keep you close all week. Not to punish you. To keep you safe." A wry smile touched his lips. "Though I'm not surprised you've ignored my wishes. You're as strong-willed and stubborn as your mother."

Addie wiped away her tears with her thumbs. She'd misjudged her father. He wasn't afraid *of* her. He was afraid *for* her.

"I understand your concern," she said. "I know you

want to protect me." He wanted to warn her too, with that hair-raising tale of Frieda's horrible fate. "But your effort to keep me safe has frightened me away from learning about my ability and who I am. *I've* kept myself from who I am. But not anymore."

Several sharp raps on the door ended the conversation. Father stiffened. Addie jumped and anxiety overtook all other emotion. Uncle Pat came back into the room as Father opened the door. Two men stood outside in the alley. One of them Addie recognized.

"Mr. Brandt, I'm sure you remember me, Officer Pete Bowdoin." He shot Addie a quick glance. "I'm escorting—"

"Agent Hugh Thompson. I'm from the government." The other man pushed forward and flashed a brown leather rectangle with an official-looking paper inside. Tiny type, a seal of some sort. He fit the bill for a government agent to a *T*—broad shouldered, chiseled jaw, sharp, beak-like nose, commanding voice. Sort of like Dunstan.

"From the government?" Father flashed a worried glance at Addie. "What is it? Is something wrong?"

"No, Mr. Brandt." Thompson's voice was far from reassuring. "May we come in?"

Father drew himself up but stepped back so they could enter. He closed the door. Pete's gaze swept across the room, lingering on an empty casket on a wheeled trolley near the elevator. His nostrils twitched. The chemical odor still stung Addie's nose after all these years. She couldn't imagine what it must be like for someone coming in here for the first time.

"What's this all about?" Father asked. His voice wobbled with unease.

"I'll get to the point," Thompson said. "The government's mobilizing all departments to verify the security of our coastal defenses. I've been assigned to check the defenses along the New England seashore. I'm meeting with law enforcement to address their concerns as well as speaking with local businessmen, to ensure they understand the seriousness of the threat."

"The German businessmen, you mean," Uncle Pat muttered under his breath.

Thompson jerked toward him. "What was that?"

Father held up his hands. "Agent Thompson, my brother-in-law has a valid point. Which local businessmen do you mean? All of them? Or just those businesses run by men of German and Italian descent?"

"No need to worry on that score, Mr. Brandt. I'm sure your loyalty to this country is unquestioned." Thompson's smile revealed even white teeth. "I'm merely stopping by to acquaint myself with you, your employees, and your family members." He nodded at Uncle Pat. "Mr. Feeney. And Miss Brandt."

He pinned his gaze on Addie. Not long, but long enough for her nerves to tighten in alarm. Was there some significance to his stare?

"There's someone missing," he said. "Your cousin, I believe. Mr. Eben Brandt?"

A long pause, then Father said, "He just stepped out."

Addie gaped at her father. Uncle Eb hadn't stepped *in* all week.

"I see." Thompson's voice went cold, and his gaze probed Addie again. She shifted, feeling exposed. "Well, thank you for your time. If you have any questions or concerns, please don't hesitate to contact me through the local police. Pleasure to meet you."

As Agent Thompson clasped hands with Father and Uncle Pat, Pete caught Addie's eye. He jerked his head toward the door, his eyebrows drawn down. She frowned. What did he want? Perhaps something to do with the way Thompson kept looking at her. Surely Pete didn't want to apologize again.

"I'll see the gentlemen out," Addie said. Father scowled at her but didn't protest. She followed their visitors out the door into the alley. Without her coat, she shivered from the cold. "What is it, Pete?"

"It's something vitally important." He licked his lips. "Is there somewhere we can talk in private?"

Her teeth chattered. How maddening. Why didn't the man just spit it out? "I have work to do." She crossed her arms, for warmth and to show Pete she wasn't going to budge. "Please, just tell me."

Pete exchanged glances with Thompson, who gave a blunt nod.

"We've received a tip that concerns us greatly," Pete said. "You've been seen with a man. A stranger in town."

She sucked in a breath. "So? Why does anyone care who I'm seen with?"

Agent Thompson stepped closer, eyes keen on her face. "You might have a care about this particular man. I understand from Officer Bowdoin that Jack Dunstan came into town last week and started asking questions about you."

"Well, he'd heard about..." Addie glanced at Pete. "You know. About what I saw."

Pete shook his head. "Addie, he came to the police

station asking about you *minutes* after you left. How could he have heard anything?"

Thompson frowned. "Miss Brandt, I'm sorry to say Mr. Dunstan came here with one purpose in mind. To find *you*."

Addie hugged her crossed arms tighter to her chest and tried to shush her roiling stomach. After everything that had transpired between her and Dunstan, she wasn't fool enough to think running into him had been a coincidence. But the way Pete and Thompson spoke, it sounded beyond shady. As if Dunstan had stalked her, as a hunter stalks a deer.

She shuddered, suddenly frightened. "But-but he says he works for the government."

"A lot of folks work for the government, miss." Thompson's voice softened. "I'm not trying to alarm you. I don't know Mr. Dunstan personally, but I know what he does, and what he's trying to convince *you* to do. I want to caution you. He has a reputation for being rash with the people who work with him. His group is on the fringe of respectability. A year ago, Mr. Dunstan was at the center of a terrible tragedy. Several of our best men were injured. One woman was killed. From what I hear, Jack Dunstan's the reason why. As far as I'm concerned, the man should be in jail."

The world reeled under Addie's feet. Bile rose in her throat.

"It's true, Addie." Pete nodded, his eyes wide. "Sergeant Gillis has confirmed everything Agent Thompson is saying. That man is bad news."

Addie's head hurt. It couldn't be true. Dunstan was a good man. There had to be an explanation.

Thompson flashed a glance at the hearse and its busted windows then stepped so close to her they nearly touched. He smelled of cloves and wool.

"Listen to me carefully." His gaze on her turned steely. An icy hand seemed to squeeze her heart. "That man is not to be trusted. Stay away from him, Miss Brandt, or you could end up dead too."

Chapter Twenty-Five

Addie brushed off Father's and Uncle Pat's questions and left work moments after Pete and Agent Thompson had departed. Stopping only long enough to exchange her pumps for her boots, she escaped before her father could order her to stay put. And before Dunstan could arrive. She didn't want to see him. Not now, perhaps never again.

Her boots thumped the pavement as she moved down Holmes Street to Ocean Boulevard, thinking a brisk walk along the beach would help her sort through her chaotic thoughts. At the boardwalk, she spotted the reporter Benny Hirtle, seated on a bench by the fishermen's memorial. She pulled her hat brim down and ducked her head so he wouldn't see her and turned left, hurrying down the sidewalk.

Noontime traffic puttered by, leaving the smell of exhaust in the cold air. Addie passed dozens of pedestrians. A few stared at her, but no one bothered her until she'd almost reached the path to the beach. A slim young woman in a deep-purple coat with wide lapels stepped in front of her, making Addie jump.

"Oh, Addie, you've *got* to help me!" the woman said in an urgent rush. "My little Calliope's gone missing. Will you help me find her? I can pay. Not much, but I have some money. Please, will you help me?"

Addie's annoyance gave way to concern. "Calliope? Is that your daughter?"

"No, my dog. She's a sweet little beagle and she's been missing for two weeks. I'm *frantic*." Tears sprang into her eyes. "I can't imagine where she's gotten off to."

"Oh, I don't think I can—"

"*Please*. I'm sick with worry for the little dear." She clicked open her pocketbook and reached inside. Addie thought she might pull out a picture, but instead she took out a well-worn leather leash. She held it out, desperation in her eyes. "Calliope's all I have in the world. I'd be ever so grateful if you'd help me find her."

Addie gazed at the woman's narrow, worried face and the dark circles under her eyes. She wore no hat and even her tousled, unkempt brown hair seemed in distress. Addie's heart twisted in sympathy. She'd never had a pet, outside of that bird Marta had nursed back to life years ago, but she knew she'd be devastated if her dog or cat went missing.

Out of the corner of her eye, she saw Benny Hirtle heading her way, moving fast down the sidewalk. Addie did *not* relish another encounter with him, or anyone. She just wanted to be left alone.

"I'm sorry, miss, I can't help you," she said to the worried woman and darted toward the beach path before Hirtle could reach her. The woman began to follow, calling to her, then fell back and shuffled away, clutching the leash.

Addie breathed a sigh of relief to have evaded them both and climbed the snow-dusted path over the dunes. She paused at the top. South Point Beach spread out before her. The scents of seaweed and ocean water carried on the chill breeze. The tide swelled, nearing high. A few people strolled along the sand, some combed through the debris pushed up by the breaking waves, looking for interesting bits of sea glass, shells, and driftwood.

Several policemen also walked along the beach, scanning the horizon. On the lookout for German submarines, Addie guessed. U-Boats they were called. She shuddered to think the enemy could be skulking just off the coast, searching for a ship to sink, or a ripe target on land to strike. Or *many* targets. She wouldn't put it past her German relatives to try to best the Japanese and launch an even more massive assault on the American mainland.

She scrambled down the other side of the dune, careful to avoid the sea grass bordering the path. Sharp as knives, those grass blades could do a splendid job slicing up a girl's legs, even through her stockings. On the beach, she saw a man who looked like Wilhelm staring out at the ocean, so she turned and went the other way.

Sea spray coated her face and she tasted salt as she walked close to the water, sinking into wet sand, daring the long fingers of the breaking waves to catch her. Her emotions heaved like those waves. Mr. Hirtle seeming to follow her and being accosted by the woman with the missing dog had rattled her. Father's story about his aunt Frieda had rattled her even more. But what Agent Thompson had claimed about Dunstan had gutted her.

A woman, dead. Dunstan at fault. Had he killed her? That's what Thompson had implied. *That man should be in jail*, he'd said.

Addie sighed. For maybe the thousandth time this week, she wished Mother was here to comfort her, to tell her what to do.

One thing she had to do—tell Rosa what she'd learned about Dunstan. Or perhaps she already knew? She'd never come to Addie's house before yesterday. Maybe that was why. She'd seemed upset and out of sorts. Addie had been so focused on denying any interest in Dunstan, she'd barely given Rosa a chance to speak before she'd abruptly left.

Winded from her walk, Addie slowed her pace and headed for a telephone pole lying at the foot of a steep dune. The pole had been coughed up with a lot of other debris by the big hurricane's high tides. Weather and time had eaten away at the wood and turned it slate gray. She picked a section least abused by seagulls, smoothed her coat under her bottom, and sat. The wood held a hint of warmth from the winter sun.

She gazed out at the ocean, her heart aching. How could she trust Dunstan now? Did she want to trust him? She barely knew him. She only knew he'd left home far too young, and she burned as hot as a coal fire whenever he got close. Distracted by the stars in her eyes and her racing pulse, she hadn't questioned anything he'd told her.

She felt so...naked. And, somehow, betrayed.

A shadow passed over her. Wilhelm, she expected. He'd no doubt spotted her and had followed her. She looked up, bending her hat's brim to shade her eyes from the sun, surprised when Dunstan's rugged face came into focus.

"Mind if I sit down?" His voice rumbled, tickling her insides.

"I don't think that's a good idea," she said, adopting an icy tone.

He sat anyway. "I waited for you outside the funeral parlor," he said gruffly. "I figured you got tied up at work, so I went ahead and..." He coaxed a well-chewed pencil out of his overcoat's breast pocket and held it up with a tentative smile. "I told you any fool can steal a pencil. Here's your proof."

She did her best to ignore him. She stretched out her legs and examined the toes of her ankle boots with great interest.

"Addie, what gives? What's wrong?"

She looked at him then. She knew what she had to do, and she had to do it fast. Before she lost her nerve. "Mr. Dunstan, I think it's best for you and me to part company. I've heard girls die when they're around you."

He went as still as death. A long time passed before he spoke. "What do you know about that?"

He sounded so bleak. Dead inside. "Only what a government man told me."

"*What* government man?"

"A man named Thompson. He's in the city checking on coastal defenses. He's with the FBI." Or maybe he'd said he was with the Navy, or the Coast Guard. To be honest, she'd been so nervous, the way he'd been eyeing her, she couldn't recall.

"Never heard of him."

"Well, he's heard of *you*. Is it true? Were you responsible for a woman's death?"

Dunstan tucked the pencil back into his pocket and leaned forward, elbows on his knees. He stared out at the rolling waves. She watched his profile, his expression as unsettled and dark as the ocean. Finally, a curt nod.

"Oh." Her belly burned. "Why didn't you tell me?"

He turned his head to look at her. "Would it help for me to say there wasn't time?"

She searched his face. "You don't trust me."

He let out a breath. "Believe what you want to believe, Addie. I'm just trying to protect you."

Like her father. Did no one believe she could take care of herself? "Protect me from what? The truth? Dunstan, if I'm going to join your precious team, I have to know what I'm up against. I have to know about *you*. Don't you think I deserve that?"

His eyes flashed. "Yes."

She stiffened in surprise. She'd expected an argument from him.

He shifted and gazed at her. "There's this man, Addie. His name's Woden. I doubt it's his real name. He's one of us. Or used to be. He was my boss, in fact. Several years ago, he talked the brass at the FBI into letting him form a team of gifted folks. Probably used his gift to stir up their fears about the coming war. Stoked their bloodlust, too. Easy to do. Don't old men always want war?"

He sat up straight and patted his pockets until he found what he was looking for. His lighter clicked as he lit the cigarette.

"Woden's power is the darkest I've ever seen," he continued. "He pushes into a person's mind and takes control of them physically. He can make them do things they don't want to. He stokes a person's rage and fear, too. He feeds on it. It fuels him. The angrier or more fearful a person grows, the more pleasure he absorbs. You follow?"

She nodded shakily. All the moments of fear and anger that had surrounded her this past week crashed into her mind. Could this Woden be here even now, tweaking her terror?

"Addie, that bastard's power is the only genuine thing about him. Turns out, he was a double agent, put in place by the Nazis years ago, tasked with finding people like you and me. Gaining our trust, then recruiting us. If he couldn't convince us or force us to join his side, well... He's too proud to admit failure, so he killed anyone he couldn't turn."

He took a long, slow drag and exhaled just as slowly.

"Woden had been doing well, amassed a small crew. Most he sent to Germany. What happened to them there, I have no idea. Put to work for the Nazis, I imagine. Then I came into the picture. Someone he couldn't manipulate, someone who could neutralize powers, even his. That intrigued him. Woden and his assistant, Madelyn, taught me to respect my gift, showed me that I could make a difference in people's lives. I looked up to him. Madelyn and me...we became close. I trusted her, trusted them both. Until she came to me with Woden's offer."

Dunstan's voice dipped as low as a neap tide. Addie had heard the same grief-stricken tone from mourners filing past an open casket. She wondered if he could turn his gift of tranquility inward.

"Woden's plan to turn me failed. Miserably. Apparently, I'm unfailingly patriotic." A corner of his mouth tugged.

"Woden raged. Tried to kill me. Unsuccessfully, as you can see. His fury knew no bounds then. His anger is his weakness. When he loses control, no one is safe. To punish me, he used his power to make Madelyn..."

His voice trailed off. He stared at the horizon and drew hard on his cigarette. Smoke shot from his nostrils in an angry gust.

"Addie, I saw him walk her into a burning building. She'd turned against her own country to join him. She was gifted, a valuable asset, loyal to *him*. And he used his power to kill her." He slumped, looking broken. "He killed her to get revenge on *me*."

"Oh, Dunstan." Her heart swelled. So did her outrage. Agent Thompson was nothing more than a malicious gossip, spreading stories without all the facts. Small-minded, judgmental, like the villagers who'd turned on Father's aunt Frieda because they feared something they didn't understand. "That Agent Thompson made it sound like *you* killed her."

He shrugged. "Can't say I fault him for that. I took the blame for the whole mess, including Madelyn's death. To keep the team together. The few of us who are left."

"What happened to Woden?"

He let out a bitter snort. "He escaped. I was injured trying to save Madelyn. Garrity and Vir—" He stopped and cleared his throat. "The others on the team pursued but couldn't catch him. He slipped away. We heard he went to Germany. Now, with us in the war, I have my doubts he'll stay there, if he isn't here already."

He eyed her and his expression filled with anguish.

"Do you see why I told you it's important to fight, Addie? As hard as you can. Madelyn had a gift, a force as strong as yours, and she barely had the will to block him from her mind. She couldn't fight him. I couldn't save her." He flicked his half-smoked cigarette into the sand and gazed down at the burn scars on the backs of his hands. "I tried to, but I failed. And she died."

"It wasn't your fault," she murmured. "You know that don't you? It wasn't your fault."

In her words, she heard the echo of his own, outside the Bijou after the attack when he'd tried to comfort her. Addie stripped off a glove and ran her fingers over his hand, caressing the rough skin. She wished she could ease his pain and give him some of the peace he'd given her.

"I suppose you're right," he said after a few moments. "But I can't help blaming myself for what happened." He studied her face, something in his eyes she'd never seen before. Doubt. "Now you've heard the terrible truth about me, about Woden, tell me I haven't lost you. Tell me you still want to help, and you'll still consider joining our team. I need you in this fight."

Her belly fluttered. No one had ever needed her before. No one had ever spoken to her or treated her as Dunstan did, either. As someone important, of value. Someone who could contribute in a meaningful way. She wanted so desperately to live up to his faith in her.

"Let's take a walk." She stood and started along the beach. He fell in step beside her. "I need to know a whole lot more before I decide. About you, about the team, about everything. No more holding back. For me to trust you, you have to trust me, and that means telling me the truth."

His expression barely changed, but she could almost feel him relax. "I think I can do that. One favor, though.

Next time you hear something nasty about me, you come see me. I'll give you the straight dope. You can find me at the Savoy Hotel, apartment 603. Deal?"

"It's a deal," she said, and he flashed a grin that made her head spin. Would it always be this way when she was with him?

"Good. I'm ready to talk. What do you want to know?"

The selfish side of her wanted to know about Rosa and where she fit into his plan. Did he plan to take her to Washington too? She pushed that line of questioning aside for something more practical. "Let's begin with your team. Who are they and what gifts do they have?"

"The team." He let out a heavy breath. "We're down to bare bones now. Mostly just me, two or three others. One of them is Pearl, who can make animals do what she wants."

"How does she do that? Is it like hypnotism? You said emotions make our gifts work."

"Her gift's kind of like hypnosis, based on trust. She pets an animal, talks to them and pushes into their minds, building a loyalty to her. Whatever she commands, they obey. She's trained monkeys to slip into tight spaces and unlock doors. Dogs to retrieve one specific item out of dozens. Cats...?" His lips quirked. "She's still working on cats. They don't like to be told what to do. Hasn't figured out how to use her gift on humans yet, either."

He bent down and plucked a sand dollar off the beach then tossed it into the surf. Two seagulls swooped in and began to fight over it. He straightened and looked at her again, his expression darkening.

"Our gifts are powerful," he said. "But they also make us vulnerable. Pearl's vibrations are flooded with trust, leaving her wide open to manipulation. I had to stash her in a safe place after Woden escaped. No telling what could've happened if he'd gotten to her."

Addie imagined a host of gruesome images filled his mind. Like her with the Sight.

"I put our strongman Garrity on the job of protecting her," he went on. "He makes the Superman look like a weakling. I worked with him in a sideshow when they found us. He hoisted barbells weighing hundreds of pounds for two bucks a day. His gift is strength, but his vibrations hold a lot of negative energy, feelings of worthlessness." He slanted Addie a glance. "He can be unpleasant at times, but he's damned loyal."

"They? You said, when *they* found you in the sideshow."

"Woden. And Madelyn."

His voice softened when he said her name. She pretended not to notice. "What was her gift?"

"Sorrow. She could push grief and guilt into a person's mind with the touch of a finger."

Addie laughed softly, mystified. "How can grief be used to chase after spies?"

"You'd be surprised. Steep a man in his most sorrowful thoughts and memories for one hour and they're ready to confess to every crime under the sun. Our team broke up a counterfeiting ring and solved a kidnapping thanks to Madelyn's gift. Worked a damn sight better than thumbscrews."

But equally cruel. Would such callousness be expected of her if she went to work for him? Admiration filled his voice as he spoke of Madelyn and how they'd used her gift. Could a timid, fear-filled girl like her measure up to someone so bold?

"How long did you know Madelyn?" she asked.

"Two years, a little more."

"Did you..." Addie couldn't meet his eyes. "Did you love her very much?"

He hesitated. A pause so brief she might have imagined it. "I thought I did."

She'd steeled herself for a mournful *yes*, but the way he bit that off, bitter and raw, surprised her.

"She used me, Addie," he said, any hint of admiration gone. "Woden used me *and* her. He convinced her to come to the Nazi side, convinced her to try to bring me over too, and everything went to hell. Can you see why I have so much trouble trusting folks? Why I held back with you? Why I keep hammering at you to fight if the time comes?"

"I do and I promise you, if the time comes, I'll be ready. I'll fight," she said with more confidence than she felt.

They'd reached the Point, the rocky spit of land that jutted out into the Atlantic, separating Goveport's north and south sides. Mackey Light stood at the Point's end, with Samuel's Cove beyond, and after that the abandoned Wentworth house up on the cliffs. Farther north, across the Perkins River, more cliffs, with the fire spotting station Hans was helping to build just visible through the trees in the distance.

Addie stopped walking and glanced behind them. A couple of beachcombers strolled a fair distance away. She couldn't see Wilhelm, and no one else was around. She turned back to Dunstan. "The coast is clear, we're alone. Why don't you hand over that pencil and let me go to work?"

He blinked, as if stunned, then laughed. "Addie, how was I lucky enough to find you?"

From what Agent Thompson had said, luck had nothing to do with it. A conversation that would have to wait for another time.

Addie led him toward what used to be a jetty before the hurricane's fierce tide had swamped it. The few stones left visible stuck out of the sand like a row of crooked teeth. She perched on a flat-topped rock. She still had one glove off. She pulled off the other.

Dunstan stood in front of her, looking down, holding out the pencil like a priest offering a wafer at Sunday mass. She took it and closed her eyes. In an instant she plunged into the Sight. Darkness gripped her. A second later, she flew forward, as if shoved from a tunnel into a blaze of light.

"Tell me what you see," Dunstan said, his voice far away.

She saw everything, and nothing. Sensations flooded her mind and poured through her veins. She moved as rapid as lightning into and out of dozens of men. A penetrating cold chilled her bones, followed by searing heat. Images flickered, words tumbled from her mouth. She sobbed with joy as she slid into a man seeing his newborn son for the first time, then ached with another man's loneliness. Too many emotions to comprehend, threatening to drown her.

Addie opened her eyes with a frustrated groan. She looked up at Dunstan, fearing his disappointment. She'd failed again.

She rested the pencil on her lap. "I'm sorry. I couldn't

make out anything clearly. Couldn't find Gillis. There was too much noise, too many men who've used this pencil."

"Don't give up," he said. "You're still getting used to your gift. You're like a newborn colt learning how to stand. Be patient and soon you'll be off and running."

She gave him a tremulous smile. He sure had a way with words. "I think I may have to touch the man himself to get a proper image, to have anything make sense."

"Why don't you try again before doing anything that drastic." He squatted in front of her and pinned her in his gaze. "I *know* you can do this."

Addie looked down at the pencil, bolstered by his faith in her. She took a deep breath and picked it up. The Sight took hold again. Light blazed and, as before, a host of sensations bombarded her brain.

"Remember, Addie, *you* have control." Dunstan's voice echoed from a great distance.

She nodded and squeezed the pencil tight. She concentrated. She flew up, above the noise and emotions vying for her attention and looked down at the undulating mass. It took all her energy, but she managed to gather the raging sensations together and shuffle them into a neat pile, like a deck of cards. Then she laid it all out in her mind's eye and searched for Gillis. *Felt* for him.

"He's here," she managed, though it seemed to take great effort to speak. She steered toward the sergeant's mind but couldn't control her fall. She pitched downward, spiraling and spinning like a kite on a blustery day. She slammed into his consciousness with a force that made her yelp.

A long time later, dizzy and out of breath, she did her best to bring her surroundings into focus. "I see...I see a building on fire. Flames crackling, reaching to the sky. It's night."

"Where are you? When?"

"I don't know." Several fuzzy figures were ahead, writhing, or perhaps that was the heat of the fire undulating behind them. They were screaming. Yelling. Addie as Gillis ran toward them. Her belly bounced. Her heavy topcoat beat against her knees. She got too close to the blaze. The heat of the flames scorched her face. Her lungs filled with smoke. She hacked and coughed so hard her whole body contorted.

"Easy now," Dunstan said.

She could barely hear him. Fear clutched her brain and her blood rushed, thundering in her ears. Her throat burned from the smoke.

"There's a man on the ground," she choked out. Flame seemed to leap like a living thing from the burning structure and latch onto the man's trousers. Addie said what Gillis said, "He'll burn to death." Her voice shook with fear.

Dunstan's anxious voice sounded in the distance, as if miles away. "Pull yourself back, Addie. Jesus Christ, step away."

An ominous *crack* cut across the panicked voices and the roar of the flames. Her head whipped up. The burning structure groaned as it buckled. "It's falling!" she shouted, panicking.

She felt Dunstan's hands on hers, pressing down. His gift of calm pushed into her brain, but too late. Terror flooded her being. Frantic, she searched for a pinprick of light in her consciousness, the escape corridor out of the Sight, but she saw only blackness. She moaned and thrashed, caught in the sergeant's future. Trapped in his mind, just as she'd been trapped inside the man having the heart attack and Jimmy Gallagher's terrible fate.

Facing death with no way out.

She screamed. Everything went dark.

～

A ddie came to, cradled in Dunstan's arms.

Not as romantic a scene as she would have imagined. She flopped like a rag doll in his hold, coated with sweat. She coughed, her lungs seemingly on fire. Beach sand clung to her coat and stockings, twigs and dried seaweed tangled in her hair.

She'd fainted, by golly. And not only that, she'd failed again. She'd lost control and let the Sight consume her. She'd given in to her fear.

She gazed up at Dunstan's worried face. "I'm sorry." Her throat burned and the words came out in a pained whisper.

"Don't be," he rumbled, his voice curt. "That was a rough ride you went on."

He helped her to sit up and then to stand, keeping his arm around her waist until her legs stopped shaking. The beachcombers had caught up to them. They stared as they strolled by. Addie flushed, embarrassed and annoyed. Dunstan kept his attention fully on her, which made her flush even more.

When he released her, he bent down and picked up the pencil, poking out of the sand.

"I can try again," Addie said, eyeing that dratted piece of wood. "I'm *sure* I'll see something useful this time."

"No." He stuffed the pencil into his pocket. "I won't put you through that again. Not today, anyway."

She wanted to argue with him, wanted to insist she could and *would* make the Sight work, but the steely note in his voice held her back.

He took her arm and walked beside her down the beach and up the path over the dunes, all the way to the funeral home. They didn't speak. There was nothing to say. He stared straight ahead, probably regretting asking her to join his team. Probably regretting coming to Goveport, too, or ever hearing the name Addie Brandt.

Dunstan turned to her at the opening to the alley. He took her gloved hands and held them tight. "You rest now, Addie. Don't even think about the Sight for the rest of the day."

He bent and gave her a lingering kiss on the cheek. She leaned into the warmth of his soft lips on her skin. He drew away and gazed down at her with a troubled look.

"We can try again tomorrow," he said, then strode away before she could answer.

She watched him disappear around the corner, heading for his car. She feared there would be no tomorrow for them, no more chances for her to prove her worth. Dunstan's faith in her had been sorely misplaced. She'd let him down again. He'd had to rescue her. *Again.*

Addie opened the door and stepped inside the preparation room, letting out a bitter breath. She'd wished for so many years for the Sight to go away, and now, when she needed it most, her dubious gift refused to cooperate. Actually, *she* refused to cooperate. She let fear get the best of her. That weakness kept her from embracing the full measure of her power.

She peeled off her coat and hung it up, glad she'd said no to the woman who'd begged her to help find her dog. The way things were going, Addie would've found herself locked in the dogcatcher's van and trapped in the Sight— without Dunstan there to save her.

Chapter Twenty-Six

The smell of something greasy and delicious greeted Dunstan when he entered the hotel suite.

The aroma came from the small kitchen where Virginia, wearing a white apron over a blue dress, stood by the narrow stove. She wielded a long fork and poked at a couple of pork chops sizzling in a frying pan. A glass of whiskey sat on the counter next to her. The box radio on top of the icebox played Lionel Barrymore performing as Ebenezer Scrooge in *A Christmas Carol*.

The cozy, homey scene did little to lighten his mood. Today's events had him reeling. Addie, gone when he'd showed up at Brandt's to pick her up. Finding her alone and unprotected on the beach. Her questions about what Agent Thompson, government man, had told her. Recounting the details about Woden's betrayal and Madelyn's death. Addie's vision of a fire and Gillis crushed by a collapsing inferno.

All of that had unnerved him, but what happened when Addie held that pencil had shaken him to the core.

She'd gotten trapped in the Sight again and tortured by it, until he'd pulled her out. The terror he'd absorbed from her still beat against his brain, making him jumpy, agitated. A minor concern, compared to the fear that no doubt still tormented Addie.

"Smells good," he said, hanging up his coat. He unbuckled his gun holster and set it on the coat closet shelf next to his hat. "You know I would've gone out for something. You didn't have to make a fancy meal."

"You've truly been deprived, darling, if you think this is a fancy meal." Virginia turned off the gas flame then reached up to the cupboard over the sink and took out two plates. "Sit down. I need to talk to you."

He tensed. He didn't need any more bad news today.

He poured a drink then headed back to the kitchen area. He sank into a chair at the small dining table and gazed at her expectantly. "What's on your mind, kid?"

She twisted the dial and turned off the radio with a click. "It's Hans. I'm worried about him. We made a date for Tuesday night, but he stood me up. I tried phoning him. Twice." She handed him plates and flatware to lay out then pattered back to the stove. "I spoke to his mother who told me in no uncertain terms that Hans was not at home. I don't know how else to contact him, save storming over there."

She carried the frying pan to the table. She speared a pork chop and shook it free of the fork onto his plate.

"I've got to do something," she said. "You *know* I have to unwhammy him. What do you think I should do?"

Dunstan let out a weary sigh. Do nothing, he considered telling her, though he knew Virginia's tender heart wouldn't allow that. She had to lift her whammy so Hans could move on with his life. If not, he could pine for her for years before her spell faded. *She* would pine for him, no matter what. The terrible secret of Virginia's gift. She fell in love with everyone she pushed, and the feelings never fully went away.

"Go over there, see Hans," he said. "But be discreet. Don't bump heads with anyone but him."

She stopped spooning a mushy goo he suspected could be creamed corn onto their plates and met his gaze. "You mean don't bump heads with Addie, don't you? Dunstan, when are you going to tell her the truth about me?"

He gulped a mouthful of scotch. This afternoon when he'd been in a confessing mood would've been a dandy time to tell her about Rosa and Virginia and the lies he'd told. Why hadn't he? He didn't have the brass, plain and simple. He feared losing Addie. Not as an asset. He didn't want to lose *her*. Her trust and respect. Her laughter and spirit and that look in her eyes when she gazed at him, a look that seemed to grow more tender every day.

The thought of losing all that terrified him.

He sliced into his pork chop, unable to meet Virginia's eyes. "I'll tell her soon enough, all right?" He relented and softened his tone. "We have more important things to discuss."

She put down the pot of goo and settled into her chair, picking up her fork. "Oh? Like what?"

"Ever hear of an agent named Thompson?"

She shook her head, but that didn't mean there wasn't one. Washington was an alphabet soup of departments and divisions, each its own secretive rat's nest competing for the same funds and status. Nobody shared a kernel of information with anyone else. Especially if it would help.

He hoped that would change with a war on, but he doubted it.

Virginia studied him with a guarded expression. "Is this Thompson someone I should know?"

He shrugged.

Her brow furrowed, creasing her makeup. "What's going on? You've been growling like a bear with a thorn in his paw since you walked through that door. Your vibrations are a mess. Is something the matter?"

"No, nothing's wrong. I'm fine." He turned his attention to his food, though each bite tasted like ash in his mouth.

Virginia shot him a stinging glare. "Have it your way, Dunstan." She stabbed a piece of pork. "But I'll tell you one thing, your habit of keeping secrets will be the death of you."

He ground his teeth. Keeping secrets had become almost a mania with him. He'd been holding back a lot, starting with the mob that attacked Addie at Schulman's. Was that Woden's doing? Could he be here? Had he stoked the crowd's rage? That would be Woden's way, concoct some elaborate scheme to catch Addie in his net, as he had with Madelyn. The man enjoyed playing games. The more dramatic the better.

Wasn't he equally guilty of playing games? Keeping secrets from Virginia, from Addie. Addie's words echoed in his ears. *For me to trust you, you have to trust me.* He wasn't in the habit of trusting people, not since Woden. Maybe not even since he was a kid.

Time to break down that wall of mistrust. "Look, Virginia—"

Someone pounded on the door, a barrage of fists that threatened to splinter the wood.

Virginia dropped her fork onto her plate with a clatter. "What in heaven's name...?"

Dunstan signaled to her not to move. No one beyond Addie and Radcliffe knew they were staying at the Savoy. Neither of them would pummel their door like that. He went to the closet, took his revolver from its holster and crept to the door.

More pounding, followed by, "Virginia! Open up. I know you're in there."

Dunstan frowned and pocketed his gun. He swung the door open to see Hans Brandt, about to make another assault on the wood. The lad threw himself into the room. An angry fire reddened his pale skin and his hair stood on end as if he'd been tearing at it with no mercy. Hans gaped at the table and the cozy meal for two then glared at Virginia.

"How could you do this to me?" He spun on Dunstan. "With this flat tire!" He flung up his fists like a middleweight boxer posing before a bout. "Put 'em up."

"Simmer down," Dunstan said. "Before someone gets hurt."

Hans took a wild swing. Dunstan stiffened at the whisk of air too close to his jaw for comfort. He moved fast and wrapped Hans in a headlock. Virginia hurried over, her eyes wide.

"Let me go." Hans writhed and twisted, clawing at Dunstan's arms.

"Hold still," Dunstan demanded. "Don't make me snap your neck." Virginia let out a soft shriek and he scowled at her. Did the minx think he'd really do it? "If you'll stop squirming and listen to what my *cousin* Virginia has to say, I'll let you go. I might even let you walk out of here alive. Deal?"

Brandt wriggled again, swearing a blue streak in German and English. Dunstan admired his tenacity, but it bordered on stupidity. He shoved his forearm into the man's windpipe, making him choke.

"Do we have a deal, Mr. Brandt?"

He squeaked a yes and Dunstan let go so fast the man staggered.

Hans cursed and rubbed his throat. "Stupid ape," he snarled.

"I've been called worse." Dunstan stepped out of his reach. "Now, why don't you tell us what in hell you're doing here."

"A friend told me you were untrue, so I followed you," he spat at Virginia. "You lied about staying with your aunt. You've been with *him* the whole time. You played me for a sap."

Dunstan winced. Had he been so painfully, nakedly wounded when he'd learned of Madelyn's betrayal? Had his last words and angry accusations sounded like this to her? Desperate, full of impotent rage.

"How can you think such a thing, Hansie?" Virginia cooed, taking his hand.

The fury should've drained from him like air from a balloon. It didn't. Brandt's eyes flashed with fury. His body remained rigid, his expression murderous.

Virginia set her chin and tried again, reaching up to stroke his cheek. "Think about how much you love me, darling. How I'm the only person in the world that matters to you."

Hans howled like a maimed tiger and shoved her so hard she thumped to the carpet. Dunstan itched to throttle him again but settled for trying to push some calm into the man's brain. He hit a solid wall.

Then Hans bolted from the room. The door banged shut behind him.

Dunstan helped Virginia up. She clung to him, trembling. "What happened? My whammy didn't work at all. I've never felt vibrations that angry."

Dunstan scowled at the door. "I have."

He didn't have to explain. "Woden!" she cried. Terror laced her voice.

He nodded. His nemesis was here. Dunstan knew that beyond a shadow of a doubt. Woden had incited that frothing mob at the store. Only Woden could turn a man's vibrations as dark and angry as Brandt's were. Only a power as strong as Woden's could block Virginia's gift, and mute Dunstan's own.

Cursing his stupidity for not realizing it and acting sooner, Dunstan went for his coat and shrugged it on. "Virginia, make sure you lock the door. Don't open it to anyone but me. Understand?"

"Of course." She twisted a blonde curl, her hand shaking. "If you catch Hans, please don't hurt him."

"I'm not going after him." He grabbed his cigarettes and lighter and shoved them into his pocket. "I'm going to Addie's. To keep an eye on *her*. To keep her safe. I wasn't sure about Woden before, but I am now. That fucker's here. He's gotten his claws into Hans. I'm sure as hell not going to let him get to Addie."

He paused outside the door long enough to hear the lock click into place then took the stairs two at a time—

the elevator was too slow.

His heart pounded like a drumbeat, his blood pumped with fear and anger and despair at the thought of losing Addie. He fought to corral those feelings before they joined with the emotions he'd absorbed and exploded into crippling terror. Or uncontainable rage.

Dunstan had to focus on only one thing. His duty. He had to keep Addie from falling into Woden's hands, at all costs. The enemy would be unstoppable with a seer as powerful as her on their side.

He reached the lobby. Steeling himself for what was to come, he dashed out into the frigid night.

Chapter Twenty-Seven

Michael Feeney squeezed his jalopy between two spanking new cars parked at the curb. He got out, unfolding his long legs, and headed for the Brandt family's townhouse. He hated coming here, probably as much as the Brandts hated seeing him here. The Brandt and the Feeney families weren't exactly bosom pals, despite Michael's old man working at that stiff house all these years, and his brothers playing pallbearer a couple times a week.

He preferred his family's bungalow on the south side. The heat was busted more often than it worked, and they needed new slate on the roof, but it had something this stuffy old pile didn't. Love. And laughter. These ghouls never cracked a smile in their lives. He didn't know how Addie could stand living here.

Frau Brandt answered the door. She wore a black dress, a dark sweater, and an unwelcoming expression. "Yes, Mr. Feeney?"

Funny how vile his name sounded on her thin lips. "Uh, is Hans at home?"

Her pale blue eyes poked him. "Certainly not. You of all people should know he is at work."

Swell. She didn't know her precious boy hadn't been to work since Monday. Didn't know he'd been fired, and Michael had the kid's final pay envelope in his pocket. And she obviously didn't know where her son had gotten off to.

He shifted from foot to foot under her stare. Now what? No way would he break the bad news to her. She might be five-foot-nothing and so thin she'd blow out to sea in a stiff wind, but she scared Michael half to death.

"Yeah, you're right. I forgot, Mrs. Brandt," he said, backing down the steps. "Sorry to bother you."

Michael dragged toward his car, his gaze pasted to the sidewalk, as grumpy as hell. Fat Charlie had been riding him and the crew like they were a nag on its way to the glue factory. Da said he might be out of a job soon if they couldn't scare up more customers. And Michael expected a notice from the draft board any day now. He had enough to worry about without having to chase down Hans to give him his dough.

His gut churned most when he thought about his brothers. They'd filled out the enlistment papers. Next step, a doctor's checkup. After that, a one-way trip to the regular Army. Heading to the Pacific by the end of the year, or maybe marching in Da's bootsteps into a muddy trench in France. His brothers thought it a big joke, especially Danny, who blustered about all the enemy sons of bitches he'd kill once he got hold of a rifle.

"You on the hunt for Hans, too?"

Michael jerked to a stop and looked up, tempted to rub

his eyes to make sure he wasn't seeing things. The girl from the bus stop last week stood in front of him. He'd never forget that face. Or that figure, even buried under a heavy coat with a thick fur collar. A compact little number wrapped in golden ringlets and balanced on the highest of high heels.

"Yeah, that I am, sis," he said. "What's your beef with Hans?"

"We had a date and that devil stood me up. Do you know where's he's gotten to?"

She had a soft, Southern purr that tickled his spine. "Now I know Hans is off his nut. How could he leave a looker like you standing in the cold?"

"My, aren't you fresh." She stepped closer, giving him a sly smile that got Michael's blood pumping. And his head humming. "What's *your* beef with our absent friend?"

Michael hesitated. He didn't want to confess he had the kid's pay burning a hole in his pocket. For all he knew, that could be what blondie was after. He hated to think this dolly could be involved in something hinky, but you never could tell.

"Just stopped by to say hello," he said finally. "Hans is my cousin. I mean, he's my cousin's cousin."

"Addie? Addie Brandt is your cousin?"

Michael frowned. "She is, and no, I won't ask her to tell your fortune."

"Oh, it's not like that at all." She flashed a blinding smile. "Addie and I are friends. She's a delightful girl." She held out her hand. She wore lacy gloves, the same color as her green coat, which was the same color as her eyes. "My name's Virginia."

He raised an eyebrow but shook her hand anyway. She

had a solid grip for a girl. His head droned like an idling engine. Christ, he had to ease up on the whiskey this early in the day. "Pleasure, Virginia. I'm Michael."

"You have a gift." She smiled again, a grin so infectious he couldn't help smiling back.

"Of course I do. I'm Irish."

She laughed, a sound like an angel. "That's not what I mean." Sleet began to fall. It ticked off the parked cars and the pavement. She glanced up at the gray sky and clutched her collar. "You have the most horrible weather in these parts. I know it's been nearly a week since we last met, but is your offer of a ride still good?"

Michael waffled. He didn't want to leave her stranded, but he also didn't want to torture himself, driving with this beauty close by his side. Inhaling her sweet perfume, having her gaze at him with those saucy green eyes, all the time knowing he couldn't touch her. Or run his fingers through those curls. And never, ever, taste those inviting lips.

"Please?"

Her sugar-coated appeal went right to Michael's heart. He groaned inwardly. Let the torture begin. "All right, sis, you've got a ride. Where you headed?"

She slipped her arm through his and his breath nearly stopped.

"Wherever you want to go, sugar," she said.

$\sim$

Addie settled in her usual seat at the end of the counter and took off her coat. Sal's was stuffy and warm today, but she kept on the wool cardigan she wore over her long-sleeved white blouse. Father had lowered the heat at work to practically zero to save on gas and she'd been shivering all morning. She feared he'd douse all the lights next to save electricity.

He might even close the business altogether if what happened overnight continued. Vandals had egged the front door and several windows. Because of the war with Germany, or because of Addie, she couldn't be sure. Perhaps both. Upset and angry, she'd helped Uncle Pat clean up the eggshell mess. She'd never seen her uncle so rattled. Father, too, but he still refused to call the police.

Sally, the waitress with the aching bunions, limped over with a cup of coffee, interrupting Addie's gloomy thoughts.

"Where's Rosa today?" Addie asked.

Sally shrugged. "Beats me. I only know she didn't come in and left me with all the work."

"Didn't come in? That's not like her. Do you know what's wrong? Is she sick?"

"How should I know? Look, you gonna flap your gums all day or you gonna order?"

Addie resisted the urge to snarl back at her and ordered the tuna salad, silently wishing Sally's bunions a speedy recovery.

She sipped her coffee, wondering what to do now. She'd come here today to see Rosa. Well, actually, she'd come here hoping Dunstan had stopped by to see Rosa, hoping she could see *him*. Selfish, she knew, but she hadn't heard a peep from him all morning and was growing desperate. Growing more convinced Dunstan had decided he didn't want her for his team and had cut her loose, as if she were a puny minnow caught in his net of robust cod.

Perhaps the wise thing to do. What good would she be to anyone if she kept floundering around inside a test subject's mind, panicking until Dunstan pulled her out? Or if she continued to swoon like a frightened, weak-livered fool. Maybe she should give up trying to use her gift at all. Father would like that.

She frowned. But would she?

Then there was her other predicament. For the first time in her life she'd gotten close to a man, and she couldn't have him. Rosa wasn't the only woman in the way. Addie had heard the ache in Dunstan's voice when he spoke of Madelyn. He still cared for her, and the guilt he felt for her death weighed heavily on him.

Why couldn't she have fallen for a more conventional man, like good old stiff and stuffy Wilhelm? Or Pete Bowdoin? He was a policeman. They didn't come more solid than that. But no, her treacherous heart just *had* to dance a jig over a man Agent Thompson had warned her to stay away from. A man Father would never accept.

A man who didn't give two figs about her.

Addie sighed. She couldn't do anything about her feelings, but she could demand an answer about her future with Dunstan's team. She made up her mind. As soon as she finished lunch, she would track him down and ask him. She remembered he'd given her his address, a hotel on the south side. She'd start there.

Her sandwich arrived moments later, delivered by Sal

himself. Almost as tall as Dunstan, the restaurant's owner had meaty arms and a belly that proved the chef sampled his own wares.

Addie tensed. Surely Sal's personal delivery wasn't a social call.

"Here ya go." He slid the plate in front of her then hesitated. "I wonder if you have an inkling of where Rosa might be?"

She shook her head. Sal sighed. His breath smelled like an overstuffed icebox, heavy on the onions.

"She's been out of work for two days," he said. "Didn't call, or send a note, or nothin'. I sent the busboy round to her place. Her mother hasn't seen Rosa since Wednesday when she left for work. Sally thinks she's with a man she's been gumming about, Dunstan or something. I know Rosa's no angel, but that ain't like her to run off with some fella without telling me or her ma." He wiped his hands on his greasy apron and gazed at Addie in frustrated appeal. "You sure you don't know where she's got to?"

Addie's heart thumped in alarm. "No, I'm sorry, Mr. Mancini. I have no idea. The last time I saw her was also Wednesday."

Shoulders drooping, Sal went back to work. Addie picked at her sandwich, fretting. As dependable as rain in April, Rosa rarely missed work. She'd been upset when she'd come to Addie's house the other day. Could that be related to her vanishing act?

Perhaps Dunstan knew.

Addie pushed her half-eaten lunch away and stood, now even more anxious to see him. She placed two bits on the counter for her sandwich and a tip, put on her overcoat and headed for the door, hoping he could answer all her questions.

~

Dunstan sat in his car, munching on peanuts he'd picked up from a street vendor. Trying to stay awake.

He'd never spent so much time in a vehicle as he had on this mission. He'd slept fitfully in the driver's seat outside Addie's house last night then followed her father's car to the funeral parlor and made sure she got into the building unscathed. After a stop at the Savoy to wash up, change clothes and to check on Virginia, he'd hurried back to Addie. He'd followed her to Sal's, and now sat parked outside.

Edgy enough about Addie, he didn't need Virginia to worry about. They'd argued. She wanted to find Hans, he wanted her to stay at the hotel. She'd won. Virginia was like a small dog with a large bone. Tenacious as hell. He couldn't stop her. The main reason he and Madelyn had recruited her, but her stubbornness could be damned inconvenient, especially now, with Woden on the loose.

What that Nazi creep wanted with Hans, Dunstan didn't know. He knew what the man wanted with Addie, though, and if he hadn't been following her that day at Schulman's, Woden would have her now. He knew one more thing. When he saw Woden, he wouldn't hesitate— he'd kill him. Be done with him once and for all. No one but Hitler would cry for that bastard. Radcliffe would probably give him a medal.

He sat up, alerted. Addie stepped out of the restaurant.

Too soon after she'd arrived, not enough time for a meal. Something was wrong.

His car started with a grumble, and he eased into traffic. He followed slowly. His heart told him to pluck Addie off the sidewalk and bundle her inside his car, warm and safe. But his head insisted he let her be. Even as it started to sleet and she turned up her coat collar, hunching against the cold. Even as traffic began to back up behind him.

God help him, he was using her as bait.

He rolled forward. Icy pebbles of sleet tapped against the windshield. He turned the switch and the wipers beat a steady rhythm across the glass. Addie rounded a corner. That was when Dunstan noticed him. He'd been so focused on watching for Woden, he nearly missed the other fella on her tail.

Couldn't be a coincidence. The man matched Addie's pace, crossed each street she crossed, turned each corner she turned. Why? What in the Sam Hill was he up to?

Dunstan slowed his car even more, earning him an angry horn honk from behind. His car fell back until he drew alongside Addie's bloodhound. He shot the man a glare that would defrost an iceberg, earning him a scowl in return. There could be a logical reason the fella shadowed her.

Dunstan felt for his gun, holstered under his arm. Or the man could be a threat.

Crunch.

His attention snapped forward. Damn it. He'd knocked into the car in front of him, stopped at the light. He looked back to the sidewalk. Addie's pursuer had vanished. Ahead, Addie crossed the street at an intersection. He swung his car around the Chevrolet coupe he'd dinged and stepped on the gas. The driver shook his fist at Dunstan as he flew past. He had no time to deal with that. And he'd deal with Addie's shadow later.

Dunstan knew where she headed in such a hurry—to see him.

Chapter Twenty-Eight

Addie hadn't been in this section of Goveport in a long time, not since she and Mother had shopped for fabric swatches at Weintraub's to make a quilt. For Mother to make, really. Another of Addie's failings. She was all thumbs when it came to stitching. Wearing gloves had put a crimp in her pursuit of that activity. That had to be five years ago at the least, and the south side had only gotten seedier since then.

She stopped at the corner, waiting to cross Sherwood Boulevard. The Savoy stood across the way, eight stories of crumbling brick, bay windows with peeling paint, and turrets with rusting gargoyles peering out to sea. The hotel had once been the height of luxury, its swanky restaurant the meeting place for the city's elite shipping magnates but had gone to pot along with the rest of the neighborhood.

The light changed and Addie stepped off the curb. Mother Nature couldn't make up her mind today and had decided to deliver a delightful mix of sleet and snow this afternoon. She shivered. Not from the weather. The back of her neck had prickled the whole walk here, as if a hundred pairs of eyes followed her. Dunstan's story about Woden, and now Rosa's disappearance, had her as jumpy as bedsprings.

The Savoy's wide oak door opened with a squeal of hinges, and she stepped into the building. She shifted her focus to a real fear, going to see Dunstan. Alone. At his hotel. Aunt Trudy would be scandalized, maybe Marta too. Father would lock her up forever if he knew.

There was no elevator man, so Addie slid the creaking gate shut herself and pushed the button for the sixth floor. The car took a hundred years to shudder to its destination, further tasking her already taut nerves.

She padded down a carpeted corridor that smelled of boiled cabbage. A radio blared from down the hall. A woman's voice shrilled through a nearby door. At number 603, she raised her hand to knock when her belly tightened at an aching thought. What if Rosa was inside, with Dunstan? What if she'd been here since Addie last saw her on Wednesday?

She ground her teeth. So what? At least she would learn where Rosa had run off to and put everyone's mind at ease.

Addie rapped on the door. Nothing. She knocked again.

"No one home but us mice," Dunstan said, striding down the hall. His hat and coat were speckled with wet, and he breathed heavily, as if he'd just run up the stairs.

"Oh, Dunstan, I—" Her heart pounded a breathtaking tempo, seeing him. "I-I need to talk to you."

He released a soft, almost nervous chuckle. "No conversation ends well that begins like that."

He seemed unsettled as he fit the key in the lock. His hand shook. He finally got the door open and stepped back, gesturing her inside. Her nose told her everything she needed to know about him, the smell of cigarettes and liquor. And perfume. Addie stiffened. *Not* Rosa's brassy perfume. A sweet, flowery scent that seemed familiar, but she couldn't quite place. Could he be seeing another woman? Or was the scent a remnant of the suite's previous occupant?

She fidgeted as she watched him peel off his overcoat and unbuckle a gun holster slung over his left shoulder. He hung them both in the closet, then did the same for her coat and hat. He dug his cigarettes and lighter out of the coat's pocket and closed the closet door.

"Take a seat." He went to a small table laden with bottles. "Want a drink?"

She shook her head. She went goofy in his company sober. She couldn't imagine the puddle she'd become with alcohol in her belly.

She settled on the sofa and took off her gloves, careful not to touch anything. She took in the shabby suite, noting the tidy kitchen area, the bathroom next to it and two closed doors on either side of the parlor. Bedrooms, she presumed. Why did one man need two bedrooms? Why did he need an entire suite?

He came over and tossed his cigarettes and lighter on the coffee table. The lighter fell off and bounced onto the carpet, but he didn't seem to notice. The sofa cushions dipped as he sat beside her. He slugged back a good amount of his drink, as if trying to douse a fire.

"What do you want to talk about?" he asked, his voice

deeper, huskier than usual. "Is it your vision? Do you remember any other details?"

Of course, business. Why did she think he'd be happy to see her? "It's Rosa. She's missing."

He put down his glass, his brow furrowing. "What do you mean, missing?"

"Her mother hasn't seen her since Wednesday. Neither has Sal. He's concerned. She rarely misses work."

He turned toward her. His knee brushed hers and he quickly moved it away. "Are you sure she's not off with some man?"

She gazed at him steadily. "Dunstan, that's why I'm here."

His cheeks darkened and his eyes glimmered with anger. "As you can see, she's not here. I haven't seen Rosa since last Saturday when we went to the Oceanside."

"But she said... She said the two of you were seeing each other every night. That you were crazy about her."

"Look, Addie, I'll put my cards on the table," he said after a painfully long pause. "I wanted to get close to you and I thought the only way to do it was through Rosa. I used her."

A strange mix of excitement, hurt, and disappointment flip-flopped in her belly. "Oh, Dunstan."

"Yeah, I know. I'm a louse." He ran his hand through his thick hair, pushing it in all directions. "I'm not proud of what I did. I'm not proud of a lot of things I've done. Rosa's a nice girl and I saw the mistake in leading her on right away. I haven't seen her since Saturday."

"I see," she said slowly. "Well, where could she be? Everyone's worried about her. Perhaps I could get something of hers and use the Sight to see if I can find her."

"No," he blurted. "Don't do that. I mean, it's not a good idea."

"Why not? Why don't you want me to?"

"Because..." He downed the rest of his drink and slapped the glass on the table. He locked his eyes on her, his gaze smoldering with a fire that seemed to scald her from head to toe. "Because I care about you too much to put you through that again."

"Oh?" *Oh.* Oh!

Addie's breath caught and every heated thought she'd ever had about him burst to the surface. He held her captive in his gaze. She moved closer, almost on instinct, and tipped her head back. A heartbeat passed then he drew her into his arms—and they kissed.

Excitement and joy raced through her, exploding in every part of her body at the unfamiliar sensation of a man's lips pressed to hers. He tasted warm and sweet and tangy, whiskey and tobacco. He shifted and deepened their kiss. Trembling, she gripped his broad shoulders and turned her head to better welcome his exploration. Turned her body too and pressed against him with blissful abandon, releasing all fear and doubt, giving herself to him. Like a normal woman tasting her first kiss.

The first kiss, she hoped, of many to come.

Dunstan had never tasted lips so sweet, never felt a body so pliant. Never felt such electricity. Never felt anything like this before. Cripes, he wanted to hold her and kiss her all afternoon. Maybe forever.

But he couldn't. He had to put the brakes on this foolishness he'd started. It took every ounce of will he possessed to detach himself from those willing lips and pull back.

Addie's cheeks flushed bright pink. She blinked at him, surprised or maybe disappointed. "Sorry, I shouldn't have—"

"No. *I* should apologize." He snatched up his drink, realized he'd emptied the glass and put it back down.

"I shouldn't have come here, shouldn't have bothered you," she said, her voice strained.

"No bother. My fault." He grabbed his Luckys off the table and shook a cigarette free from the package. He looked around for his lighter, frantic and unsettled. How could he let himself kiss her? A woman under his care. He couldn't take advantage of her like that. He beat at his pockets. Where was that damned lighter?

"Are you looking for this?" Addie gestured to a glint of silver on the floor.

She bent down and scooped it up. Her body suddenly stiffened, and her breath came in short gulps. Her fingers curled around the lighter, holding it so tight her knuckles whitened. She flopped back against the sofa and her eyes rolled back into her head.

Dunstan dropped his cigarette. He went as still as a statue. Son of a bitch.

She'd been pulled into the Sight.

∿

A ddie propelled down a dark tunnel. She pinged back and forth and every which way, spinning like an out-of-control carnival ride. Terrifying images and sensations bombarded her. People shouted and screamed. A voracious fire devoured a towering structure. Snow fell and the wind blew, but the inferno heated the air as if it were summer.

Sgt. Gillis stood near her, drenched in sweat. Addie focused, reached deeply into her mind—if the Sight hadn't dropped her into the sergeant's body, then whose skin had she slipped into?

"You fool, it's sabotage," Gillis cried, glaring at someone behind her. "Why did you do it?"

Addie tried to turn and see who Gillis accused, when a flash of movement dangerously close to the burning structure seized her attention. A man silhouetted by the flames crumpled to the ground. The fire leapt out at the fallen man and in an instant, flames shimmered up his legs, devouring him whole.

Quaking in terror, the woman Addie inhabited raced after Gillis and another man toward the blaze. Her lungs scorched from the smoke. Her shoes sank into the slushy snow as she ran. A woman's shoes, dressy pumps not suited to winter.

Addie struggled to make sense of the chaos. Someone else would be at the fire with Sgt. Gillis. A woman who'd touched Dunstan's lighter. Not Rosa. She was tall, buxom. This woman felt smaller.

Suddenly, a tremendous force slammed into her mind. She fought to free herself, desperately tried to tear away, but the energy latched onto her like a vengeful undertow and pulled her down. The force gave one last satisfied tug and yanked Addie out of the vision as if it jerked a rug out from under her feet.

Fuzzy images and muffled sounds and scents of a different scene began to take shape. Voices murmuring, the crash of waves breaking on the shore. The smell of wet beach sand, kerosene, and musty, rotting wood. The feel of the new being she'd sunk into. Another woman. Addie tried to dig deeper into her consciousness, but the woman's energy threw up a wall, blocking her.

She concentrated on her physical surroundings instead. She paced the floor of a frigid hole of a building, a shed or boathouse, maybe. She wore trousers and boots with heels that slipped on the slick wood-planked floor. She stopped moving and turned her gaze on a dark figure, sitting against the wall and lit by a dull glimmer from the kerosene lamp. He wore no shirt. His muscled chest rose and fell in measured breaths.

Dunstan.

Addie's heart lurched. What was he doing here?

"Did you enjoy undressing me, sugar?" he asked, his voice muted and echoing.

Addie as the woman took a long, slow drag on her cigarette, eyeing him. "Oh yes. Just like the old days." She flicked ashes to the wet floor. "You remember the old days, don't you Jack? When we were in love."

Addie moaned, awash in aching emotions. She tried to flee, to break away from the painful images and a future she couldn't bear to see. She heard Dunstan call to her from the physical world. She tried to edge toward his voice, but the woman's energy held her like a grasping hand. It curled around her mind, trapping her.

Dunstan's image wavered then sharpened. "What happens now?" he asked.

"I'm sorry, Jack," Addie as the woman said in a heavy, mournful voice. "But you have to pay for what happened to that Italian girl."

Shock raced through Addie's veins, followed by dread. *Rosa*. What had they done to her?

Dunstan's expression went as cold as death and he spoke, his words drowned out by Dunstan from outside the Sight calling her name again, anxious, fearful, begging her to return to him. The woman stiffened and glanced over her shoulder. Addie shivered. Had she heard him? Could she feel Addie here, in her mind?

No. Voices from beyond the shed's door had caught her attention. A breath of fear broke through the barrier the woman had put up between her and Addie. Fear for herself, and for Dunstan.

She turned back to him, hiding her turmoil. "I've got to go. Don't go anywhere."

"I wouldn't think of it," he said then looked her in the eye with a challenge. "Tell me. Did you ever love me?"

The woman dropped her cigarette and ground it under her heel, avoiding his gaze. "No, Jack. I never loved you."

Dunstan from the real world called again. He touched Addie's face and a gentle wave of calm rolled in. The wall the woman had erected began to buckle. As the energy binding the two of them together splintered, the woman's emotions gushed through in a torrent that took Addie's breath away—and exposed the woman's lie.

She had loved Dunstan. She *still* loved him.

And she hated him for it.

Chapter Twenty-Nine

"Addie, come back to me," Dunstan called again.

He hovered over her, his chest tight. What did she see? What visions tormented her? What was wrong with her? The other times she'd gone into the Sight, she'd thrashed about, quivering in fear. This time, she barely breathed. She slumped back against the sofa, as still and pale as a corpse.

He pried his lighter from her grip, cursing himself for letting her get hold of the damned thing. She couldn't have gotten a vision off it from him, but she could from Virginia. She'd handled this hunk of metal a few times. Only days ago, to light a cigarette for him.

Could she be trapped in Virginia's mind, in a future of untold horror? His blood stilled. Was something awful going to happen to Virginia? Or did Addie see another attack? The Germans this time?

"Addie." He grasped her cold hands. "Addie, wake up."

Nothing. She didn't stir. Her body temperature seemed to have plummeted, and her breathing slowed to near nothing. Frantic, he cupped her face and rubbed his thumbs over her icy cheeks.

"Come back to me. *Now*." He reached into her mind and gave a hard jerk. The emotions rushing along her vibrations abruptly changed course and shot into him like a bullet from a gun. Fear and heartbreak flooded him. His vision clouded, but he remained focused, draining every ounce of those feelings from Addie's mind.

She moaned and stirred. What seemed like eons later, her eyelids fluttered open. "I never loved you," she murmured sleepily.

Dunstan jerked back as if she'd punched him in the mouth.

No time to mull that over. She came out of it for real. He let out his breath as her stiff posture relaxed and she sat up. Her gaze darted around the room. Her cheeks were still deathly white, but her breathing had returned to normal.

"Welcome back," he said. "I thought you were gone for good." His smile of relief faded. She stared at him like she didn't know him. Like a stranger who meant her harm. "Addie, what's wrong?"

She pushed him away and leapt off the couch. She turned and gaped at him, opening and closing her mouth several times. Good god, the Sight must've shown her something unspeakable.

"Out with it," he demanded. "What happened? What did you see?"

"I-I saw you, with..." She shook her head, as if to clear her mind. "Rosa." She clenched her fists by her side, her accusing eyes on him. "What did you do to her?"

His blood ran cold. "Rosa? What did I do—?" He

struggled for control. "Damn it, what did the Sight show you? Tell me."

"Oh, Dunstan, you're back," Virginia sing-songed as she sailed into the suite. "Don't be peeved I was out so long. I couldn't find Hans, but found another one like—"

She spotted Addie and snapped her mouth shut. Dunstan groaned. He'd been so wrapped up in Addie he hadn't heard Virginia at the door.

Addie's gaze darted back and forth between the two of them. Shock, anger, and the pain of betrayal flashed across her face. A booshwa explanation for why a woman Dunstan had supposedly just met suddenly waltzed into his hotel room died on his lips. So did the truth. Why bother? Addie had figured out the most damning part of the story.

He'd lied to her. Over and over again.

"Addie darling, please," Virginia cried. "It's not what you think."

"Yes, it is." Addie bolted to the closet, nearly knocking Virginia over, and flung open the door. "It's *exactly* what I think. And *worse*." She tore her coat from the hanger and whipped it over her shoulders. She glared at Virginia. "How could you lead my cousin on like that? When you've been here with him? You should be ashamed." She swung on Dunstan. "And *you*! You lying, deceitful, murderous snake!"

A rock the size of Gibraltar settled in his stomach. That about covered everything.

"Where is she?" she demanded. "Where's Rosa? What have you done with her?"

He held up his hands. "I don't know what you're talking about."

"Really, Dunstan? *Another* lie?" She reached for the door handle, jerked her hand back and fumbled with her gloves, trying to put them on in a hurry.

"Addie, stop," he ordered. His sternness had the desired effect. She froze and turned those baby blues on him. "You're wrong about me, about Virginia, about *everything*. Now sit down and we'll talk it over like normal adults."

The wrong thing to say. He knew that as soon as the words clunked from his mouth. His heart broke to see her hurt expression, and the way she drew into herself, like a flower's petals curling for protection from a storm.

"Dunstan," she said, tears in her voice. "You of all people should know, I'm not normal. I'm Addled Addie, freak of nature. Sometimes I don't like what I see, but at least I know it's the truth."

She threw open the door and stormed from the room.

He wanted to chase her, but he couldn't move. Fear—his own and Addie's—weighed him down, turning his feet to stone. The elevator's bell dinged a moment later, followed by the rumble of the doors closing.

She was gone.

He exhaled in frustration. "Great timing, Virginia."

She shut the door with a soft click. "I'm so sorry. If I had any idea she was here, I'd have stayed away."

He knew that. He shouldn't bite her head off. It was *his* fault. The whole goddamn mess. He went to the window and pulled the curtain aside. Sleet ticked against the windowpane. He looked down, watching for Addie. The roads were shiny and icy slick, and so was the sidewalk.

"Dunstan," Virginia said, tentative, as if afraid he'd

snarl at her again. "I have news, about Hans. Well, a little about him, it's more about this man I met."

He frowned at her, not really in the mood. "Get on with it," he bit off.

"Well, this man, his name's Michael Feeney." She hesitated then blurted the rest. "He works with Hans. Well, used to. Michael says the poor boy's been fired. On account of not showing up all week. Michael says he saw Hans get into a brawl on Monday. A fight that happened out of thin air and stopped just as fast."

Dunstan nodded and turned back to the window. "Woden. You know he enjoys causing a scene." He saw Addie come out of the building. She bent against the pelting sleet and rushed up the sidewalk.

"There's more," Virginia said. "Michael Feeney is Addie's cousin. He has her gift. We don't need her now. I'm certain we can recruit him—"

"I don't want him. I want Addie."

"Oh, really? Since when do you want *her*? I remember you said you had no interest in Addie. That she was only an asset to be used."

"I did," he said with a bitter sigh. "And by god I meant it." He flung the curtain back into place and eyed Virginia, his heart as heavy as lead. "But isn't it time we both admit I'm the biggest fool on earth?"

Chapter Thirty

"Feeney, you remember Walt Nowak?" Fat Charlie said around a mouthful of pastrami sandwich. "Worked that job with us at the shipyard last year? He got married last week. Wife's got headlights like goddamn bowling balls." He cupped his hands in front of his chest and laughed. "Lucky bastard. She'll be keeping him busy, that's for sure."

Seated across the small wooden table, Michael bent over his egg salad sandwich, eating with his gloves on. Trying to ignore his boss. Hard to do. For the first time in a long time, Michael was sober. Stone sober and he didn't like it much. He didn't much like being drunk either, but better to be soused than having a clear head. Sober, he felt the bitter wind whipping off the ocean, smelled the pine planks being laid across the tower's wooden skeleton, and every pop of the hammer was like a blow to his brain.

But the downright worst thing about being sober—he caught every word flapping from Fat Charlie's mouth.

Michael had decided to take a break from booze after

he'd met Virginia yesterday. That little blonde had given him a reason to try being sober. Whiskey made him forget, and right now, he wanted to remember. Remember every detail of his afternoon with her and everything she'd told him about her power and his own. They'd spent an hour chewing things over in his car, then picked up some sandwiches and talked for another hour.

It seemed fantastical. There were others out there like her, like Addie and him. A gift, Virginia had called the Sight. She called the love potion she could turn off and on at will a gift too. Hadn't always been that way. She'd told him before she'd learned to control her power, men fought over her wherever she went, and she had no idea why.

"I think I inherited my gift from my granny," she'd said. "She was a fierce and practical Polish woman who got accused of being a shameless flirt. Poor dear, she had no idea why men circled her like moths around a flame."

Michael thought about that long and hard. Except for Addie, no one else in his family had shown even a hint of the Sight. But Da liked to spin a yarn or two about the relatives back home in Ireland, folks who told fortunes and were right nine times out of ten.

When he and Virginia were all talked out, he'd dropped her at the Savoy Hotel. She promised she'd be in touch after she told her boss about him and could arrange for them to meet. A fella called Dunstan, who'd already explained everything to Addie and could show him how to use his power too. And tell him how he could help win the war.

Michael stared over Fat Charlie's right shoulder into the trees, his thoughts whirling. If he could learn how to tame the Sight, he could hug Ma again. Hold Virginia's hand or kiss her good night when he walked her to her door. Do a hell of a lot more when they were alone, without fearing what he might see.

Most of all, if he could control this strange power, he'd use it to find out when and where his brother Danny was going to get hit—and save his life. He would look into his other brothers' futures too, before they marched off to war.

A movement in the distance caught his eye. His skin prickled. Someone was there. Not *there* as if he'd lost his way. More like lurking, peering out from behind a tree. Spying. Michael glanced at Fat Charlie, who dug at his gums with a toothpick. Maybe he'd been fretting about sabotage and troublemakers all this time with good reason.

Michael decided he'd go take a look. Excusing himself, he faked like he headed for the outhouse then swung left and doubled back through the trees. He ducked under low branches and slipped on pine needles and icy patches of ground to the spot where he'd seen the movement.

He found nothing.

He pushed out an aggravated breath. He hadn't been mistaken. He'd seen someone. The fella had probably heard Michael coming and bolted. Better tell Fat Charlie, anyway. Maybe get the cops up here for a thorough look-see.

He turned back, when a fist came out of nowhere and bashed him in the mouth. His head snapped back and his lip split. Blood gushed down his chin. Pain rippled across his face. Michael staggered. He swiped the back of his hand over his bloody mouth and gaped at the fella who'd popped him.

Hans Brandt.

"What the fuck—?"

"Don't try to stop me," Hans cried.

The boy's body twitched violently, and he breathed like a stuffed-up engine. His eyes were wild, glazed with madness. Words fell from his mouth in a waterfall of languages. Michael heard the German words for *father* and *tonight*, and in English, "My duty...prove my loyalty...I'll show you all."

Michael's heart pounded. *I'll show you all*. That didn't sound good. Sounded bleak and lethal. He got an idea. A terrible idea he wished he could talk himself out of. The Sight. He had no idea how to use it, but he could try. He might be able to find out what had gotten Hans sputtering and riled up.

Michael threw off his gloves and put up his dukes. "Come on then, you stinker. You wanna fight? Let's fight."

No hesitation. Hans charged like a bull and slammed Michael to the ground. The kid started pummeling. Michael's nose broke with a crack and burst of pain.

Blessed mother, I hope you're on my side.

He grabbed Hans's throat with his bare hands and let the Sight rush in.

Chapter Thirty-One

Addie pulled up a stool and opened her makeup basket. They had a client. An elderly widow from a German family in town, her corpse so small she barely put a dent in her casket's lining.

Having completed his part of the preparation, Uncle Pat sat reading the afternoon newspaper in a chair he'd pulled up to the window. As usual, Uncle Eb was absent, but Father had been busy upstairs, making arrangements with the grieving family. He'd just left to go to the bank to deposit their payment.

Addie bent over her task in the silent room and tried to focus on painting Frau Klein. It had been so long since they'd had a customer, she feared she'd forgotten how. She tucked her tongue into the corner of her mouth to help her concentrate. Would've bitten her tongue too, if the pain could keep out the agonized thoughts swirling through her mind.

Dunstan and Virginia. The fire the Sight kept showing her. The woman she'd inhabited who'd run toward the blaze. Addie felt certain that woman was Virginia. The woman in the boathouse with Dunstan, though—who could she be? That being's vibrations had simmered with great power. Whoever she was, she'd used Dunstan's lighter, and many times, to leave such potent energy behind.

Addie's heart ached, for herself, and for Hans. He must have found out about Virginia and Dunstan and their love nest at the Savoy. That would explain why he'd been so angry all week. Perhaps Rosa had found out too and why she'd come to Addie's the other day, to cry on her shoulder. Maybe she'd run off to lick her wounds or found someone else to help her forget.

Or maybe...

I'm sorry, Jack, but you have to pay for what happened to that Italian girl. The woman's stark accusation repeated over and over in Addie's mind. Surely that didn't mean Dunstan...? She could barely think the word. Had Dunstan *killed* Rosa?

Dunstan was a lot of things. A two-timing skunk, clearly, the way Virginia had sashayed into the suite yesterday like she owned the place. A liar, certainly. He'd claimed to care about Addie, pretended not to know Virginia when they met at the nightclub, and who knew what else he'd been untruthful about. And though he'd been quick to say no when Addie had suggested using the Sight to find Rosa, she refused to believe the man could be a murderer.

At least, she hoped not.

Addie touched the swan brooch Rosa had given her, pinned to her blouse, and a chill ran up her spine. To think, she'd let that louse kiss her. No. She'd kissed him with as much conviction as he'd kissed her. A mortified blush warmed her face. She'd kissed him with abandon, in fact. *He* had put a stop to it. She had no idea how far she would've gone if he hadn't.

The worst sin of all, Dunstan had gotten her to hope. Hope she might have a future. That she could be someone, could use the Sight to do good. Instead, she'd wither away in this basement, with no one but the stiffs and Uncle Pat to keep her company.

She felt a presence at her elbow and looked up to see her uncle standing by her stool, staring at her. "What?" she demanded.

He lifted an eyebrow. "I said she's got enough paint on her face. She's red as a boiled lobster."

Addie stiffened. Frau Klein looked more like a circus clown than a lobster, with red splotches on her cheeks.

"You're awful distracted today. Care to tell your old uncle your troubles?"

She shook her head. What would she tell him? That she and a handsome, two-timing liar who may or may not have done away with her best friend, had kissed? At the Savoy Hotel, of all places.

She bit her lip to stem the tears that threatened to fall and picked up a cloth, bending over Frau Klein and wiping the excess rouge from her cheeks. "I really don't want to talk about it," she muttered.

"Suit yourself." He wandered back to his chair and his newspaper, pretending disinterest, but his concerned gaze lingered on her.

A few minutes later, someone rapped on the alley door. It couldn't be Dunstan. He hadn't come after her when she'd left his hotel and she thought she'd seen the last of his guilt-stricken face. Still, her heart kicked up at the thought he might be at the door, eager to explain and beg her forgiveness.

She closed her makeup basket with a decisive snap. Unless Dunstan had an armful of convincing explanations and Rosa in tow, she doubted she could forgive him. Ever.

"I'll get it," she said, slipping off her stool. Uncle Pat grunted in reply. She opened the door to see... Not Dunstan. For the fourth time in a week, she faced Pete Bowdoin.

He took off his hat, his expression grave. "Addie. I need to speak with you. It's, uh, a delicate matter."

Uncle Pat regarded her with twinkling eyes. "Oh, *now* I know why you been distracted. Go on, I'll hold down the fort."

Addie cringed. He thought Pete was sweet on her. One look at Pete's somber expression and she knew romance was the furthest thing from his mind.

She snatched up her coat and hat, pulled on her gloves, and followed him out the door. "What is it, Pete?" she asked, somewhat shakily as they hurried along the alleyway. "Has something happened?" Her family's faces swam before her eyes. "Has someone been injured?"

"I'm sorry, Addie." He took her arm and led her down the sidewalk toward the waterfront. "Sergeant Gillis asked me to fetch you. We need your help."

Shoes and boots thudded on the pavement as people dashed past them down the hill. Addie's heart leapt. "Is it an attack?" It couldn't be. Everyone ran toward the water, not away. Pete wouldn't lead her toward danger.

"The sergeant wants to ask you a few questions," he said, and nothing more.

Fear threatened to paralyze her. She pushed it back. She couldn't, *wouldn't* be afraid. She shook off Pete's hold and hurried her pace.

He trotted next to her and soon they reached Ocean Boulevard. A fierce wind whipped off the water. She didn't feel the cold as much, because today she'd finally worn her trousers. She spotted a half dozen police cars and an ambulance near the fisherman's memorial. The vehicles' flashing lights cut through the murk of the gray, overcast afternoon. Addie's stomach cramped.

They ran across the street. Pete steered her to the right, along the boardwalk. A crowd had gathered near a gap in the seawall, where a short pier had once stood but now was nothing but two rows of thick, beaten-down pilings.

It seemed as if half of Goveport had turned out. Mostly men, they stood shoulder to shoulder, eerily still, as quiet as church. They looked down into the water. Benny Hirtle, the reporter from the *Goveport Herald*, stood in the crowd, notepad in hand. He swung his gaze Addie's way and licked his lips.

She held her breath and stuck close to Pete as he shoved through the broad-shouldered swarm. Pete hung onto her so she wouldn't slip on the pavement, slick with ice and sea spray and coated with gull droppings.

"What is it?" Addie asked in a shaky voice. "What's down there?"

"There's a body by the dock," a man with a bushy beard said. "Towed in from the north shore by Maheu's boat." He gestured to a rickety fishing boat bobbing nearby, with its painted name, *Mere Marie,* faded and peeling.

"Dead?" Addie managed to ask.

The man snorted. "Cops are fishing it out with a gaffe, so better be."

They came upon Sgt. Gillis at the front of the gawking group. He scowled at her. Pete pointed down into the water eddying around the remains of the old pier. Dread coiled in Addie's belly. She'd seen a body before. Scores of them, some in pretty rough shape. Why should the thought of seeing just one more terrify her so much?

She forced herself to look. The tide rolled in, near high. Gray-blue water lapped at the salt-scored, barnacle-coated pilings. Several policemen had inched down the mucky bank and were nearly hip-deep in what had to be freezing water. Their topcoats floated around them. One of the policemen extended a pole with a sharp-pointed hook on the end, reaching for...

What?

Something bloated and grotesque thwacked against a piling. The creature's coat and green dress were twisted and shredded. Its face had been pecked away by fish and other ravenous things looking for food in the murky brine. Seaweed tangled in its hair.

Hair once black and as shiny as polished onyx.

Bile nicked the back of Addie's throat. She knew whose body floated there. Her knees buckled and she hit the ground with a thud.

Rosa.

∼

Dunstan's head dropped back against the car seat as he struggled to stay awake. He'd been shadowing Addie for days, including last night, and now teetered on exhaustion. He pushed open the car door and climbed out to stretch. The cold slapped him in the face, waking him up.

He lit a Lucky and stared at his lighter for the umpteenth time. What had Addie seen? Something dark and heartbreaking. A sorrow he hadn't absorbed since... He clenched his jaw. Not since Madelyn. *No.* He shook off his foreboding. She was dead. He knew that for a fact.

He squinted at the Brandt building down the street, picturing Addie inside, fuming at him. Her words yesterday had cut him, but her expression had nearly killed him. He'd lost her trust. Lost *her.* Lost her with something he hadn't done. Yet.

He longed to storm in there and demand she tell him what she'd seen, demand she let him explain. He doubted that would work. He'd already had to explain himself too many times for her to believe him now.

Damn it, he'd let things slip from his control because of his own fear. Since Madelyn, he'd been scared. Afraid of screwing up again, afraid of losing his team, the only real family he'd ever known. He'd let that fear cow him. Make him weak.

No more. Time to take charge. He'd win Addie back. He would find out what the Sight had shown her and fix it. If he could convince her to come to Washington with him, he'd tell Radcliffe to take his plan to lock her in a room and stick it in his hat. She would work by Dunstan's side where she belonged. They'd be a team.

And he'd never lie to her again.

He straightened, eyes narrowing at a policeman who loped up the street and steered into the alley to Brandt's side entrance. He'd seen that cop earlier this week, bothering Addie near Colby Park. What brought him here now?

After a tense minute, the cop popped out of the alley with Addie in tow. She threw her coat on and let the man lead her down toward the waterfront. Something was happening down there. Dozens of people rushed along the sidewalk. Police cars screamed up to the curb.

Dunstan's gut squeezed. He flung his cigarette to the ground and followed Addie and the cop at a brisk pace. The pair merged into the crowd. He moved faster to catch up, then stopped dead.

Woden stood at the bottom of the hill.

He wore a long coat and a black hat and stood with his shoulders squared. Dunstan couldn't see Woden's face clearly, but he knew a challenge flashed in the man's eyes. *Come, my friend. Try and stop me.*

Dunstan's blood rushed in fear and fury. The emotions dammed up in the reservoir in his brain surged forward. He set his jaw and mentally held back the raging tide. If he gave in to the anger, terror and even grief now, his feelings would consume him. He'd lose his only chance to stop that son of a bitch.

Woden nodded, as if reading his thoughts, then spun around and moved into the crowd. Toward Addie.

Dunstan raced after him.

Chapter Thirty-Two

Rain started to fall. Droplets splattered Addie's face and joined the tears running down her cheeks. She still sat on the cold ground. Sgt. Gillis helped her up.

"I'm sorry, Miss Brandt," he said. "Did you know the woman?"

Wasn't that why he'd sent Pete to get her? To identify the body? "Yes. It's Rosa. Rosa Conti." Her voice came out hollow, empty.

"Come with me." He took her arm in a strong grip to lead her away from the crowd when someone called his name. He glanced back and winced in annoyance. "Stay here, out of the way."

Addie nodded absently to his broad back as he left. She collapsed onto a nearby bench. Rain had soaked the seat, but she didn't care. Barely noticed. Rosa was dead. Drowned. How could this be?

"Addie," a deep voice rumbled.

She lifted her gaze to see Dunstan eyeing her, his

expression grim. He breathed in shallow gasps. Raindrops rolled around his hat brim and dripped off the edge. He looked like hell. Unshaven, drawn, like he'd been on a bender for a week.

"Rosa's dead," Addie said, her voice flat, wrung of emotion.

"I know," he said gently. "I'm greatly sorry. Please accept my condolences."

Addie turned to the sound of urgent voices at the dock. The policemen hoisted up Rosa's body, wrapped in a sopping blanket and strapped to a board. They laid her on a stretcher while the onlookers gawked. The crowd had swelled to nearly a hundred people, Uncle Pat, Wilhelm, and Agent Thompson among them.

Sgt. Gillis followed the stretcher as its wheels thump-thumped along the pavement to the ambulance at the curb. Addie watched him help Pete and the other men lift then slide the stretcher through doors that gaped like an open mouth.

"She's dead," Addie repeated. New tears threatened. "Everything's changed. The Sight showed me Rosa as an old woman. Married and grown old. But then it didn't. I tried to see her future again and saw nothing. Emptiness." She looked up at Dunstan. "Her future changed. I should've figured it out. I could've stopped it."

"Not your fault, Addie. Woden did this, I'm sure of it." He leaned down and held out his hand. "We need to leave. *Now*."

A knife seemed to pierce her brain. Anger surged and she slapped his hand away. "Don't touch me, you murderer."

He flinched. "What?"

"Woden didn't kill Rosa. You did!" She leapt up off the bench, her fury mounting. "She found out about you and Virginia. She found out about that other woman, too, so you drowned her."

Dunstan swore. "This is Woden's handiwork. He's in your head. Pushing you. Making you angry." He flicked his gaze to his right and spoke in an urgent rush. "He's here, Addie. Right here. He's trying to get to you. Come with me, we need to leave."

"Stop telling me what to do! You can't control me anymore. I've been blinded by my feelings for you—" Another sharp jab to her mind and the words stopped on her lips. What feelings? She felt no love or tenderness toward him. Only hatred. He was a lying snake. He wanted to use her. Like he used Rosa. "Get away from me."

He didn't. He grabbed her wrist and pinned her with a look so intense her breath stuttered to a stop. "It's Woden, Addie. *Fight him*."

Calm crept into the boiling pool in her mind. Her heart urged her to latch onto Dunstan's gift, but another shock of pain speared her brain, then another, again and again like a sharp blade, poking holes in the lid of a tin can. Fury turned Addie's heart dark and bleak.

She broke from his hold and shoved him away. "*You* drowned Rosa!" she cried. "You monster. You *killed* her."

She ended on a shriek of rage that boomed across the boardwalk. The onlookers and policemen swung around. An ugly murmur rippled over the crowd as they surged toward them. Dunstan didn't run, even with the mob closing in, hissing and jeering.

His eyes held fast on her, never wavering. "Fight, Addie. Damn you, *fight*."

More calm flickered through her, shoving against the fury. Both energies vied for control, twisting her every which way, as if she dangled from a kite's tail in a raging storm, pummeled by the winds. Addie took a breath. She had to focus. She reached out to Dunstan's gift and pushed against Woden with all her strength. After what seemed an eternity, she broke free. She blinked away the red haze of fury, but too late.

The mob ripped Dunstan from her side and swept him away. His shouts and commands for them to stop fell on deaf ears. They screamed, tore at his clothing and his hair. They snatched off his hat and stomped it to pieces. They pulled off his overcoat. His cigarette lighter fell out of the pocket and hit the pavement with a metallic *ting*.

Pete shoved to the center of the mob, followed by several other policemen. "Careful boys, he's got a gun," he cried as Dunstan's shoulder holster flashed into view.

Pete swung his Billy club and bashed Dunstan's temple with a sickening thwack. Blood spurted and gushed down the side of his face in a crimson stream. He staggered but remained upright, buffeted by the jeering mob.

And yet, Dunstan's gaze still held hers. "Addie, *run!*"

Pete swung again. Another stomach-turning crack and Dunstan toppled, felled like one of those massive redwoods she'd once compared him to. The mob cheered. Pete worked Dunstan's gun out of its holster and pocketed it. He slapped a pair of handcuffs on him then snapped his wild-eyed gaze toward Addie.

"We warned you about him. He's dangerous," he snarled.

"No, Pete! Please listen." But he didn't. He jerked away from her and helped the other policemen hoist Dunstan off the ground and carry him away. Addie's heart shot up her throat.

Dear lord, what have I done?

She had to help him. She clawed through the crowd, calling out, but the cops tossed their bulky prisoner into a police car's back seat before she could reach them. Pete slammed the vehicle's door and the mob cheered again.

Addie cried out in anguish and frustration, looking around for someone who could help her. The crowd had swelled. People mingled on the walkway, chattering, full of speculation. Uncle Pat was still here but she couldn't see Sgt. Gillis anywhere. Benny Hirtle scribbled furiously on his reporter's notepad. He spotted Addie and steered toward her.

"Don't fret, Miss Brandt. The man was guilty," Agent Thompson said, appearing at her elbow. His eyes held hers. "You did the right thing, turning him in."

"I didn't mean to. A man named Woden made me say those things. I think Woden's responsible for Rosa's death. And he used his power to make everyone here so angry."

"Power?" Thompson's bushy eyebrows drew down. "You've spent too much time with that conman, I'm afraid. Don't tell me you believe Dunstan's ridiculous tales of people with magical gifts."

Addie puffed in indignation, but before she could snap a retort, someone behind her spoke.

In German.

"I am sorry about your friend, Adelaide."

She spun to see Uncle Eb, holding an umbrella, his expression pained. Her eyes widened. He'd been missing for a week. Now, of all the places he could be, he showed up here.

"You don't mean that, Uncle." She knew she sounded like a sullen child, but she didn't care. He seemed ten times more cut up about Rosa than he had about the death of her own mother.

He frowned. "You've had a shock. Come with me. I will drive you home."

She watched the police car pull away from the curb. Could that be Sgt. Gillis behind the wheel? Raindrops spattered the windows so she couldn't see the driver clearly, but she could see Dunstan in the back. She caught his gaze and his expression turned to terror. He threw his shoulder against the car door, trying to get out, shouting something she couldn't hear.

Uncle Eb took her arm, gingerly, as if she might break. "Come along, child. You must come with me."

She eyed her uncle, confused. Maybe she should go home. A cold, empty bitterness settled in the pit of her stomach. She'd gotten Dunstan into this terrible mess, she had to get him out of it. She needed a quiet place to think. To figure out what to do next.

"I suppose you're right, Uncle," she said. "Let's go home."

~

Dunstan struggled to keep his eyes open as the police car rumbled away from the curb. That cop's nightstick had packed quite a wallop. His ears rang like church bells on Sunday. His head spun and blood dripped down the side of his face, clouding one eye.

But he could see clear enough through the window for terror to grip him to the core.

Addie, on the sidewalk—with Woden.

Chapter Thirty-Three

The elevator wobbled slowly upward. Michael paced the car, willing the damned thing to move faster. He'd gotten away from the worksite as soon as he could and hustled over to the Savoy. Frantic to see Virginia, to tell her the fearsome things he'd heard and felt and seen in the mind of Hans Brandt.

He closed his eyes, dredging up every detail of the Sight. The smell of the gasoline Hans would sprinkle at the base of the fire tower. The scratch of the match being struck, the pop of air as the fire burst to life. The crackle of the flames eating the wood like a starving beast.

And that last, angry breath Hans would take as he stepped into the blaze.

Holy hell, Fat Charlie's jitters about sabotage had come true and Hans Brandt was the fella going to do it. For a reason that made some kind of sense in the fool's cock-eyed mind. Michael had heard his jumbled thoughts. Hans had been told the fire tower was really a lookout tower, a place to watch for invaders from the sea. Destroying it would create a blind alley north of Boston, a stretch of ocean close to shore where enemy craft could lurk undetected.

He shuddered. Destroying the tower could help the Axis powers inch closer to victory.

The elevator finally reached the sixth floor. He knocked on Virginia's door, but she wouldn't open up until he'd identified himself. Her eyes widened when she got a look at him.

"Good grief, Michael. What happened to your face?"

He touched his swollen nose and his split lip. He'd almost forgotten about his fight with Hans. "Kissed by a pair of fists. You gonna let me in?"

"Of course." She closed and locked the door once he stepped inside.

She looked as pretty as a picture in a Christmas red dress that hugged her figure and a frilly white apron tied around her waist. She glowed, full of energy and life and smart as a whip. He was smitten, and she hadn't even used her love spell on him.

"I was just fixing dinner for Dunstan, though I doubt he'll be back anytime soon." She untied the apron and tossed it over the back of a chair at a small dining table. "Don't look so surprised, Michael. I *can* cook. You're welcome to join us if you'd like."

He pulled off his hat. His gaze strayed from the table to the kitchen. He caught the smell of chicken frying. She'd told him about her business partner, about how they'd been staying here in separate bedrooms, but the cozy scene lit a jealous fire in him.

"Now Michael, I won't have you going green," she said, resting a fist on her hip. "It doesn't suit you. I told you there's nothing between me and Dunstan. I think his heart's been stolen by your cousin Addie." She took his hat and coat and dropped them over the apron on the chair. "A good thing, I say. Dunstan's *such* a pill when he's broody. Drink?"

She shimmied toward a drink cart loaded with bottles. He caught her by the arm, stopping her. His throat was dry, and he wanted nothing more than to wet it, but he needed a clear head.

Worry lines creased her doll's face. "Dear me, it must be something terrible to put you off mother's milk. Tell me what's happened. Why are you here? And why are you all banged up?"

He swallowed, trying to find the words. "I saw something today that scared me sober. Something the Sight showed me."

She bit her lip and nodded for him to continue.

"I didn't know who to tell," he said. "I thought about going to the cops, but I been in the clink before. I go in with this, they'll probably toss me in the nut house. So, I'm telling you."

He ran through the story as clearly and calmly as he could, but still she went pale.

"He got away from me," he said, finishing up. "Hans is a strong son of a bitch. Flipped me off him like a piece of driftwood. Hightailed it into the forest. I would've stopped him if I could, you know that." She murmured some kind of agreement, and he went on. "We gotta stop him. There's not much time. I heard him babble something about tonight. He's gonna torch the tower tonight, and then..."

He couldn't say the rest, though it scorched his mind.

Then Hans would walk into an inferno. Kill himself, for what? For the fatherland and for ultimate victory? It made no sense.

"That poor boy," Virginia said. Then she gasped. "So that's what Woden's up to. Dunstan thought he'd come to Goveport for Addie. But he's stooped to sabotage now. He's a wicked man, to use Hans like that."

"Woden?" She'd said that name like a curse.

"He's a Nazi agent with an odd fascination with fire. He doesn't care who he kills to get what he wants." She leveled a gaze at him that made goose flesh prickle up and down his arms. "Michael, Woden's mind control powers are *very* strong. He's a formidable foe. You need oodles of strength to fight him. Do you think you can do it?"

"Me?" *Now* he needed that drink. "I came here to tell you. Thought you and that Dunstan fella could take care of the rest."

She stamped her foot. "Michael Feeney! I never took you for a coward. We'll *all* stop this. You, me, and Dunstan. Together."

Michael looked toward one of the windows. Rain hit the panes, making the outside seem as blurry as he wished his brain could be right now. Virginia had him pegged. He was a coward. A yellow belly who'd been running from the Sight, from his feelings, and from his life for so long he didn't know how to be brave.

He swung back to her. She glowered at him, magnificent in her anger. Maybe this girl could show him how. She'd already gotten him to put aside his beloved Old Crow. For the time being, anyway. She'd got him looking at the Sight, and himself, in a new way. Hell, he'd gone after Hans instead of turning away like he always did. Maybe a new, gutsier Michael Feeney lived somewhere inside him. A man ready to take charge.

He made his decision. She wanted his help. She *needed* his help. And by God, he was going to help.

"Stop shooting daggers at me," he said, holding up both hands in surrender. "Count me in. What do you want me to do?"

Her smile lit up her face, and his heart. "First, we need to find your cousin Addie."

"Addie? Why?"

"Because Dunstan will be wherever Addie is. Let's go. I'll tell you everything on the way."

Chapter Thirty-Four

Uncle Eb practically dragged Addie across the boulevard toward his car.

"Wait, stop." She tried to shake him off, but he had a surprisingly iron grip. His fingers dug in, holding her arm as tight as a vise. "I changed my mind. I don't want to go home."

"But Adelaide—"

"No." She finally tore herself free. She'd had it with people telling her what to do, people manipulating her. She had to help Dunstan and she had to help him *now*.

Uncle Eb shouted her name as she dashed back across the street, his cry drowned out by the noise of traffic splashing in puddles as the cars rolled by. She reached the sidewalk on the other side and looked around wildly for a cop who could tell her where they had taken Dunstan, but they had all gone. So had Uncle Pat. Benny Hirtle lingered, talking with the remaining eyewitnesses, his reporter's pencil busy taking down their words.

Perhaps he could help.

She moved toward him when she saw Agent Thompson leaning against the back of one of the benches, mopping his rain-wet face with a handkerchief.

"Please, Agent Thompson," she cried, rushing up to him. "You have to help me. Dunstan didn't do it. I know he didn't. He couldn't hurt anyone. A man named Woden is responsible. You have to believe me."

Agent Thompson folded the handkerchief and slipped it into his overcoat pocket. "Miss Brandt, *I* don't have to believe anything."

Addie's shoulders sagged. She was on her own then. She might as well go with Uncle Eb. If anything, that would get him to stop yelling her name and making such a stink.

"However." Thompson gave her an encouraging smile and her heart lifted. "Since *you* believe so strongly in Mr. Dunstan's innocence, I'll help you to whatever extent I'm able. This is a local matter and I have no jurisdiction, but I can escort you to the police station. I'll stand by you, while you plead your case. Would you like that?"

She bristled at his tone, as if she were a child to be indulged. Nevertheless, Addie would take any help she could get. "I would. And thank you."

She hurried behind Agent Thompson to a smart black Packard. Uncle Eb trotted after them. He called to her in German, turning heads in the lingering crowd, few of them friendly.

Something crunched under her foot. Dunstan's lighter, the thing that had started all this trouble. She scooped it up and slipped it into her coat pocket as Agent Thompson opened the car door. He ushered her inside with an almost theatrical wave of his gloved hand. The soft rain had changed over to snow and big flakes dusted his hat and coat. She settled into the seat, and he closed the door, drowning out her uncle's now frantic voice.

Thompson smiled at her as he climbed into the driver's seat. He started the car and maneuvered into traffic, leaving Uncle Eb fuming on the sidewalk. Addie sat back and put her uncle out of her mind. She tamped down the horror of Rosa's death as best she could. And she tried not to think about the way she'd betrayed Dunstan.

She focused on only one thing. How she could fix what she had done and set him free.

Dunstan stared at the back of the driver's fat head. The guy had two heads, actually, since he was seeing double. But he saw enough to recognize the policeman behind the wheel. His heart sank. Had that bastard been one of Woden's men all along?

"We're not going to the jail, are we?" Dunstan asked, struggling to lean forward. His voice slurred worse than a drunkard's.

The cop snorted. "You got that right."

Dunstan flopped back against the seat. Damn it. Woden had caught him in his net. Caught Addie too. His nemesis had won again.

Blood oozed from his temple and rolled down his cheek to his jaw. His hands were cuffed behind him so he hunched a shoulder, wiping as much of the blood away as he could. His head spun with the movement. And throbbed.

Worse, the emotions he'd been keeping a tight lid on

had started to break free. Madelyn's grief, Woden's fury, the disgust and self-loathing he'd absorbed from Garrity, desperation, envy and a host of other sensations dripped into his mind like water from a leaky waterspout. Even a shot of happiness, and love. For Addie.

But fear hit him hardest. Addie's fear, and his own mounting terror. What would happen next? He was still breathing, so Woden must have a plan for him. And Addie? Send her to Germany as he had the others he'd turned? He'd intended to send Madelyn there until he decided punishing Dunstan by killing her was more important than handing her over to the Reich.

He struggled to push through the din in his aching brain, struggled to think clearly as the police car cruised along.

Sometime later, he had no idea how long, the car bumped off the road onto what felt like a dirt track. Trees bent over the road, shrouding them in darkness. Branches scraped the windows. The car bounced down a rocky slope, making him dizzy and nauseous. He dug his fingernails into his palms, trying to stay conscious. He had to get out of this car, out of these cuffs, and get to Addie before she disappeared with Woden for good.

The trees thinned out. He leaned against the window and looked out. He saw open sky above the treetops, dotted with dark clouds. The car jounced through a rut. His head whacked the doorframe and pain screamed through every inch of his body. The car slowed, seemed to be moving through mush. Beach sand? Was this bastard going to drive him into the ocean? Hell of a way to dispose of a man.

Dunstan would be damned if he'd let that happen.

The car jolted to a stop. A brute with a mug like a bulldog pushed up to the door. Where did Woden find these thugs? Dunstan swiveled on the seat and lay like a turtle on its back, drawing his legs up. Panting from the effort, he stilled, ready to attack. The handle clicked. The door began to open. He finished the job. He kicked like a furious mule and the door bashed into Ugly's face, sending him flying.

Dunstan ran. He didn't count on his driver. That bastard of a cop moved fast and tackled him with all the finesse of a steamroller. Dunstan's old pal the nightstick came down, and the Fourth of July burst in front of his eyes.

He drifted in and out as Ugly and the driver half-dragged, half-carried him along a stretch of snow-crusted beach. His shoulders bumped over the concrete threshold of a wide doorway as they lugged him into some kind of building. Bone cold, smelling of kerosene and seaweed. Dunstan tried to stand, tried to swing his fists, but he was like Samson after the haircut. Useless.

"Put him over there. And give me that gun," a voice said. A low, whiskey-soaked voice that stabbed him in the heart. "Now, go. Woden wants you back at your post."

A face appeared above him. A beautiful face. A familiar face he could never forget. Sculpted cheekbones, full lips, thick, brown hair tumbling over her shoulders.

"Why must you always cause so much trouble, you big ape?" Madelyn said.

The darkness swallowed him.

Chapter Thirty-Five

Michael had never been the best driver, sober or not. Speeding made it worse. The snow and the darkening skies didn't help. He nearly flattened several pedestrians as his jalopy flew up Main Street. Seemed like everyone in town had decided to jaywalk tonight. How he made it to the funeral home without killing anyone, he didn't know.

He and Virginia ran up the alley in time to see his old man closing up. Michael heard the rattle of the key in the lock.

"Michael!" Da strolled toward them, smiling. "Just the man I want to see. How about lifting a few with me at Reilly's?" He eyed Virginia. "You're welcome to join us, little lady."

"Sorry, no time," Michael said in a rush. "Where's Addie?"

"Gone home." Da frowned. "Terrible thing, her friend Rosa was drowned. Found in the shoals on the north shore. Towed into town by Fishy Maheu like she was the catch of the day. Murdered. Pushed off the cliffs or something, the cops are thinking."

Virginia gasped and his father eyed her with a frown. "Don't worry, sis, they have the man they think done it. Big fella with a kisser like a headstone."

"Dunstan." She squeezed Michael's arm. He didn't need any special power to know that bit of news scared her stiff. "And Addie? Was she with him?" she demanded. "The man they arrested I mean."

Da shook his head. "She's home by now. That G-Man Thompson gave her a lift. What's this all about?"

"Tell you later," Michael shot over his shoulder as he and Virginia sprinted back down the alley toward his car.

Minutes later, his jalopy fishtailed on a patch of ice as Michael took the corner at Pine Street. They squealed up in front of the Brandt home to see Addie's cousin Marta scoot down the front steps, dressed like she toddled off to church—checked coat with big buttons, dressy gloves, a half-moon hat that wouldn't stop the weakest breeze, never mind the winter cold.

The girl nearly jumped out of her fancy shoes when Michael and Virginia rushed up, calling her name.

"Where's Addie?" Michael demanded, wasting no time.

Marta looked surprised. "Why, she's at work, I expect. Which is where I've got to get to before I'm late." Her gaze bounced between him and Virginia, her surprise turning to alarm. "What's wrong? Where's Addie?"

Virginia's breathing turned ragged and nervous. "We don't know. She's not at work. Mr. Feeney said she should be home by now."

"Look, Marta, I won't mince words," Michael said.

"Your brother's in a hell of a lot of danger. Maybe Addie, too."

"What do you mean Hans is in danger?" Her voice pitched upward in fear. "How do you know this?"

He froze her with a look. "You know how. The same way Addie knows things. The Sight."

Michael sketched out the gruesome story as quickly as he could. Poor Marta went as pale as milk and swayed like she was going to faint. Virginia touched her shoulder, steadying her.

"B-but why would my brother do something so awful?" Marta asked.

Michael gestured to Virginia. "She thinks Hans is under some kind of spell. A mean cuss named Woden's got some kind of power, like me and Addie. Except this Woden can poison a fella's mind, make him so angry he'll do just about anything."

"Well, *that* explains a whole lot," Marta said.

"Now Dunstan's got himself arrested and Addie's gone missing." Virginia wrung her hands. "We need to find her and stop Hans. And we need to do both right *now*."

"I think we should go to the police," Marta said.

Michael snorted. "A fine idea, except they won't believe us."

"Probably not, darling, but that's a good idea," Virginia said. "At least we can spring Dunstan from jail."

Marta announced her intention to go with them, even if it meant getting fired. Michael didn't balk. There wasn't time to argue with an obstinate girl. They piled into his car, and he steered toward the police station. The three of them must've looked a sight, pushing through the front door. Even more of a sight as they stopped and stared at one another. Now what?

Sgt. Gillis sauntered up to them. He eyed them one by one, lifting an eyebrow when he got to Michael.

"Feeney," Gillis said with a nod.

"Sergeant," he replied, unhappy Gillis recognized him. They'd met only once, when Michael had spent the night in the drunk tank. Gillis had been mighty judgmental about that, for an Irishman. "We're here to report an act of sabotage—"

"I want to bail out Jack Dunstan," Virginia said at the same time. "He's been framed—"

"Quiet!" Marta's voice cut through the chatter. She faced Gillis, a tiny thing next to his bulk. "Sergeant, you have a great wrong you need to correct. You turned my cousin Addie away when she needed your help. You *can't* turn us away now. Mr. Feeney has the same power Addie has and he's seen something terrible. Something you and Mr. Dunstan can help us stop."

Gillis scowled. Michael tossed Marta an admiring look. She'd hit the man squarely in his big gut.

The sergeant cleared his throat. Several times. "I can't promise anything. I'll need more information. Specifically, when and where this terrible thing's going to transpire?"

"The new fire tower near the quarry," Michael said. "Tonight. He's going to burn it down tonight. We have to stop him. *Now*."

"We?" Gillis said.

"Yes, *we*," Virginia bit off, her green eyes snapping with anger. "Including Dunstan. Release him. He'll know what to do."

"We need Addie, too," Michael said. "She's with that government man, Agent Thompson."

"Whoa, Nellie." Gillis held up both hands. "Two things. One, I can't release Mr. Dunstan, because he never made it to the lockup. And two, who in the hell is Agent Thompson?"

Chapter Thirty-Six

The sky darkened as night closed in. Agent Thompson had turned the Packard's heater up all the way. The wipers scraped across the windshield, flicking away snowflakes and water kicked up by passing cars. The warmth and the steady swish should've lulled Addie, but too much had happened for her to relax. Her stomach churned, her heart ached, and her temples throbbed.

Rosa, dead. Dunstan arrested for her murder. The way she had turned on him, trapped in what Addie now knew as Woden's power. She burned with shame and disgust. Dunstan had warned her. He'd told her she needed to fight. And she had failed him.

Agent Thompson glanced at her and flexed his gloved fist, as if stretching achy fingers, then gripped the gear shift. The car jerked as he took the right fork onto Shore Drive, passing the arcade and several restaurants. Addie watched the Oceanside Club go by. The doors were open, but the outside lights had been turned off due to the new blackout regulations.

"Agent Thompson? You're going the wrong way. This isn't the way to the police station."

"I know, Adelaide. I'm taking you home." His voice had gotten deeper, ominous.

"My home's not this way either," she said, eyeing him in growing alarm.

He chuckled. "I am taking you to your new home."

She sat up straight. He'd spoken in German. That's when she heard it. Became aware of it, actually. That hum that had been softly tickling her brain since... Well, since she'd been with him.

"Wh-what do you mean?" she said, barely able to breathe.

"I'm taking you to Germany, Adelaide. Once this mission is complete, I shall accompany you personally to Berlin." He flashed a smug look. "You've been a difficult quarry to bring to heel, but I succeeded in the end. Despite the incompetence of the others I employed to assist me."

Addie struggled to keep up with his German. She would think him stark raving mad if the chilling truth hadn't already sunk in. He hadn't taken leave of his senses. Not one little bit. He was no government agent named Thompson.

He was Woden.

"The others?" she managed to say through the fear rising in her throat.

"My people. Falcon, and my man Smith," he said, full of disgust. "Officer Bowdoin to you. You saw through his clumsy attempts to draw you in."

Addie cringed. No wonder she kept running into Pete and why, each time, he'd tried to get her to go with him.

He worked for Woden. Who else had this Nazi seduced to his side? Many faces swam in Addie's mind, people who'd sidled up to her these last weeks, begging her to come away with them. Wilhelm, Benny Hirtle, even Uncle Eb.

"Bowdoin failed. They all failed," Woden spat. "I thought I had you when I reeled in your friend Rosa, but she refused to bring you to me as I instructed." His voice hiked up in outrage. "She disobeyed me."

Mother Mary. That must explain Rosa's visit to Addie's house and her strange behavior.

"Disobeyed?" Addie cried. "You mean she fought you and your power. She defied you. Good for her." Grief speared her heart. Rosa had protected her, at the cost of her own life. "And you drowned her, you monster. You killed my friend."

"I did what had to be done. Regrettable, but let this be a lesson, Adelaide. You must learn to guard your emotions. People like us can't afford to have friends. We must let no one get close." He stretched his fingers again. "In the end, Miss Conti served me well. Her death has been useful."

"Useful?" Addie swallowed bile. "You mean, useful to blame on Dunstan. You made *me* blame him. You ginned up the crowd against him."

The whole sordid story clicked. Woden had toyed with her from the beginning. He had used Pete and manipulated Rosa. He'd come to the funeral home himself, bold as brass, to spread malicious gossip about Dunstan, to make her doubt him. He'd murdered Rosa and arranged the rest. At the seawall, Addie had heard someone say the body had been towed in. The *Mere Marie's* captain had probably been told exactly where to find her.

And Pete. Woden sent Pete to the funeral home to

fetch her. To help identify the body, he'd said, but really so she could be there when they fished poor Rosa from the sea. Woden had somehow managed to get Dunstan there too, so Addie herself could point the finger of blame.

She groaned. *Stupid, stupid Addie*. She'd walked into the man's net with her eyes open. *She* had helped him trap Dunstan.

"I have done it all in service to you, Adelaide. You will soon thank me. I'll bring you to our beloved homeland. I'll train you and guide your power to heights Jack Dunstan can only imagine. You will no longer fear your gift. Or feel shame. You must practice your German, for I intend to present you to the Fuhrer. When he sees how well I've groomed you, what you are capable of, we shall earn his respect." He glanced at her and his beady eyes glimmered. "Our kind will no longer follow in the fight to win this war. We shall lead."

"That will never happen," she said in English. She wouldn't give him the satisfaction of hearing his mother tongue on her lips. "You may have framed Dunstan, but you forgot one thing. The police can't prove he killed Rosa. They'll have to let him go. It's only a matter of when. And when he's free, he'll come for me. He'll stop you."

He *tsked* like Aunt Trudy when Addie said something she thought absurd. "Jack is not in police custody. Do you think I'm foolish enough to hand him over to them? Officer Bowdoin has taken care of him."

Her stomach turned to stone. What did that mean?

"It won't be long before my family knows I'm missing," she said, trying to sound calm, though far from it. "My uncle Eb saw you with me. They'll come looking."

"No one will come looking, I'm afraid. Soon, all of

Goveport will turn their attention to a fire near the Perkins River. That structure your earnest cousin was helping to build is going to burn. Every fireman and lawman and Boy Scout in the city will run to extinguish the blaze. While they're occupied, my real mission will unfold."

Addie ground her teeth. The inferno she'd seen in Gillis's future—the fire tower. "Your real mission? The fire's a distraction?"

"Certainly." He sounded offended. "Do you think I'd waste so much of my time in this place for one act of sabotage? My mission's much larger in scope. Everything is going forward as I planned, down to the smallest detail. Thanks to your cousin Hans."

"Hans?" She could barely choke out his name.

"He's key to my success. I've commanded him to set the blaze when it's full dark. The fire will draw off the law and anyone else who can get in my way." He shot Addie a greedy look. "Get in *our* way. Pity Hans won't live to learn of our triumph, but he will have the satisfaction of sacrificing himself for our cause."

Sickened, Addie struggled to breathe. *He'll burn to death*, Gillis had said, or *would* say when he got to the scene and spotted the man on the ground, his clothes in flames. *Hans*. Her cousin had roared like an angry lion all week, lashing out at everyone, and now she knew why. This villain had filled him with rage. He controlled him.

"Why are you doing this? Hans never hurt anyone."

Woden's eyes narrowed. "He has hurt his father. He's turned against his country. It's fitting that he gives himself up to ensure Germany's success in this war."

He downshifted and turned the steering wheel. The car

careened onto a bumpy, sloping track. She pitched forward as the vehicle descended. Night had fallen, and the evergreen trees bent overhead made it darker still. No light penetrated, except a dull beacon in the distance. Mackey Light. They were headed down to Samuel's Cove.

Soon she would have no escape.

Her fear threatened to explode into panic. What had Dunstan said about the man feeding off churning emotions? Woden *wanted* her to give in to her terror. She bit her tongue and willed herself still. She needed a clear head. She had to get away. Had to stop his evil plan and save Hans. Had to find Dunstan. If he was still alive.

Addie touched the door handle. Not a great option, but her only option. She pushed down and the latch gave with a soft click. The door opened a fraction. Wind whistled through the crack. She could smell car exhaust and the ocean.

"*Stop*. Don't move."

Woden grabbed Addie's shoulder and his energy shot into her. She slammed back against the seat. Her arms thudded to her lap as if they were made of concrete. She couldn't lift them, couldn't move. Fear tore through her, spiked by his power. Terror that burrowed bone deep, pinching every pore and nerve ending.

"You're strong," he said, his voice dropping to a husky murmur, laced with admiration. "Rosa was strong too. She tried to repel me, but she was no match for my superior power. She failed, and so shall you. You will not escape."

He moved his hand back to the steering wheel, but his energy still pulsed into her brain. Her vibrations hummed with fear. She choked on it. The urge to give up pulled at her. To give in to her terror and to give in to him. If only Dunstan was here to help her.

No. Woden had said it himself—she was strong. Stronger than the fear. Strong enough to block his power on her own.

Her captor stared out at the road, his blocky face lit by the sickly green light of the instrument panel. He breathed heavily and sweat slicked his cheeks. His hands trembled. He winced when he touched the gear shift and turned the steering wheel, as if in pain. The great Woden might not be as invincible as he'd bragged.

Addie had the strength to defeat him.

She closed her eyes and took control. Shoved away her fear and shoved against Woden's angry storm. Fought with every ounce of energy she had left. She edged him out of her mind bit by bit. Slowly, her right hand moved. She touched the door. The trees thinned out, the car rolled past scrubby pitch pines and beach rose bushes into the open. Now or never.

"Do not persist in fighting me, Adelaide. I do this for your own good. For your future. The Americans are weak. Their military is weak. Their defeat is inevitable. I'm sure you would prefer to be with me, on the side of the mightiest nation on Earth. On the side of your own people."

Something Father said a while back nicked at her. *These are my people.*

"You don't know me at all, Mr. Woden," she said. "Germany may be in my blood, but my heart is *all* American."

Addie threw open the door and jumped.

Chapter Thirty-Seven

Dunstan woke up. To what, he couldn't be sure.

He sat on solid ground, his bare back against a cold, wet cement wall. From the sound of breaking waves and the smells—barnacles, rotting fish, kerosene—he could be in his uncle Jerome's bait shop. From what he saw in the light of the gas lamp suspended from the crossbeam, he could be in a boathouse or fisherman's shack. His hands were still cuffed, secured to the wall behind him with a chain attached to a thick metal ring. That made him think of a dungeon.

"Did you have a nice rest, Jack?"

Madelyn.

He hadn't been dreaming. A nightmare, actually. Madelyn was alive. The world tipped and spun. Or maybe that was his aching head. Madelyn, alive? Then who rested in that coffin they'd put into the ground at Arlington Cemetery?

Ugly memories pushed through the chaos in his mind. He'd watched her go into that building. Then, an explosion that shook loose every brick on the structure. He'd raced across the street to save her, flung open the door and flames shot out. He ducked, covered his face protectively, and the fire had scorched his hands. He'd nearly choked to death on the smoke.

He couldn't save her.

He'd drunk himself into oblivion trying to erase that bitter fact. Trying to drown everything out. The sight of the coffin lid closing on her charred body. Madelyn's grim-faced family members gathered around as the casket slowly lowered into the ground. Their accusing stares. His superiors' interrogations about what had happened and the finger-pointing that followed. Dunstan's own rage and regrets.

"If you could see your face," the very much alive Madelyn said, her voice sharp, amused. "I mean, aside from the bruises. I don't know why you're so surprised to see me, Jack. Faking one's death is the oldest trick in the book."

She began to pace back and forth in front of him, her long, slim body clad in a plain wool coat, pinstriped trousers, and short boots. No hat. Madelyn hated hats. She walked close enough he could smell her perfume and her cigarette. Far enough away he couldn't grab her if he somehow broke free. He moved his hands and arms, testing his bonds. The chain tethering him to the wall clinked but stayed rooted in place.

"Don't even try," she said. "You're not going anywhere." Her gaze darted over him, head to foot. "Especially not like that."

They'd removed his overcoat, his shoes and socks, his suit coat, shirt, and tie, leaving him in just his trousers.

The wet and slime coating the floorboards soaked through the seat of his pants. The handcuffs binding him froze his wrists like rings of ice. Were they planning to let him freeze to death? He shivered. An effective plan, if they were.

"Did you enjoy undressing me, sugar?" he asked, glowering.

Madelyn stopped pacing and took a step toward him. He felt her energy, grief that weighed down her vibrations like an anchor. Her sorrow ignited his own, aggravated by the absorbed emotions he could now barely control. His chest constricted. *Damn it.* He'd be bawling next.

"Oh, I did, Jack, just like the old days." She flicked ashes to the wet floor. "You remember the old days, don't you? When we were in *love.*"

She made the word sound vile. Fitting. What they'd shared didn't even come close to love. He'd lived a life without love. When he'd met Madelyn, he'd been like a dog grateful for any scrap of attention from its master.

"I try to forget as much about the past as I can," he spat. "Especially you."

"Don't make me laugh. You enjoyed it as much as I did."

"Fibber Magee and a dozen circus clowns couldn't make you laugh."

She took a slow drag on her cigarette. Dunstan watched her, remembering how he'd once felt looking at her. Being with her, hearing her voice. He'd once loved that throaty, sexy voice and her extremely persuasive purr when she said his name. For a long time after what happened, he couldn't bear for anyone to call him Jack. Now her voice rankled. His name on her lips turned his stomach and everything about her infuriated him. Every second of his life with her had been a lie.

And now she'd joined up with Woden.

He yanked fruitlessly at his bonds. "Jesus Christ, Madelyn. How can you be working with that bastard?"

"I'm called Falcon now." She took another drag and exhaled. Smoke poured from her mouth like steam from a boiler. "As for joining Woden, I have my reasons."

He snorted. "Falcon? A good alias for you. A bird of prey, doing its master's bidding." He couldn't keep the venom out of his voice if he tried. "So now you're a Nazi. You've thrown in with Woden's glorious cause. Does it matter to you at all that he killed an innocent young woman who'd never hurt a flea?"

A long pause as she gazed at him. An emotion he couldn't place flickered across her face. He thought he might be getting under her skin.

"She got in the way," she said. "Woden only did what he had to."

"You tell yourself that," he said, with a bitter laugh. "What happens now?"

Her cool mask slipped. He saw worry on her face. "I'm sorry, Jack, but you have to pay for what happened to that Italian girl."

"What does that mean? Is Woden turning me over to the cops?"

She gave a delicate shrug. "I honestly don't know." She seemed put out by that fact. "But I'm sure whatever he plans to do won't be pretty. Or painless. He might go easy on you if you agree to help us. If you share whatever information you've picked up about American intelligence and defenses, Woden may show you mercy."

He grunted. As if that would ever happen. "You think I'll believe anything that comes out of your lying mouth?"

Another hard pause. "Why, Jack, I'm wounded."

"I bet."

Raised voices and the sound of a vehicle outside cut through the pound of the surf. Madelyn turned toward the door, listening, then back to him.

"I've got to go. Don't go anywhere." She smirked as if she'd cracked a hilarious joke.

"I wouldn't think of it." He looked her in the eye. "Tell me. Did you ever love me?"

Her vibrations went as dark as midnight, emotions full of regret and remorse and something else that sliced him to the core.

"No, Jack," she said finally. She flicked her cigarette to the floor and ground it under her heel. "I never loved you."

She left, leaving him gutted, inside and out. He stared at the remains of her cigarette, crushed to bits. He'd be crushed next. Woden would kill him. Or leave him here to freeze. Or...did Woden have other plans for him? He'd lusted after the peace Dunstan's gift gave him from the moment they'd met. Maybe that bastard had something else in mind for him.

And Addie? He didn't want to think about what Woden had planned for her. Didn't want to feed the fearful emotions boiling in his brain. He had to stay calm, had to focus on one thing.

Getting out of here.

He jerked his arms apart again and again until his wrists were raw, hoping to snap the links holding the handcuffs together. No luck. He went to work on the chain attached to the wall next. He tugged and yanked until his head throbbed, trying to wrench the metal ring free. He felt it give, but not enough.

A woman's scream tore the air outside. Dunstan froze. Terror filled his heart.

Son of a bitch. *Addie*.

~

A ddie landed on her hands and knees with a painful thump. Stones and pebbles jabbed into her gloves and pierced her knees through her trousers. A low branch scratched her face and her lungs yelped from the sudden cold.

But she'd broken free. From the car, and Woden's power.

She scrambled to her feet to see the Packard slide to a stop farther down the slope. Its headlights lit the beach all the way to the water's edge, shining across the snowy sand. Addie knew where she'd been brought, Pott's Beach, at the far end of Samuel's Cove. The tide rushed in, coming in fast. The tops of the jagged boulders that made navigating the cove so treacherous were barely visible.

She saw Woden's silhouette push out of the car. A flashlight popped on as he turned toward her. She didn't hesitate a moment longer. She dashed up the narrow road. She slipped on the snow and twisted her ankle when she stumbled over a large stone, but she kept moving. A figure loomed out of the darkness ahead of her. She skidded to a stop.

Uncle Eb. He clutched a tiny flashlight.

"What are you doing here?" she asked, nearly breathless.

"Hush, Adelaide. I've come to save you. Now let us go."

Save her? The uncle who hated the very sight of her had come to her rescue? "But how did you—"

He grabbed her arm and tugged. They started up the steep hill. The flashlight's narrow beam lit the way.

"I met that man Thompson in Germantown weeks ago," he said. "I discovered his views on world matters are as mine. As we spoke, he began to ask about our family, about Hans and particularly about you. My doubt grew." He puffed from exertion. "I feared he meant you ill, so I have been following you for days, looking out for him."

"Uncle, you risked yourself for me?"

He clucked. "Politics are one thing, child. Family is another—"

He gurgled to a stop as something blurred by Addie and struck him in the head. He fell. She gasped. A man with a face like a broken vase, all to pieces, stood over her uncle. She knew him, even in the low light. The tough with the ratty sweater in the mob outside Schulman's. The man who would've ripped her apart if not for Dunstan.

"Thank you, Jurgen," Woden said to the man in German, coming up to them. He barely spared a glance at Uncle Eb, crumpled on the snowy ground. His flashlight flared into Addie's eyes, and she squinted. "Come along, Adelaide." He gestured with his free hand down the hill. "Walk."

Her blood rushed, followed by a piercing stab to her brain. Her legs stiffened. One knee began to lift. She pushed against his power, refused to let him violate her mind again. Woden eyed her with a cool expression, but she felt his anger. He wasn't as controlled as he pretended to be.

"You are a willful child," he said. "I'll break you of that on our journey, never fear. Jurgen, bring her."

Before Addie could move, the tough seized her around the waist and grunted as he picked her up. She screamed, for all the good it did her. The wind caught her shriek and blew it out to sea.

Jurgen followed Woden down the hill, carrying Addie. She didn't make it easy for him. She flailed, kicked, and punched. She screamed again and again. Jurgen dropped her. Her face scraped against the icy, gritty sand. She tried to crawl away, but he seized her by the wrists and dragged her. Her coat tangled around her hips and her trouser pockets filled with sand as she squirmed and shouted, but Jurgen didn't let go.

He hauled her past Woden's car. Its headlights still shone, illuminating the falling snow. Jurgen stopped when they got to the beach and released her near a small building with cement walls, a wide door, and a tarpaper roof pockmarked with holes.

Addie sat up and shook sand and debris out of her hair. She rubbed her wrists to get her blood flowing again. A tall, slim form appeared above her. A woman, her face turned from the light and too dark for Addie to get a good look.

"Is this Jack's new bint?" the woman asked. "How charming." She spoke in English.

"She's not Dunstan's, she's *mine*," Woden said and prodded Addie with his boot. "Get up Adelaide."

"No!" she cried, with fury and a lot of moxie.

He cursed. "I said, get *up*."

He bent down and grabbed her shoulders, pinning her in his gaze. His energy surged and anger and fear stabbed

Addie's brain like an ice pick. She pushed back with all her force. Exhausted from fighting, she weakened quickly, and he won. She shot to her feet.

"This way," he spat, panting. He touched her back and propelled her toward the boathouse. She fought him all the way, to little success. He marched her like a wooden soldier to the small building.

The woman followed. "My goodness, Woden." She let out a bitter laugh. "You'll use up all your energy on this one. Are you sure she's worth it?"

Woden shot her a frigid stare. "Oh, yes, she's worth it." He breathed heavily, his voice strained, irritated. "Stop your questions, Falcon, and open the door. I want her secured inside so she won't slip away from me again."

Falcon. Woden had mentioned that name as one of his people who'd tried, and failed, to capture her. The woman stepped to the door and threw the rusty bolt. She turned. Light from the car's headlights touched her face. Addie's blood stilled to see the woman who'd asked her to find her lost dog.

The hinges squealed as the door opened, revealing a small, square room with crumbling concrete walls. Despite the dim light, Addie found Dunstan right away. Exactly as she'd seen him in the Sight, sitting against the wall, hands behind his back. His bare chest rose and fell.

Their gazes connected. "Dunstan, you're alive," she cried, with a hefty measure of relief.

"Seems so." He gave her a brash grin. A confident smile that lifted her heart.

Woden shoved Addie inside.

Chapter Thirty-Eight

Michael's car rocked to a stop near the supervisor's shack. A squad car with Gillis at the wheel raced up the access road on his tail. Another police car was already here and had been for a while. Snow covered it like a white blanket.

Probably the patrol car that came by every night to check on the site. Michael couldn't see the driver, but he did see Hans, lit by their headlights. He stood by the fire tower and poured liquid from a metal can along the base of the structure.

Michael let out his breath. They weren't too late. They still had time to stop him.

They spilled out of their vehicles and ran toward him, hollering and calling out. Michael and Gillis took the lead. Marta and Virginia sprinted behind them. Their shouts filled the night. Their shoes and boots thudded against the snowy, winter-hard ground as they tore up the rise. The bitter smell of gasoline grew stronger as they closed in on the tower.

"Stop. In the name of the law," Gillis bellowed.

No dice. Hans tossed the gas can away. He lit a match and touched it to a rag. The cloth flared. Suddenly, Marta screamed. Michael skidded to a halt and looked behind him. Gillis did the same. He swung his flashlight beam and found Marta—squeezed in a policeman's grip.

"Pete!" Gillis cried, a mix of horror and surprise. "What are you doing?"

"Get back, Sarge. Don't move, any of you." Pete shifted. Gillis's flashlight glinted off the long blade of the knife the man held to Marta's throat.

Michael stopped his headlong rush toward Hans and cursed a blue streak. Not only was Marta in danger, Virginia stood a hair's breadth away from the bruiser with the knife.

"That's it, stay where you are," Pete shouted. "Let Brandt complete his mission. Try to stop him and she dies." His hand shook and the knife blade's tip poked Marta's neck, drawing blood. She squeaked in fear.

Michael grimaced. Who would move a muscle after that threat?

He watched helplessly as Hans flung the burning rag. It arced like a shooting star and landed near the foot of the structure. The flame flickered against the wood for the space of a breath, then *whoosh*. The tower and its scaffold ignited like a fireball. Reflected in the firelight, Hans watched the blaze come to life with the intense gaze of a man under an unbreakable spell.

"Christ almighty," Michael breathed. The tower would be nothing but ashes in no time. Fat Charlie was going to be one angry son of a bitch tomorrow.

Gillis swung on the cop holding Marta. "You fool. It's sabotage. Why did you do it?"

He didn't get an answer. Marta struggled as Pete tightened his hold around her middle.

"Dear God," Virginia cried.

She pointed and everyone's attention snapped back to Hans. The boy began to walk toward the fire. Michael tasted bile. The gruesome end to his horrifying Sight was about to come true.

"Hans, stop!" Marta wailed. She fought against Pete's hold. "Let me go. Someone stop him!"

Michael swore. That someone was him. He was the closest, the only one who could reach Hans in time. He could change what the Sight had shown him if he acted *now*. He dug deep, dredged up every bit of courage he could find, and ran.

His feet flew, his legs pumped. He covered the space between him and Hans in the blink of an eye. Heat scorched his arms as he circled Hans in a bear hug and yanked him out of the flames. Michael moved back too fast. He stumbled and fell. Hans landed on top of him with a crushing thud. Above them, the fire roared. The flames popped and crackled, the heat nearly unbearable.

Gillis and Virginia rushed up. They rolled Hans off him, and Michael scrambled to his feet. Virginia shrieked. He'd pulled Hans away too late. Fire licked at the lad's trouser cuffs and ran up his legs.

"He'll burn to death," Gillis shouted, panicked.

He whipped off his coat. Michael did the same. Broiling from the heat and choking on the smoke, they beat at the flames eating away at Hans's trousers until the fire died.

A brief triumph. The burning wood above groaned, as if throwing in the towel. Gillis looked up. The structure began to crack, about to fall and crush them under an inferno.

Michael swung toward Virginia. "Get back."

She ignored him. She seized Hans by the arm and tugged. Gillis pitched in and so did Michael. Coughing, struggling to breathe, the three of them dragged Hans away from the tower to safety just as the structure gave way.

With a final, pitiful moan, the blazing wood plummeted to the ground, collapsing with the force of a boulder hitting water. The crash boomed through the trees and across the ocean. A scorching wind blew in a mighty gust. A wave of sparks and pieces of smoldering embers rocketed outward and showered the ground around them.

"Jesus Delano Christ!" Gillis cried. He sank onto the ground, panting, his face slick with sweat. So was Michael's own.

"Michael, you're a hero," Virginia said.

Her smile froze and Michael followed her terrified gaze to see Pete and Marta duking it out. She'd somehow broken free and flailed at him with the skill of a champion bantamweight. She got him in the chin with a left hook and Pete staggered back. He recovered fast and lurched forward, the knife held low, poised to stab.

Virginia screamed. Gillis shot to his feet and ran, but Michael moved faster. He thundered across the ground and barreled straight at Marta. He shoved her aside. He swung a fast fist at Pete. He missed.

Pete did not.

The knife caught the firelight as it sliced upward—and sank into Michael's gut.

Chapter Thirty-Nine

Dunstan scanned Addie, taking a quick inventory as Woden pushed her into the room. Her clothes were torn and coated with wet sand. She'd lost her hat and leaves tangled in her hair. Scrapes slashed the side of her face. She was a mess, but thankfully alive.

Her appearance paled in comparison to Woden's. Ashen-faced, droopy, dripping with sweat, he rasped out heavy breaths, as if about to keel over and meet his maker. Knocking on death's door or not, Woden met Dunstan's gaze with a triumphant grin, a cocky bastard to the end.

"Hello, old friend," he said.

A hundred emotions flooded Dunstan's vibrations now that the dam in his brain had burst, but rage rose above the chaos and filled every vein, pore, and blood cell in his body. He yearned to rip the man apart, but he forced himself to still. Had to. Woden's gift didn't work on him, but that didn't mean the man couldn't feed off his fury.

He eyed Woden, as cool as he could muster. He

wouldn't fall into that trap again. He'd save his anger and hatred for later, when he broke free.

"What are you doing here, *old friend?*" Dunstan said. "What are you up to?"

"He's burned the fire tower," Addie cried. "He's k-killed my cousin Hans." She choked on an agonized sob, her furious gaze on Woden. "He says the tower's a distraction, so he can bring me to Germany."

That was not going to happen. Dunstan yanked at his bonds with vigor, his aching head be damned.

"Not quite correct, Adelaide. You're vitally important to *my* plans, but not to this mission." Woden turned from her and met Dunstan's eyes with a smirk. "This will delight you, my friend. Since we last met, I've been overseeing an infiltration. In a short time, men with powers you can't even dream of will land on this beach. They'll fan out across the nation and insinuate themselves into war industries. They'll destroy them from within."

"Is that all you've got?" Dunstan's flippant words could hardly disguise the terror building inside him. Nazi agents with incredible gifts committing acts of sabotage would be a disaster. "You risked everything for that?"

"I risked very little. The mission has proceeded flawlessly. Soon we'll have men in place at manufacturing plants and shipyards across the country. America's defeat will be inevitable."

"And Madelyn?" Dunstan tugged at his bonds again. "Why is she here? What's her part in this plot?"

Addie stiffened. "Madelyn? She's alive?" Her stricken gaze shot from him to Woden. "Is she Falcon?"

Woden let out a blat of laughter. "Indeed she is, my dear. Wasn't that a splendid trick we played on Jack? We placed the body of a Jane Doe at the warehouse. After the explosion and fire, no one suspected she wasn't Madelyn, least of all the heartbroken Jack Dunstan. How we laughed about the tears he shed over an unknown woman's coffin."

That stabbed him in the heart. A tidal wave of grief crashed over his vibrations.

"You might think you're clever," Addie said heatedly. "But she's *not* very good at her job. I saw through her flimsy attempt to kidnap me. Lost dog, indeed!"

Woden's laughter sounded forced this time. "Spite doesn't become you, Adelaide. Madelyn is cunning, and extremely capable at what she does. I wouldn't entrust this operation to her if she wasn't. My saboteurs will receive their orders from her, since you and I will be leaving the country. She's proved herself invaluable. I know I can trust her to see this mission through."

Addie looked at Dunstan, her expression distressed, her eyes filled with questions. He damn well didn't have any answers. His former lover, a Nazi mastermind? That was news to him.

"How'd you get her to go along with you?" Dunstan asked, his voice betraying bitterness. "Couldn't have been easy to convince her to turn on her own country. Or to try to drag me into your mess. Or fake her own death."

"Do you think I had to stoop to threatening or coercing her? Madelyn's quite rational for a woman. She understands the stakes, she knows who has the upper hand in this battle. She *chose* to join me and the winning side. As for attempting to bring you over to our cause, that was *her* idea." He watched Dunstan closely, his eyes glimmering. "She was so sure you'd bite, so sure she had you wrapped around her finger. You're a great disappointment to her, Jack."

Dunstan flinched. He'd thought he knew Madelyn. He'd been wrong. He didn't know her at all. And she didn't know him if she thought her scheme would work.

"But that's water under an old bridge," Woden said. "She's moved on, and you... Well, you'll not be here to witness her triumph. You'll be coming with me."

Dunstan flinched again, in surprise this time. He'd been sure he would breathe his last in this dank hole. "To Germany? For what?"

"To help me."

"For the last time, I'm not turning traitor, you bastard. Not for you, or anyone."

"I have no expectation you will." Woden grimaced as he slowly removed his gloves. He held up his hands. Veins stuck out all over, and his fingers were black as pitch, rutted like a plowed field. "As you can see, there is a price to pay for a power as great as mine. The blight is spreading. *You* will cure me. You'll draw out the poison and make me whole."

Addie gasped. Dunstan stared at those hideous hands. How could he do that? His gift drew away mental anguish, not physical. And even if he could figure a way to cure him, he wouldn't. Wouldn't risk drawing the poisoned debris of Woden's gift into his own body, not for a million dollars and Lana Turner's hand in marriage.

"You know, you could've *asked* me," he said. "You didn't have to put on a big show to capture me. Didn't have to kill Rosa." Guilt rose up, joining the emotional jitterbug in his head.

Woden glowered. "I *had* to destroy you, in every way.

353

Had to drag you into the gutter and ruin your name. Now, you're branded as a murderer who's escaped justice. Radcliffe and the Bureau will disavow you. No one will trust you. You have no one to turn to but *me*. You help me and I'll give you power you've never known before. We'll make a new team. With my gift, Madelyn's brains, your ability to turn people to sheep, and this lovely girl's gift of sight—" He gripped Addie's chin and tipped her face toward the light, admiring her with a ravenous expression. "We will be unstoppable."

Addie tried to bite him and Woden wrenched his hand away. Her teeth snapped at air.

"Atta girl," Dunstan said, his heart swelling. "Consider that my answer too. I'd rather go to hell than help you."

"Silence." Woden's arm shot out, reaching toward Dunstan.

"You're slipping, old friend. You can't control me, remember?"

"No, but I can hurt *her*," he snarled. "And I will if you don't do as I say. My people in Berlin won't care what shape she's in, as long as she arrives alive."

Dunstan went as still as the grave. Even the cyclone battering his vibrations froze as the horror of Woden's threat took hold. "You hurt her, you'd better make peace with whatever hell beast you worship," he said through gritted teeth. "Because I'm going to kill you."

Woden wheezed with laughter. "You've threatened that before, Jack, and yet, here I stand, still alive. When will you learn it's useless to fight me?" He turned to Addie. "That goes for you too. You will obey me. The boat will arrive soon. We shall all board, and we will leave. If you give me trouble, I'll order Jurgen to put a bullet into Jack's leg. A wound that won't kill him, but I'll allow to fester during our journey. If you come willingly, he won't be harmed. Is that clear?"

Trembling, Addie nodded.

"There." Woden pulled on his gloves, his movements careful, as if not to aggravate his pain. "I'm pleased we have reached an understanding. Now, sit down." He gestured. Addie banged to the floorboards on hands and knees as if he'd shoved her. "You won't have long to wait. We leave on the high tide."

The door thudded shut behind him, followed by the rusty squawk of the bolt sliding into place. They were locked in.

"Swell guy, huh?" Dunstan said.

Still on hands and knees, Addie scrambled over to him. "You're alive!" She threw off her gloves and cupped his face. "I was so worried. You're so cold."

His gaze caressed her troubled face. The cold didn't bother him now. Not with her here. Hope sparked, lifting some of the gloom choking his vibrations.

"Did Pete do this to you?" She touched his bruised temple, making him wince. He felt *that*. "You look like a palooka who lost his last fight." She searched his face. "Can you ever forgive me? I mean, those terrible things I said to you at the Savoy. What the Sight showed me, I didn't understand. Then they found Rosa, and I accused you of... I didn't fight, Dunstan, when you told me to. I let Woden into my head, and I said such awful things."

"Hey," he murmured. She quieted, gazing at him steadily. "There's nothing to forgive. You're safe and that's all that matters."

She leaned in and their lips touched in a kiss. Funny

how his head didn't hurt now, with her soft lips tasting his, her warm hand pressed to his bare chest. His head buzzed. Electricity rushed through him. He felt he could do anything now.

They parted too soon, though for the best. They had work to do.

"Addie, think you can get me out of this?" He bent forward and shook his cuffed hands. The chain clinked. "What am I connected to, anyway?"

She leaned around him to look. Her body heat warmed him, and her vibrations hummed along his own, filled with fear, remorse, a little anger, and something else. Something he also felt. Warmth and affection. Emotions he couldn't think about now. They both needed to be on guard and focused.

"Well?" he demanded, somewhat gruff.

"It's a metal ring. It's used to chain up a boat, I think, so it doesn't get stolen. It's pretty solid, but the cement is crumbling. I might be able to yank it from the wall."

He shook his head. "Already tried. How about the handcuffs?"

"I'll need something sharp to pick the latch." She stood and touched her head. "My hat had a bow on the brim with a pin in it. Lost it, somewhere out there."

She sounded so put out he wanted to laugh. He held it back. If he let even one emotion loose, no matter how pleasant, the rest would rush out.

"I'll buy you a new hat when we get out of here," he said. "I'll buy you twenty hats when we get to Washington." He did a quick glance around the room. "Maybe there's something in here you can use."

She nodded and began to search. He watched her, hope growing stronger.

"This place was flooded in the hurricane," she said, glancing over her shoulder. "You can see the watermarks on the wall. Used to be a dozen boathouses along this cove, but the rest were made of wood. Smashed like toothpicks by the storm's surf. I'm surprised there's any floorboards left in here." She stopped moving, looking down. "A nail. That ought to do the trick."

She squatted and picked at the nail with her fingers for what seemed like weeks before giving up with a frustrated sigh. "It's in there good, won't move." Her face suddenly brightened. "Oh, Dunstan, I'm such a dope. My pin. The one Rosa gave me."

She stood and unbuttoned her coat. The light cast a dull gleam on a brooch in the shape of a swan fastened to Addie's blouse. Dunstan's bubble of hope blew up to the size of a zeppelin.

She came back to him, removing the brooch and staring at it. "No Sight. Not even a flicker," she said mournfully, then gazed at him with tears in her eyes. "Rosa's truly gone, isn't she?"

"I'm afraid so," he said gently, a lump in his throat.

He leaned as far forward as he could, and she went to work, the *tick-tick* as she poked the pin into the latch the only sound.

"That woman, Madelyn," she said, sounding tentative and unsure. "I saw her. I *was* her, in the Sight. I saw her with you." Addie said that last part so softly he had to strain to hear. "You were here, as you are now. The vision wasn't clear. Or maybe my thinking wasn't clear. I thought you two were together. Thought you'd both done something to Rosa." She sat back on her heels and gazed at him. "I didn't know who she was."

"I didn't know who she was either. Now I do. I've been mourning a woman who didn't exist." He hoped Addie couldn't feel the fury that squeezed his vibrations. It might alarm her.

She turned back to her task. "Sometimes I hate the Sight and what it shows me," she said in a way that made him think there was more she wasn't telling him. "Sometimes I wish I didn't have it at all."

"I'm glad you do. I never would've met you."

A soft click and one of the cuffs swung loose, freeing his right hand. He shook it vigorously, trying to encourage the blood to flow again. Icicles stabbed his fingers.

Addie went to work on the other cuff, but he twisted and grabbed the brooch from her. "Check the door." He attacked the handcuff's lock. His fingers were stiff and cold. "Let's see how strong the bolt is. Check the window too. I'm too big to slither through, but you might be able to if you can loosen that board. If you can, you run."

"What about you? I think Woden needs you more than me. You saw his hands." She shuddered. "He's just using me to keep you in line."

"He's using both of us. That's what he does, uses people. But I mean it. Run if you get the chance. Don't worry about me."

She shot him a mulish look. "I *will* worry. I don't want to leave here without you."

He struggled to bite back his irritation. "Addie, listen. That knock on the head the cop gave me shook loose every damned emotion I've ever absorbed. They're haunting me like ghosts in an attic right now. I'm trying to hold on, but it's a battle I'm losing. I don't have time to be polite and I don't want to bite your head off. Just do as I ask. You get a chance to run, you run."

She hesitated an infuriating five seconds then stood and went to the door. She rattled the handle and it held fast. She threw herself against the wood. It didn't budge. Might budge with his side of beef crashing into it, though. He poked and prodded the handcuff lock, willing it to give way. The brooch's pin bent under the pressure. The glass beads came loose from the setting and pinged the floor.

Addie moved to the window. The panes were long gone, the opening sealed with a plank of soggy wood. Snow fell through a hole in the roof, settling on her hair.

"The board's nailed down pretty good," she said. "Not even slightly loose."

"Sh! Listen." Woden and another man were close to the building, talking. He heard Madelyn, too. They were speaking German. "Can you hear them, Addie? What're they saying?"

"Dunstan," she said, lowering her voice. "You've been a spy all this time and you haven't learned any German?"

Clearly Madelyn had. Or had spoken the language all along. Another thing he hadn't known about her.

"I know enough to order sauerbraten," he said. "Now shut up and listen."

She frowned but moved back to the door and pressed her ear close. "They're talking about the boat bringing the men. The captain's a...what's that word? A drunkard, I think. Woden's afraid the man will foul up. Especially with the snowstorm making it hard to see. Falcon's asking what's going to happen to you. Woden won't say. She's worried. I hear it in her voice."

Dunstan perked up, intrigued. Not by Madelyn being worried about him, which he doubted, but by Woden's reluctance to share information with her. Did she know about the horror eating away at the man's hands?

"Now he's saying it's time to retrieve the packages. He'll bring out the girl first." She swung toward him, her eyes going wide. "We're out of time, Dunstan. He's coming for me."

Chapter Forty

Michael didn't feel the knife go in. Not at first. The blade pricked him, a dull pinch, and he thought the cop had grazed him. Then Pete drove the knife in all the way and a blistering pain seared his stomach like a son of bitch. Hot waves of agony pulsed through him as Pete yanked the blade out.

Michael fell and hit the ground on his back. He couldn't move. Couldn't feel his arms and legs or anything except the pain and the warm liquid that pumped out of his gut with each beat of his heart. Blood. *His* blood. It bubbled from the wound, soaking through his work shirt, staining it crimson.

Time seemed to slow, or speed up, he couldn't tell. The sound of panicked voices and the roar of the fire blended together. His vision grew fuzzy, but he saw one thing clear. The lovely, worried face that came into view above him. Virginia, her saucy, laughing eyes now haunted and wet with tears.

He tried to lift his hand to touch her cheek but didn't

have the strength. Damn his luck. The first time he'd used the Sight, the first time he stuck his neck out and tried to help and look what it got him. A hole in his belly and a beautiful woman dripping tears onto his chest.

And no way to tell her goodbye.

"We need to get you to a doctor," Virginia said, sounding desperate.

"Hans, too," Gillis piped up from behind her. "Both men need a sawbones." He glared at Pete, who he'd tackled and now held by the collar. "*You'll* help me carry Feeney to my car, Pete."

The ratfink had the nerve to choke out a protest.

"We need to staunch the bleeding first," Marta said, dropping down beside Virginia and shouldering her out of the way. "Find me a cloth or something for a bandage."

Virginia wriggled out of her slip as Marta tore open Michael's shirt. She grimaced, looking like she might upchuck her supper all over him, but that didn't stop her. She placed her hands over the gaping wound, one on top of the other in the shape of a cross, as if blessing him. She pressed down. Michael moaned, would've screamed loud and long and with no shame if he could. It stung like a million pieces of glass had shattered inside him.

"Hold on, Michael," Marta murmured. "We'll take care of you. You'll be all right."

Gillis frowned and shook his head. Virginia held her slip limply in one hand. Despair flashed across her face. Michael had his doubts too, but Marta sounded so sure, so cool, so *certain* he'd pull through, it gave him hope.

With an energy that echoed her words, Marta pressed down hard on his wound. She locked her gaze on her blood-soaked hands. Sweat beaded her forehead and streaked her face. Her eyes glittered and her breathing turned ragged.

The stab in Michael's gut began to ebb. The glass shards slicing into him became a soothing tickle that seemed to flow like a gentle tide from Marta's hands and into his wound. He blocked out all sight, sound, and thought except that sensation. He focused only on Marta's determined eyes and the pressure of her hands on his stomach.

"It won't work, Marta. We're losing him," Virginia said, her voice full of tears. "We *must* get Michael to the hospital."

Gillis released Pete and stepped over. He bent down, took Marta by the shoulders and tried to pry her from Michael's side. "Come now, child. Move away," he said, gentle but firm.

Marta shook him off and pressed down harder. The tickle in Michael's gut grew stronger. His insides squirmed, as if silky fingers threaded through his wound, pulling the torn pieces together, stitching them into a whole. Making *him* whole.

It didn't hurt at all. He felt joy. Joy that spread from his belly to his torso, into his limbs and all the way to his toes and fingers, like an electric current humming through his veins. Lighting him up, freeing him.

His vision dimmed. The world around him dimmed too. Virginia's sobs and the feel of Marta's hands faded. He was done for, sure enough. What else but the journey to the Pearly Gates would make him feel such bliss and freedom?

He stretched out as if settling in for the night, ready to

meet his maker. He let out a happy sigh as everything went dark.

$$\sim$$

Michael woke to the face of an angel gazing down at him.

"Welcome back, sugar," Virginia said, smiling, sounding relieved. "I thought we'd lost you for keeps." She leaned down and kissed him, then pressed her tear-streaked cheek to his.

He blinked strands of her snow-wet hair out of his eyes and gazed up in confusion at Gillis, who grinned from ear to ear. Michael wasn't dead. He was still alive. Still here at the worksite, on the frozen ground, breathing in smoke from the fire that raged at full force.

"What happened?" he asked, dazed and his voice rough. He needed a drink.

Virginia sat back on her heels and took his hand. "I'm not quite sure." She glanced up at Gillis, who stood beside Pete, keeping an eye on him, then shifted her gaze back to Michael. "But I think Marta has a gift. She healed you."

Someone, probably Virginia, had gone for Michael's coat and dropped it over him to keep him warm. He pushed it off his chest and looked down to his stomach, where his bloody shirt gaped open. He went ice cold. The bleeding had stopped, the stab wound covered over. Sealed, as if Marta had placed a bandage over it. An ugly, purple-red skin bandage, but the wound had closed up nonetheless.

"I'll be damned." He touched the healed patch in disbelief. It felt solid, inside and out, petrified like those ancient stones he'd seen in the Goveport Science Museum on a school trip long ago. "Marta did this?"

"She most certainly did. She saved you, and she's going to save Hans." Virginia helped him to sit up and he followed her gaze up the rise to Marta, bent over her brother, lit by the flickering flames. "I never heard of a single gifted soul who can heal, and here she was, living in the same house as Addie. There's *tremendous* power in your family, Michael. Dunstan will be beside himself to find out."

Her relief and excitement turned to worry. He guessed at her thoughts. Where was Dunstan? And Addie? What had happened to them?

Michael fastened his bloody shirt as best he could with a couple buttons missing. He stood, leaning on Virginia's arm though he didn't need her help. He didn't feel a lick of pain. His head whirled a bit and his legs wobbled some, like he'd had a couple snorts and not a knife shoved into his breadbasket.

Virginia picked up her slip, then his coat and handed it to him. He put it on, scanning the area. The collapsed fire tower had become a massive bonfire. The blaze rumbled like a speeding train. The flames and black smoke billowed up into the night sky, spreading an ugly orange glow over everything and everyone.

All this destruction, for what? Michael had almost died. Hans too. Dunstan and Addie were missing. For an act of sabotage? There had to be something more to it, some piece of the puzzle they hadn't found yet. And Michael feared Addie was the key.

"Do you hear that?" Virginia said, cocking her head. "Sirens."

"I've been hearing them for a long while," Gillis said. "The fire department will be here soon. The police are coming too. For *you*." He aimed a stern look at Pete, a cross between a threat and a promise.

"Sounds like every fire engine and ladder truck in Goveport is headed this way," Michael said, exchanging glances with Virginia.

"I get it now," she said. "This is only part of Woden's plan." She twisted her hands together, agitated. "To call the authorities away. To distract."

"From what? From where?"

"From whatever he plans to do with Addie and Dunstan." Virginia eyed Pete, next to Gillis, looking uncomfortable. "I bet he knows."

The sergeant gestured to Pete and stepped back. "The man's all yours, Feeney."

Michael started toward him, but Virginia grabbed his arm, hauling him to a stop. "Are you batty?" she said. "You had a knife in your belly not ten minutes ago. You should take it easy."

"Doll, I'm feeling fine," he said with a wink. And he did. A little winded, maybe. Nothing a swig of Old Crow couldn't cure.

He crowded in close to Pete and grabbed him by the collar. Michael wouldn't need the Sight or any other special power to knock the truth out of the man.

Just his fists.

"All right, you bastard." The fella stared at him with frightened eyes. "You're going to answer, and you're going to answer true. Where the fuck is my cousin Addie?"

Chapter Forty-One

The boathouse door bolt shrieked open. Addie jumped, her terror mounting.

"Go with him," Dunstan said in a furious whisper. "I'll be right behind you. Remember, if you get the chance, *run*."

She didn't have time to argue, though she wanted to. Dunstan barely had a moment to slip his now-free hands behind his back before Woden stood in the doorway.

"Time to leave, my Adelaide," he said.

Ugh. Her name on his lips, his voice full of avarice, turned her stomach. She swallowed her panic and stepped toward him. Behind her, Dunstan cursed, with a ferocity that shook her all the way down to her toes. Woden chortled in glee and led Addie outside, slamming the door. The bolt *thunked* back into place.

The night had grown colder. The wind had picked up and so had the snow. Icy flakes fell, caught by the wind, their swirling dance illuminated by the light of a kerosene lantern someone had set on the ground nearby. Woden held Addie's arm and guided her across the snow-covered sand toward Madelyn like a doting father with a fragile child.

"Falcon, send the signal," he said to Madelyn in German.

"You haven't answered about Jack." She also spoke German, her voice strained. "What are your plans for him? Surely you're not going to leave him here to freeze."

Woden's eyebrows rose. "What is this sudden concern? Don't tell me you still care for that man."

Madelyn stared at him like a rabbit caught by a hunter. "I don't give a fig about Jack Dunstan. You know that."

A lie. Addie knew the woman's true feelings.

"Perhaps you need to reassure me," Woden said coolly. "You have an important job to do in the coming months. I don't want feminine sentiment to distract you. My plan for Jack is simple. He is coming with me. Jurgen will bring him once the men have landed and Adelaide and I have boarded the ship."

Woden's gaze lit on Jurgen, standing nearby with his muscled arms folded across his chest. Addie's belly burned to see Jurgen's puffy lips spread in a menacing grin. She suspected that brute wouldn't be as gentle with Dunstan as Woden had been with her.

Madelyn nodded and cast her eyes downward as if cowed, but Addie caught the glint of defiance in her expression.

"No more delay," Woden said. "Send the signal and be quick about it."

Madelyn spun and tracked through the snow up the beach to Woden's car. She climbed in and flicked the headlights on, then off, then on again. Three times in rapid succession. Seconds later, a pinprick of light flashed on the dark water in response.

Addie kept her eyes glued to the spot, waiting. The beam from Mackey Light swung around and caught a large fishing boat bobbing just off the cove. Victor Maheu's boat, no doubt. The next time the beam spun around, a rowboat lowered from the *Mere Marie*. Moments later, the small boat bounced over the waves toward shore. Several silhouetted figures huddled inside.

Madelyn left the headlights on and came back from the car. Woden turned to Addie. She cringed as he slid his arm around her waist. "Come along, my lovely—"

The boathouse door crashed open, and a dark shadow flew out. Dunstan's howl of rage carried across the beach. Addie's skin prickled. He pounced on Jurgen in a flash. A nauseating crack and Jurgen's body buckled, straight down. Dead.

Dunstan fixed his gaze on Woden. Addie shuddered to see the almost inhuman look blazing in his eyes. His body trembled, as if he could barely restrain the fury about to explode. He flexed his fists. His knuckles cracked.

"Addie. Run."

She did, with no hesitation. Her shoes dug into the snow-wet sand as she pelted up the beach. She glanced back to see Dunstan throw himself at Woden. The car headlights lit the two men, grappling like mighty elk fighting to the death. Behind them, in the lighthouse beam, the rowboat rose up on a breaking wave. Woden's saboteurs were almost to the shore.

Addie jerked to a stop and gasped as Madelyn stepped into the headlights' glare. She held a gun, pointed at the wrestling men. Thinking fast, Addie tore to the left. She bashed Madelyn's wrist and knocked the gun from her grip. The weapon thumped to the sand.

Madelyn growled in frustration. She flung off her glove and seized Addie's hand, yanking her close.

"You're not worthy of Jack," she said, her hot, tobacco-tinged breath gusting over Addie's face. "He doesn't need you. You're in his way. You're in everyone's way."

Madelyn slithered into Addie's brain and her energy took hold, ten times more powerful than when Addie had held Dunstan's lighter. Her vibrations keened with ten times the sorrow. An overwhelming cold, a forlorn ache pushed into Addie's mind, shrouding her with anguish. Loneliness. Despair.

"Jack despises you. You're a burden to him," Madelyn whispered. "A burden to everyone. No one wants you."

Addie's vision clouded with tears. All the light and hope rushed out of her, like sewage pouring down a drain, leaving her hollow and empty. Her thoughts echoed Madelyn's words. Dunstan hated her. She was a burden to him. To everyone.

Grief-soaked memories flooded her mind. Hugo Nunes, sobbing and frightened, dying in that hole. Rosa's bloated body. Mother, seconds after she'd passed, so small and lifeless. Her coffin slowly lowered into darkness. Moist, black earth shoveled onto the casket's lid with a mournful thump. Addie yearned to crawl into that grave with Mother, to lie down and close her eyes forever.

A gut-wrenching sob shook her as she gave herself fully to the grief that had battered her heart since her mother's death. Madelyn sucked in a long, shivering breath. Somewhere deep down, Addie knew the woman had triggered her sorrow and now fed on her pain. Took pleasure from it.

"Run away," Madelyn purred into Addie's ear. "Run away from the grief and sadness and Jack's hatred. Never come back."

Addie trembled. *This isn't right.* She needed to stop Madelyn, needed to drag herself back from the darkness. She'd been trapped by this woman's energy once before, during the Sight in Dunstan's hotel. She wouldn't allow it to happen again. She took a breath and focused. She walled up her grief, shoved through the sorrow, and stomped on the anguish.

With a tremendous mental thrust, she pushed the pusher from her mind and slammed the door after her.

Addie opened her eyes. Madelyn gaped at her in disbelief.

She grabbed Madelyn's hand and squeezed. "Turnabout is fair play," she said and gave herself to the Sight.

Chapter Forty-Two

Michael pounded down the rutted, tree-shrouded road to Samuel's Cove, with Virginia close on his heels. His injury had been all but forgotten. He felt nothing except a cone of numbness from his navel to his backbone. A frozen emptiness he suspected would be with him the rest of his life.

But at least he had the rest of his life, thanks to the miracle-worker racing down the path behind him. Marta had brought him back from the brink of death, then she'd gone and cured Hans too. She'd danced around, as giddy as a puppy when her brother sat up and asked what had happened.

Michael still had trouble figuring it out. Marta had a gift. A power different from his and Addie's and even Virginia's. How could that be? One of the many questions he meant to put to Virginia as soon as they freed his cousin from Woden's clutches.

One big question had already been answered. The Sight had shown Hans dying. They'd changed that future.

And Michael was bound and determined to change his brother Danny's future, too. No matter what anyone said.

He put that out of his mind for now and picked up his pace, urging the girls to run faster too. Sgt. Gillis had taken Hans in for questioning—and Officer Bowdoin to jail—with a promise to come to their aid like the cavalry as soon as he could, but Michael feared the cops would be too late.

"Shit!"

He stumbled over something on the path and nearly planted his face in the dirt as he stopped fast. Virginia skidded to a halt next to him. Gillis had given them a police flashlight, and she aimed the light at the obstacle. A body, dusted with snow. The man groaned as Michael rolled him over. Michael swore again when he recognized the face in the light.

Marta rushed up behind them and gasped. "Father!"

"Anyone from your family *not* involved in this affair?" Michael said, eyeing her.

He got a glower for an answer and rightly so. He bent to help Brandt up, but Marta waved them on.

"I hear sirens," she said. "The police are on their way. You go on. Find Addie. I'll help Father then catch up."

Michael nodded and he and Virginia took off. The trees thinned out and the snow cover thickened, making the path slippery. She held onto his arm. He liked that, having someone depend on him. He'd tried to convince her to go with Gillis, for safety's sake, but she would have none of that. She wanted to be at the center of the action. With *him*.

The path opened onto the beach, and a scene of utter chaos. A surging wave pushed a rowboat filled with shadowy figures to the shore. The boat's prow slid into the sand. The men on board leapt over the side and splashed into the foam. Two ferocious-looking fellas duked it out on the beach, one of them without a shirt. Nearby, another man was laid out like a corpse.

And there in the glare of a car's headlights he saw Addie, his timid little cousin, fighting with a tall, skinny dame. The pair of them danced a desperate kind of two-step.

Michael let out a relieved breath. Addie was alive, anyway.

"Who's the bad guy?" he asked Virginia. The sirens got louder, closer, but Michael figured he'd already played hero once tonight, why wait for the cops? "Who do I tackle?"

Virginia took in the scene, cool as ice. "Tackle anyone but the big fella without his shirt," she said. "That's Dunstan." She shifted her gaze toward the skinny woman brawling with Addie and gasped. "My god! It can't be her. She's dead—"

She dashed toward the two women, cursing a blue streak. Words that might offend some prudish old priss, but not him. He raced after her, his heart swelling with pride.

Virginia was everything he'd ever wanted and dared to hope for but never thought he'd find. She lifted him up, got him thinking he could be something more than a drunk with a fearsome melodrama playing in his head. He could see himself with her forever, if she'd have him.

And if she would, he intended to make himself worthy of her, every day.

Chapter Forty-Three

Madelyn fought desperately to free herself from Addie's mental hold, twisting and turning like the falcon she resembled caught in a net. Addie held on, taking in as many snippets of the woman's future as she could, unfocused images and smells, unclear sounds and vague emotions that snapped like an elastic band and vanished when her quarry finally managed to throw her from her mind.

Addie blinked rapidly, bringing the present back into focus. The wind had picked up and pelted her face with icy crystals of snow. Through the haze she saw nearly a dozen men dressed in hats and heavy overcoats make their way up the beach from the rowboat. The darkened figures of a tall man and a petite woman shot out of the trees and raced toward her from up the road. Madelyn glared at her, breathing heavily.

And Dunstan...

Addie gasped. He and Woden still fought, trading bruising kicks and gut-stinging blows, but Dunstan's injuries had taken a toll. Sweat coated his face and chest. He moved clumsily and swung his fists as if punching through wet sand. He weakened and Woden took advantage of it, pressing in.

"Dunstan!" Addie cried, but before she could run to him, Madelyn shoved her to the ground. She hit the wet, snowy beach with a painful thump.

"You've fouled things up enough," Madelyn snarled.

She lunged and Addie braced for a blow when Madelyn snatched up something from the ground beside her.

The revolver.

A second later, the weapon exploded. The bang echoed across the beach and boomed in Addie's ears. The smell of gunpowder filled the air.

Addie froze. Her blood turned to ice. The world went still. She barely registered the wail of police sirens closing in. Barely saw Madelyn's stunned expression, or the gun that fell from the woman's limp hand. Vaguely noticed Woden's bloodied face as he dashed by, grabbed Madelyn by the arm, and ran off with her into the night. Took little note of the men from the rowboat who disappeared into the trees behind them.

She saw only Dunstan.

Saw his large hand close over the buttonhole burst of red in his upper chest. His confused face as he gaped down at the wound, then up at her. Their eyes locked. He dropped to his knees, wavered, then fell face first into the sand.

"No. No, no, no, *no!*" Addie couldn't stand. Her legs wouldn't work. She scurried like a dog on hands and knees to where Dunstan lay. She called his name again and again, a dozen times. She tried to flip him over but didn't have the strength.

"Help me, please," she begged, not sure anyone could hear her cry.

"I'm here, Addie."

Michael, his voice a reassuring murmur. Virginia Beach hurried up behind him. Working carefully, they all three turned Dunstan over. Sand and snow stuck to his sweat-soaked skin and clumped around the wound. Blood gushed from the bullet hole above his heart like water from a spigot.

"I'll get help," Michael said.

Addie thanked him but he'd already gone. She took a ragged breath and struggled for control. Michael returned with Marta. Her cousin knelt at her side and placed her hands over Dunstan's wound, pressing down.

"I can heal, Addie." Marta smiled into Addie's eyes. "I have a power, like you. I can heal him."

A blossom of hope lifted her heart until Virginia leaned down and touched Marta's shoulder. Tears streaked her face. "Your energy won't work on him," she said gently.

Oh. Addie remembered now. Dunstan's gift. Marta whimpered in frustration as Virginia drew her away. Only Addie remained.

She took Dunstan's hand and kissed his knuckles. "Jack Dunstan, don't you dare die on me."

He groaned. His eyelids fluttered open. "Can't...get rid of me...that easy."

He coughed and more blood spurted from the wound. Addie bit back tears. His face had paled to the color of slate.

"Addie." His eyes opened again, seeking hers. His vibrations reached out to her own. His emotions had quieted. All anger and fear had drained away, replaced with deep sorrow.

She touched his face, his skin bitter cold. Colder than before, in the boathouse. "I'm here."

"Stay with me."

Addie's heart lurched. She could finally admit to herself what she'd perhaps known from the very beginning. She'd fallen for this man. Fallen for every gruff, tender, exhilarating, and complicated bit of him. And now she was going to lose him.

"I'll stay with you, Dunstan. I'll stay with you, always."

His mouth quirked in a smile. Her belly fluttered, and her heart broke. Then he closed his eyes.

Epilogue

A ddie crossed the room and gazed down at Dunstan, his long body stretched out and so very still. The white sheet had somehow slipped off. She picked it up and tenderly covered him, tucking in the edges.

His eyes were open—and very much amused.

"I'm not an infant, you know," he said.

"Well, if you wouldn't keep kicking off the covers, I wouldn't have to do this."

She'd done too good a job tucking him in. He had to struggle to get his arm out from under the tight sheet to reach for her. She took off her glove and laced her fingers through his. His *warm* fingers. His body had finally reached a normal human temperature.

"You're here," he said.

And you're alive. She couldn't hold back a smile even if she wanted to. He was banged up and bed-ridden, but alive.

She sank down on the edge of the bed, still holding his hand. "I almost wasn't here. The head nurse refused

379

to let me in to see you because I'm not family. The obliging Miss Beach came to my rescue. Now there's a mighty confused nurse out there who's crazy about Virginia."

He laughed then winced in pain. "I'm in a hospital? How long?"

"Two days."

"Damn it. Woden's got a head start on us."

He struggled to sit up. Addie gripped his big shoulders and gently eased him back down. Not a difficult task in his weakened condition.

"Don't, Dunstan. You have a bullet hole in your shoulder that needs to heal. You have a concussion, and you almost froze to death. The doctor thinks you'll be here for the better part of a week."

"A week?" His gaze flicked around the small, spare room then settled on a potted poinsettia on the bedside table, the only spot of color in all the white. "Is this a private room?"

Addie nodded. "Virginia insisted. Only the best for you, Dunstan."

"That girl sure knows how to spend money." He sighed and searched her face. "I'm already in my sickbed, might as well give me the rest of the bad news. Woden got away. What about Madelyn?"

Addie took his hand again and stroked the scarred patch on the back with her thumb. "Gone too. After leaving you with such a delightful Christmas present."

He touched the thick bandage above his heart. "Madelyn's a crack shot. I don't think she meant to kill me."

Addie snorted. Maybe not, but she almost had. And she'd tried her best to get Addie out of the picture. But she wouldn't tell him that. Not now. When he'd fully healed, she'd tell him everything.

"The men they brought ashore got away too, save one," she said. "My Uncle Eb tackled him. I believe he thought the man was Woden. I don't think he's yet realized he stopped one of Hitler's spies. His friends in the Bund will probably give him the dickens when they find out."

That earned her another laugh and another wince. "What about Hans? The fire? And Gillis?"

She stood. "You need to rest. I'll tell you all about the fire when I visit tomorrow. Hans is fine. Gillis let him go. So did Virginia. She took her love spell off him yesterday. And we suspected Gillis for nothing. Turns out, we were following him to his favorite restaurant. The only thing he's guilty of is straying from his reducing diet."

Dunstan growled. "Wasting our time with him when Woden was right under our noses." His voice turned bleak. "And Madelyn."

Addie reached into her skirt pocket and took out Dunstan's lighter, scratched and scuffed from being stepped on. "I found this on the sidewalk by the seawall after Rosa... Well, I thought you might want it back."

She held it out, but he made no move to take it. "Madelyn gave me that. Toss it. I never want to see that thing again."

The pain in his voice and his expression twisted her heart. "Does it hurt much, what she and Woden did? You loved her once." Her chest tightened, saying that.

He scoffed. "Love? I was a fool who didn't know any better. I don't think I ever loved her. She sure as hell never loved me."

Not true, as Addie knew, and she wondered about

Dunstan's heated denial. She stepped to the bedside table and put the lighter down with a soft *clink*. He must have been in love with Madelyn. Deeply in love. He seemed not just angry about what she'd done but wounded to the core. Perhaps he still cared for her, deep down. Could those feelings be why he insisted people call him Dunstan, and not by his first name? The name *she'd* used for him. Did he struggle with the intimate memories the name evoked?

Addie moved the poinsettia a fraction. Would those feelings get in the way of what she felt growing between them? She hoped not, but she couldn't be sure.

She moved back to the bed, pushing those doubts away. There would be time for worries later. Today, she basked in happiness that he was alive. That when he looked at her, she saw only tenderness and hope. That her heart sang, just to be near him.

"Never fear," she said. "Woden and Madelyn may have gotten away, but they won't be free for long. We'll catch them."

He quirked an eyebrow. "We will? How?"

"While you were going ten rounds with Woden, I got to know Madelyn. Or Falcon, or whatever she likes to be called now. I used my gift..." She paused, letting out her breath. The word felt somehow liberating. "I used my gift to read her future. I have an idea where she's going. We'll catch up to her."

"*We'll* catch her?" A smile pulled at his lips. "Does this mean you're joining the team? You're coming to Washington with me?"

Father didn't want her to go. In fact, he was dead set against it. When he found out what had happened, what Addie had endured and Michael's role in the whole affair, he'd been livid. He'd demanded to meet Dunstan so he could punch him in the nose for putting his daughter in such danger.

His protective anger convinced Marta to keep her gift and how she'd healed Michael and Hans a secret. At least until she finished high school and could make firm choices about her future. Virginia had said she could join their team, but Addie knew Marta's destiny lay elsewhere. She would defy her mother's wish that she marry the shoemaker's son. She would follow her own path and play a different role in this war.

Michael had declared himself raring and ready to take up with Dunstan's motley crew. Addie suspected Virginia had a lot to do with her cousin's newfound conviction. A true feeling, not an infatuation sparked by Virginia's gift.

He'd made a complete recovery from his injury, though the same couldn't be said for Marta. She'd endured terrible abdominal pain since healing Michael and had trouble breathing after tending to Hans. A side effect, Virginia had said, assuring them Marta's distress would fade, like the terror that lingered after Addie used the Sight.

As for Addie, she knew she had a lot to learn about people with gifts and her own ability but stood ready to accept the challenge. No more hiding, or giving in to her fear. She would follow in her ancestor Frieda's footsteps and embrace who she was, no matter the consequences or what the world thought of her.

She glanced at Dunstan. But unlike Frieda, she had support and encouragement and even a possibility of happiness.

She would go with him. She would embrace her gift and use it to do good. She would become the person she was meant to be. A person Father could let go of. A person Mother would be proud of.

And she would keep her promise to Dunstan. She would stay with him. Always.

She sat back down on the bed and took his hand again. "Yes, I'm going to Washington with you. What do you think of that?"

His eyes blazed with heat. "Addie, I think I could kiss you."

She glanced over her shoulder, toward the open door and the nurses bustling about in the ward. She looked back at him and bent close, flooded with emotion.

"Well then, Mr. Dunstan, what are you waiting for?"

- The End -

Afterword

Thank you for reading *A Moment After Dark*. I hope you enjoyed it! If you did, please help others find this story by leaving a review.

And please don't forget to visit my website, where you can sign up for my newsletter group and get the latest news on what's happening with me, my books, and what I'm working on next (hint: plan a trip to 1946!), plus exclusive content, free books, and all kinds of other goodies.

Just stop by my website to join the fun! (Link www.janetrayestevens.com)

Also by Janet Raye Stevens

***Time flies when
you're on the run***
A WWII time travel adventure

***They can't say no
to the mistletœ***
Winner, RWA's Golden Heart® Award

Coming April 2022!

IT'S BEEN A LONG, LONG TIME - A Beryl Blue, Time Cop
adventure

www.janetrayestevens.com

About the Author

Meet author Janet Raye Stevens – mom, reader, tea-drinker (okay, tea guzzler), and teller of fun, adventurous, occasionally heartbreaking, and stealthily romantic tales. A Derringer Award nominee, Janet's work has been recognized multiple times, including the Daphne du Maurier award for the World War II paranormal suspense, *A Moment After Dark* and RWA's Golden Heart® award for the sweet holiday romance, *Cole for Christmas*.

Janet writes mystery, time travel, WWII-set paranormal, and the occasional Christmas romance, all with humor, heart, and a dash of suspense. She lives in New England with her husband, who's practically perfect in every way, and their two sons, both geniuses and good-looking to boot.

www.janetrayestevens.com